"THE STORY'S A GOOD ONE . . .
the reader is quickly gripped and looks forward to the
brutal, brow-to-brow, bullish clashes between little-
tough-guy Hoffa and slim, fearless Kennedy."
The Kirkus Reviews

"A MIGHTY INTERESTING BOOK . . .
The mighty Titans, Robert Kennedy and Jimmy Hoffa,
stand face to face in the battle of the ages. Silhouetted
against the backdrop called USA, they move around
each other, snarling, sniffing, and striking out for each
other . . . Jimmy triumphed, then Robert triumphed
. . . they stalked each other, and liked each other . . .
Jimmy H. was the heralded leader of the Teamsters
Union. Robert K. was the Investigator who dared to try
and pin bribery charges on his opponent. Robert was
forever after the criminals within the Teamsters with
his hard working investigative team, unearthing evidence wherever he could, traveling wherever he had to
for interviews, meetings, in faraway offices, on bowling
alley runways. Jimmy was always out after the votes,
the popularity contests, needing everyone's backing. And
they continued their mighty battling until their ultimate
triumphs and tragedies."
The West Coast Review of Books

blood feud

Edward Hannibal
and Robert Boris

BALLANTINE BOOKS • NEW YORK

Author's Note

Although certain scenes, characters, names and chronological sequences of events have been altered for dramatic impact, the basic facts in this novel are as they happened.

Library of Congress Catalog Card Number: 78-11951

ISBN 0-345-31238-4

Manufactured in the United States of America

First Edition: April 1979

Paperback format
First Edition: June 1980
Second Printing: May 1983

Combat

The chief counsel wore his eyeglasses high on top of his head, and leaned forward as he fired questions at the witness. The witness, black hair combed straight back from his wide, clear forehead, sat still and relaxed, cold hatred in his eyes; he had taken the measure of his young adversary and decided that the kid was a pushover. So far the questions thrown at him seemed like so many weak punches, easily batted away, not worth any serious counterpunching yet; let him wear himself down.

Frustrated, the questioner began moving in closer; the faint sneer on Jimmy Hoffa's mouth and in his replies was heating up the anger in Bobby Kennedy's chest. "Do you know Joe Holtzman?" he asked again, impatient, wishing he had a deeper voice.

"I *knew* Joe Holtzman," Jimmy answered again, playing cat-and-mouse and enjoying it.

"Then *was* he a close friend of yours?"

"I knew Joe Holtzman."

"Was he a close friend of yours?"

"I knew Joe Holtzman!"

"Was he a close friend of yours!" He wanted to grab the man's throat and shake him.

Jimmy wanted to belt him in the mouth. "Now listen here!" he finally shouted, loud and tough. "I knew Joe Holtzman! But he wasn't any particular friend of mine!"

Wanting to scream and curse, Bobby smiled into Jimmy's reddened face. Then he turned away and tried for a change of pace.

1

"I'll ask you again, until I get a proper answer." He turned back, locked eyes with Jimmy, and demanded, *Do you know Joe Holtzman!"*

"I knew Joe Holtzman!" Jimmy spat, fuming.

Calmly, smiling: "Was he a close friend of yours, Mr. Hoffa?"

Jimmy had a pencil in his hand. He snapped it in two with his thumb and pitched the pieces onto the tabletop in front of him. The sound of spectators' murmurings spread through the Senate Caucus Room's high overhead spaces like a drumroll.

This old room had seen a lot in its day, but nothing ever quite like this Kennedy-Hoffa cockfight. The television cameras and equipment mixed oddly with the stateliness of the chamber off the marble stairway on the third floor of the Senate Office Building. Its ceiling was vaulted, its carpets red; light through the high, arched windows met electric light in the crystal droplets of the great chandeliers and threw brightness everywhere. Here the sinking of the *Titanic* had been investigated in 1912. Here, under the Harding Administration, a Secretary of the Interior, Albert Fall, fell, caught in corruption. Here J. Pierpont Morgan had sat with Tom Thumb perched on his lap, and here Senator Joseph McCarthy had both soared to fame and plunged to disgrace.

This now was not the McCarthy Committee, though he was a member of it, but the McClellan Committee, officially known as the Senate Select Committee on Improper Activities in the Labor and Management Field. What was "improper" and what was not, as Robert Kennedy was to learn in his grapplings with James Hoffa, was often a matter of opinion; not everyone shared Bobby's clear, black-and-white vision of right and wrong. Their joustings played across the networks to the whole country, and reviews were mixed. Truckers held to their basic view of Jimmy as "the finest man God ever put a pair of shoes on." A lot of women couldn't quite understand what Bobby was so mad about, but thought him "very cute" anyhow. Bobby had picked up some courtroom experience from his short-lived tour of duty under Joe McCarthy himself, just before the Fall, but Jimmy on the stand

2

proved a dervish a Clarence Darrow or Perry Mason would have found befuddling. When Bobby would try to nail Jimmy for bugging his own people, he would get a classic dose of the labor leader's amazing abilities to cloud men's minds.

"We have here an expense voucher for twenty-three Minifons," Bobby began. "Mini-phones, small German tape recorders purchased by the Teamsters . . . for *you,* Mr. Hoffa. Could you tell this Committee now what were they used for?"

Jimmy hid a grin beneath his hand, squinted in thought, pinched his nose—and returned the serve to Bobby. "What did I do with them? Hmm. What did I do with them . . ." Then he brightened. "Well, what *did* I do with them?"

Some in the audience laughed. Bobby didn't; he moved closer. "Yes. What did you do with them?"

"I am trying to recall."

"You could remember that."

"When were they delivered, do you know? That must have been quite a while—"

"You know what you did with the Minifons! And don't ask *me!*"

"Well, well. Hmm. Let me see—what *did* I *do* with them?"

"What did you do with them, Mr. Hoffa!"

As a parent to a child: "Mr. Kennedy. I bought some Minifons. And there is no question about it. But I cannot recall what became of them."

"Yes, it must be difficult to remember with such a *selective* memory."

Jimmy wet his lips and, with a twinkle in his eyes, looked straight into the larger, blue eyes of his young opponent. "Well, I will have to stand on the answers that I have made in regards to my recollection and I cannot answer different, unless you give me some other recollection other than I have already answered." Put *that* through your head and see what comes out, sonny!

The audience roared over Senator McClellan's rapping gavel. Bobby stared unsmiling at Jimmy. Jimmy stared back. They held this stare long after quiet had returned to the room. Jimmy finally ended it, without losing the match: he winked at Bob. Furious, Kennedy resumed his attack.

"Mr. Hoffa. Did you ever wear a Minifon yourself? In order to record a fellow Teamster?"

Curious, Jimmy leaned forward. "You say 'wear.' What do you mean by 'wear'?"

The "uneducated" workingman sidestepping the rich Harvard lawyer at every turn. Aside from the personal chafing, what irked Bobby most was that he *had* the goods; he'd done his homework—one of his prime nemeses was unpreparedness; it was what had pitted him against Roy Cohn when they both worked for Joe McCarthy, then later pitted him against McCarthy as well: interrogating witnesses on hints, rumors, half-truths, incomplete information. Now here he was, documented to the teeth, and Hoffa was still dancing rings around him.

Bobby accosted Jimmy: "Now here we have two Teamster officials. Mr. Keating and Mr. Linteau. Both were convicted of taking kickback money from employers. And yet you continued paying them while they were in prison! What were you afraid of, Mr. Hoffa?"

Righteous, outraged, indignant, Jimmy burst. "I was not charged with any crime connected with them! Nor was I on trial! I was not afraid of them going to expose me, because they have nothing to expose! But, insofar as they were concerned, we felt—*I* felt—they had been with the union sufficient time, worked the hours they had worked . . . We knew their families, and decided to recommend that they be taken care of. And so we did."

Bobby was on him. "Mr. Hoffa! If you're looking around for charitable organizations to contribute union funds to, I'm sure you can get a better group than two individuals who *violated* their union trust! They received money from *employers!* These were not people out on the picket line who got into a fight—these were people who *received money from employers!* How can you possibly explain being so solicitous of them—unless you received some of the money yourself? Can you explain that?"

Words, words. "I think I have made my statement," Jimmy replied calmly.

"You don't have anything else to add to it?"

"Nothing."

Bobby riffled pages of his notes loudly. "Later, when they got out of jail, they *continued* to receive their money! All from union funds! Do you have anything to say to that?"

Jimmy, almost bored: "I have made the statement that I care to make for that answer. Unless there is some other question"—looking up at the row of Senators—"I suggest we move on."

The audience chuckled. Bobby let his glasses fall down from his hair to his nose. A recess was called. Bobby headed for the outside hall to get some air. He took a different door from the one Jimmy was going toward. Outside, Bobby ran into newsman Clark Mollenhoff and grinned malevolently.

"He's an *eel!* Come on, you got me into this, what do I do now?"

"Just keep punching, Bob."

"But my God, it took so much to get him up there! We've come such a long way . . . he *can't* slip through."

Clark Mollenhoff's shoulders were higher than Bobby's head; his voice was heavy and reassuring. "Don't let him get your goat. You're getting the stuff out into the open. Don't forget that. He can tap-dance on your face, but he can't stop the evidence from being heard."

Such a long way didn't say half of it. It had been no quick, easy thing to get Jimmy Hoffa from International Teamsters Headquarters in the Marble Palace to the witness chair.

In fact, it hadn't been any quick, easy thing to get Bobby Kennedy interested in Organized Labor at all, much less Jimmy Hoffa himself.

After all we've been through didn't say half of it, either.

BOOK ONE

Basic Training

Nineteen twenty-nine. The Stock Market had just crashed.

Since the mystical moment when the Jazz Age began, the Market of the Roaring Twenties hadn't been the preserve of investors, it had been the greatest floating crapshoot of all time.

It was like a national lottery, a what-the-hell sweepstakes into which everybody and his brother threw a chunk of their paychecks, gambling for the Big Score that would lift them out of their workaday world and up to where the nifties played: Easy Street, USA.

A dead end, as it turned out, to almost everybody's shock.

Some chose despair and even death over failure and poverty.

Others did not.

When the noon whistle blew at the nearby factories, the stock boys at Frank and Cedar's Department Store in Detroit broke for lunch. One was a sixteen-year old kid named Jimmy Hoffa, the other his friend, Walt Murphy. As usual, they bummed some milk from the kitchen crew and copped some bulk chocolate for dessert out of the Candy Cage, to which Jimmy had the key, and took their lunch pails outside to the loading platform. But today they didn't dig in very heartily. Jimmy especially was down in the dumps, disillusioned and scared. He bit into the sandwich his mother had made.

"You hear anything new, Murph?"

"Yeah. Another five this Saturday, maybe more."

"Christ. Us, you think?"

"I dunno. One of these days, though. Me first, prob'ly."

Jimmy had been there longer, two years. It was a good, clean job and he liked it: just enough heavy work from the unloading and the baling, just enough moving around and chewing the rag with the people who stocked the counters. Twelve bucks a week, six days a week, ten hours a day. No great shakes, but not bad, either—when he dropped the envelope on his mother's kitchen table every week the look on her face was worth it right there. Not for a second did he ever regret his decision of two years back, when, in September of '27, he sat against the gym wall with all the others entering Western High, waiting for the old fogey to get to the H's. He didn't know whether he was going to yell "Here!" when she called his name or not. By then he had it down to his mother or school. Work or school. She herself was all for his going on —he was smart and a good student. But it wasn't up to her, so far as he was concerned. It was up to him.

Only too well could he remember the earlier days. His German-Irish coal-drilling old man, dead. Jimmy was seven then. That was back in Stringtown (for stringing clams), their section of Brazil, Indiana. Jimmy had been born there, on St. Valentine's day, ha ha. Two weeks later his mother left him and his brother and his two sisters to go cook in the restaurant on Main Street, do housework for the big-house rich-ies up the Hill, then bring home washing on top of that. His sister, Jennetta, helped her do the ironing; he and his brother, Billy, did the delivering, but it wasn't enough: he watched her, pale and thin, start to dry up before her time, never complaining but buckling under it all.

Steely and all-Irish, in '24 she'd picked them up and moved after bigger money in Detroit, and found it: first she worked in a laundry, then got on the pro-duction line in an auto-parts factory, finally landed a job in Fleetwood, polishing radiator caps for Fisher Body. Like the rest, Jimmy kept chipping in as best he could, first as a fifty-cent bag boy weekends in a gro-cery store, then as a delivery "man," which meant a

9

nickel or dime extra in tips. Still, his ma kept looking so tired. When the hell would the day come when he could look at her and not see that goddamn tired look on her wonderful face?

By the time the registration monitor got to the G's, Jimmy was long gone out of his seat and away from the school forever. Frank and Cedar's hired him the very next day, and after two years they were giving him enough smiles and hints to let him give in to his dreams of moving up . . . clerk, floorwalker, assistant manager—the whole American stairway to the stars.

His mouth full of banana, Murph on the loading platform said, "I figger, fug the Crash, though, y'know, Jimmy?"

"Oh yeah? You gonna learn how to eat skins?"

"No, but you're gettin' warm. I figger, if things is good or if things is bad, what's the one thing people *hafta* keep on doin'?"

Jimmy thought, *Screwing?*, but kept mum. He hated talking or even hearing about dirty stuff. It wasn't religious with him—he already hated any and all religions, keep you down, fill your head with bullshit—he just didn't like that kind of talk, that was all.

"Ya got two guesses, Jim."

"Shut up and say it—what?"

"Eat. People always gotta eat."

"So?"

"So get into the food business."

Jimmy slid his sharp, gray-green eyes away from the truck yard and onto his friend's face beside him. *Out of the mouths of babes,* he thought. Murphy's statement made more sense to him than anything he'd ever heard before in his life.

Less than a thousand miles east, a skinny four-year-old boy lay belly down on the blue-green rug of the living room—not the formal living room, the informal one—in his parents' mansion in Bronxville, New York. To the boy, the rug was water, and he was swimming through it expertly and ferociously, better than his older brother Jack, just as good as his oldest brother, Joe; his four older sisters didn't count.

Watching from the adjoining study, his father

thought he was having a fit or throwing a tantrum and shouted, "Bob! Bobby!" But then he noticed how the kid was kicking his feet and moving his arms, and he chuckled. Only a moment ago he had been thinking, *That's no way for a millionaire to behave!* But now he realized that his seventh child and youngest son was practicing an ability. *Good,* he thought. *That's exactly the way for a Kennedy to behave, millionaire or not!* And, although he didn't know it yet, Bobby was indeed a bonafide millionaire. His father had just that week made him one. Likewise each of his brothers and sisters. Trust accounts for all. Joseph P. Kennedy, Senior, late of Boston, now of New York, wasn't called the Wolf of Wall Street without reason.

"Any man who holds out for top dollar is a fool" was the senior Joe's motto so far as the stock market was concerned. Out of taste and compassion he would not, of course, now say this to any of his colleagues who had got hurt or gone under; and, to his few fellow survivors, it didn't need to be said. But he'd say it anyway and often to them, for wasn't he the strapping, living, prosperous proof of its wisdom? Granted, he had been more of a manipulator than a speculator, but nevertheless and simply: Joe Kennedy had seen Black Tuesday coming and got out, six months before the roof caved in.

He went in and scooped Bobby up out of the water, held him high in the air over his head until the boy laughed, then brought him down in and close to his chest. Bobby hugged his neck. His father said, "Take a walk?"

"Okay."

Hand in hand, they passed through the French doors to the terrace, across it and down onto the spacious, manicured lawns. The father knew enough not to intrude upon the child's imaginings, which could embarrass him, so he talked in parallel terms: "Know what I was thinking about today, Bob?"

"No, what?"

"The Cape. Boy, I can still see you and Joe off the boat. You must've jumped into that drink a hundred times in a row! You remember that?"

"Yeah."

11

"And you were a hundred percent right, too! Only way to learn how to swim is to get wet! You'd jump in, Joe'd pull you out. You'd jump right back in, Joe'd—"

"I didn't want him to pull me out!"

The father laughed, big white teeth beneath circle-lensed spectacles; he was forty, looked thirty. "I know you didn't, bud. Still, we were all a little scared for you. Your mother said—"

"I'm not little!"

"Didn't say you were! Just young, that's all."

"I'm not young, either! And I swam, Dad! I learned to swim!"

He squeezed the boy's tiny hand even tighter. "You sure did, my man, you sure as hell did! I was very proud of you."

"And it was cold, too!"

"It certainly was. Well, the Sound, you know, gets—"

"And it was deep!"

"Well, sure! Heck, you were—"

"And dark!"

"Ha! Were you scared?"

"No!"

God, how I love this kid, Joe thought, not quite admitting, *He reminds me of me.*

They passed the girls' croquet court and came to the gazebo, beyond which the grass wasn't so thick any more: the boys' sports had brought the earth through. A ball, a bat, and a couple of mitts lay in a heap. "Dammit, I've told you a thousand times not to leave good equipment lying around! That stuff costs a lot of money, you know!"

"I didn't do it, Dad!" He picked up the damp football and threw it hard at his father. His hands were still so small he had to hurl it like a shot-put or a grenade. But he could catch the thing, and after a few easy lobs he yelled, "I'll go out for it! Throw it higher!", turning the game of catch into screen-pass drill.

His father kept throwing it, farther and harder, to see just what would be considered too far, too hard, too high for the boy. He had to feel great sympathy for

12

Bob: the runt, the last of the lineup, unless Rose was getting any more bright ideas, four girls between himself and his idolized brothers, and physically a peanut to boot. But talk about gung ho! As hard as everything came for him in a brood where everything came so easy for the others, or seemed to so far, this little guy—Oops, he had tripped and fallen three times now. "That's it, I'm beat!" Joe called. Over the boy's protests he said, "C'mon, let's raid the icebox. I'll tell you all about the movies, how's that? Want to hear about Hollywood?"

"Aw, Dad."

"Give me a break. These are my best shoes."

"Okay, if you wanna give up." They took hands again and headed back to the huge house. "Did you see Tom Mix?"

"Yup! One day I was . . ." Mix had been the least of it for Joe out West, but he'd tell the boy only some of the adventure-and-glory parts now. Which would definitely not include Gloria Swanson and her dadratted *Queen Kelly!* As much as he liked and admired her, how he could ever have let *that* bundle of whoopie get produced under his auspices he'd never know. He'd got his name disassociated from it just in the nick of time. Setting up RKO was one thing, but let anybody in the Church in Boston or New York get a whiff of his being involved in the making of anything that red-hot and . . . He shuddered to think of the consequences.

Still, now that he was back in the clearer, colder air of the East, and could see better just what a terrible thing it was that was coming down upon the country, he had to think, hell, let them run it if they want to. All those millions of less blessed, less fortunate people beyond his hedges were going to need all the diversion and distraction they could get.

A crony in the City that day at lunch had, with the awareness of a decapitated chicken, asked him, "What now, Mr. Kennedy?"

"What *what* now, Eric?"

"What's the best thing to invest in now?"

"Children," Joe had replied, deadpan. "That's where my money's gone." He had meant it, at the

13

time quite literally and now, walking with Bobby, he realized he had meant it in all senses: for once, what was true for the millionaire was just as true for the most destitute farmer or apple peddler: the people of the thirties would have only one going concern in which to invest—their hopes, now that their money was gone, were in their children.

All Viola Riddle Hoffa's children were now working but ends were still not meeting, so she began taking in boarders as well as laundry. One was a young guy named Jim Langley; he was in the food business, a driver for the Kroger grocery chain. The night of the day Jimmy had talked with Walt Murphy, Langley and Jennetta were as usual behind the closed doors of the parlor doing what engaged couples did in those times. Jimmy knew and didn't care: he knocked just once, then sent the sliding wooden doors crashing back into their wall slots. "Jim, I gotta talk to ya!"

Langley didn't give it a second's thought—yes, yes sure he'd talk to somebody down at Kroger's about a job for him.

Langley did, lying that Jimmy was eighteen, and the next afternoon Jimmy showed up on time at the giant warehouse on Green Street. The night foreman was a bitter, sadistic little man named Gus Cantling and, as Jimmy was to learn, known by all the men working under him as "the Littlebastard." Jimmy himself was only five five and a half, but next to Cantling he felt tall. There were no applications to fill out, no real personnel procedures at all besides confronting the Littlebastard face to face, which Jimmy did.

"Mr. Cantling? I'm a friend of Jim Langley's, and he said he—"

"Who cares. Whatta *you* want, punk?"

"A job."

"Why?"

"Why? I'm hungry, that's why, and my family's hungry."

The Littlebastard kept making checks on his clipboard. "Who isn't. How old are ya?"

"Eighteen, like Langley—"

"Bullshit."

14

"Okay. Sixteen. But I'm strong as anybody eighteen. Stronger! Show me something you want lifted and I'll lift it."

"What about school?"

"I quit."

"Listen, I got enough stupid gorillas."

"I ain't stupid! Come on, my mother works in a factory and takes in laundry and my old man's dead. Whaddya say?"

Cantling took the cigar stub out of his mouth, spat brown onto the loading platform's deck, put the cigar back in, and said, "H-O-F-F-A?"

"Right."

"Start now. Five at night to five in the mornin'. Thirty-two cents an hour, but ya get paid just for the time ya work. Work enough and at least ya'll eat regular. Still want it?"

"Yeah! I want it! Thanks a lot, Mr. Cantling, you won't be sorry."

Walking away, the Littlebastard snuffed. "I know *I* won't."

Elated, Jimmy took a walk for a half hour. Arriving back at five, he was told to take a number and get on line. It was a long line, some forty men and boys. At five-thirty Cantling appeared and read off numbers, slowly. Jimmy studied the faces around him: fear, longing, supplication, cold cynicism, fiery hatred —all aimed at the Littlebastard's face. When he heard his number, Jimmy's heart leaped, and he bounced up to join the others on the platform. It felt like being picked for a team, and he started throwing grins around. Nobody answered him. Then it dawned: more than half the guys were being sent away. The numbers had been chosen strictly by Gus Cantling's whim. Watching the losers straggle off, downcast, muttering, cursing guardedly, Jimmy found himself praying to his luck that he'd never be one of them; it made a taste in his throat that he hated. The Littlebastard looked at his night work crew, hollered "Rest period!" and, grinning, disappeared into his office.

Jimmy sputtered, "Rest period? We ain't done any work yet! What the hell's that supposed to mean?"

A weary-faced old-timer said, "Means there's no

15

trucks or freight cars in yet," and wandered off to join one of the card games being started. Some men dozed off, some read newpapers, some just smoked and stared into the middle distance, a few dropped down into the darkening cobblestone yard and began tossing a torn old football around. Jimmy grabbed a broom and started sweeping out the floor of the huge freight elevator behind the loading dock. A kid about Jimmy's age came over, smiling.

"Name's Bobby Holmes, what's yours?"

"Jimmy Hoffa." He quit sweeping and shook the guy's hand.

Bobby said, "Spare a cig?"

"Don't smoke. Sorry."

"What do you think you're doing, anyhow?"

"I came to work, I'm gonna work. I hate hangin' around."

"Like to work for nothing, do you?"

Jimmy stopped and met Bobby Holmes's amused eyes. "Oh," he said then, "I get it." He let the broom handle go slapping down against the corrugated-metal, straw-dirty floor and followed Bobby Holmes outside to wait.

Jimmy learned a lot more that first night. An engine rolled two freight cars up to the platform at about eight o'clock, and the men went at them, Jimmy lagging back only long enough to get the lay of the land, see how it was done. The cars were loaded to the brim, stem to stern with wooden crates full of lettuce. One set of three or four men would start off-loading the crates onto wooden flatbed wagons with huge wheels, wood-spoked and steel-rimmed. As the hole in the car grew, so did the number of men, until they had two "bucket brigades" going, one from each end of the car to the wagons. They alternated every half hour or so between being inside men and outside men, the latter not only loading the wagons, but also pushing them inside the vast, half-lit, freezing warehouse to be unloaded.

Halfway through the second freight car, the Little-bastard appeared out of nowhere and answered the question Jimmy had been about to ask Bobby Holmes: "You goldbrickin' sons of bitches! You try

16

pullin' a slowdown on me, you whores, and you've seen your last piece of work from me! I want these fuggin' cars empty and the hell out of here in ten minutes or you can all look someplace else tomorrow night! If you slime don't wanna work I got a thousand outside who do! Now speed it up!"

So it went through the night. In the morning Jimmy dragged his aching, but not that strained, body homeward, figuring: out of the twelve hours, they'd worked only six, meaning he'd made $1.92—eight cents less than he would have got at Frank and Cedars! Two hours more, eight cents less. But that was a fool's arithmetic, he decided. Cedar's was going to close down any day now, and Kroger's was going to stay in business. People had to eat. So he'd eat it, and hope things got better.

By the end of his first week he had made $15.36 for his forty-eight hours. The only snag was, he'd put in eighty hours. So this was how it felt to be a workingman.

In mid-thought and only half a block from his house, Jimmy dropped to the sidewalk and started ripping off pushups. It was a habit he'd started to keep his hydrant-like body hard, but by now it had come to be an escape valve for him, a surefire way of stopping thoughts that bothered him. Pushups were beautiful. You could do them anytime, anywhere—if you didn't care what people thought, which he didn't. And they worked for him again this cold early morning, except for one sickening thought that just wouldn't leave his mind: Gus Cantling.

Jimmy had never seen anything like him. He'd seen tough men and plenty of them, hair-trigger guys who'd just as soon hammer your face in as not. But the Littlebastard wasn't like that. Physically, Jimmy was sure, he couldn't fight his way out of a paper bag, and after studying him for a week Jimmy felt even surer that he'd yellow out to a cocker spaniel. But the bastard, the little tin Jesus, had something that made size and guts beside the point: his job. Cantling had authority, and authority meant he could hire and fire, and that meant power. The guys had talked about taking him out: down the elevator shaft, a grappling

17

hook in his throat, a push under a rolling freight car or truck, a tire iron across his skull. Nobody'd ever know who did it, and there'd be a thousand likely suspects—half the men in Detroit would confess to it gladly.

And even after only one week, Jimmy could see the sense in doing it. He couldn't imagine how some of the guys had taken the mental's shit for years. The only time he ever smiled, if you called that dirty little sneer a smile, was after he'd finished reading numbers or just fired some starving skeleton who had to go home empty-handed to face six kids and a wife eating bread smeared with lard, with salt and pepper if they were lucky. Jimmy could see Cantling on a slave ship, happy as a pig in shit. Sometimes Jimmy could practically see a bullwhip in his hand at the warehouse: how he'd love to open your back for you, instead of just yelling threats or laying you off.

Whenever vengeance talk got too crazy, the one guy who'd always cool it was Sam Carson, the oldest worker on the crew, the one who had once belonged to a union someplace. Sam would say, and they would believe him, "The Littlebastard's a doozy, all right. Bad as they come. But belay it. They got plenty more where he come from. You'd just be buyin' yourselves one we wouldn't know his habits. Least we know what that snake's gonna do."

Still, Jimmy dreamed of making mincemeat out of Cantling. How could you slave away under a crazy like that and still look yourself in the mirror? Made you feel like some kind of animal, hard times or not.

Jimmy sprang to his feet and sprinted home. The house was still asleep. He opened the icebox and leaned his pay envelope upright against a bottle of milk, then went to bed. He'd keep on. He was different from the next dozen or fifty guys. His time would come. He'd get the Littlebastard, no matter how long it took.

America in the thirties. The decade of the Depression. Worse did come to worst. The hallowed, ingrained American spirit of "it's bound to be better around the next corner" came to one too many corners, weakened, dropped and died. Flappers, jazz, rollicking family picnics in the country, dreams of owning a motorcar, a farm, a house, a shop, of sending one's kids to college—all turned to ashes overnight and blew away with the wind. Life narrowed down to the holes in your children's shoes and where were you going to find the cardboard with which to patch them. People turned to the religions in unprecedented droves, but only those most thoroughly conditioned to approve of and abide life as a valley of tears, anguish, want, and grief found much comfort or strength there.

Where had the God of the New Testament gone? Only the God of the Old seemed to be still operating, the God of locusts, pestilence, famine, blood, vengeance. No manna came. Drought made a dustbowl out of the nation's breadbasket. People yanked harshly at their roots, and a country of settlers perforce became a country of nomads. Mass exoduses, with no Promised Land to head for, only rumors and myths. Hoovervilles grew like fungus: whole cities of families living in cardboard-and-tar-paper huts in public parks, defecating into dug holes. Humans who had tasted steak now clawed like dogs into swill buckets and garbage cans. No Welfare, no Unemployment benefits, no relief, no Aid to Dependent Children, no nothing. The vivid image of ex-bankers peddling apples from a cart survived to become a cartoon in later years, as "Brother, Can You Spare a Dime?" came to be sung lightheartedly. But in the thirties they were real, and anything but funny. What apples the man didn't sell he ate and fed to his family, and they kept no doctors away, and the doctors worked on the cuff or for barter —the ones who didn't close their black bags and join the millions of others in scrounging, waiting, begging, fighting for a job, any job, any work. If you are what you eat, you are what you don't eat; it took an alarmingly short time for the corroding body to wizen the soul. The universe took over. Gaunt, bitter, hopeless, *stopped,* America lapsed into a coma.

Even in the best of times the lives of the immensely rich seem, like those of royalty, to be tales sung by a troubadour who has visited the dream place of supermen or angels: enviable, entertaining, imaginable, but not quite believable. In the worst of times those lives become totally unbelievable and unimaginable by the masses of ordinary people; hearing about them would cause hate and a wish to destroy. Thus, the prudent prince closes his castle gates to the eyes of the starving peasantry.

Through most of the Depression decade, the Kennedys continued to live in Bronxville, winter at Palm Beach, and summer at Hyannisport, Cape Cod—but quietly and privately. After all, when equality gets pushed too far, everybody loses. If everyone on the foundering ship lay down as equals on the deck to wait for the sinking, who would mend the holes and repair the engines? Franklin Delano Roosevelt, rich as hell, was President of the United States and using everything he had to bring the people a New Deal, his name for saving the ship and getting it back on course. And Joseph P. Kennedy, Senior, was one of the ones trying to help him. Likely he still had political ambitions of his own, the urge toward public service and power being in his genes. Whatever, he saw FDR as America's last best hope. In 1932 and again in 1936, the Wolf of Wall Street worked hard and used all his resources to help keep Roosevelt in the White House.

"Mother!" yelped one of the girls. "That pig stinks! Tell him he's got to get rid of it!"

Rose Kennedy smiled. "Porky's quite clean, and he's Bobby's piggy bank. You should all be so resourceful."

In addition to Porky, Bobby had uncountable white rabbits and a paper route going for him. His father had put Bobby and the rest of them (now including another sister and another brother: he was no longer the youngest!) on strict allowances. Bobby didn't think his was adequate, and so had branched out into sidelines of his own devising, like the pig, the rabbits, a magazine route. He fast saw the law of diminishing returns at work in the magazines and promptly lost interest in them. First, he quit walking door to door and started using the chauffeur to cruise him on his appointed rounds; then, he finagled the driver into doing it for him. Finally he gave it up as a lost cause.

He was indifferent to school and was kept back in the third grade. He was a Cub Scout. He was a kid. And as such he was in a world of his own. That being given an actual childhood was a luxury in those mean years was something he couldn't yet know. To him, a kid, there were only two worlds, the one inside him and the one outside; and, since he was a Kennedy, the one outside dwelled within the same walls he did: his family. The births of the two youngest, Jean and Ted, seemed to blur rather than define his particular place in the lineup. He no longer enjoyed so much direct attention from his father. His mother kept reminding him, "The seventh child is the lucky one," but he'd have to take her word for it, it sure didn't feel very lucky to him. A pragmatist, he paid attention to and extracted from the whirlwind around him, noting what pleased and what did not, and set his will to doing what pleased. One thing that invariably pleased was punctuality.

He was playing with one of his sisters just before lunch one day. "Lunch!" He jumped up and dashed for the dining room—straight through the glass door, which happened to be closed at the time.

HailMaryfullofgracetheLordiswithTheeblessedart ThouamongwomenandblessedisthefruitofThywombJesus

21

*HolyMaryMotherofGodprayforussinnersnowandatthe
hourofourdeathamenHailMaryfullofgracethe . . .*

He said it over and over to himself, going up on the
lift, getting into his skis, waiting his turn, looking down
the slope, then going off and down. He won. It
was the first clear, earned-with-agony-and-practice-
and-will victory of his life, and it tasted so sweet he
wanted to yell, and did. It was St. Moritz, 1939; he
was fourteen.

That was where they wintered now. They summered
in Cannes, on the Riviera. They lived at No. 14
Prince's Gate in Grosvenor Square, London. The place
was a gift from J. P. Morgan to the American people.
It had thirty-six rooms and a staff of twenty-three, plus
three chauffeurs. It was the American Embassy, and
Bob's father had been appointed Ambassador to the
Court of St. James's by FDR the year before. They
weekended at Astor, where their seven horses were
kept. They met the King and the Queen and the
Princesses. They saw their pictures in the papers all
the time, for England loved them: their looks, the life
they had brought to No. 14, the dash they displayed.
Just the past March they had all, except Joe Jr., gone to
Rome for the Coronation of Pope Pius XII, who, as
Cardinal Pacelli, had been their guest back in Bronxville.

Didn't everybody live this way? No, not everybody.
Very, very few lived this way, and now Robert Francis
Kennedy knew that. And knowing it was to eventually
change and fix his life, and the lives of others.

The two guys crossed the yard, heading for the
lunch wagon parked outside Kroger's gate. Jimmy, still
passing crates from the truck back to the platform,
yelled after them, "And a doughnut or somethin' too,
if he's got it!" One waved an okay. They were two of
the guys whose numbers had been called for the day
shift, which wouldn't start for another half hour. Those
turned away didn't break up and move off as quickly
as they used to. It was 1931, and the men were different in other ways as well. There were more of them,
for one thing, but that wasn't what caught the
eighteen-year-old Jimmy Hoffa's eye: it was how they

looked like refugees off a boat from some island of Hell. Their cheekbones bulged and their eyeballs stuck out from their sockets; their hair was long or scissors-chopped, and "rags" was too good a word for the clothes they showed up in.

Jimmy, Bobby Holmes, and Sam Carson were the only ones left of the original bunch. God knew why. Each did the work of two men; that must've been it. It sure wasn't any love for them on Gus Cantling's part. If anything, he'd grown even more vicious. The little bastard was out on the platform near them right now. In May, the sun rising through the mist of first light, cutting through the nighttime freeze and wet with yellow light and warmth, looked good even in Detroit. Maybe the prick was enjoying the spectacle. No such luck. He was merely waiting. When the two dayworkers reached the loading platform with the trays of coffee and doughnuts, Cantling waited until the food had been dispensed, then spat at the top of his voice, "You two! Turn in your slips! You're fired!"

They were stunned speechless. By the time one had come out of it enough to start sputtering, Cantling was back on the other side of his office door. He had paused only long enough to call out two new numbers. From the lingering job hunters, the waiting day crew, and those still working, bubbles of words broke anonymously in the air.

"Why?"

"What the hell they do?"

"That cocksucker!"

Jimmy whispered to Sam Carson, "He can't do that, can he?"

"He just did."

"But, Sammy!"

"Yeah. He went too far this time."

At about nine that night, Gus Cantling pricked up his ears. His door was closed, but he could hear them. He hadn't heard that sound in a long time, but he knew exactly what it was. Something thick and sweet twisted in his chest, and he felt the smile curl on his lips.

He opened the door. The yard was empty. Six workers hung around on the platform, waiting for the next truck to pull in. The rest were inside the warehouse, talking low, huddled close in the light of their cigarettes and the low-watt bulbs overhead.

Jimmy was talking. "Yeah, but, Sammy, he's got all those lepers out there! They'd *kill* to work! They're fuggin' starvin'! If we go—"

"We don't go, kid. We strike. That don't mean go. You stay and you fight."

Bobby exhaled. "Union! Anybody give a shit that it's illegal in this state?"

"So's slavery," Sam grunted.

Inside his office, Cantling hung the receiver back on its hook. He went outside. A truck had come in, and the whole crew was going at it. He lit a fresh cigar and yelled, "Carson and Hoffa! We're heavy by two! You're through for the night!"

Jimmy and Sam walked down the dark Detroit streets, past warehouses and shut factories. Jimmy tried to laugh. "Like I said before, all we got to lose is our jobs or our life. Now I guess it's just our life, huh?"

"Yeah? And what the Christ's that worth, livin' like this?"

"I don't know, Sammy. Nobody could ever organize those—"

"Anything unorganized can be organized. Anything! Don't ever forget that, Jimmy."

"That's bullshit, Sam."

Sam never got the chance to answer.

The long black car shot out of the next cross street, cornering with a scream of rubber on wet cobblestones. It came straight at them along the curb, lights blinding, doors coming open like wings. "Goons! Take off, Jimmy!"

When the footsteps behind reached his heels, Jimmy threw up both hands behind his head. The sap hit so hard he was sure his wrists had broken, and he went down. The kick to his groin came at once, and he vomited. He curled his knees up to his chin and played dead, drunk with pain. Through tears he saw his man run across the street to join the other two, working Sam against the post of the streetlight. Sam's face was already spaghetti sauce in the yellow light. One man held his arms back behind the pole. One hammered his kidneys. The other kept punching his face. Jimmy crawled to the middle of the narrow street, but still couldn't make it to his feet. Fire burned in his intestines, and his hands felt dead. Then he couldn't crawl any more. He yelled, "I'm coming, Sam," but it came out a whisper. He saw no more, only heard.

Flesh and metal against flesh finally stopped. Sammy's voice rattled up out of some deep hole: "You ... boys ... finished now?"

The hammer of a pistol cocked. A voice, a little out of breath but clear and deep, said, "Not yet, Carson. You're takin' the whole trip."

"Kill me ... and you gotta kill the witness."

A laugh. "Tough shit for the witness."

Jimmy in the street felt the cold muzzle of a gun under his left ear. "That was fuggin' smart, Sam. Thanks!"

The goons laughed.

But Sammy was still maneuvering. "Wait, wait, what's your hurry? Listen, you gettin' paid for this? How much?"

"Plenty!"

"I mean it—how much? I know the rates!"

One goon laughed. "Go ahead and tell 'im. What's the dif?"

"Yeah," the second voice agreed. "Dyin' man's last wish!"

"Five. Five big ones, Carson. Thanks for the—"

"Not the bonus, you asshole," Sam said quietly and evenly. His voice sounded kind of gurgly, but strong again. "The job. I mean the job—how much for findin' me?"

The lead goon hesitated, then said, "Two and a half a week."

"Startin' tonight, right?"

"Right."

"Jerks!" Sam snorted. "So if ya knock us off now, you're outta work, right? No two fifty. Just the five. For the three of ya! Jesus!"

Jimmy felt the gun barrel separate from his neck. The night air hung heavy with silence.

Sam filled the gap: "Just keep on lookin', why don't

yez? Two fifty a week for hide-and-seek ain't bad! Makes ya wonder if ya ever wanna find, y'know?"

Jimmy thought the silence would never end.

Finally: "Christ, you're right. Carson's right. See you around, Sam."

Sammy laughed. "Not if you're smart."

Jimmy heard shoe soles, car creaks, door slams, then the car roaring off into the night. He looked up in time to see it was a Packard, then rolled over and lay flat on his back, staring up at the starless sky. Then he began to laugh. It hurt, but he couldn't help it. He hooted to the rooftops.

"Sammy, Sammy, Sammy, you old bastard, you *did* it! You fuggin' organized 'em! *You organized goons!*"

Sammy stopped wiping the blood off his face long enough to light a smoke. He chuckled into his dripping, crimson handkerchief. "Well, they were unorganized, weren't they?"

Jimmy thought for a long while. Then: "Sammy?"

"Yeah?"

"What was that bump-off-the-witness shit? Why?"

"Sorry, kid. I was buyin' time, or tryin' to. But you know somethin' else?"

"What?"

"You're always alone, Jim. It's always just you when it comes down to the hard place."

"Sam?"

"Yeah, kid?"

"I'm in, Sam. What do you want to do?"

The next night their numbers weren't called, but the night after that they were. The load was called reefers. They were iceboxes on wheels, full of fresh strawberries, to be moved into the warehouse's cold-storage rooms as fast as posible. Cantling needed all the ablebodied, undiseased help he could get, and he was out there with them cracking the whip all night. Beyond the tracks in the yard was what looked like a hobo jungle: some ten or a dozen bent figures around a small fire. Job hunters with no place better to go, they'd hang around all night sometimes, praying for an accident or a heart attack or some other break from God that might mean work for them. Near midnight, they were joined by two new men—Sam Carson and Jimmy Hoffa. Jimmy was the first to get work.

The guy slinging the heavy crates opposite Jimmy on the line looked like a bag of bones to begin with. He'd started getting the shakes about an hour before, but now it looked as if he was going to conk out altogether. "Steady," Jimmy sang to him, "steady, keep the swing, just keep the swing, forget how heavy they are . . ." But it was no good. The guy caught a crate and held it, swaying in place. "Pass it! Swing it!" He couldn't. He dropped it. Shovelfuls of ice and hundreds of red, ripe strawberries went dancing all over the platform. A hand, Cantling's, pulled him off the line by the back of the neck. "That's it! You're home! Clear out!" Then he cupped his hands to his mouth and yelled to the men at the fire, "First one up here works!"

Sam moved only his head, to watch the sorry race. Incredibly, the first hand to touch the platform belonged to one Sam had figured was already dead but didn't know enough to lie down. *Starving'll do it,* he reflected. *Give you speed you don't have.*

Gus Cantling barked into the skeleton's face, "Ever handle berries before?"

"Plenty," the man croaked, "lots of experience!"

Cantling stepped back to let him climb up. "Jesus Christ, you don't look like you can lift a feather!"

"I'm thin, that's all. Always have been. I'm strong enough, though, you'll see, honest." Then he coughed.

"Shit—you got TB, right?"

"No, no! It's nothing. A cold, that's all. Too many smokes, you know."

"Okay, I ain't got all night, you was first, so get your ass in there. Any trouble and you're right back out again, got it?"

The cadaver ran over and filled the empty space. Jimmy looked at him and thought, *You think it's good luck, but it ain't.*

Take, swing, pass. Take, swing, pass. After another ten minutes, the guy next to Jimmy reported, "Okay, the word's all down the line, Jimmy."

"They all with me?"

"Yeah!"

27

"You sure?"

"Yeah!"

"Beautiful. Wait on me, now, just wait on me."

The new man said, "What's up?"

Jimmy smiled, letting the word seep through his teeth: "Strike."

"Oh my God, no!" the man cried. "I have to get some money! My—"

"Shut up! It's on, and you're in it."

Cantling screamed from behind him: "You can talk at home, Hoffa! Shut up and move that—"

A full crate in both hands, Jimmy straightened up, saying lowly, "This is it."

As he turned and walked toward Cantling, every man played statue, causing an abrupt silence so weird that even the men at the fire turned their heads, as if at some loud noise. Sam Carson got to his feet and made for the warehouse.

Cantling's teeth almost cut his cigar stub in half at the sight of Jimmy Hoffa's deadly face coming at him. Only one figure kept moving behind him, and that was the starving man, pathetically running crate after crate from reefer to wagon by himself. Sam vaulted to the platform and went over to him. "Put it down, bud," he said quietly.

In tears, the baffled man whined, "No . . . no—my kids, I got kids they've got to—"

Sam dug his right hand into the bones of the man's shoulder and squeezed once, like a vise. "You want them to be orphans?" Then Sam dug into his pants and brought up a dollar bill, slapped it into the victim's hand, and shoved him gently toward the yard. "Come back tomorrow."

"After we win this thing!" Jimmy yelled back over his shoulder.

Cantling blinked and looked away first. Over Jimmy's shoulder he yelled, with a crack in his voice, "Get back to work, you eight-balls!"

Nobody moved.

Jimmy grinned. "Sorry. We're on strike."

The cigar dropped entirely. *Strike! Strike?* Listen, men, this ain't you. I know that. You get your asses

28

back to work and I'll forget it. This is between me and Hoffa now!"

"Now!" Jimmy said. Each man set his crate down gently.

"You're a dead one, Hoffa," the Littlebastard was hollering, but his voice said he was over his head now and knew it. "Them's ripe strawberries!" He was still yelling at the men but looking into Jimmy's waiting, smiling, flint-eyed face. "They're ripe strawberries! If they stay out, they spoil!"

Jimmy snarled. "*We* know that." Then he lifted the heavy crate straight up his chest and past his eyes until it was over his head, turned slightly and pitched it crashing down onto the platform. The berries spread like bloody buckshot.

"All right!" Cantling yelled. "We'll talk!"

"We will," Jimmy said, "but you won't!" He turned away and faced his men like a bandleader, starting the chant: "Blough! Blough! Blough!" Blough was Cantling's boss. "Blough! Blough! Blough! "Move your ass, you slime!" Jimmy barked at Cantling. "No Blough, no strawberries."

Cantling ran to the phone.

Blough was there in ten minutes, obviously pulled from sleep. Sam Carson started to walk to him. Jimmy caught up and passed him. "This is all mine now, Sammy. Stay out."

Jimmy made a deal with Blough: they'd finish unloading and storing the fragile strawberries that night in exchange for an open hearing of their grievances the next day at Kroger's main offices downtown. Blough agreed. He was nailed and he knew it.

Sam, Bobby Holmes, and another man named Hardy accompanied Jimmy, who did all the talking. Blough at his desk was flanked by other company officers. Cantling leaned against a wall in a corner, looking yellow and lilac, as if he had frostbite. Jimmy laid it out, and as he talked he found himself starting to move around, and he realized that their eyes and attention kept following him so long as he kept his gaze locked with Blough's.

"Point four, Mr. Cantling himself. He yells at us like he's herding swine. Well, we ain't swine. He's gotta stop that. And another thing he's gotta stop—no, this *you* have to stop, Mr. Blough. This man can no longer have the right to hire and fire! He—"

"Like hell," Cantling muttered.

"Quiet," Blough said. "I made a deal. They loaded the strawberries, and now we're by God going to hear their complaints."

"*No!*" Jimmy heard himself shout; he saw his index finger aimed between Blough's eyes. "No! These are not complaints! These are demands, sir! Yeah, we unloaded your strawberries, and now these are our *terms*. For not shutting you down dead as a Thanksgiving turkey!"

Cantling weaseled forward. "Mr. Blough, give these bastards an inch and they'll—"

"You!" Jimmy stopped him. "Our next demand could be that they fire you! Now, if you don't clam up, we *will* demand it, and we'll goddamn *get* it!"

Cantling looked at Blough. Blough's eyes were still glued on Jimmy.

"All right now," Jimmy continued, not yelling but speaking at the exact same pitch at which this Mr. Blough had spoken. Some sixth sense inside Jimmy had detected the man's frequency and informed him that it would be smart to speak to Blough on it. "Five. We know you can't do much about our waiting times, but you can fix where we have to wait. There's no place to sit, and no fit place to eat our meals. We demand both. Six. We're all still puttin' in seventy, eighty hours a week to get our forty-eight. That's okay when we know for sure that work's comin' in. But sometimes it don't. So. We demand a call time and a guarantee of half a day's pay."

Blough had begun nodding yes to the call time, but the pay demand froze him. "Question!"

"Yes, sir."

"What if I just say no?"

"What if I just say you got two more carloads of ripe strawberries comin' in tonight?"

"I could hire other men to unload them, my friend."

"Mr. Blough, men don't work too good with busted heads."

30

Carson, Holmes, and Hardy chuckled.

"Quiet!" Jimmy whispered, still looking into Blough's eyes.

Without consulting any of his men, Blough leaned back in his swivel chair and said, "All right. You've made yourself a deal." He extended his hand. Jimmy's was already there. As they shook, Blough said, "Mr. Hoffa. You win . . . this time. But take an older man's advice. Don't push it."

Jimmy let go of his hand abruptly. "I'll go put my men back to work now."

"Your men?"

"Our men."

Blough's voice stopped him at the door. "Mr. Hoffa."

"Yes, sir."

"How old are you?"

"Eighteen."

"Think you'll ever make nineteen?"

Outside, the others started to burst out in jubilation, but Jimmy said, "Hold it. Wait." They grabbed a trolley to the warehouse. There, fifty or more men were waiting. Jimmy mounted a crate. His face was granite; it looked like bad news. Then he dropped the mask, let his face break wide open with shining eyes and teeth, threw up both his arms, and sang, "We did it! We won! We won! We beat 'em! You got it all!" Under the tumult that followed, Jimmy side-mouthed to Carson, "You were right, Sam. Blough and all his cronies. . . it's just one thing, like one person. And all these guys. There could be a hundred of 'em, and they're all just one thing. Just one, whole beautiful *thing!*"

Sam Carson chortled. "I never said that, Jimmy. But if you say so." He was about to call him kid, but stopped. "If you say so!"

The snakes that infiltrated the dune grasses were harmless, but they were long and black and swift, and almost everybody was afraid to go near them. As the two young men walked along the sand paths through the dunes to the beach, their family house high behind them, the shorter one stopped abruptly. The other one said, "What?"

"Ssh!" This one had a round head and the sharp-edged face of a falcon; his body, tanned now, was thin but wiry and looked made of nothing but bone and gristle. He remained poised in mid-step, looking to his left. Then he suddenly shot forward and downward. When he came up he had a four-foot adult snake by the tail. Yelling "Hay-ya!" he whip-cracked it in the air, breaking its back.

His brother laughed. "Terrific! It'll be a great comfort to know I'm leaving Saint Patrick back here in charge!"

Bobby blushed. "They frighten the little kids."

Jack was taller, broader, square-headed, his face softer and more open than Bob's. He was going away soon. To war. Neither said it, but both knew this was probably their last time alone together for God knew how long. They resumed walking. Jack said, "God, I'd never touch one of those slimy bastards."

"They're dry, actually."

"I'll take your word for it."

Both were bareheaded and naked except for faded chinos rolled to their knees. The intervening years had somehow closed the abyss between them; Jack didn't seem so much older any more, which was both nurturing for Bob and maddening: with war going on now, Jack could go and he couldn't. It had been Jack who'd made the first move to friendship. Before that, it had always been the oldest, magic Joe, who had looked him in the eye, said he knew he was there. But then Jack just said it one day, about a year before: "You know, I never met you until you were there?"

"Come on. You were there, I was there."

"Yea, but no . . . no, I can remember it. I was eleven, I guess, and one day in you walked. Into my room. And I said, 'Holy mackerel, this little turd's my brother!' "

Crossing the beach now through the morning fog, Bob remembered exactly when Jack had told him that and blurted, "Jack? I want to say something. I'm sorry about me with the *Victura*."

"Aah, you raced all right."

"Sure, terrific, coming in thirteen out of fifteen's just outstanding! You always won on that boat! So *I* take

32

your boat, and . . . Well, it sure as hell wasn't the boat!"

They had reached the tideline. Jack picked up a driftwood stick and belted a pebble one-handed into the surf. "I told you then and I'll tell you now—and Dad knows this too, he's said it all your life—your odds are more even than mine or Joe's."

Bob also found a bat-size stick and started whacking stones into Nantucket Sound. The name suggests that it is a calm bay, perhaps, but there, off Hyannisport, it is open ocean, with thunderous surf. "My odds are even! Lovely, lovely."

"You know what we mean. I'll admit it in a minute —I have yet to break my ass over anything. Neither has Joe. The odds seem to be for us, that's all. It even scares me sometimes. But you, they're not against you, they're more . . . well, they're more even, as I said. It's a deadlock with you, so you have to break your ass very time out. You have to work twice as hard as anybody else. For everything. And, of course, nobody's ever accused you of being unwilling to bust hump."

Whack! "Ha, gotcha! Nothing short of the third tier counts, right?"

"Right." *Whack!*

"Yeah, but I bust hump and still lose half the time!"

"Less than half, Bobby."

Whack! "Yeah, that's true."

"You little—" *Whack!* "There! Over the fifth! Right on the sandbar!"

"Okay. From now on, *over* the sandbar."

Jack threw his stick into the waves. "Uh-oh, way short. You win." Grinning.

Bob looked at him. "You want to walk?"

"Yeah, let's walk. I miss this beach already."

"Watch it!" A tern had dive-bombed out of nowhere, straight at Jack's head, then looped and soared straight skyward again, followed by Bob's stick. "God I don't think I'll ever get used to them doing that."

"Well, they've got their nests and eggs right in the dunes there."

"I know. They're kind of like Dad, huh? Don't mess with *my* kids!"

Jack laughed. "You said it. 'Course, it's Joe doing the real flying now. He's up there someplace right now."

"You going to try to fly too, Jack?"

"Fantastic sailor like me? You kidding? Uh-uh— I'm putting in for a PT boat, if I can get it."

"Are you scared at all, Jack?"

"Of what? Hell, no! . . . Well, actually, to tell you the truth, kid, there are times . . . about three o'clock in the morning, usually, and I can't sleep . . . when I begin to see the vague glimmer of wisdom in our father's isolationist position."

Both brothers laughed loudly into the wind.

Then Bob said, "You want to run?"

"No, I don't want to run. If I beat you, you'll be depressed. And you have to be *it* for the duration around here, so we can't have you in a mope. And if you beat me, I'll get too depressed to end the war in two weeks!"

They sat down on the sand and gazed seaward. Jack pulled a crumpled pack of Luckies from his chinos. "Bobby?"

"No thanks."

Jack smoked. "By the way, heard about your noble attempt to get sprung out of Milton Academy—close but no cigar, huh?"

"Well, it worked once before, got me out of St. Paul's and into the Priory. Thought I'd give it another go."

"No harm trying. Mother's a pushover for that Catholic spiel, but you might as well swallow the fact that Dad's never going to let you go to an R.C. school. Christ. how long did he let you stay at Portsmouth?"

"Three seconds."

"As religious as he is, and with all the priests and bishops around all the time—don't ever forget his real side. He wants the world. And he wants it for us, too. When he was at Harvard himself, being a mick mackerel-snatcher kept him from the clubs he wanted to belong to. Well, it didn't keep me and Joe from them, and it won't keep you from them either. He loves that kind of progress."

"I did like the Benedictines, though."

"Of course. You're a fanatic. Forget it, though, as far as education goes. See you in Hah-vad Yahd, bozo. You're going to get all the right credentials whether you want them or not."

Bob sighed. "Aah, credentials for what, though? I'm sure as hell never going to Wall Street, or have a goddamn ticker tape on the goddamn porch of my goddamn summer house!"

"What language—some Catholic! But you've still got a lot of time, Bob, don't worry so much."

"Well, what are you going to do when you get back? Do you know?"

"No, but I don't worry about it. Write, maybe."

"Oh lord. *While England Slept . . . And With Whom?*"

Jack roared and shot his cigarette into the sea. "Aah, who knows. Maybe I'll be Mayor of Boston, like Fitz."

"Yeah, that's a good idea. You could do it, too."

"Thanks."

"Listen, Jack, when you're Mayor, can I have the Cape or Worcester or something?"

"Absolutely. Just name it."

"Terrific."

"But you'll have to go to law school first."

"God damn it!"

The long white Cadillac oozed to a stop at the curb. One man got out from the rear and crossed the street. He kept his right hand in the pocket of his suit jacket. When he reached the picket line he asked the first sign carrier who came near him, "Hoffa here?"

"Yeah, over there."

"The guy in the hat?"

"No, the other one."

He walked over to the other one. "You Hoffa?"

"Yeah."

"You business agent, Local Two Ninety-nine?"

Before the man could say no, the right pocket had exploded. Jimmy's brother, Billy, dropped to the sidewalk, a bullet in his stomach. He was out of commission for a while, but he lived.

35

A few days later the white Cadillac found the right Hoffa, supervising another picket line outside another trucking firm in another industrial outskirt of Detroit. This time the man said, "You Jimmy Hoffa?"

"Who wants to know?"

The man nodded toward the marching truckers. "Don't your boys get paid, Hoffa?"

"Yeah, they get paid, they get paid chicken shit."

"Uh-huh," the stranger grunted. He walked back to the Caddie. As he closed the rear door, the horn sounded three soft, musical notes. Like elephants, two trucks roared up, men dropping from their tailgates even before they stopped. Over a hundred heavy-weights wielding baseball bats and pick handles descended on the fifty strikers, swinging wood at faces, heads, shoulders, legs. Skin burst like overripe tomatoes. The sound of bones breaking cracked sickeningly in the air. Wading in, his powerful arms and fists flying, Jimmy kept yelling, "Don't run! Give it to 'em, give it to 'em!"

The driver of the Caddie yawned. "Enough?"

The man in the back said, "Nah, a lotta them stayed. There's a few still standin'." He lit a cigar and rolled his window down a crack to let the smoke out. "Okay. The mood I'm in is generous."

The three soft, musical notes sounded again, and the goons climbed back into the trucks, which sped away, followed slowly by the long white limousine.

Bleeding from a gash over his right eye, Jimmy helped his new union buddy Sandy Farrell to his feet. "You okay?"

"Yeah. Few of them are gonna have headaches to-night too, I'll tell ya!"

"All right—what's with the fuggin' white Caddie?"

"Christ, Jimmy, don't you know nothin'?"

"No, I don't know nothin'—who *are* they?"

"They're the Purple Gang, Jim."

"Jesus." The old-new Capone mob. "All right. Where they hang out, you know?"

"Yeah, I know, but we ain't—"

"Can it. Take me there. Enough's enough. Bobby! Sam! Get these guys fixed up and back on line!"

They grabbed a trolley. Jimmy didn't have enough

money for taxis or cars yet. Two Ninety-nine was supposed to pay him fifteen dollars a week out of the dues, but there weren't many dues yet. In fact, when he took it over he'd found a ten-thousand-dollar debt staring him in the face. He'd quickly got the dues to begin coming in, but was still taking only five bucks a week for himself.

In a doorway across from the First Street barroom, Sandy said, "That's it."

"Okay, wait here."

"Don't mess with 'em, Jim."

"Who's gonna mess with 'em? I'm gonna talk with 'em!"

"You're signin' your own death warrant."

"Bullshit. This ain't 'twenty-five, it's fuggin' 'thirty-five, and I ain't exactly empty-handed!"

"You're crazy."

"Yeah, like a fox. What the bosses can do, *I* can do! Money don't care who makes it, earns it, or spends it. You're talkin' me off my peak. Wish me luck."

"Wish you luck? Wish *me* luck—in findin' all the pieces."

Jimmy left him, crossed the street, and disappeared into the tavern, his white socks flashing in the sunlight as he walked.

In less than fifteen minutes, Jimmy was back out, strutting as cockily and jauntily as when he went in. "It's okay. They're out of the skull-cracking business. Ours, anyhow."

"What'd you do, Jimmy?"

"Reached an accommodation."

"I don't know. I don't like it."

"What's the matter?"

"I don't know, just—I mean, how the fug can hoods be bad for the bosses but good for us?"

"Ah, don't be an old woman. Listen, I'd make a deal with the goddamn devil himself if it meant this union quits losin' and starts winnin'! We're gonna win, and we're gonna keep on winnin', I don't care who I hafta use to do it. See all that blood today? See them poor bastards beat to the ground, when all they want's a decent day's pay for a day's work? You wanna keep

37

seein' that every fuggin' day of your life? Not me, brother."

"Well, let's get outta here, before they change their minds."

"No, you go. I got a second phase I gotta attend to." As he said it, the white Cadillac poured onto the street from behind the tavern, swung into the curb, and opened its rear door. The door was lined with fur. The seats were burgundy. The suit on the smiling, waiting man was silk. Jimmy got in, the door closed, and the car moved off down the one-way street. Sandy Farrell watched it go, block after block, until he couldn't see it any more.

When Jimmy struck the huge tobacco company for union recognition, no Purple Gang came to harass him, but he had a little trouble anyhow. A small gang of scabs had been hired by management to break the strike. But they were amateurs, and when Jimmy first spotted them he could read it in their gait. He pulled half a dozen of his toughest men off the line and said, "Look natural. We're havin' a smoke break. Give 'em the first punch, then we'll take 'em.'" This was for the benefit of the cordon of police overseeing the picketing.

The lead scab pulled a kid off the line and threw him against the plant's cyclone fence. "That's it," Jimmy said, and led the counterattack. He ducked under the swinging billy club and came up inside the big guy's defenses, punching away with both fists. The guy went down bloodied, but as Jimmy was looking to see where else he could help, the official billy club landed on the back of his neck. He came to inside the Black Maria running him in. "What the hell's this?" he protested to the sergeant. "They started it!"

The captain at the station said, "You can't pull a man in for defending himself, Donlan. Take him back."

As soon as Jimmy got back to the line and shouted his first word of encouragement, Donlan clapped him back in the wagon. In all, Jimmy made eighteen trips between the police station and the strike site that day. Around the tenth or so, they quit giving him the ride back and he ran out of money. On the last, he looked

38

up at the weary captain and said, "How about a dime for a coffee-and, huh?" The captain gave him the dime, with which he paid his trolley fare back to his striking truckers.

Then one early morning he showed up at a little laundry being struck. Although it was the girls who operated the mangles who were organizing against their seventeen-cents-an-hour wage and generally deplorable conditions, the outfit employed four drivers, all Teamsters, so Jimmy was called in to help things along. He'd threaten to pull the Teamsters out in sympathy, and the boss would have to listen to the girls. He saw two sights that day that he would never forget the rest of his life.

The first happened right away. A trolley line ran right past the laundry. Shortly before work time, a car clanged to a stop, loaded with female scabs. But the pickets had been tipped off and knew what they were going to do. Just as the last woman stepped down off the trolley, the strikers dropped their signs and charged the gaggle of scabs, stripping each and every one of them stark naked and sending them scattering with whacks across their behinds.

The second came later in the day and was of an entirely different and higher order of beauty: the blondest hair and the bluest eyes in the most beautiful face James Riddle Hoffa had ever seen. Up to now, until this vision, Jimmy hadn't had overly much to do with girls. He lived by a very nuts-and-bolts philosophy: what added to the efficiency of your performance, you did; what didn't, you didn't. For him, smoke, booze, and dames had fallen into the latter category. But Josephine Poszywak had looks to make an angel hide its face. They fell in love and got married and stayed married ever after.

Jimmy had been right: he was as different and as special as he felt, and it didn't go unnoticed. First Detroit saw it, then New York. They gave him room, and when he had it filled, they gave him more. He was dispatched out of state, to Ohio, to Illinois, to Minnesota, to wherever the International Teamsters were having trouble that they couldn't handle without the "little guy's" magic touch. Nobody asked too many questions about how Jimmy Hoffa did what he did. His helpers? Union men, it was presumed, who were particularly loyal to Jimmy and particularly adept at street-fighting. And anyhow, it was wartime out in those streets, on those docks and loading platforms. It was us against them, and us was in the right because us was the little guys being screwed and abused, and in wartime a different set of rules comes into play: you fight fire with fire, and you fire first if you want to win—and winning was everything.

But Jimmy, tough as he was, was more than a mouth and a set of fists. In his first engagement with Blough at Kroger's, he discovered there was something else different and special about him: he had a mind. He learned that when he trusted it, it worked like some kind of safe-deposit vault. It would take in and store nearly everything spoken or written. All he had to do was tap it and the information would be there, weeks, months, even years after he'd taken it in. He still had that inner-ear sixth sense, too, and he learned as he went that it did more than tell him how to deal with a particular face and voice; it kept tabs over both his body and his mind. He learned to trust and listen to it, and when it told him that he was beginning to go around on the same carousel, that he had a big piece missing, he believed it. Having a loving wife, close pals, powerful allies, encouraging superiors, and the ability to organize *things* of men to do what he wanted was a lot, but ultimately not enough. He had to learn what went on the paper the bosses put their John Hancocks to. Getting the contract was nothing if what was in the contract wasn't truly "better and more."

In Farrell Dobbs Jimmy got the mentor he needed —and more. Dobbs came close to being the father Jimmy never had. Dan Tobin of Boston had been head of the Teamsters since 1905, but out in the country, out on the roads, the king of organizers was Farrell Dobbs. Since Jimmy had made the union's life his own, its success had spread from city to city until it had reached the point where two breakthroughs were needed. One was the landing of uniform contracts, by which a trucker in one state would get the

40

same pay and benefits as his counterpart three states away. This meant bargaining on a consolidated basis at the highest levels. The other was the signing up of the over-the-road teamsters, the big-rig, long-distance, interstate high-ballers, in addition to the city-limits short-haulers. Tobin back East wasn't all that sure that this wasn't biting off more than they could chew, but the train was already rolling. Jimmy himself was already on it, waylaying over-the-roaders out at the highway truck stops, far from the intimidation of the boss-run warehouses.

A big-rig driver would pull over, lock his cab doors, put a lug wrench in one hand and a lit cigarette in the other, and nod off for a snooze. When the cigarette burned his fingers, it was time to get rolling again. If you put a foot up on his running board and rapped against the window, you had to jump back fast and start talking even faster, lest you learned the hard way the risks a hijacker took. Jimmy was good at it. Sometimes he'd have a driver out and talking, only to be bushwhacked by gangs of hoods waiting in the trees. Just as often, he wouldn't have to miss a syllable, secure in the knowledge that his own gang of brawlers was in that car tearing into the pull-over even as he spoke. When he didn't have backup, he'd run like hell if he could; if he couldn't, he'd stand and mix. He gave as good as he took, thanks to pushups and attitude, but his head still got opened a lot.

Farrell Dobbs was already king in organizing the over-the-roaders, when Detroit farmed Jimmy out to support him in Minneapolis, and their first handshake was like the opening of university ages for Jimmy. For once in his life, he kept his mouth shut and listened and watched; for his sixth sense told him that Dobbs's way was the way to get the Teamster message across the entire nation. Dobbs took him under his wing, and from the older pioneer he drank in the basics of the institutional framework and imaginative ideas that would later become his own trademarks in the world of collective bargaining. From Dobbs he learned the tools of his trade.

Hoffa, Dobbs and the Dunne brothers— Vince, Grant and Miles—moved out from the latter's strong

41

Local 544 in Minneapolis, and traveled the roads into the Dakotas, Iowa, Wisconsin, upper Michigan, organizing. Jimmy teamed with Farrell. They virtually lived in their car, eating in it, often sleeping in it, and Farrell would explain excitedly to the younger man: "Once you have the road men, Jim, you can get the local cartage, and once you have the local cartage, you can get anyone you want."

"Yeah, but that'd be just one town. What if it's out in the boondocks someplace, like where we are now?"

"Aha! No place is really in the boondocks. That's when you start your leapfrog. Your dock men, for instance, don't accept freight from drivers who aren't organized—they go back home with the news, and there you have your start, *there!* See? And you do the same with the interliners. Your organized carrier suddenly won't transfer to his link-up unless the link-up goes union. It's *leverage,* Jimmy. It lets you choose the battleground. One city jumps you into another, which jumps you into another state."

"And into other businesses too, right? I mean, who don't need trucks? They deliver everything!"

"You've got it. 'We won't pick up or deliver unless everyone in your company belongs to *some* kind of union!' "

"Christ!" He was getting theory and application all at once, and they took all the more deeply because they succeeded. By January, 1937, they had organized thirteen locals in six states. By the spring of the next year, they had penetrated and added Ohio, Indiana, Illinois, Missouri, and Nebraska, for a total of forty-six locals in eleven states, which the International Brotherhood of Teamsters solidified into the Central States Drivers Council. Farrell Dobbs was named its negotiating chairman. His teacher-friend-father's great victory thrilled Jimmy Hoffa. It was also to be the big break of his life and career; it came soon and in a way he never would have expected.

In 1940, Farrell Dobbs abruptly quit it all. President Dan Tobin was astonished and tried to talk him out of it; he took him to the top of the mountain. "You can have money, Farrell, more than you've ever touched. And power—I guarantee you the first vice-presidency that comes available in the International."

"Thank you, Dan, but I have more important things to do."

Farrell Dobbs then turned his organizing skills to help his first love, the Socialist Workers Party, trying to raise money to hire bodyguards for his mentor and idol, Leon Trotsky. Dobbs visited Trotsky in hiding in Mexico, then went to New York City's Greenwich Village to devote himself full-time to the causes of the Communist Party, anti-Stalin branch. The Dunne brothers were also staunch, committed Trotskyites, but remained in power in Teamsters Local 544, Minneapolis. Dan Tobin gave Dobbs's job to a dark-horse contender. Young Jimmy Hoffa of Detroit leapfrogged overnight into the negotiating chairmanship of the mighty Central States Drivers Council.

In 1941, serious trouble started in Minneapolis. The Dunne brothers, under the red banner, turned Five Forty-four into a rebel local. They broke from the AFL and went independent. Tobin immediately slammed them into a trusteeship, but it was an ineffectual gesture. John L. Lewis's brother, Denny, descended upon Minneapolis on behalf of the rival federation, the member-hungry CIO. He came with carloads and truckloads of organizers and began signing up members left and right.

America was on the brink of a world war. A mammoth, united industrial effort would obviously be necessary to mount, sustain, and above all win such a war —and, in the process, put the nation back on its feet economically. The Teamsters were a vital link in that chain. The loud, leftist revolt in Minnesota was a serious crack in that link. It had to be blowtorched shut, President Roosevelt told his old friend, Dan Tobin. Tobin agreed, and promised that it would be done. He knew exactly who he would use to accomplish this volatile piece of business. One was a man named Dave Beck, the Seattle strongman, mogul of the Teamsters' powerful Western Conference and odds-on successor to Tobin's presidency. The other man was this little whiz of a scrapper from Two Ninety-nine.

Jimmy didn't like it. It would be union man against union man. It would be breaking up a healthy, militant local. Worse, it would be going in against his friends. "That's Farrell's outfit, Dan. I love that guy, sir. I owe him. And the Dunnes are my pals, especially Vince."

Now old Dan Tobin went once again up the mountain. "It's your Rubicon, Mr. Hoffa."

"My what, sir?"

"Your main chance, son. It can mean everything for you, everything you want, and more." He made Jimmy Hoffa the same promises Farrell Dobbs had resisted.

Jimmy did not resist. "You mean it's them or me?"

"You could put it that way. Yes. You could certainly put it that way, Jim."

The Minneapolis truckers themselves were scared and confused. Most carried two buttons in their pockets. When the CIO squads came trooping around the taverns, loading platforms, and truckstops, they'd put the CIO button on; when the Teamsters came, they'd wear the AFL button. Minneapolis-St. Paul citizens that summer saw street war as bloody and vicious as anything many of them would see later overseas. It was hand-to-hand combat. Guns, billy-clubs, blackjacks, pickhandles, brass knuckles, knives. Jimmy landed even heavier than Beck. Teamsters, ad-hoc deputy organizers from the Purple Gang, the Mafia, and other sources of mercenary soldiers. Even the city's police and the FBI were on his side this time.

The shiny blue truck said GINZBERG BROTHERS PAPER PRODUCTS in gilt letters on its sides. It pulled to a stop at the curb outside Rogan's Luncheonette and Beer Parlor. Twenty CIO "signers" dropped calmly out of the truck and entered in two's and three's. The place was crowded with its usual patrons, truckers from Five Forty-four. Pens and pencils flourished, papers were signed, buttons were passed out.

Outside, five black Cadillacs and one unmarked meat truck filled the street. Jimmy Hoffa went in with the advance wave. He was using a length of tire tread this evening; the summer heat helped it stay supple. Denny Lewis's troops fought back. The beering, card-playing truckers ran for their lives through every exit. Rogan stayed down in his cellar, listening to the heavy crashing of his money being lost. An AFL face went onto the hot grill. A CIO head bounced off the edge of the beef and pastrami cutter. They used chairs and bottles.

The arrival of the second and third assault waves behind Hoffa pushed him toward the rear of the place. There was a back room. "Moose!" he yelled. "Kick it in!" Moose kicked it in, and Jimmy flew through the doorway, swinging. He caught one guy trying to squeeze through the small window, pulled him back, and got in two good ones across the back of his head and neck. He swung around and stopped, tread in mid-air over his shoulder. The thin face was bruised.

"Jimmy!"

"What the hell are you doin' here?"

"How can you *do* this, Jim?"

"Farrell, I—Moose! The window!"

Moose deglassed the window.

"Go ahead, Farrell, get out!"

"I came back to try to prevent this, Jimmy, it's—"

Jimmy turned away. "When I get back in here, you better be gone, Dobbs!" Parts of bodies in the jumbled main room felt the tread-whip's sting. He never went back into the rear room.

The Teamsters-AFL prevailed. The killing blow was dealt by the Federal Government. Dobbs and the Dunne brothers were indicted for conspiracy to overthrow and sent to jail.

When it was over, Tobin was good to his word. "Well, Jimmy, how will it feel to be the newest and youngest vice-president of the International Brotherhood of Teamsters, the largest, most powerful—"

"I don't want it," Jimmy said.

"Excuse me?"

"I said I don't want it."

"An international organizer then?"

"No. I don't want that either. Sir."

"Then what in God's name do you want, my job?"

Jimmy looked at him cold-eyed, not laughing. He knew exactly what he wanted. The Farrell Dobbs massacre had been the wildest, bloodiest, most brutal clash he'd ever taken part in, made worse by the spectacle of union man going hand-in-hand against union man. He hadn't needed that to know that fists, guns, and clubs, no matter how necessary they could be in certain times and places, were not the real key to power in the Teamsters, not the way such a gigantic organization was *really* run. "Mr. Tobin," he said, "make me a trustee."

"How old are you, Jimmy?"

"You are wise for your years, in any case. Very well, a trustee it is."

There were only three trustees. Now Jimmy would be one of them—while continuing to run his home Local 229. The trustees were the ones who examined the books of the Teamsters each year.

And the books were where the money was.

The man who knew where, why, and how the money went would know how the enormous union really ran.

If that man happened to also have all other things going for him, the money would show him not only how it ran, but how it could be run.

Jimmy Hoffa happened to also have all other things going for him.

And now they were going to show him the money. With long, whole years of war ahead of him in which to study it.

Having dropped out of school before high school, Jimmy Hoffa finally got to hit the books, and he hit them hard. For he wanted to come out the top in his class, or not come out at all.

The Operations Officer at the map gave the two pilots their last-minute-run-through briefing on their secret mission. "Again, here, on the Belgian coast, is the target. *Here*"—pointing to an X grease-penciled over coordinates in the English Channel—"is where you bail out. Any questions?"

The plane was a PB4Y Liberator outfitted with enough explosives to make it a missile, and with a special guidance system that made it a drone: after they bailed out, it would fly itself over the German target.

"Nineteen, twenty-nine, something like that."

Ensign James Simpson was completing the final checkout of the Liberator when its pilot ran up from

46

the Ops shack. They shook hands. Simpson yelled into the wind, "So long and good luck, Joe!"

Joe Kennedy adjusted the parachute he'd never get to use and closed the cockpit window. Just short of their bail-out X, the PB4Y Liberator drone-missile exploded in midair.

The phone rang in the hallway of the Harvard dormitory. Robert Kennedy's roommate, Dave Thatcher, answered it. He laid the receiver down and walked back into their rooms, where Bob was nearly finished packing. "It's himself again, Bobby."

"I told you to tell him I'm gone, didn't *I*?"

Thatcher grinned. "Ah, this time he says that right after you tell me to tell him you're gone you're to get your bony little ass to the phone."

"Dad, hi . . . I'm sorry, but it's too late. I'm going, and that's it. I know I'm the only one! But now I'm not going to be the only one! Dad? Dad? . . . Listen, Dad, you can go see the Secretary of the Navy till hell freezes over! I already saw Forrestal myself . . . Yes, a couple weeks ago . . . I hitched, what the hell difference . . . No, don't blame him, he was great . . . No, I didn't tell him you were all for it. We didn't mention you at all, as a matter of . . . Dad. I love you, but I'm hanging up. I have to report in, and I'm already late. I'll write to you from sea!"

The sea he got wasn't the sea he wanted. He got the Caribbean, and spent the rest of the war chipping paint and getting into brawls in San Juan. His duty ship: a destroyer named the *Joseph P. Kennedy Jr.*

Back at Harvard, though he was built for light-weight boxing or chess, he made the varsity football squad. After one particularly sorry scrimmage, the coach pulled him aside and started to chew him out. Then he noticed something odd about one of his legs: it had been broken for several hours. He was an end. He couldn't block, tackle, or throw, but he could run and he could catch, which is what an end is supposed to do. He displayed a will and ferocity that any coach would have to acknowledge and reward, and this one did. In his senior year, in the last minutes of the game, Bobby was sent in against Yale and won what

47

neither his father nor his brothers before him had: his letter.

He never bothered to collect his diploma.

His first job was a temporary one: rent collector for one of his father's banks. But the territory assigned him was Easty—East Boston, the Sicily of Boston Harbor. He walked up the steep hills and down them, up and down the steep stairs of the two-deckers and the three-deckers. He had learned long before that only a small percentage of humankind lived life in the Kennedy style, but he had never known what want and poverty meant until he had his nose stuck in it in Easty. Families of nine and eleven and more living in five rooms, three, two. The end of the war had ended much of the available work in the area: Bethlehem Steel, the Navy Yard, the various waterfront shipyards and warehouses. In the neutral gear before the downshift to postwar prosperity, unskilled labor was the first to get laid off, and most of these immigrant men were unskilled. The pennies that children could earn or scrounge were too needed to let the children go to school. Bob Kennedy saw this up close, and the seeing made something stir way down deep inside him. Old and young, all these hurting people seemed to him like so many hurting children. "Public service," the idea instilled in him and in his brothers and sisters by their parents their whole lives, began, at last, in Easty, to take a tangible shape in his consciousness, and it was human. He was one lousy rent collector.

When Jack ran for Congress from the 11th District, against eight other Democrats, Joseph Sr. masterminded the campaign from a suite in the Ritz-Carlton, overlooking the Public Gardens and the Swan Boats. Friends of Jack's from school and from his PT-boat days showed up from all over the country to help "Shafty" run. John Hersey had written a piece for the *New Yorker* of Jack's heroic PT-109 escapades. The *Reader's Digest* had condensed it, and reprints were mailed to virtually every voter in the district, with pictures for those who couldn't read. One of Bob's jobs was to tack these up on every lamp post and fence in the area assigned him, East Cambridge—another Easty, only flat, with Irish as well as Italians jammed into the blocks of tenements between the factories. Uneasily integrated squalor.

Lechmere Square, Inman, Kendall, Central—this was East Cambridge, and it belonged to Mike Neville, its Mayor and Jack's major opponent. The odds against Jack here were estimated at five to one; if Bob, under the direction of Jack's chum Lem Billings, could reduce them to four to one, he could come home satisfied. Here at least he didn't have the hills to climb, but after he'd wallpapered the streets with the posters, he had no idea what to do. He tried sitting in his office waiting for politics to happen. He got a lot done—a lot of pushups and knuckle-cracking. Bored stiff, he said the hell with it and hit the streets. It felt good to go door-to-door with something to give people, rather than wanting rents, and East Cambridge thought it was just a riot having this millionaire Kennedy kid coming to their doors with all his hair and teeth and everything, to talk about his wonderful, handsome, war-hero brother. He got offered and ate a lot of meals at kitchen tables and at dining-room tables with the best movie-china. Reporting in, he said, "Hurry up and win! I'm spaghetti from the waist down and corned beef and cabbage from the waist up. *Marone! Jayzus!*" What came a lot easier was playing with the kids—softball in the parks, touch football on the glassy empty lots, stickball in the streets. Kids bring news home; they talk a lot, and they talk loud. Jack swept East Cambridge—he got it all. He was on his way, and Bob was thrilled. There was nobody else in the word that he'd rather help, and he had; he had.

As high, bright, and animated as he could bounce, Bob could likewise go way down, pensive and brooding. At such low moments he could sometimes actually envy, not the poor, but the ones with all the odds against them. More than once in Easty and in East Cambridge he had spotted some young faces in the crowds, sharp eyes burning with ambition; they had only one place to go, and that was up, up and out, and they were by Christ going to do it! The simplicity of it. Whereas he knew it already—he could do the greatest thing in the world and people would always say, "Well, hell, with all that money . . ."

Having practically every imaginable avenue open to him agonizingly amounted to having none. What in God's name was he supposed to *do* with his life?

If anything, he was a mover, to whom any action was preferable to none. After Harvard, he got an assignment from the Boston *Post* and went to the Near East to report on the Arab-Jewish war. There, he nearly got a taste of the action he'd missed in the Caribbean. This time he was glad to miss it. Scheduled to go from Tel Aviv to Jerusalem in a Jewish convoy, Bob met a British armor officer who'd been friends with his sister Kathleen back in England. While Bob was grinding through by tank, Arab raiders demolished the convoy.

Home, he went to the University of Virginia Law School about the same way he'd gone to Harvard: halfheartedly. He never talked much in class, when he went, because to talk you had to have done the work. He knew he was considered just another rich kid, but went along, not caring much what the hell anybody thought of him. He was going only because Jack had said he ought to. Who in hell wanted to be another lawyer, anyhow?

He did get into harness and dazzle them when he felt like it. When he turned his attention to the all-but-dead Student Legal Forum, button-down shirts popped all over the campus, and Charlottesville as well. Showing no compunction against getting his father to pull all the fabled strings he could, Bobby brought to the Forum speakers straight out of the headlines. Among them were Thurman Arnold, one of FDR's original New Dealers, running the Administration's antitrust endeavors; Supreme Court Justice William O. Douglas; Arthur Krock of the New York Times; Seth W. Richhardson. Chairman of the Subversive Activities Control Board; the President of RCA, Frank M. Folsom; a legend named Joseph P. Kennedy, Senior; a Congressman named John Fitzgerald Kennedy, and two others.

One was Ralph Bunche, the first black Nobel Prize winner, now a top United Nations official. *He thinks he's gonna bring a Negro here?* When the smoke cleared, graciousness prevailed, and Mr. Bunche was accorded all Southern hospitality. As if to return the courtesy, in his speech Bunche lashed into a Yankee. Without naming names, he attacked one of the Forum's previous speakers for trying to drag isolationism out of hiding and back into respectability right while the Korean "conflict" was being waged. That previous speaker was, of course, Bobby's father. And the loudest round of applause came from Bob Kennedy himself.

Bob's real coup, the speaker he not only invited but hosted a huge party for, was a star of stage and television. Campus liberals burst blood vessels because he was also the Republican junior Senator from Wisconsin and Chairman of the Senate Subversive Activities Control Board, whose hearings were watched like soap opera and sports by practically everyone everywhere in America, on their home and tavern and club TV sets: Senator Joseph McCarthy in his heyday of finding and exposing Communists and Communist sympathizers practically everywhere he looked.

Hero or demagogue, the Joe McCarthy who arrived to address Bob's Student Legal Forum was hardly what the outraged liberals dreaded. He was affable, charming, reasonable, and gave a calm, toothless, bland speech. He'd come without TV or Cohn, of course.

Bobby was married by now, to Ethel Skakel, richer even than he, "more Kennedy than the Kennedys," smart, vivacious, funny, and in love with politics. She, too, had worked for Jack's 1946 election in Massachusetts. Together, they met Joe McCarthy up close, and could not help liking him. When Bobby made a friend he never unmade him, and Joe McCarthy became a friend then and there. Later, the bachelor Senator even squired both Pat and Eunice Kennedy. Now, leaving after his speech, he told Bob, "Ever find yourself in Washington, look me up."

Washington. Why not? Right, wrong, or in the middle, it seemed the one place left in the snoring country where anything was going on. It was where the action was. Elsewhere, these were the years of the Silent Generation. Eisenhower's in the White House, all's right with the world. Industry, both mercantile and personal, was the order of the day. Since the Soviets had launched *Sputnik,* the sciences had pushed the humanities aside. The low silhouette prevailed.

Bobby had had school up to here. He was itchy. Burning. He wanted to play some ball. In a big game. Against somebody really tough. Anybody really tough.

So he went straight from law school to Washington. To the Justice Department. Which happened to be situated across the street from the "Marble Palace"— the gleaming, ostentatious new headquarters of the International Brotherhood of Teamsters. From which Jimmy Hoffa was now operating part-time, flying high, as ninth vice-president of the world's largest labor union.

The universe again took over and brought the two of them together.

Robert Francis Kennedy, a rebel in search of a cause.

James Riddle Hoffa, a rebel still in search of "better and more."

Irresistible forces, unmovable objects.

Kennedy and Hoffa.

It had to mean war.

BOOK TWO

Skirmishes

Robert Kennedy went from law school to a $4,200-a-year job in the Internal Security Division of the Justice Department, where he proceeded to go nuts researching the status of the nation's coastal lighthouses. When Jack ran for re-election against Henry Cabot Lodge, Bob was more than delighted to quit and once again help his brother win office.

When he went back to D.C., it wasn't to lighthouses but to Senator Joe McCarthy's staff as an investigator, only to come up against Roy Cohn, McCarthy's recently appointed chief counsel. It was loathing at first sight.

Whether it was their similarities or differences that most bothered Kennedy about Cohn is moot. Roy Cohn was young, brilliant, and attractive in a faintly jaundiced, surly-eyed way. The Senator doted on him, as he would later dote on Cohn's friend and assistant, G. David Schine. In any case, what clearly rankled Bobby was Roy Cohn's methods. In Bob's opinion, he shot from the hip; he'd build a case on innuendo, in Bobby's estimation, and if anything was holy to Bobby it was method. For him, means were ends in themselves; he was confident that if you made sure the means were right, the results would take care of themselves. When Cohn took charge of the entire staff, displacing Bob's boss, former FBI man Francis Flanagan, Bobby left.

G. David Schine, young and very rich, got drafted. Roy Cohn tried to get him a commission, and when that failed he tried to get him into the CIA. The military establishment failed to co-operate, and Cohn, in retaliation, vowed he'd "get" the Army. Senator McCarthy backed him up. Once the McCarthy-Army hearings started to turn so sour, the Democrats on the committee walked out in protest.

They came back, though, and when they did they brought along a new minority counsel: Robert Kennedy. That he and Cohn were not going to coexist peacefully became vividly evident. Cohn had Mrs. Anna Lee Moss on the stand, questioning her about an alleged Communist named Bob Hall. Kennedy interrupted Cohn. "Mrs. Moss—this Mr. Hall. What color was he?" Mrs. Moss was black. "Take your time, Mrs. Moss, and please be certain—was Mr. Hall a colored gentleman, or—"

"Yes, sir. He was."

With that, Bobby spun to Cohn. "Then there is some confusion, is there not, Mr. Cohn? The Rob Hall we were talking about—was he a white man or a colored man?"

Cohn looked as if he'd just tasted something rancid. "I never inquired into his race. I am not sure. We can check that, though."

"But I thought I *just spoke* to you about it?"

"My assumption has been that he is a white man, but we can check that."

Senator Stuart Symington addressed Mrs. Moss. "Let me ask this—the Bob Hall that you knew, was he a white man?"

"He was colored," Mrs. Moss repeated. "The one I knew of."

Symington looked at both counsels. "Then let's decide which Robert Hall we want to talk about."

"Mr. Cohn," Bob said, "when you spoke about Rob Hall, the union organizer, we all felt that he was a colored gentleman."

Cohn was indignant. "I was not talking about a union organizer, Bob. I was talking about a *Communist* organizer."

"Then evidently it is a different Rob Hall."

Cohn got angry. "I don't know that it is! *Our* information is that it was the same Rob Hall."

The courtly Senator McClellan smiled. "If one is

black and the other is white, then there *is* a difference."

Cohn replied, "I think . . . I think that might be something we should go into and get some more exact information on."

Bobby nodded. "Yes. I think so too."

On another occasion, Cohn cornered Kennedy outside in the corridor. "You can tell your pal Scoop Jackson we're going to get *him* on Monday!"

Bobby was incensed. "Don't you make any warnings to us about Democratic Senators!"

"I'll make any warnings I want. Any time, any place!" Bobby was already walking away. Cohn called after him: "You shouldn't be here! You have a personal hatred for one of the principals! You have a personal hatred!"

Bob whirled. "If I have, it's justified!"

Cohn was yelling now. "Do you think you're qualified to sit here? Do you think you're qualified?"

By now, reporters had begun to gather round. Bob gone, Roy Cohn muttered, as much to himself as to the newspeople, "Oh, we got a real cute kid here. A real cute kid!"

In his quarters, Senator McCarthy paced the floor. He was drinking. "Sure you don't want, Bob?"

"No. Thank you, sir."

"Come on, little coffee royal without the coffee? No? Bob, you should learn how to relax more."

As he talked, Bob couldn't help noticing the smile. The Senator had a ready, wide smile; a slight gap between his top middle teeth lent it a boyish, pixyish charm that was hard to resist, even when it flashed on a television screen. But now it seemed to happen at unlikely places. In the heat of the hearings in session, the Senator had begun smiling even when he was being most bitterly and derisively attacked. It seemed he had lost control of it, and this was disconcerting to the young, perplexed minority counsel.

". . . And, ah, I wish you and Roy wouldn't go at it like that, either. Not around the front-page boys."

"Joe, I told him he was following a blind lead. I tried to warn him. He disregarded my warning. I had to cut in. He needs harder information before accusing—"

"Aw, forget the Rob Hall question for now. It's the bickering that's bad for business!" Smile. "It's . . . it's all changing, isn't it, Bob. You can, I can almost *feel* it out there. It's the climate, the feeling. It's not the same any more somehow."

"No, sir, it's not."

"I'll say it again—I am sorry you quit my team, Bob. I miss these little talks of ours."

"I miss them too, Senator. And you . . . I, uh . . . Joe, no matter what happens, I, uh, I want you to know how much I have always basically admired you. I still do."

As Bobby was leaving, the Senator poured himself another drink and said, "Yes, you've got to have a cause. Windmill or not. A cause. A direction." Smile. "Something or somebody to *go* after! Get something *done* about something. You, Bob. What's yours? You know yet, or still looking?"

"Still looking, I guess, Senator."

McCarthy smiled again, and then he stopped. He looked down and away. "When did it all start going wrong, Bob? When did it all start going wrong?"

"You really want to hear it from me, Joe?"

"Yes."

"When you stopped playing it by the rules."

The Democrats won control of the Senate that next January, and Bob became chief counsel. Bobby Kennedy could stand his nose in books and his body in cramped offices for just so long before he wanted to climb the walls. With a little authority now, he could make a little room for himself, and do business his way. This meant that a lot of meetings with staff and far-flung investigators that might have taken place in stuffy Senate Building rooms took place instead on the sprawling, scruffy lawns of Bob and Ethel's home ten miles outside Washington: Hickory Hill, in McLean, Virginia. To work for and get along with Bobby, it didn't hurt to have a love for touch football, tennis, kids, dogs, word games, grab-ass by the pool, raucous meals, practical jokes, open bars, noise, quick wit, supreme confidence, willpower, idealism, and buffoon-ery.

Evenings, Saturday mornings, Sunday afternoons. Bring the wife and kids. And the reports, the news, the word. One Saturday, Dave Thatcher was supposed to bring a pickup team to challenge Bob and Ethel's mighty touch-football squad. They were running scrimmage, warming up for Dave's challengers. Ethel was their main runner, Ol' Swivelhips herself. Many a big, rough former combat man lived to regret being too gentlemanly to tag her or otherwise slow her down-field advance. Here she comes, there she goes—she'd leave him waving at air. They had run through their basic set of plays when Dave finally appeared, hustling down from the house. For his benefit the Kennedy team was chanting its tigerlike readiness: ARE WE READY? ARE WE READY! WE ARE READY! WE ARE READY!

Dave stopped above them on the hill and an-nounced, "Gentlemen, lady—I have had to search high and low, the highways and the byways of fear-ridden Washington, to find a team willing to risk mayhem at your hands! Cowardice, I must report, runs rampant through our capital. The press corps re-fuses to play you . . . the freshman Senators refuse to pick up the gauntlet . . . even the Pentagon has failed to produce eleven volunteers!"

"Boo! Hiss! Excuses, excuses! Where's your navy, Davey?"

"However, it just so happens the right man was on the case. Undaunted, intrepid, I just so happened to come across this gang of little kids in town for the weekend. They're from Maryland, so maybe that's why they don't know any better, and here they are now . . . Thatcher's Hackers!" With that, the door of the house opened and out trotted the entire first string of the Baltimore Colts in full workout gear. Every-body fell on the ground. One player came forth to Bobby and smiled shyly, "Mr. Kennedy, we wanted to present you with Sunday's game ball, and Mr. Thatcher, well, he thought this'd be a good way to do it."

Grinning, Bob glanced sidelong at Thatcher and said, "The bet's off."

"Like hell."

Ethel hollered, "Okay, let's huddle!"

Bobby tossed her the ball and, catching Dave's head signal, followed him off to one side. "I just heard, they're going to vote censure on Monday."

"Where'd you hear it?"

"The Sans Souci."

"What the hell were you doing there?"

"Eating lunch."

"Rich sissy. Well, I could've saved you the lunch money. The vote'll be at least sixty-six to twenty-three."

"Well, that's the end of Mighty Joe at last, huh?"

"Yeah. The minute he put himself in the hands of those goddamn yo-yos . . ."

"Well, you can't say you didn't warn him, Bob."

"Aah, he was seeing headlines and hearing 'Hail to the Chief'—he never heard me."

Dave sighed. "It is kinda sad. Well, where do we sell our snake oil now, boss?"

"Senator McClellan wants me as chief counsel on his Permanent Investigating Committee."

"Move it, Bob!" Ethel yelled.

"We're coming!"

"You gonna take it?" Dave asked.

"Already took it."

"What'll we be doing?"

"Investigating everything. Permanently."

"Beautiful. Big, big! I love it. Guess we'd all better start playing Saint Peter as far as McCarthy goes, huh? I never heard of him myself."

"Baloney. Hate the sin, not the sinner, Dave. I liked him then, and I like him now, and I don't give a rat's ass who knows it."

"That isn't political expedience talking."

"I don't care."

"Hey, who got to do the writing of the actual death sentence? Who completed the minority report?"

"I did. Come on, let's hustle."

Eddie Cheyfitz, dapper, wavy-haired lawyer and public-relations man for the Teamsters, was brimming with good will and cheer when Bob pulled into the parking lot of the Marble Palace in his powder-blue convertible. He had invited Bob to a tour of the glittering, white, five-story International Headquarters building, and Bob had accepted. Nobody needed Eddie Cheyfitz's bubbling enthusiasm to be impressed by the place; five million dollars shows, wherever you put it. The Palace had a movie theater, a penthouse terrace, private washrooms, drapes custom-designed with the Teamsters' team-and-wheel logo, finely carved furniture, walnut paneling, a fountain, Scandinavian chandeliers, a French chef, and secretaries and receptionists hired for their looks. "Check that marble, Mr. Kennedy—flown in from Italy and assembled a piece at a time! That job alone took over ten months."

"It's quite a place, Eddie. Quite a place."

"It's a monument to Labor, Bob. A monument to the American workingman. Here, up these stairs, now. Your interest is most gratifying, Mr. Kennedy. I feel it's very important for you, and everyone in Government for that matter, to learn more about unions in general, and of course us Teamsters in particular. I know I don't have to tell you that the relationship between Labor and Government is a sacred trust. We're embarking on a new era of growth in the country, the war in Korea's over, and as we see it, the people are turning to their leaders for new . . . well, leadership, and . . ."

Bob smiled. "And my Committee is thinking about an investigation of corruption in Labor."

Eddie Cheyfitz laughed. "And your Committee is thinking about an investigation of corruption in Labor. Ah, here we are now!" Eddie opened the door to President Dave Beck's office, and Bob stepped in.

"Holy God!"

"What do you think?"

"What's under the desk, the White House?"

"Funny you should ask. Let me show you something." He led Bob across the immense room to the windows, and there, perfectly framed and seemingly no more than an arm's length away, loomed the domed Capitol building. "Beautiful?"

"Yes, very beautiful. It's all very beautiful." He scanned the elegantly stocked bookshelves, the built-in hi-fi and TV, the forty-eight-button intercom, the exquisite carpeting.

"Dave's sorry he couldn't be here himself, of course, Mr. Kennedy, but when you're president of the world's largest—"

"That's okay."

"He did ask me to request a personal favor of you —may I?"

"Sure."

"Well, Dave's read so much about your brother's book, *Profiles in Courage* . . . He'd be honored to have an autographed copy. If it's no trouble."

Bob grinned. "I'll ask Jack. I'm sure he'll be delighted. We want Mr. Beck to know he has a friend in the Senator."

"Those words are music to our ears, Bob. In these times, you know, the relationship between Labor and Government is a sacred—"

"Excuse me. Eddie?"

"Yes, sir?"

"Where does one find a john in a Marble Palace?"

Inside, Bobby stepped up to the bank of sinks and washed his hands. Water flushed almost silently somewhere behind him; then there was another face in the wall of mirrors, smiling, its eyes crinkling.

"Ever take a leak in a goddamn shrine before?"

Bob laughed. "It does feel kind of sacrilegious."

"You're the Kennedy kid, aren't ya. The Senator's little brother."

"That's me. How'd you know that?"

The man washed his hands vigorously, still looking straight at Bobby in the mirror. "I make it my business to know anyone who can help me, and anyone who can hurt me. The rest, I forget about!"

Bobby laughed. "And who are you?"

"I'm Jimmy Hoffa, Ninth Vice-President of the International Brotherhood of Teamsters, Chairman of the Thirteen States Central Conference of Teamsters, Chairman of the Michigan Conference of Teamsters, Chairman of Joint Council Forty-three, and President of Teamster Local Two Ninety-nine, Detroit."

"What do you do in your spare time?"

"No such thing as spare time," Jimmy said, drying his hands and pitching the towel at the wicker basket. "Put 'er there, kid."

They shook hands.

When they let go, Jimmy grabbed Bob's hand again, hard. "Hey! Take a tip! Don't let go so fast, huh? It's a sign of weakness."

"I'll remember that."

"Your name's Robert, right? What is it, Bob? Bobby?"

"Either one."

"Okay. Call me Jimmy. Can I call you Bobby?"

"Sure."

"Good. Listen, I'm not just mouthin' off. I been watching your work, Bobby. The Talbot thing, the clothing-procurement megillah, the shipping scandal. I want you to know something, and you can tell this to Senator McClellan, too—I think you guys are doing one terrific job. You carry a big broom and you ain't afraid to use it, and that's what this country needs right about now. A clean sweep. You keep up the good work, hear? You keep the flies from walkin' into everybody's food."

Bob laughed. "Well, thanks for the endorsement, Mr. Hoffa."

"Jimmy!"

"Jimmy."

"So. Tell me, who do you go after next?"

"Uh, you, possibly. Well, not you personally, but some people think we should start looking at the Labor Movement. We're hearing talk about possible corruption in—"

"Good! It'll do us a world of good! There's not an ounce of hankypank that I know of, and I'd love the whole country to get a good gander at how a labor union's supposed to run! You scratch my back, I'll scratch yours! You find any rats, you tell *me* where they are and that'll be that! Yes, sir, a clean sweep! Good luck to ya, Bobby. Ya know where to find me if ya need anything, right?"

"Right!"

Bob told Dave Thatcher all about it on the tennis court at Hickory Hill. "... So this time I give his hand the hardest squeeze I can manage, and he says, 'That's more like it! Almost no weakness at all that time, kiddo!' *Almost!* Ha!"

"Net ball"

"Like hell!"

"You could see it!"

"Oh, okay."

"So you liked him."

"Yeah. He's cocky as hell, and tough, but—"

"And all for an investigation of his own nest?"

"That was in!"

"I know, I know."

"Yeah—that's what surprised me."

"Well, it shouldn't have."

"Why not?"

"Hell, any fool knows investigating big Labor is political suicide. Point!"

"Damn! Okay, your serve, and try to get it over the net this time. You think so too, Dave?"

"What?"

"That it's suicide?"

"Christ, Bobby, you'd be cutting Jack's throat!"

"Damn!"

"Ho! A new racket for Mr. Kennedy, please! Or can you play with a hole in it?"

"I can whip you with the handle. Shut up and serve. Really think there'd be trouble, huh?"

"You tell me—does Jack have his eye on Chicago or not?"

"There's some talk, nothing definite."

"Listen, if Labor wasn't trouble, why hasn't somebody else got their hooks into it?"

"That's no reason for us to back off, we're not somebody else."

"It's reason enough to slow down, my friend. Thirty-love! Take a break?"

"No!"

"You that sure McClellan wants it? He's never been big on messy political wars."

"Why should it get messy?"

"You think there's corruption to be found?"

63

"Clark Mollenhoff guarantees it."

"If he's right, you'll be between the rock and the hard place. An absolute no-win situation. Half the people won't believe you, the other half'll say you're anti-Labor. Bingo. Half the voters in the country out the window. Bye-bye, Jack."

"Ha! Bye-bye, Thatcher!"

"Good one. A beauty, Bob. Thought I had you distracted."

"You did. That was one of my distracted shots."

"Take my advice, Bob, and hold your horses. It'll keep. And stay the hell away from Clark Mollenhoff. Crusading reporters never helped anybody get elected."

"That's hard. He's camping out on my doorstep."

"He got anything real?"

"I'll tell you later. I'm having lunch with him in an hour. But I think so, yeah."

"Oh God. So why the hell are you giving *me* the third degree?"

"To distract you! And it worked—game, Mr. Kennedy!"

To Bob, Clark Mollenhoff resembled the young Raymond Burr as Perry Mason, only bigger. Bobby met him at the Colonial Arms, a meat-and-potatoes place. Bobby's appetites and instincts were telling him no, but he was still running hot and cold. "I'm not even sure it's in our jurisdiction," he told Clark. "Doesn't it belong to the Senate Labor Committee or the IRS?"

"IRS is playing three monkeys. Financial records are being destroyed, and they don't want to know about it. Bob, there is sworn testimony, under oath, that union financial records have been shredded every year for God knows how long. False reports are filed with virtually no danger of prosecution. Go talk to SLC yourself. They're buried in paper. There are reports of goon squads still being used. There's Mob infiltration, and I'm not going to kid you—people have been killed when they got too close to this thing. It's crying for investigation. I've been sniffing around this long enough to know I shouldn't be surprised if some acid finds its way into my face, and I know this—if anybody ever gets up the nerve to do it, it'll go big."

"If it's so big, why haven't the Labor Committees jumped on the bandwagon?"

"Simple. Everybody's afraid of the Teamsters. Half a dozen Committees have come away with bloody noses over the years. The trick that nobody's pulled is to get two things working. One, a public figure with clout, and two, a responsible press to support him. So far, the Teamsters never fail to muscle the press."

"So who could Robert Kennedy count on?"

"Clark Mollenhoff, for one. He's not much, but he's a start, and responsible as hell. I've been eating and sleeping this for a long time, Bob. It's my story and I want it."

"I don't know. Beck and that bunch . . . they seem pretty decent to me."

"Look, I have my suspicions, but I can't honestly say how far up into the inner circle it goes, or even if it does. But there's a pattern working out there. Out in the small podunk towns, out in the paper Locals. At least, it's something the Teamster brass would want to know about. How long are you going to be in California?"

"How did you know I was going?"

Mollenhoff smiled. "I've got a friend out there working on a story. Maybe I can convince him to share it with you."

"I'll think about it, Clark. I'll let you know."

"Bob, it can't hurt to look."

"Other people tell me it can hurt like hell. Tell me something—why me?"

"You don't need my answer to that."

"I just want to hear it from a Republican."

"Sparing you the compliments, you're tough, you're thorough, and you're still enough of a babe-in-the-woods to be excited by the dangers instead of scared by them. You're too rich to be buyable, and you're too Catholic to compromise. Besides, it's a very worthy and moral cause."

Bobby whistled. "Phew! For a minute there I was afraid you were going to say Holy Grail."

Clark Mollenhoff's mouth laughed, but his dark-ringed, sharp eyes didn't. "All right, it's the goddamn Holy Grail. Will that do it?"

"Would you say anything to get me into this investigation?"

"No, nothing untrue."

After Labor Day, Cape Cod brings its finest beauties out of hiding to reward its year-round natives as well as its part-time loyalists, such as the Kennedys. Indian summer can be balmier than August, and even more pleasant, with the mugginess scrubbed out of the air by the fresh, clearer sea winds announcing autumn. Then the fall itself glistens and invigorates, not with the fiery colors found inland, but with the more subtle palings and blanchings of scrub pine, beach plum, compass grass. Joseph P. Kennedy, Senior, was seeing the winter of his life approaching close; his hair had already gone to snow. He would linger longer at his beloved Hyannisport these years, and come back to it more often. His son Joe had dubbed them the Kennedy Clan years before, and now the clan would grab any and every chance they could to gather at Hyannisport. Journalists labeled it the Kennedy Compound, but it was really just a bunch of beach houses whose backyards met.

Here, never waiting until Thanksgiving or Christmas, the Kennedys would meet—the brothers and sisters, the husbands and wives, and now more and more children—to share huge meals, play touch football, sail, run on the beach, gossip, and, mostly, let age-defying Rose and Joe act in person Mother and Dad for them all.

As dependable as the tides, the talk would never stray for long from their commonly shared passion, politics. Tables would be cleared, and amid the familial sounds of china and silver clinking in the kitchen, cigars would be lit, drinks poured, lamps lit. The father could look about him now and see that it was at last happening. The years had taken severe wages of them, but now here were the survivors, strong and hale: they were *his* and they were *in* it.

On this particular evening Jack was gleeful. ". . . No, no, what *really* pulled Mr. Lodge's shade was Bobby! Archbishop Cushing baptized the baby when—the day before the election? And it was over, we were home! Keep 'em coming, Bob."

"Do our best."

"All right, but that's done," the father said. "It's Mr. Kefauver in the news right now."

"Yup. He's got the inside track," Jack said.

His father protested. "Out in front, yes. But he can be taken."

"Yes, I think Stevenson's opening the door, Jack," Bob said. "He wants you to make the nominating speech. That's his way of saying if you want the convention you'll have to win it on the floor."

"At least he isn't supporting Hubert," Dave Thatcher put in.

Jack grinned. "He enjoys watching a pleasant round of vicious infighting."

"He'll get his fill of that," Joe said, smiling, "with Eisenhower and Nixon!"

Jack stopped the laughter: "But when all's said and done, he'll turn to Kefauver. There's your next V.P. I'm sure of it."

"I'm not," Bobby said. "Kefauver isn't charismatic enough. He alienates the North on anti-crime and the South on civil rights. He isn't . . . unifying. He isn't perfect."

Jack winked. "He isn't Catholic, either."

Bob shrugged. "I still think your smartest move is a try for the number-two spot. Even if you lose—"

"Do my ears deceive me?" their father snorted. "Did I just hear what I thought I heard? *What* was that word?"

Bobby laughed. "To rephrase—in the event that sheer bigotry denies you a place on the ticket, you won't be some obscure Senator from Massachusetts any more. You'll come out of it a national figure."

Jack turned to Dave. "Did he actually say obscure?"

"Speaking of national figures," Joseph Sr. interrupted, "I was speaking with John McClellan, and he tells me, Bob, that you're leaning towards an investigation of Labor?"

Bob and Jack exchanged fast glances. Bob looked down. "It's, uh, still just exploratory, Dad."

Very softly, the father said, "I assume you're taking into consideration the timing involved?"

Bob had been sprawled, one leg up, in a wicker rocker. He swung to his feet and walked to the mantel, relieved that he was being challenged on it openly at last.

"Okay, let me spill a few things, then you tell me. I read a report last night. Some union officials in Portland, Oregon, have gone into the jukebox business for themselves. If a nightclub or bar won't take their machines, these *union officials* simply belt them with a picket line! They shut the guy down! He can't get food or supplies or whatever he needs to operate. Truckers won't take away his dirty linen, taxi drivers won't deliver patrons to his place . . . and the police won't answer his complaints."

Sensing the effect his words were having, Bob went on, the blood rising audibly in his voice.

"One guy, one nightclub owner, decided to see the Labor Relations Board in Salem. Well, he never got to make the trip. His son's best friend"—glancing at Dave—"got killed in an automobile accident. So then the poor bastard got a phone call saying they're sorry about the mistake. And that the *right* kid would be dead in a week. Now, what the hell does that sound like to you?"

"Murder, Inc.," Jack muttered.

Their father looked up at his walls of books. "There are some things, so many, many things . . . in this world . . . that cry out loudly to be corrected." Then he removed his glasses and began polishing them with the handkerchief from his blazor pocket. "It sounds, to me, like a complicated, entangled investigation with clearly no guarantee of success."

"Listen to the man who always says the good fight has to be fought!" Bob snapped.

Joe put his glasses back on, the hanky back into the pocket, sat up straighter in his chair, and said it flat out: "Yes. Sometimes. Sometimes. The question *I* have right now is this—is this the time? With Chicago right

68

ahead of us, is this the time to go looking for toes to step on? I asked, you answer."

Bob slumped. "I can't. How can I? God, does it always have to come down to politics?"

His father paused long, then said, "Yes. In the end, it always comes down to politics."

Jack took the tiller, Bobby manned the lines. They moved the *Merlin* out past the breakwater under power; then Jack killed the engine and Bob raised the mainsail. There was a good wind up. The sun hadn't yet broken clear of the horizon, wasn't round yet. It was deep red, like molten lava. Together in the cockpit, the brothers took spray in their faces from the heavy chop. Beyond the whitecaps the sea was smooth, and Bob raised the jib. Now they were *sailing*.

Jack said, "You know what gets me most out here? The quiet. To reach this kind of speed on land, you need engines. Noise. But this—all this power with all this quiet. Fantastic!"

His brother's equanimity always amazed Bob. They were drinking coffee from a Thermos. Their mother had made them sandwiches for later. "Yeah, sometimes I wish we could just go sailing all the time."

"And that's all?"

"Well, race, probably."

"Ha, that's the idle rich, remember? We're the others."

"Oh, that's right, too. Well, anyhow, if you want to know what I think, I think Stevenson's—"

"Speak right up, Bob."

"I think he's going to throw it open to the convention, that's what I think."

"Why would he do that?"

"Because it's the smart play."

"Then I'll tell you—if that happens, I want you to handle the floor fight for me."

"Great. You sure?"

Jack laughed. "You mean your ruthlessness? Listen, what they call ruthless I call playing hardball. And I'll tell you about the union thing. I've thought about it. I'm the politician, I'll worry about the politics.

69

I know how bad you want it. and I think you're right. Go get them, Bob."

"Thanks, Jack."

"Besides, there are other considerations. I am on the Committee, am I not?"

"You are."

"And the hearings will be televised, will they not?"

"They will."

"I rest my case. I'll obscure-Senator *you!*" The wind shifted. "On your toes now, Bob, we're coming about."

On the morning of November 12, 1956, wearing only a suit against the bitter wind, Robert Kennedy arrived again at the Marble Palace, ten minutes early for his appointment with President Dave Beck. But, keeping her eyes down upon the correspondence in her hands, Mr. Beck's personal secretary told him, "I'm sorry, Mr. Kennedy, Mr. Beck cannot be disturbed now."

"But I have an appointment."

"Which Mr. Beck has had to cancel. We're sorry."

"How about later, then—this afternoon?"

"Do try again, if you like. I can't promise you'll be any more successful, though."

Bob was getting the message. As he was about to push her again, a door to his right suddenly opened. Seeing Bobby, the man abruptly began to close it. Recognizing him, Bob rushed and stopped the door with a straight-arm. "Mr. Mohn!"

"Uh, yes? I . . ." He was Einar Mohn, a Teamster VP and Dave Beck's executive assistant.

"I'm Robert Kennedy, and I want to know what the hell is going on."

"I wouldn't know. Now, if you'll excuse—"

"I had an appointment, and I believe I'm entitled to an explanation."

"Appointments can be broken, Mr. . . . ."

"I'm not some salesman, I represent the U.S. Senate!"

Cornered, Einar Mohn blustered, "And we do not

appreciate the U.S. Senate or anybody else insinuating there's corruption in the Labor movement!"

"We aren't insinuating anything. We're thinking of looking, period."

"Does that explain this little fishing expedition of yours on the West Coast?"

This stopped Bob. "I'm going to the Coast, yes. On Congressional business. I have formally asked for your help while I'm out there in checking out certain information that might involve your union. Can I count on your assistance or not?"

Mohn sat at his desk. "This union is not happy about your investigation. We don't like the way you handle your friends. You can count on us for nothing. And if you persist, your brother might be reminded that he's jeopardizing what could be a meaningful relationship!"

Well, that was telling him. Bob forced himself to relax. Then, smiling, he placed the gift-wrapped package he'd been carrying on Mohn's desk. "Here. Mr. Beck asked for an autographed copy of my brother's book. Would you please see that he gets it, and wish him a Merry Christmas from us? We do not mistreat our friends, Mr. Mohn."

Going down the marble staircase, Bob ran into Eddie Cheyfitz coming up. Big smile. "Bob!" Great to see you. You're looking splendid!" Big handshake. "Hey—congratulations, too. Damn good thing Jack didn't get the VP nod after all, huh?"

"Well, we were glad he came as close as he did."

"Sure, but he can thank his lucky stars he wasn't any part of poor Mr. Stevenson. What a bloodbath, phew!"

"Adlai was still the right man. The time was wrong, that's all."

"Ahem—any ideas on who's the right man for nineteen-sixty?"

Bob laughed. "Ask me in 'sixty."

Eddie laughed, then spoke lower. "Now, what's this I hear about your career? Investigating Labor on the West Coast?"

"Good thing I'm not working on National Security!"

"Well, it's a small town, Bob." Rolling his eyes up the stairs: "How's Dave taking it?"

"You tell me. Mr. Beck is not in for Mr. Kennedy."

Eddie put his arm around Bob's shoulders lightly. "Aah, don't take it wrong. You have to understand Dave. He's a grand old man—and he sees himself that way. Respectability is the most important thing in the world to him. The union's his baby, his family, and a man automatically protects his family. It's human nature. Mr. Beck doesn't want to see anybody trying to drag his loved ones through the mud."

"Then, Eddie, he should know I couldn't agree with him more. *If* there's anything amiss somewhere, it should be handled internally, of course. I just want—"

"I'm glad to hear you say that, Bob. Leave it to me, now. Let's see what Eddie can do for you. You know the old union story about the last man on the line?"

"No."

"Owner of the factory's gonna die. Ran it like a family his whole life. Decides he wants to leave his workers some real goodies to remember him by. Tells his lawyers to give 'em all a big raise. Lawyers say, 'Okay, but we gotta get all the workers to sign for it. Union regs.' So they go, and everybody signs, naturally. All except one old crank, last man on the line. He don't sign nothin'. The owner hears this and says, 'I didn't offer enough. Throw in an extra week's vacation.' Same thing. One guy won't sign. On it goes, until finally the old man gets bullshit, goes down the line, grabs the old gink by the throat, and says, 'Sign, or I'll bash your head in!' Duffer signs on the spot. Owner says, 'Now what did you make me do that for? Why didn't you sign before?' Last man on the line says, 'Nobody explained it before!' "

Bob laughed with Eddie.

"You catch my drift, Bob?"

"Got you, Eddie."

"Okay. Don't worry. I'll be talking to you."

Shoving reams of paperwork into his attaché case, Bob told his secretary, "Angie? Carmine and I need plane reservations to L.A. for as early as you can get

73

them for Friday. And put us into the Hyatt House. Call us O'Rourke and Benson."

"O'Rourke and Benson—are you kidding?"

Bob blushed. "That's Carmine's idea—can I disobey Carmine?"

"Oh, brother!"

"All right, change it then. Make it Rogers and Basilio."

"Now you're talking. Oh, I have a message from Senator McClellan."

"What is it?"

"Be careful."

"Terrific."

The phone rang. Angie answered it. Covering the receiver, she asked, "Bob? Are you in for an Eddie Cheyfitz?"

"Eddie. What can I do for you?"

"Actually, Bob, I think *I* can do something for *you*. Got a pencil and paper?"

"Go ahead."

"Frank Brewster. Head of the Western Conference of Teamsters. Mr. Corruption on the West Coast. Talk to Dutch Woxburg."

"W-O-X?"

"Right. He's Conference Treasurer, L.A. He'll give you the big picture."

"Wow. Thanks, Eddie, I—"

"Don't thank me. We just want you to know we're after the same thing you and the Senators are. A clean union."

Angie said, "You look as if you just saw a ghost."

"Get Carmine in here, fast. I think something's happening."

Aboard the TWA Constellation, Carmine Bellino and Bob both held attaché cases open on their laps. Bellino was in his forties, dark, intense: "the investigator's investigator." An ex-FBI agent and accountant, he was gifted with a near-photographic memory and had acquired from experience the patience and persistence of a bloodhound. He read from his papers: " 'Woxburg, Arthur, a.k.a. Dutch. Four-two-eight Del Mar, North Hollywood. Can be reached there or at

Teamsters office.' Why don't I contact him, Bob, while you start with the others."

"Okay. How do we hit Brewster?"

"Well, formal or informal. Formal, we go through a Sam Bassett. Attorney for the Western Conference. Informal, we walk into Brewster's office in Seattle and say hello."

"Let's say hello."

"Let's say hello."

An unmarked car was waiting for them at the L.A. airport. In the terminal, a tall plainclothesman intercepted them.

"Mr. Rogers? Mr. Basilio? Captain James Hamilton, Intelligence Division, LAPD. This way, please."

At the car, Hamilton introduced them to the driver, Lieutenant Joseph Stephens, who informed them, "It's reached us that certain parties know you're in town. I'm Police Labor Squad. This could scare people away, so we've changed your hotel as a precaution. Hope you don't mind."

Driving, Hamilton said, "If you'd rather, the interrogation room at my precinct is at your disposal."

Carmine said, "No, hotel's better—easier for subjects to relax."

But when they saw the Colonial Arms in downtown L.A., Bobby grinned. "It's not the Colonial Arms *we* know. Who'll feel relaxed here, the bedbugs?"

"Well, sir, if you want to stay incognito . . ."

"It's fine, I was only kidding."

"We can change you to a better place easily."

"No, no, let's get the goddamn ball rolling!" Bob said.

Hamilton replied, "The *ball* is already *rolling*, sir."

Bob turned. "Wait a minute. Did I just say something wrong, Captain?"

"Well, no, sir, but this isn't a game. We're, uh, wondering if you know just how serious—"

"We know," Carmine grumbled.

Bob said, "I'm starting to know—all right? And it's not a game for me, I promise you."

They split into teams. Carmine went with Stephens, Bob went to the hotel.

75

The rooms in the Colonial Arms were even starker and grimier than its façade promised, but they served the purpose: a no-man's-land where nameless people, for their own motives, could unburden themselves to sympathetic ears. Of the many faces and voices that rendezvoused with Robert Kennedy and James Hamilton, these three were typical: the Frightened Man, the Gangster, and the Angry Brother.

As it evolved, their procedure became basically watcher-and-talker, with Bob doing most of the talking. But with the Frightened Man, Bob faltered. The man was jittery, obviously terrified. Bob was afraid he'd bolt. As it happened, the man showed up when Bob was wolfing down a deli tuna sandwich. The man sat uneasily on the edge of the rickety straight-back chair, kneading his fingers between his legs and jabbering uncontrollably. Bob quickly sensed that so long as he kept on eating, saying nothing, the better his chances the man would stay.

The Frightened Man babbled, ". . . And I don't really know why I'm here at all! I'm afraid I've misled you guys. I don't have anything to say, I don't know a thing that means anything. I mean, I'm no liar, I said some things happened and they did, but I don't feel like talking about it any more. I am sorry, Mr. Kennedy. I know I've put you to all this trouble for nothing, but . . . I mean, I can't afford any more trouble with the unions, you know? You have to understand that. You can appreciate my problem, can't you? I mean, put yourself in my shoes for a minute and you'd zip your lip too! I mean . . . Oh God, half of me's dying to tell you how they muscled into my cleaning business . . . The bastards. It's what? It's nothing, a pukey little operation, but it's mine. I've worked my ass off twenty hours a day for years and they just walk in off the goddamn street. They poured *acid!* On the clothes! People's clothes! They trust them to me to clean them. Do a nice job. People's clothes! I can't talk about it, I just can't tell you. I'm sorry, I . . ."

Bobby swallowed and said nothing.

"For instance, Mr. Kennedy, I could tell you about the time they. . . ."

Carmine Bellino/Basilio came out of the Teamsters building and got back into the car. "Woxburg isn't in."

"Out to lunch, right?"

"Yeah, for the rest of my life."

"They say when he'd be back?"

"Wouldn't even say if."

"That stinks. Bum lead? Somebody wild-goosing you?"

"Maybe. They told me one thing I didn't know."

"What?"

"They were expecting me. Not a hint of surprise."

The spring finally cut through the slipcover and bit Bob in the leg. He moved to the sofa, next to Hamilton.

The Gangster arrived so well dressed that Bob felt the weird urge to apologize for the surroundings. This was Bob's first successful hood, and he was fascinated by him. Either the movies hadn't exaggerated after all, or else this dude had taken his style straight from them. The Gangster paused inside the door, took a day-long inventory of its every detail in one sweep of his eyes, moved the chair back against the wall, then stayed standing, putting one highly polished black shoe on its seat. With his four-hundred-dollar pinstripe suit, indigo silk shirt, silver tie, freshly barbered face and hair, if he'd uttered, "Psst, hey you, c'mere!" Bob wouldn't have been surprised. But he wouldn't have laughed, either: the man's mahogany eyes shone with *I survive.* He gave Bob a friendly leer and cracked, "Nice place you got here. It's a privilege to participate in a big-time Senate investigation."

Bob was cowed.

Hamilton got it going. "We don't want to take up too much of your time. We understand you've been double-crossed by somebody we're interested in. Here's your chance."

"Okay. There's a strip joint in the Valley. The English Muffin. Guy called Philly Federico . . ."

In North Hollywood, Carmine Bellino scanned the mailbox names in the lobby of 428 Del Mar. He was about to push the doorbell opposite APT. #5. A.

77

WOXBURG when a little girl opened the inside door and ran past him. He caught it before it closed, and was in. He took the stairs and came to the door of #5. Judging by the halls, it was an expensive place. Music played on a radio inside, very loudly. Carmine knocked, then knocked again, harder and louder. "Mr. Woxburg? Arthur Woxburg? Dutch?" Suddenly the radio went dead silent. But no footsteps approached the door. Carmine yelled, "Woxburg? I've traveled three thousand miles to see you, Mr. Woxburg. My name is Carmine Bellino and I represent—" The radio came back on full blast, drowning him out. He tried some more, then quit and walked away, down the way he had come.

The Angry Brother was a trucker in his mid-thirties, well built and good-looking, dressed neatly in denim workshirt, khakis, Marine garrison belt, clean white T-shirt showing at the neck, heavy leather work boots. He conspicuously ignored Captain Hamilton and told Bob: ". . . But no names, all right? Now, I want you to get a couple things straight. One, I'm no chicken. I did forced recon with the Corps in Korea, and I'll mix with fucking anybody, and I want to do what's right. But two, this sucks. This scares me, and I don't mind admitting it. Not for me, you know? But you don't know who they'll take out. I mean, they'd rather hit your wife or your kid instead of you anyhow. That's why I'm here—they already got my brother. Fucked up his drive shaft. He's . . . Christ, there he is, highballing along up in the Sierras, and blooey. End over end straight down! Tore him clear in half at the belly before he lucked out and it blew up!"

Hamilton probed. "How do you have the details down like that? Did the Highway Patrol . . . ?"

"Highway Patrol bullshit—I was fucking there!" the Angry Brother told Bob. "I was behind him! I watched my own goddamn little brother die!" He choked; he wasn't that tough. He looked away toward the filthy windows, his eyes glistening.

"That's a terrible thing," Bob said softly. "I know what it is to lose a brother."

"Your brother died fighting goddamn Nazis in a goddamn war, Mr. Kennedy!" the stricken man yelled, his voice close to breaking. "Mine died fighting slime. Fucking two-bit hoods who—" He at last spun around to Hamilton. "And where were the cops? Nowhere! And what'll the goddamn bought cops do? Zilch! Zero! Expect help from you guys? Shit—*neverhachi*, GI!"

Hamilton tried. "The report said insufficient evidence."

"A drive shaft split with acid is insufficient evidence? Goddamnit, why didn't you people *do* something?"

Bob waited for silence. "I'll do something."

"How do I know that?"

"Because I'm telling you. But I can't do much unless you talk to me. And I mean name names."

The man slumped. "Okay."

Driving back through the L.A. traffic, Carmine said, "He's hiding, all right. But I can't tell if it's because he's guilty or scared or—"

"Or just subletting his apartment," Stephens blurted impatiently, "or just waiting for your 'Mr. Rogers' to get his ball rolling!"

"Hey, wait, lieutenant—"

"Look, Mr. Bellino, I live day-by-day with creeps out to lunch. And I've also lived through enough politico clean-ups to make me puke. There's shit going down, and I'm just not in the mood any more to watch another hotshot use us to get headlines!"

Carmine sighed sympathetically. "I know the feeling. All I can tell you is what I smell. This little guy is no hotshot. He'll go all the way. It's why I'm aboard. When I was— uh-oh." He'd been checking his side-view mirror. "Lieutenant, do you see what I see?"

Without looking, Stephens said, "Black Caddie. Big silver grill. Standard Teamster escort. They *do* know you're in town."

At the Colonial Arms, Hamilton told Stevens and Bellino, "Got one guy allergic to the badge. Bob took him for a walk."

79

Bob and the Angry brother walked the sidewalks of the commercial district, talking.

". . . And the third guy's a Mike Richards. Real name's Ginsberg, and they call him the Gent. He was the— Hey, will you look at that." They were crossing an alleyway. Deep down it, a huge garbage truck was working, several men unloading full fifty-gallon drums of an ice-cream factory's refuse into its broad lift-bucket.

Bob said, "What about it?"

"Well, that's where it all started for us. Any idea how much garbage the average American family has to get rid of in a year? Tons. And businesses have even more."

"Never gave it a thought."

"Nobody does. But me and Al did. Al was my brother. We were sick of over-the-road. You know how it is when you start having a wife and kids. So we pitched our dough together, got a loan, and opened a garbage route. Called it Saladwagon, Inc. Not officially, just as a joke. And we were doing pretty good, too. One guy puts you on to another, and pretty soon we had a list of stops big enough for two trucks. Me on one, Al on the other.

"That's when the union put the gorilla on us. Said it was time to organize. We say, why organize? Christ, it's just me and my brother, what are we gonna do, hold each other up for a raise?"

"They . . . insist?"

"Yeah, they insist—they blow up one of our trucks! They tear the electricity out of our office! Al and me get the message. It's definitely time to go union."

Bob looked at him fascinated. "That ended your troubles, right?" They stepped into the alley and leaned against the wall on the sunny side.

The trucker lit a Pall Mall and snuffed. "Mr. Kennedy, you got a long way to go."

"Go on." He was calling the man by his first name now.

"Hell, that's when the real shit started. The union starts using us to organize the outfits we service. They call up in the morning and say so-and-so don't get his garbage hauled away today. The poor bastard calls

80

us then, mad as hell, but what can we do? Before we know it, we're hurting bad. We're down to one paying client, this huge processing company in east L.A., makes all these little doodads that go into airplanes or something. Good for two full loads a day easy.

"So the union decides to organize *them* next! Same old tune. We're sitting on our hands three whole months. Jesus, Al was a funny guy, always with the jokes, but this time we're both ready for a Section Eight. We're both mortgaged up to here, the banks start coming down heavy, the goddamn *food's* running low, so finally we say fuck this, we're goin' back to work. And we do. For one day. That's when they torch our second truck. They torch our office. They shoot at Al's wife with a goddamn rifle one night! They call my wife and say I'm dead, she should go to the morgue and get the corpse."

"My God."

"Oh, yeah. Well, that's when we said screw it, and went back to over-the-road. Ha, thought we were home free! That's when Al . . . Al . . ."

"Was he going to talk?"

"Mr. Kennedy, Al was more than my brother. He was my best friend, you know? But even if he wasn't, he was the bravest human being I ever come across, Korea or anywhere. Yeah, he was going to talk. And you know what? I'm ashamed to tell you. I was the one who turned woman on him. I was scared of dying. And I pressured him out of it. For me, he was going to forget. Only they didn't know that."

"And that's why you're here."

"That's an affirmative."

"Did you try going to the Joint Council? The Western Conference? The NLRB?"

He laughed. "Come in, world—how do you like America so far, Mr. K? Oh, uh, I think that's the car I saw parked outside your hotel."

Bobby turned. He was right. Stephens had come looking for them. Bob stepped out to the curb and waved. The car pulled up, and Carmine got out. Bobby was all excited now and turned back to call his informant over. But the alley was empty. Even the garbage truck was gone, out the other end. Bob said, "Oh, dammit, you scared him off!"

"We didn't," Carmine said. "They did. I'm afraid he spotted our escort service.'"

Bob stared down the block at the Cadillac with the silver grille. "Jesus, they're subtle. Looks like a funeral car. Wait here."

"Bob, no!"

"Mr. Kennedy!" Stephens called.

Bobby double-timed up the sidewalk, straight at the limousine. He saw the driver's window start to roll up, and broke into a run, yelling, "Tell your employers! You're interfering with a Senate investigation! And that's a crime! Punishable by—"

The Cadillac roared away, burning rubber and leaving him standing in a purple cloud of exhaust fumes, grinning.

Stephens had whipped a U-turn and came screeching up. Again, Carmine got out. He was calm, Stephens was gasping. "Jesus Christ Mr. Kennedy!"

Carmine smiled. "Bob, I suggest we continue your ... education back at the hotel."

"No," Bob said icily. "I suggest we continue it up north, and now."

Mollenhoff's friend was there to meet them in the pouring rain at the airport. Like Clark Mollenhoff and Dave Thatcher and so many others who were to find themselves signing on for active duty under, around, and behind Robert Kennedy, this man bore the look and attitude of a breed of man produced by World War II and Korea: the combat officer of the lower ranks. Not of the career, lifer, professional soldier type, but rather of the get-in-do-it-get-out kind of fighter. Tough and smart and brash enough to cut through bureaucratic bullshit when it got in the way. If you want to contact somebody, grab the nearest phone, run up to the Cadillac, walk into the fire-fight. He walked up to Bob Kennedy and Carmine Bellino. "Mr. Rogers, Mr. Basilio, welcome. Clark Mollenhoff sent me."

He drove them into the cold, drenched city. They

mutually agreed to skip the pleasantries. Bob or Carmine asked; the man answered. It was that simple.

"Teamsters Local One Seventy-four—how many members?"

"About four hundred."

"Four eighty-three sound close?"

"Sounds exact."

"How many attend union meetings?"

"Less than a third."

"How many care about the dirty stuff?"

"Less than that."

"My report says that fourteen people attended the most recent meeting," Carmine said.

The man laughed. "Then fourteen attended. You already have all these specifics, why do you need me?"

Bob smiled. "How much do you know about Frank Brewster?"

"He's President of the Western Conference, and he's into crooked deals. I know enough."

"How much of what you know will you tell me?"

"I told Clark and I'll tell you. I don't trust Congressional investigations. They're all flash and no substance. They vanish in the night. Never been surprised yet."

"Then stick around, we may surprise you."

The man took an investigator's look at Kennedy and was impressed. "We have to pass One Seventy-four on the way—want to take a look?"

"Absolutely. Terrific."

He stopped in front of it and turned off his lights, but kept the motor idling. Bobby said, "Good Lord, it looks like the Little Red Schoolhouse!"

"Quaint, isn't it."

"Yeah—hard to believe there could be anything crooked going on inside."

"No, not hard at all." The man pointed. "Notice the parking lot, please."

Bob snuffed. "Ah, yes, the inevitable Teamster Cadillac."

"*Ten* inevitable Teamster Cadillacs, to be precise."

Bob asked him, "What the hell is it with them, anyhow? Do they *want* to look like the Capone Mob or what?"

He explained, "Actually, it started on fairly sensible reasoning, Mr. Kennedy—"

"Bob, please."

"Okay. Anyhow, the logic went that if you wanted to negotiate seriously with management, you couldn't go in with your hat in your hand. If he lived on Elm Street, you bought a house on Elm Street, or the equivalent. If he belonged to the Junior Chamber of Commerce . . . and so forth. Then, of course, the illustrious Dave Beck made his famous speech, 'If the head of General Motors can drive a brand-new Cadillac, why can't the head of a Teamster Local!' Our illustrious Frank Brewster, staunch union man that he is, naturally took his President's advice, quite literally."

"And then some."

"Yes, he's got quite a stable, and not just Caddies, either. Encouraged by his very generous union expense account, Frank has developed a taste for the finer things in life. Shall we go?"

Driving again, Carmine asked, "What else besides the Caddies?"

"Would you believe a stable of thoroughbred racehorses? Monthly tab more than sixteen hundred bucks —which Local Number One Seven Four picks up."

Bob whistled. "Can you prove that?"

"Want me to?"

"No, I'm all flash, no substance."

"Touché. You're damn right I can prove it."

"Terrific."

Bob went alone to Local 174 early the next morning. A secretary told him sweetly, "I'm sorry, but Mr. Brewster isn't in."

"Do you mean he isn't in to me or he's out?"

"He's not . . . um, I mean, he's . . ."

"Can *I* help you?" Though he didn't introduce himself, this was noticeably well dressed Samuel Basset, lawyer for Brewster's Western Conference.

Bob said, "I hope so. I'm Robert—"

"Kennedy. I know. Chief Counsel, Senate Permanent Investigating Committee. We get television out here. Mr. Brewster is literally out. Of town. Will there be anything else? Judy, please get me the Thompson Brothers file."

"How long will Mr. Brewster be away, Mr. . . . ?"

"I can't really say. Judy . . . ?"

"All right, I don't need to see him. Not yet, anyhow. I'm also here to examine the records of the Western Conference of—"

"That's nice, I'm sure, young, uh, man, but for that you would definitely have to see Mr. Brewster. I am his attorney, and, as such, know that no records can ever be made available to anybody without Mr. Brewster's express approval. Now you really must excuse me. Good-bye, and thanks for stopping by. Judy? The file now, please?" He closed his office door behind him. Bobby stared at it, resisting the urge to put his foot through it. He looked at Judy pretending to search for the Thompson file in the B drawer, then left.

Teamster attorney Sandy Farrell was watching the snow fall on Washington. The Capitol was a faint outline in the distance. Like some Prussian general's spiked helmet, he thought. He grinned at his own reflection in the window. Behind him at the desk, his old friend Jimmy was in high gear on the phone, making deals. Sandy, listening, knew a stranger would be amazed by the staccato, machine-gun performance, unaware that being on only one phone at a time was one-third Jimmy's normal capacity. Jimmy's hoarse, sharp-edged, mile-a-minute barrage, which had benefited Sandy so well and so often down the years, reached his ears like a song.

". . . Then come to terms at three hundred and *eighty* thousand! Sure! That's six point two across the board, right? Well, all right then, I think we can reach an accommodation. Now feed me the numbers of the medical plan. The medical! Bullshit, 'tomorrow'— now! Okay. Yeah . . . yeah . . . but what's the base? Top dollar I'm talking about, Buzzy—he gonna pay out each month? . . . Whaddaya mean ya hafta look it up? *I* could fucking look it up! Sandy could . . . You don't know, how *come* you don't know, how come I *do* know, and *I* ain't the one suppose to be sitting on top of this goddamn negotiation! *You* are!

"Buzzy, baby, I'm tellin you somethin', don't let

this ever happen with me again, you wanta stay where you are, huh? Two strikes is all you get with me, brother. Two strikes is *out* where I come from, and don't you forget that, pally. Okay, okay, wait a second now, I gotta see these figures now . . ." He shut his lids and looked up inside his head, muttering aloud: "Guy's offering three grand in claims, that's a month, that's thirty-six a year . . ." Then, back into the phone: "That *still* falls short of present hospital costs! Tell him to up it twenty percent—that's forty-three two per annum, and that's what I want and what I'm gonna get. I know, I know, Buzzy, but listen to Jimmy —tell him he can take it or leave it. Tell him that's it, brother, that's all she wrote, and he'll meet you, he'll come to an accommodation and we'll be in like Flynn." *Slam!* No good-byes. He looked at Sandy and winked, got up, barreled out from behind his desk, and dropped to the thick carpet to resume his habitual, calming pushups.

Sandy relighted his pipe and smiled. "I still think you ought to donate that brain of yours to the Smithsonian, Jim. All those figures, and you still don't own a pencil!"

"What? That? Small potatoes, Sandy! Cherry tomatoes!"

"Come on, it's an incredible gift and you—"

"Learned it in school, Sand, learned it in school! Ha! Besides, ya write somethin' down and somebody can read it! Now. Reason I called you. The big one. How close are ya?"

"Another week anyhow, Jimmy. Those new wrinkles you threw at us—"

"Those . . . wrinkles . . . are the . . . key to the future! Wait a minute. Twenty-eight . . . nine . . . there! Enough." He jumped to his feet, patted his rock-solid belly, and returned to his chair. "Areawide bargaining, Sandy! *National* contracts is what we're talking now, kiddo." *Ring!* "Hello! Yeah—speak to me! He's in town—in town where? You in Seattle or . . . okay. He moving on Brewster? Ha, yeah, that's Frank's style, all right. How's the rich kid lookin' in the field, though—think he'll give up? He what? Right up to the car? Ha! Then that's Frank's ass in the sling all right. Yeah, yeah. Keep me informed." *Slam*.

"That teenage Irish shoe clerk! Like Pinocchio, I got him, Sandy! I told ya, didn't I?"

"This damn pipe won't stay—"

"Get rid of it!" Ya don't need it!"

"Think he'll tackle Brewster?"

"Tackle him? The brat thinks he's Palladin. A fuckin' Mountie! He'll tie Frank up in knots! Then, it's bing-bing-bing to His Majesty the Wheel! What's the puss for?"

"It's going too easy. I think Kennedy's trouble."

"Aah, you old lady, I'll eat that jerk for breakfast! Hell, I've had bigger mouthfuls at Teamster lunches. Wasn't for me, he'd be home in bed by now. And as soon as I'm finished with him that's where I'll drop him! And then, Sandy old partner, it's Christmas morning every day the rest of my life!"

One difference between Jimmy Hoffa and Bobby Kennedy was that Bob sometimes put papers on the floor and read them while he did his pushups, holding himself up on one arm while he turned the pages. He was doing this in his room at the Olympia Hotel in Seattle the night Sam Bassett returned his phone calls at last.

"What is it exactly that I can do for you, Mr. Kennedy?"

"I'm still waiting to hear from Frank Brewster."

Basset said, "So am I, what else is new?" and hung up.

Bob was still furious when he met his contact man for dinner at Tony's, a spaghetti house. The man said, "Get some of that fettuccini al Tony into your system. It'll cheer you up."

"I'll cheer up when Frank Brewster knocks off this first-level stalling action. Does he take me for a fool? What's he think, I'll give up and go away?"

"He might. I did. At first."

"Well, he's got to learn what you apparently have. I'd like to teach the unctuous Mr. Bassett a couple of things, too."

"Bob, you're doing it just right. Hang in and outlast

87

them. They'll come out, I know they will. They aren't used to having anybody serious on their tail. That's a key tactic, I think. Simple bonehead perseverance. Even after you flush out Brewster, you shouldn't . . ."

"What?"

"Nothing. Just pep-talking. Eat your meal, it's—"

"You said after Brewster. *After*—what's that supposed to mean?"

"Nothing. Slip of the—"

"You're holding out on me, dammit."

"Call it a story still in the development stage, that's all."

"How far beyond Brewster does this thing *go?*"

"I can't, Bob."

"You can't not!"

"Look, for one thing it's much too early, and for another, it . . . the story doesn't belong to me, Bob, it belongs to my publisher, and I am bound to honor—"

"You're kidding yourself and you know it."

"No, not entirely. Well, maybe I am. I don't—"

"How far?"

"I can't, Bob. Not yet."

"It's all the way, isn't it! Is it? Is that what you're not sharing with me?"

He nodded. "I think so. But there's so much I can't prove yet, Bobby."

"And why can't you?"

"There's so much material, financial records especially, that I need and just can't get at yet."

"What's this?"

"A breadstick."

Snap! "Now?"

"Two breaksticks."

"Here. One for you, one for me. You can't get the evidence you need because you're trying to do it as a private citizen. You know Clark Mollenhoff's philosophy on this?"

"All too well."

"And you still disagree?"

"Uh, less and less."

"Well, I agree with him completely. I am that guy! My Committee has the one thing you need and will never get from any paper, magazine, or network!"

"Subpoena power."

"You got that right, my friend. You have facts and no power. I've got the power and so far the flimsiest of facts. Christ, man!"

"You need me, I need you."

"You've *got* me, mister."

The man put down the fork he wasn't using anyhow. He reached his hand across the small tabletop. "Now you've got me, Mr. Kennedy."

Without finishing dinner they went straight to the man's files at his office. "Frank Brewster's an amateur. Nickel-and-dime stuff. Pads his expense accounts, even uses Teamster dues for his stable bills. But here's where I think it really starts, Bob . . ."

Bob tried to decipher the bunches of invoices and receipts. "What? He owns this mansion, too?"

"No, he doesn't. Turn the next page."

"Beck!"

"Yup. Dave Beck. Teamster president. His majesty the wheel."

"Jesus, look—nails, copper tubing, toilet seats, toilet-seat covers! Piping, a garden hose . . . sixty-nine cents for a light switch! He wouldn't even take sixty-nine cents out of his own pocket?"

"Incredible, isn't it?"

"Incredibly petty!"

"Keep going, it gets better. Here, this is more major construction on Beck's place—he added a new wing of four rooms, six-car garage, landscaping . . . Bob, it adds up to seventy-one thousand bucks. All union money. All paid to one guy, this John Lindsey, contractor, Seattle."

Bob snapped his fingers. "Wait a second! Damn, I wish Carmine was here. But I remember . . . yes! This wouldn't be the same estate Beck *sold* to the union a couple years ago?"

"Yes, it would. A hundred and sixty-three thousand dollars."

"Good God Almighty! That means the Teamsters paid for the whole thing in the first place, then *bought it back* at more than twice the price."

"Not a bad deal."

"Not bad for Beck, no."

"Now you know why Brewster took a powder."

"What can we do until he surfaces?"

"Well, *you* could go meet Mr. Lindsey. This is where I have to lay back, Bob."

"Right. Do you have photostats or something of all this?"

"I will in about twenty minutes."

Carmine landed from L.A. the next afternoon. Bob picked him up. "I'll drive, you read."

By the time they got to Lindsey's posh lakeside residence, Carmine knew why they were there. Bob went to the door, talked to a maid, then came back to the car.

"Out, no idea when he'll be back. It's an epidemic. Everybody's disappearing."

"Maybe it's us."

"So we wait again."

"Well, we've got plenty of reading material. Here are the affidavits from L.A."

Dusk came and went. They kept the engine running off and on for warmth. Bob switched on the overhead light to finish reading Carmine's reports. The last one stopped him cold: " . . . *The trucker was told there would be no independent operations in San Diego. He was then beaten and knocked unconscious. When he regained consciousness, he was covered with blood and suffered terrible pains in the abdomen. The pain was so intense that he was unable to drive back to his home in Los Angeles. He went to a hospital for help. There an emergency operation was performed. The doctors removed a large cucumber from his rectum. Later he was told that if he ever returned to San Diego, it would be a baseball bat. He never returned to San Diego. . . .*" Bob shut off the light. "Mother of God," he said wearily, "you read these things and you say, this can't be happening. Not here, not now, not in America. It can't be happening, but it is."

"It's everywhere, Bobby. L.A., Seattle, Detroit, Boston, it's like cancer."

90

"I was wrong. They can never clean their own house on this. It's too big."

"Yeah, well, that's the trouble side of decentralization. Each Local's autonomous. Has only itself to answer to."

"Where the hell has the IRS been all this time?"

"Unions are tax-exempt. The Revenue guys have no jurisdiction."

"The goddamn FBI does!"

Carmine pulled his overcoat collar tighter around his neck and ears. "Hoover's a statistical cop. He likes crimes that have high visibility. Big headlines for the Bureau. Bank heists, autotheft rings, domestic espionage. Labor stuff is dirty pool and too long-term. It's political dynamite that can go up in your face. It's not his cup of tea, Bob."

"God, look at that house. The last time my father lived like that he was Ambassador to England!" He looked away from the mansion, started the car and let off the hand brake.

Carmine said, "Aren't we going to wait for Lindsey?"

"I've done all the waiting I'm going to do! From now on, they start coming to us."

The phone was ringing when they got to their room at the Olympia. It was Stephens from L.A., and he said, "Mr. Kennedy, we just got a tip that Frank Brewster's here. At the Palmer House."

"We're on the next plane down!"

Stephens met them on the L.A. runway. With lights flashing and sirens wailing, he sped them to the Palmer House. Going up in the elevator, Bob said, "My God, Carmine. I'm nervous!"

"So'm I. Haven't felt like this since we closed on Dillinger."

Stephen's jaw dropped. "You were on the *Dillinger* case? I didn't know that, sir!"

Bobby squinted at Carmine. "Neither did I!"

Carmine grinned. "Live and learn."

"Here it is, Nine Fourteen."

Before they could knock, the door opened and a maid came out, pulling her service wagon. "Oh! You scared me!"

"Is Mr. Brewster here, ma'am?"

"Oh, no, this room's checked out."

Bob dashed to the phone and called the desk. "An hour ago! Okay, thanks a lot." He put his finger on the button and pulled his phone book out of his pocket, then dialed. "Bassett? This is Robert Kennedy. I'm calling you from the room at the Palmer House in Los Angeles where your client has been staying! Now you listen to me this time. I want to see Frank Brewster before I leave the West Coast.

"My Committee is now going to prepare for open hearings into Labor corruption. If I don't get a definite appointment to see Brewster within the next ten minutes, I can assure you he will be found by our investigators. And when he is, he will be subpoenaed to appear in Washington. I'm going to give you this phone number. If you don't call me back in ten minutes, you and Brewster might as well go out and buy plane tickets, because you'll be visiting me in D.C." He hung up.

Waiting, Stephens said, "That's one hell of a bluff, Mr. Kennedy."

"It's no bluff."

"You hope."

"Carmine—" *Ring!* "It worked."

He let the phone ring twice, just long enough to laugh in relief. "Yes. . . . Well, good. I've been looking forward to meeting you too, Mr. Brewster."

Sandy Farrell gingerly opened the door to Dave Beck's office and peered in. "So there you are!"

Jimmy was sitting in Beck's chair. He laughed. "Come right in! My door's always open!"

"I take it you got the word before I did."

"Yup. Brewster's gonna make like a canary! So's Nate Shefferman in Chicago—hear that? Told ya, didn't I? Beck's through."

"Yeah, just a matter of time now. You pegged the Kennedy kid right."

"Yeah, he's got his big thrill."

"I still don't know, though, Jimmy—thing about tasting blood, you can develop an appetite."

"Will you can that line of malarkey! Hearings! You kiddin' me? Dog-and-pony time! Lights, camera, bullshit. Then back to business as usual."

"Hope you're right."

"Money in the bank, Sandy! Look at that, would ya? One stinking phone! No wonder he lost touch!"

Across town, Bob Kennedy and Carmine Bellino were sitting in the living room of Senator John McClellan's apartment, anxiously waiting for him to finish reading their documents. When he did, he let out a long, silent whistle. "It's overwhelming, isn't it."

"Yes, sir, it is."

"And not merely Beck. He's fairly well on ice, I'd say."

Carmine said, "He's dead but still standing. All that's left is the pushing."

93

"But the *scope* of this thing!" the Senator drawled. "I had no idea. You both realize, of course, some of these charges are going to be very tough to support."

"We have to try," Bobby said, too quickly.

"I didn't say we wouldn't," McClellan said. "Don't go righteous on me, Bob. It'll be tough to support. This investigation . . . it's hardly going to make any of us very popular!"

Bob brightened. "Can we take that as a green light, Senator?"

"After reading all that? You've hardly left me many options. But listen, now—save all your hoopla for New Year's Eve. I want this *thorough*. Every t crossed, every i dotted. If we're going to become so very unpopular, it had better be for a damn good reason!"

"Yes, sir."

"Robert. I want you to sound out the other boys in advance. Start with Sam. Hell, if we can't get that good ol' country lawyer all fired up for this brawl, we'll have to take another look at it."

Senator Sam Ervin indeed got fired up. He hefted the thick Confidential sheaf and dropped it heavily onto his desk. "Unpopular! Shoot, John's a mighty fine fella, but he don't know a fish from a mongrel dog if he thinks this shindig'll make him unpopular! Gotta have a little more faith in the American people than that!"

"You'll support the investigation then, sir?" Bob asked him.

"Hell, yes! It's what we're put here for, ain't it?"

Senator Stuart Symington passed.

Senator Joseph McCarthy smiled. "Sure looks as if you've found the cause you wanted, Bob. I think the best way I can help you is to bow out of it right now."

"No, Senator, you—"

"Look. The unions are afraid of an investigation. The Democrats are afraid of the unions. And the investigators are afraid of me. I'm the ranking Republican on this Committee, and I'm me. They're bound to fear that I'll end up as Chairman of another so-called witch hunt. If half of what you've shown me will hold water, it's too critical to risk somebody's using me to sabotage it."

"Senator," Bob said, "there's something you don't

know. A new Committee is being formed. It's to be strictly bipartisan. Both Senator McClellan and Senator Ervin have stated that if there's any attempt to omit you, neither of them will serve."

"They said that?"

"They did. And I assume it includes any attempt on your own part."

Senator McCarthy laughed. "All right, I'll tell you what. Tell John this is just a suggestion, mind you, but it's a sound one—appoint Senator Ives Vice-Chairman. That way I clearly have no chance nor any intention of taking over."

"That's . . . very smart, Senator. Thank you."

"Bob, you can count on me to do everything I can for this investigation. It'll be good to be working on the same side with you again."

Bob smiled. "Yes, sir, it will."

A very worried Sandy Farrell sat watching Jimmy Hoffa pace the floors of his office in his home Local, 299, Detroit. They were waiting for Dan Ohlmeyer, Jimmy's top sergeant, to finish reading the draft of the new contract they had brought from Washington. Dan had begun making grunts of fret and doubt early on, and hadn't stopped. Sandy knew Jimmy's face was no clue to his thoughts, but he also knew how much Jimmy valued Ohlmeyer's judgment when it came to contracts that Local committees would go for or not go for, so Dan's sounds couldn't be giving him much encouragement. Finally Dan looked up and said, "I don't know, Jim. It's a bitch. I'm not sure even I go for it, myself."

"What's your problem, kid?"

Sandy prompted, "Every base is covered, Dan."

"I know, I know, but . . ."

"But what?"

"Well, it's all there all right, Jimmy. But what's there ain't *choice*."

"Ain't choice? What ain't? Christ, we're boostin' the minimum to two twelve an hour! Since when do you have problems with a forty-cent pay hike?"

"Come on. Some'll get it, but most will get fired to pay for it."

95

"Nah, that's old stuff. You're missin' the forest for the trees, Danny. It's the uniformity we're goin' for, kid. Greater efficiency! This way, the guy in Tuscaloosa makes the exact same as the bozo in New York."

"I see that, Jimmy, but . . . Take this Local right here. Ours. If we come under an areawide pact, we lose any say in the future. We just become part of a group, and what's good for the group has to be good for us. When do we get to say what we think's good? We don't. I can't *sell* it, Jimmy. It's too new, too soon. Beck's always let each Local go its own way, and the guys are used to that."

"Well, they can get un-used to it! Times are changing. Beck is goddamn *out*. It's modern times now. I know you can do it, Dan. You get your ass in gear and start sellin' that contract, huh?"

Ohlmeyer grinned fondly at his boss and went to the door. "I'll try for you, Jimmy. I'll do my best. But I'm not making any promises."

When he was gone, Jimmy slumped into his chair. "What's happening in Washington?"

"Forget Kennedy. If Dan—"

"I asked you a question."

"He's still in the process of putting a Committee together."

"How's he doin'?"

"I hear it's not too popular."

This didn't cheer him. He sighed. "Turns out areawide bargainin's not too popular either. Does he have his power base?"

"Do you have *yours*, Jim!"

Jimmy turned his chair to the window and stayed staring out at the new, clean snow gradually covering the sooty banks of earlier falls. Then he swung back around and said quietly, "I'll tell you who my power base is. The guy who knows he can put a dime in a pay phone, dial a number, and talk to me about his problems. One of these days they're *all* gonna realize what I'm trying to do for the working stiffs in this country. The little guy. If I don't protect him, he's gotta know that sure as hell nobody else will. When enough of those guys know they got Jimmy Hoffa humpin' for them, I'll have a power base I can knock

96

your goddamn Committees and councils out the window with!"

It was snowing in Hyannisport, too. They had had a joyous, white Christmas, and now it was New Year's Eve, 1956. All but the tiniest children were gathered in the parents' house, waiting to see in the new year. Three members of the family weren't yet taking part in the festivities: Bob, Jack, and their father. Bob had a problem: Jack was no longer sure he wanted to be part of the new Committee, and Joseph Sr. was agreeing with him. They were off by themselves on the heated sunporch. Piano music and singing drifted out through the closed French doors.

The father said, "You have two solid, experienced Senators, both Democrats, who want no part of it. That should tell you something, Bob."

"It does. It tells me they are making a politically sound decision that reeks of moral cowardice."

The father rolled his eyes to the ceiling.

Jack laughed. "Hey, Saint George, take it easy on the Democratic Senators, will you? There aren't enough of us to go around as it is!"

"Look, you two can laugh, and Symington and Jackson can go wash their hands, but none of you has seen what I've seen. There are thousands, I don't know, millions of workingmen out there—union men —with absolutely nothing between them and any goddamn mobster hood who feels like terrorizing them!"

"Ah, come on, Bob."

"Read the report, Jack."

"It's New Year's Eve. I want to party! We didn't come here to—"

"Just read it. That's all I ask."

"You're not too . . . close to this, are you, son?"

"No, Dad, I'm not. It is a threatening situation. Really threatening. The fear in those lives! The outright exploitation going on, every day. I'm not exaggerating, Dad. Jack. Honest to God, it makes you question who is really running this country! We have to stop it! If we don't get one more Democratic Senator to join this Committee, there won't be a Committee. You've gotta do this, Jack!"

"For you."

"Not for me! For *it*."

The father slapped both knees with his hands and stood up. "Well, I've said my piece. I'm going to sing some songs and drink some punch and talk to some pretty women. Listen to your brother."

"Who?" both brothers asked.

Without looking back, the old man said, "That's your decision." Then he left.

Jack said, "Aw, Jesus, some impartial moderator *he's* turning out to be." He sighed. "All right, where is it?"

"In Dad's den. On the desk."

"Send me in some drinks. I'll see you at midnight."

At twelve everybody yelled *Happy New Year!* kissed each other. They had just begun singing "Should auld acquaintance be forgot" when Jack came out and joined in. His eyes looked troubled. He had read the report. He winked at Bob and nodded.

Bob smiled and sang louder.

The committee had been born.

Three large trucks roared through the black, freezing Michigan night toward Pontiac, led by a long black Cadillac. Jimmy Hoffa was doing the driving. Sandy Farrell rode the death seat. They had the radio on, and the news said, ". . . With Vice-President Nixon scheduled to leave next month on a fact-finding tour of Latin America.

"In the world of organized Labor, a new Senate Select Committee is being formed, it was announced today. Called the Select Committee on Improper Activities in the Labor or Management Field, the investigating panel will be headed by Senator John McClellan, Democrat of Arkansas. Joining him on the Committee will be Senators Kennedy, McNamara, McCarthy, Ervin, Mundt, Goldwater, and Ives. According to Chief Counsel Robert F. Kennedy—" Jimmy snapped it off.

Sandy said, "Or Management. That's a good one."

"Yeah. And the little weasel even got his brother into the act!"

"Ha. He ain't running for President, Father, he's my brother!"

"Ah, that's okay. Maybe I'll put 'em both on the payroll. Oh, listen, I want you to make sure Brewster doesn't come unglued. He has to take the fall right along with Beck."

"Why Frank? He's only—"

"You can't tell, Sand. I don't want nobody to start looking like a contender, least of all Brewster."

"Okay, there's plenty enough there to hand him. How much farther, Jim?"

"To the presidency?"

"No, the Community Hall!" They laughed, driving into the night.

Dan Ohlmeyer was already there, trying to preside over the meeting, and having a hard time doing it. He had read through the proposed new contract, and the right half of the full hall had exploded in violent protest, led by a trucker named Earl Stanton. Dan's supporters also jumped to their feet. Folding metal chairs were going over, voices and tempers were growing louder and hotter, and Ohlmeyer was afraid it was going to break down into a brawl. He kept pounding his gavel and shouting for order. "Come on! Hold it down! Let's talk this out! We can go over the contract! Point by point! We can—"

"Shove your contract!" Stanton's men roared. "We don't want it, and we don't want you neither!"

Ohlmeyer's men yelled, "Hold the floor, Dan! You —shut the fuck up and listen!"

Suddenly, heads started turning toward the back of the hall. Ohlmeyer shouted, "What is it?"

The word passed: "It's fuckin' Hoffa! Himself! He's outside!"

Ohlmeyer announced, "Ten-minute recess!" jumped to the floor from the stage, and made his way through the confused truckers.

The minute Jimmy and his trucks pulled up at the hall, the headlights of five Pontiac police cars flashed on their high beams. As Hoffa's strong-arms came pouring down out of the trucks, wielding wrenches and lengths of pipe, the patrol-car doors started opening and spilling out armed deputies. Jimmy ran into the wash of light, his hands high.

"Stay back, guys! Hold by the trucks!"

The police chief met him in the middle of the lot. He said, "I've got twenty men."

"I got fifty!" Jimmy said.

"We've got machine guns."

"Then between us we'll be able to maintain law and order here tonight, won't we, Captain."

"That's what we're here for. Who are you?"

"I'm Jimmy Hoffa, and that's what we're here for too. I'm goin' inside, and I'm goin' alone."

"That's fine. We'll just stay here and keep watch."

"You do that."

Ohlmeyer met him on the steps and walked him through the crowd of Teamsters. Jimmy walked fast and talked fast. "Ya got a fuckin riot here or what?"

"I told you it wouldn't go down easy, Jim. They hate the contract, and me with it. Half of them, anyhow."

"They got a mouth?"

"Yeah."

"What's his name?"

"Stanton."

"He any good?"

"Too good, if you ask me."

"I'm through askin' you anything kid." He leaped to the stage and faced the mob, half clapping, half booing, all still yelling and flailing their arms in the air. He waited, staring down at them, not motioning at them at all, just staring and smiling slightly. When they started to simmer down, he cracked his voice at them at full volume, as if he'd been speaking and had just paused for a breath. And he galvanized them.

"All right! That's better! Now, in case there's any of you who don't know me yet, my name is James Riddle Hoffa and you can call me Jimmy. I'm a member and officer of this, the greatest union in the world —and *anyone* who thinks I'd do anything to *hurt* it should stand up and say so to my face! Because I'll break his jaw, and I don't care how big he is! And some of you boys look pretty damn big, too!" This got them to laugh. It always did.

"And if some one of you tanks should knock me down . . . I'll get up and let him taste the heel of my boot. And if he knocks me down twice, I'll get up and take a club to him! And if he knocks me down, I'll get up again! I've done it before, men, and I'll do it again. I won't stay on the ground, because I believe in what I'm fighting for, because what I'm fighting for is this great union of ours! I believe in it, I believe in Jimmy Hoffa, and I believe in you!" This got them to start applauding and cheering, a little.

"I'm *not* going to go into the contract! I won't, because it's a good contract! But *you* can go into it. And you're a fool if you don't. You can tear it apart and start from scratch. That's up to you and your Business Agent. I've never shoved anything down your throat, and I won't start now!" That got them cheering and applauding.

Somebody yelled, "We don't want Ohlmeyer!"

Another voice picked it up. "We want Ohlmeyer out!"

Jimmy looked as if they'd insulted his mother. *"Is somebody here trying to ridicule the reputation of Dan Ohlmeyer?* A man who's been a loyal Business Agent for almost twenty years? Since some of you were still in diapers? A man who fought beside me in *battle?* Who got bloodied with me in 'thirty-two, in 'thirty-three, in 'thirty-four, in 'thirty-five, and in nineteen hundred and thirty-seven? Has someone else here paid the dues that Dan Ohlmeyer has paid—in hospital operatin' rooms . . . and at the end of police billy clubs?" He paused to inhale the utter silence. "Dan Ohlmeyer is a good and a reasonable man. He loves this wonderful union, and if he don't have your respect, so help me God, I'll take a club to you myself!" They were now totally and loudly in love with him.

"But I want you all to know in your hearts there's no monkey business or shenanigans goin' on here! So you know what I'm gonna do? Right here and now? I'm gonna take one of you—one of you from the rank and file—and *move him up!* I'm gonna make him a representative and let him speak for the other side of the coin. Now, we've been hearin' about a guy . . . Stanton? Stanton—where the hell are ya?"

The astonished Earl Stanton raised his arm. "I'm over here, Mr. Hoffa."

Jimmy mimicked him. "Well, don't be *over there*

. . . be over here! Come on, boy, get your butt up here! You've just been elevated! Get up here with him, Dan. That's the way."

Onstage, Stanton turned shy and confused. "I, uh, don't know what to say, Mr. Hoffa," he said meekly, shaking Jimmy's hand, then Ohlmeyer's, in the din of applause.

Loudly, Jimmy proclaimed, "He don't know what to say? Well, don't say nothing to me, Mr. Stanton—say it to *them!* You and Dan Ohlmeyer bang your heads together, get yourselves a good contract, then say it to them!"

"Yes, sir," Stanton said. Taking Dan's lead, he backed away from the front of the stage.

Jimmy pointed his finger at the audience. "Now I don't wanna hear about any more unrest in this Local! *Nothin's going to destroy this union—right?*"

"Right!" from every throat, and as he went weaving through them they stretched to touch him, all the while cheering and laughing and clapping their big, heavy hands.

Outside, Jimmy hollered, "Back in the trucks!" Sandy stood by the running Cadillac with the photographer. Jimmy came up and said, "You get what I wanted?"

"Yes, sir, Mr. Hoffa, every license plate, every car."

"Okay. I want the names that go with 'em, and I want them on my desk by tomorrow."

The man ran.

Sandy said, "Sounded like you did it again. You should've been the lawyer instead of me, Jim."

"Nah. Attorneys corrupt too easy."

As they laughed, Dan Ohlmeyer caught up. He was very upset. "Jimmy, why?"

"Why what?"

"Why'd you have to elevate Stanton?"

"You a total moron? He's one of us now. You feed him that contract and make him understand how much he loves it."

"I still don't like it."

"*I* like it! You don't hafta like it any more, kid! You fell off someplace. You let me down. You didn't deliver your boys. If you still need it spelled out,

102

you're a dead one! Keep the job, Dan, I know you got the family. But do yourself a favor—don't ever let anything remind me you're alive! Sandy, let's get outta here. Inefficiency makes me sick."

Many were called, few were chosen, and they were the best. They were former combat men, a lot of them, former cops, former FBI agents, former newspapermen, attorneys, accountants. LaVerne Duffy, Walt Sheridan, Pierre Salinger, Jim McShane, Paul Tierney, Joe Maher—they were more alike than different, this commando squad of investigators Robert Kennedy put together and put to work. They had all tasted action-for-a-purpose to one degree or another, only to have the Flaccid Fifties come and smother it. It was take-care-of-number-one time, the era of the Low Silhouette, the Silent Generation, and these guys were going nuts. Then along came Kennedy.

As commanders before him had done to such great effect, Bob offered them "nothing but blood, sweat, and tears. It's a rotten job. We're here to help the Congress of the United States tell the American people things they are not going to want to hear. If you want out, now's the time. It'll be lonely work, boring work, and the pay is shit compared to what you all can make someplace else.

"It's also probably the most important job you'll ever be offered in your lives. That's why it's not only a rotten job but a glorious one. Being alone means you'll be your own boss. You develop your own cases, follow your own leads. We need and we demand facts. Facts, facts, and more facts. Facts that most people you meet are not going to want to give you. Doors will slam in your faces. Your lives will be threatened. *At least* threatened."

Salinger quipped, "Well, as long as there's no danger involved."

The men packed into Bob's closet of an office laughed.

Bob continued. "Truthfully, the greatest danger is not the physical one, as real and great as that is. It's in false information. Incomplete information. This investigation cannot . . . I will not allow this investigation to be discredited. I want to know everything a potential witness knows, and I mean everything, long before I ever put him on the stand before the Committee and the country. You will provide me with that information, and I will take the full responsibility for its accuracy and completeness. Therefore, the first son of a bitch to deliver me a half-truth is unemployed. No second chances. One screw-up and I'll forget your name by breakfast.

"On the other hand, my office and my home are always open to you for breakfast, lunch, or dinner whenever you're in town. Be nice and Ethel might not bill you."

After this general briefing, Carmine gave them their specific assignments and they hit the roads, rails, and airways of the country. What Clark Mollenhoff had called the Great Investigation was on.

In Detroit, Jimmy was yelling hello into one phone before hanging up another. "Yeah, this is Hoffa. Hi, Joe, good to meet ya. Spill it . . . I see. I see. You take it to your B.A.? . . . He what? That shit bum, I'll take care of him! Go over his head, Joe. Go straight to the Joint there in Austin, and you tell them Jimmy Hoffa himself sent ya!"

Sandy Farrell picked the Western Union telegram out of Jimmy's mail pile and handed it to him.

Jimmy read it. "I don't believe it! He's lost his marbles!"

"What is it?"

"Read that! Beck wants anybody called up before the Committee to plead the Fifth!"

Sandy read: ". . . The union will take no disciplinary action against . . ."

"Save it and frame it! That's Beck's death warrant, and he wrote it himself! That stupid bastard."

"I'll tell you, if anyone on the Committee ever saw this, it would—"

"Whaddaya mean *if?* Get movin', Sandy."

Eddie Cheyfitz found Bob feeding peanuts to an elephant in the Washington National Zoo.

"Morning, Mr. Kennedy, sorry I'm late."

Bob grinned. "Hope you didn't bring any photographers. Wouldn't they love to show a Kennedy buying a Republican lunch! What's on your mind?"

Cheyfitz handed him the telegram. While Bob read it, he said, "That went to every Teamster officer in the country."

"The Fifth Amendment. Beck's talking conspiracy here—your grand old man has a pretty macabre way of protecting his loved ones, Eddie."

"I'm as amazed as you are. That's why you can keep the telegram."

Bob resumed feeding peanuts into the upturned trunk. "You've been remarkably generous with information, Eddie, and I've been wondering—why?"

Cheyfitz flushed. "I'm a Teamster attorney, Mr. Kennedy. Isn't it possible that I, too, should be deeply bothered by some of the things I've seen?"

"Cut it out, Eddie."

"Now just a minute! Are Kennedys the only ones allowed to suffer moral outrage?"

Bob snuffed, but when he looked up to answer, Eddie Cheyfitz was already walking away.

Walt Sheridan was waiting for him outside the Marble Palace. Going in, Bob said, "Give me the subpoena. This is one I want to serve personally. You hit Western Union?"

"Yes. It's all there on file. Beck sent the telegram himself."

"He must be awful scared to get this heavy-handed."

"Well, the Fifth's not an admission of guilt."

"No, but most of the public thinks it is. Beck must know that."

"He mustn't give a damn."

This time Bob didn't have to force his way into Einar Mohn's office. Mohn received the subpoena politely, his face ashen. Bob said, "May I have your copy of the telegram, Mr. Mohn?"

"I . . . I believe I have the right to counsel. I'll speak with my attorney, then you'll hear from me."

"That'll be fine."

"Just a minute, Mr. Kennedy. May I ask—just where did you get this?"

"I can't divulge that."

"All right. I already know anyhow, I think. May I ask you something else?"

"Of course."

"I realize you're still very young and . . . eager. But isn't it occurring to you that all the blocks are falling for you a bit too easily?"

Sheridan thought he smelled abuse coming and said, "Let's go, Bob."

"No, wait a minute. What are you saying, Mr. Mohn?"

"Isn't it obvious? Somebody's out to get Dave Beck. And they're using you to do it. How does it feel to be manipulated, Mr. Kennedy?"

Outside, Bob stopped cold halfway down the elegant staircase. He covered his eyes with his hands.

"What's the matter, Bob? Are you all—"

"He's right!" he hissed. "Goddamnit, he's right! I'm the gun that somebody's pointing at Beck. Walt, get me the line on Eddie Cheyfitz, and fast. It's time I know his story."

Sheridan walked into Bob's office. "You'd better take this sitting down."

"Gimme."

"Cheyfitz is no longer a Teamster attorney. He's had a new client for some time now."

"Hoffa!"

"James Riddle."

"Jesus Christ, Tinkers to Evers to Chance! Hoffa to Cheyfitz to me—all to take out Beck! Damnit, I've been working for that bastard all this time!"

"Uh, speaking of the devil, Bob. I passed Cheyfitz coming in."

"He's outside now? Beautiful!" He threw the door open and barged out. "Eddie?"

"Bob! Can we talk? I've just been informed—"

"Forget it! I'm going to inform you of something! I'm going to get Dave Beck's ass, and I'm going to get it without any more help from you! Now you go tell Jimmy Hoffa that when I'm through with Beck, I'm coming after him!"

"Hoffa? I don't—"

"Yes, Hoffa! As your client, he is entitled to your

106

professional counsel regarding future legal action! See ya, Eddie!"

Cheyfitz called Hoffa in Detroit immediately. Jimmy guffawed.

"Ha! Took him long enough to catch on, didn't it! Well, well. Take a walk, Eddie, I'll take it from here." He hung up and told Sandy, "Aw, Little Lord Fauntleroy's been *used* by the baddies!"

"Call him."

"Hey, you're gettin' good, Sandy."

Bob was relaxed but still surprised when the call came. "Jimmy, hello, what can I do for you?"

"Hello, Bobby—gee, you sound right next door! Great connection, huh? So how's the weather in Washington these days?"

"Inclement, Jimmy. How's Detroit?"

"Overcast, Bob. Heavy overcast. Hey, Bobby, that was some scare ya threw into Eddie Cheyfitz! Now what'd ya wanna go and do that for?"

"I felt I owed him. I saw he was making a mistake and warned him about it. If he wants to take it as a threat—"

"And what mistake's that, Bob?"

"Trying to manipulate the Federal Government."

"Jeez, I can never get the hang of the names you lawyers put on things."

"Spade's a spade, Jimmy."

"There's a joke goes with that, but I wouldn't offend you with it. How're things goin' with your Committee?"

"Making a good start, Jim. But it looks like it's going to be a longer haul than we thought."

"That a fact."

"Yes. Much longer."

"Like I told ya before, Bob, if ya need any help, ya know who to call."

"I appreciate it, Jimmy. And I think you can make book on hearing from us again all right."

"Somethin' I wanted to get straight with you, Bob —ya know, just because the Teamsters went for Ike last time don't mean I did. Fact, I don't mind tellin' ya, I think 'sixty's high time the Democrats got their

107

turn at bat. Just don't run Stevenson again. You can think of somebody better, can't you?"

"I don't speak for the Party, Jimmy."

"Don't mention our support to your brother, now, Bobby—don't want him to get too cocksure of himself, do we."

"The Senator's too busy to be thinking much about nineteen sixty these days, Jim. He's all involved in this investigation."

"He is, is he."

Punch, counterpunch.

Bob ended it, sounding as ominous as possible. "We all are, Jimmy."

After he hung up, Jimmy said blackly, "Rich fucking playboy. Sounds like a fuckin' *machine* on the phone. How you read him, Sandy?"

"Tough, committed . . ."

"No, I mean why? What's his number in this?"

"Bleeding heart!"

"Bleedin' hearts can kill ya."

"Well, I've been trying to tell you from the beginning . . ."

"Yeah, yeah, he might be dangerous. Maybe you're right. But it oughta be kept simple! All I want is to be President of this union. His brother wants to be President of the whole United States! There's an accommodation to be reached in there someplace. Okay. When the vinegar ain't workin', ya reach for the honey. Wind up Cheyfitz again—tell him I want some peace-pipe time with the spoiled brat."

"Something personal?"

"Yeah, face to face."

Sandy smiled. "Wouldn't mind being a fly on *that* wall."

Glinting, Jimmy said, "Yeah, it should be something to see, all right."

The investigation's first major break came in the form of a slight, middle-aged, nondescript gentleman who arrived unannounced one day outside the Kennedy office in the basement of the Senate Office Building. Finding Angela Novello's desk chair empty, he took a seat and waited quietly there until Bob's other secretary, Teresa Kraus, noticed him. She said that Mr. Kennedy was in the process of interviewing somebody and was liable to be quite some time. The man said that was all right, he would wait.

Inside, Angie was taking shorthand as Portland, Oregon, racketeer Jim Elkins told Bob his story: ". . . Then, in nineteen thirty-one, I bought twenty to thirty years, hard time."

"For what, Mr. Elkins?"

"They called it assault with intent to kill."

"Okay. Now before you go on, I again want to make sure you understand—all this is for me to find out in advance how you're going to testify if we call you before the Committee. This way, we hope to avoid getting any innocent people involved."

"That's good. I want two people kept out of this. My wife and my brother. My brother's straight. He's not in the rackets. Makes an honest buck. Not much, but it's honest. And my wife's a good woman. She doesn't know a lot of things. You might as well know this, too—Frank Brewster told me that I would find myself wading across Lake Washington in concrete boots if I—"

"Will he admit that?"

"He's already denied it. I've made up my mind to tell what I know—but my wife and my brother. Those are my terms."

"Accepted. They'll be kept out. Now, on this nineteen thirty-one conviction, when did you get out of prison?"

"They pardoned me after four years. See, the way the thing went down was kind of funny to begin with. I was in partners with a cop. Cutting a little money with him. One night, we're going to stiff a place together. He goes in first. When I go in, he starts shooting. At me. I figure he wants to dissolve the partnership. So I shoot back."

"Did you hit him?"

"Not bad, no."

Bob's phone buzzed, and he picked it up. Teresa said, "I know you didn't want to be disturbed, but I've got two problems. One is Mr. Cheyfitz on the line.

He's been calling and calling, and this time he says he *has* to—"

"Okay, I'll speak with him. What else?"

"There's been a man waiting for you, and I kinda feel sorry—should he stay or come back?"

"What's he want?"

"He says he has very important information for you."

"Then see if he wants coffee or anything. I'll see him as soon as I can."

Eddie Cheyfitz said, "Bob! Can we still talk?"

"Sure. What is it, Eddie?"

"I'll make it short, but my honor's involved. I have to speak my piece, Bob."

"Go ahead."

"I want to tell you about Jimmy Hoffa. The Jimmy Hoffa I know. Bob, look—okay, maybe he was a wild kid. And he was. And maybe he did a lot of things he shouldn't have. But he came up hard, Bob. And all that's past for him. It's ancient history. He's a very important force in the Teamsters—and he could be a very important force for good, for reform. He *wants* to be that, Bob. He's as upset about this whole Beck thing as you and I are. He wants to co-operate. Please keep an open mind. Nobody ever gave you any misinformation. You can never say that. All right, maybe Jimmy got overzealous about wanting to get this clean-up going. But really, that was our only sin, and we're sorry.

"Bob, this Beck mess is bad publicity for us—and why should the innocent majority suffer for the—"

"Jesus, get *to* it, Eddie!"

"Dinner, Bob. I want to invite you to have dinner with me and Mr. Hoffa at my home. If you consent, I'll invite him. I want to redeem myself with you both, by being a civilizing agent in this. I want to bring you two together. He admires you greatly, Bob. And I feel that if you can get to know each other better as men, well, you both owe the working man in this country that kind of chance."

"You're a hard man to say no to, Eddie. Okay. I'll have my girl work out a date." They hung up. "Angie, do that, will you? Dinner some evening soon with

Cheyfitz and his client. Some weekday evening. Now, I'm sorry, Mr. Elkins, please go on."

"Where was I?"

"You were shooting somebody, but not bad."

At the end of the day, he had the patient man's business card in his hand. " 'John Cye Cheasty, Attorney.' How do you pronounce that?"

"*Chaste*-ee. People call me Cy."

"Please sit down. You're a practicing attorney?"

"Yes. In New York. Also, some investigatory work from time to time."

"Have you come for a job Mr. Cheasty?"

"No, sir. Well, in a way. I've just been offered a job, and that's what I've come to tell you about. Mr. Kennedy, Jimmy Hoffa has offered me two thousand dollars a month if I can get hired as an investigator for your Committee."

Bob was stunned.

Cy Cheasty got up and started emptying money and papers from his overcoat pocket onto Bob's desk. "He gave me a thousand-dollar advance. Here's seven hundred and sixty-three dollars and forty-seven cents. These are receipts for the difference. I flew from New York to Detroit to see him, then from Detroit to—"

"Hold it, hold it. *Angie!* Get back in here, please, and bring your pad."

Cheasty sat back down.

Bob said, "He wants to plant you on me? As a *spy?*"

"Yes, sir."

"That's—that's—"

"That's subversion of the national Government, sir. It's something I could never do and live with myself."

"My God, you're a breath of fresh air, Mr. Cheasty."

"Thank you, but I have no choice."

"Angie, please call Mr. Hoover, tell him the situation we have here, and ask him nicely if he'll come down here. Or we can go up there."

Hoover came down. Not five minutes after he arrived, a young FBI agent followed, handed him a file, and left. Hoover opened it and read aloud: " 'Cheasty, John Cye. Department of Navy, four years. Secret Service, nine years. Distinguished record. Currently rendering legal and investigative services to top New

York City law firm. Erratic finances. Mild heart condition.' "

Bob said, "Judging from that, you don't need to be told that what you've told us so far isn't evidence."

Cheasty nodded. "No, it's just my word against Hoffa's."

J. Edgar Hoover said, "We're going to require proof that he asked you to get documents for his use from classified Government files. Then we'll need proof that you delivered them."

"I guess we're offering you a job, Cy," Bob said.

"Are you willing to take it?" Hoover asked. "To do exactly what he asked? Under constant FBI surveillance? Just how bad is your heart anyway, Mr. Cheasty?". .

"It's . . . very busy right this minute, sir. I'm up to it, though. And if I get caught, well, my heart condition won't matter much anyhow, I guess."

Hoover moved to leave. "That's that, then. I'll put things in motion."

"And believe us, Mr. Cheasty," Bob said, "as far as protection for you goes—"

Hoover cut him off. *"We* will take care of Mr. Cheasty, Mr. Kennedy. You can both set your hearts at ease."

The side window of the small, parked van was opaque on the outside, but clear on the inside, where two young FBI agents were taking turns manning the camera pointed at the street activity in the cold Washington dusk. When not on the camera, the agents rubbed and blew into their hands to keep warm. Finally they started to get what they were there for.

"I'm making a car . . . Yeah, it's Cheyfitz at the wheel . . . must be the one . . . Now I've got Cheasty, too . . He sees the car . . . starts to approach it . . . car stops . . . figure getting out . . . Holy cow, it's Hoffa himself!"

"His own bag man? That's crazy!"

"It's him all right . . . Coming across . . . meeting Cheasty . . . Ah, we're getting it all, getting it . . . Oh no! Some jerk's in my line of sight! Get outta there, you idiot!"

"Should I move us? We gotta get him taking the package!"

"Yeah, move us! No, wait, he's . . . Yeah, move, move!"

Hoover waited in his office, watching the clock on the wall.

Kennedy waited in his, chin on desk, staring at his wristwatch.

Cy Cheasty met Jimmy Hoffa on the street, handed him a manila envelope, and accepted a smaller white envelope in return. Cheasty said, "They're going to subpoena one of your Portland people next week. A Murray Conner?"

Jimmy said, "Connor, yeah. Good. Keep it up."

Inside the van, the agent yelled, "We got it! We got it!"

They called Hoover. Hoover called Bob and simply said, "It's on film now. All of it."

Bob called Ethel at home. "I'm flying, yeah. He just passed his screen test! Remember now, nine-thirty on the dot! You got the number?"

"Memorized," she said. "Engraved in lead. You're sure you still want to go through with this, Bob?"

"I don't have a choice. I'm afraid if I call it off he'd get suspicious, and Cy could be in trouble."

Bob drove alone to Eddie Cheyfitz's home in Chevy Chase, Maryland. Eddie greeted him at the door and introduced his wife, who discreetly excused herself for the evening. Jimmy was waiting inside and extended his hand, all smiles and warmth. "Thataway, Bob, see ya took my advice with the handshake."

"Yes. Well, this is certainly more pleasant than the last place we met."

"Ha, I'll say. These lawyers know how to live, don't they. Lemme tell you, Bob, when Eddie here told me you wanted to set up this meeting, I was tickled pink."

"*I* wanted . . . Thought this was all your own idea, Eddie."

"It's a good idea—that's all that matters, right, gentlemen? Now, can I make us a drink?"

"Sure," Bob said. "A little bourbon if you've got it."

113

"Thought you never touched the stuff!" Jimmy said.

"Just on special occasions."

"Jimmy?"

"Not me. Go ahead, I'll just watch you two kill your livers. Still, from what I hear, Bob, I guess you and me do have quite a lot in common, huh?"

"I can't imagine what."

"Well, on keepin' in good shape, anyhow. Hear you do it all—the tennis, the football, the pushups? Pushups, they're what I swear by."

"And you're both true family men, too!" Eddie added heartily.

Bob smiled. "If I knew that, I wouldn't have worn this bullet-proof vest."

"Man's family's everything," Jimmy stated earnestly. "You don't have a wife and kids, you got nothin'. That's another thing I hear about Bob, Eddie, that I like. He don't run around on his old lady. Me neither! And that ain't always so easy, either, huh, Bob? When you're handsome and do all the travelin' around all the time like we do—"

Eddie laughed. "Aw, you're gettin' too old for that kind of stuff, Jimmy." He winked at Bob.

"Like hell! Listen, if I wanted 'em, which I don't, I could have 'em by the harem-load. And I could handle 'em, too. And so could you, I bet, huh, Bob?"

Bob looked through him, not smiling.

Eddie tried to smooth it over. "Uh, I don't think Bob likes to talk much about sex or his private life, Jimmy."

"Oh, hell, it's just boys. But I respect that too, young fella. Truth is, I don't care much for it myself."

"Gentlemen, we're having roast beef. May I ask how you'd like it done?"

Both wanted it medium-rare. They soon were at the dining-room table being waited on by Eddie's manservant. Jimmy was philosophizing on the benefits of being the runt in a family when Bob asked coldly, "Jimmy, what is your basic philosophy for dealing with employers?"

Jimmy laughed. "I believe in doing unto them as they would do unto me, only worse! Nah, I'm only kiddin'. You know what it takes in the union business? And it is a business nowadays. Organization and information. Good, strong men in all your key spots . . . and a good, strong flow of information. You gotta know what your friends and your enemies are up to. All the time. I'll give ya an example. Excuse me if this comes as a shock to ya, Bobby, but we happen to know you're plannin' to subpoena Murray Conner in Portland next week. How's that?"

Bob feigned surprise and amazement. "That's incredible!"

"Bet ya'd love to know how I come to know that, huh?"

Eddie said, "My God, *I'd* like to know!"

"That's just terrific, Jimmy. Uh, Eddie, could I get a cup of tea? Back to employers, Jimmy—how have you been so successful in running strikes when others . . . ?"

"Bob, a strike's the same thing as a war. If you don't intend to win it, don't get in it in the first place. The world I come up in was somethin' I don't expect you to understand. Poor and tough. I was arrested eighteen times in one day once! They beat your head in, you hadda get up and go in for more. It was the only way. You gotta start tough and stay tough. That's Beck's big problem, he went soft. Turned into some kind of cartoon drawin' of a big shot! Like a pig with teeth, only the teeth are fakes, they're made outta paper! Same with Reuther. Walter Reuther forgot how to run a strike! Forgot how tough ya—"

"Just how tough are you, Jimmy?"

"Put yer arm up here for a minute and I'll show you."

"I mean another kind of tough. Are you tough enough, for instance, to kick the gangsters and the hoodlums out of your union?"

Jimmy threw his knife down. "Jesus, here we go again! Gangsters and hoods, gangsters and hoods! Where are they? Point 'em out to me! What hoods?"

"What about Johnny Dio?"

"What about him?"

"Wouldn't you agree that he's a racketeer?"

"Listen, Mr. Lawyer—if he's a racketeer, arrest him! Book him, try him, and throw him in jail. If you think a guy's a crook, prove it and arrest him. And if you *can't,* then why the hell should I hafta kick him outta anything? Dio's a guy I know 'cause I hafta know him! I don't have no Congressional Committee at my disposal to go checking out every character that comes around, just to make sure he's lily-white all his life! I take people as they come! I don't go for holdin' a man's past against him, either. Man's got a right to work, in my book. John Dioguardi? I'm not sayin' he's not tough. Sure he's tough! But as far as I know he's strictly legal."

"And he *is* a friend of yours?"

"My friends are my own business. Your friends are yours."

"But doesn't a man in your position have to be extra careful in all his relationships? You're a powerful man, Jimmy. When you speak, you speak for thousands of workers . . ."

"Millions, Bob."

They both laughed. Cheyfitz started looking nervous.

Bob went on. "All right, then take the way the union deals with its lawyers."

Eddie bridled. "What about it?"

Bob smiled. "Not you, Eddie. I'm referring to the blatant impropriety of using Teamster Union funds to pay attorneys to represent union officials who refuse to account for how and why other union funds are vanishing."

"There's nothing improper or illegal about assigning counsel," Eddie said.

"But to pay for it out of union funds? That's morally and ethically reprehensible!"

Hoffa flared. "Our morals are none of your goddamn business, Bobby!"

Bob flared back, "Morals dictate behavior, and it's your behavior that I'm making my goddamn business!"

"Put your arm up here! I mean it! There's a lesson in this I want you to learn!"

Bob stared at him, not moving.

Embarrassed, Eddie tried to turn it. "Heh, that's Jimmy, always the physical competition."

"You ain't passin' my test, Bobby!"

116

That was when the phone rang. Eddie bolted to answer it.

Bob said, "It's your test, you pass it."

"Scared ya'll lose?"

"That's childish, Jimmy."

"Mr. Kennedy, it's for you. Your wife."

Jimmy called after him, "If it's your wife, she's prob'ly callin' to see if you're still alive! Ha, ha."

Laughing, Bob said loudly, "Ethel? I'm still alive—but if your hear a big explosion, I probably won't be!"

Jimmy roared, laughing. "Send her my best, kid, and tell her ya gotta hurry back for an important arm-wrestle with Jimmy Hoffa!"

Eddie whispered, "Jimmy, lay off, will you?"

Jimmy snarled, "Bullshit I'll lay off! He's a gutless wonder and he knows it, and now *I* know it! I've got his fuckin' number now, and it's a zero. That rich little pansy's gonna fold, don't you worry. This is just what I wanted to find out."

Bob returned and made his excuses. Eddie and Jimmy rose and walked him to the door. Jimmy smiled. "Aw, now ain't this too bad, now we won't get our chance to square off."

"Maybe next time, Jimmy. Eddie, thank you, I enjoyed it."

Jimmy said, "Stay in touch, Bobby."

"You can count on it, Jimmy."

"Well, now at least you can go home and tell your little lady you've met Hoffa and he ain't half as bad as some people think."

Bob met his eyes. "I wish I could tell her that, Jimmy. I wish it were true. But I have good reason to believe it isn't. Good night."

When the door had closed, Jimmy Hoffa exploded. "Did you hear that? He acts like he's doin' me some kinda favor even talkin' to me! His ass is grass, Eddie! This is it, this is goddamn war, and that skinny little son of a bitch of a mother's boy is gonna wish he was never born!"

Nosce hostem is the Latin motto U.S. Intelligence uses for it, what Jimmy himself had said at their "friendly" dinner: know your enemy.

117

A black Cadillac brought Jimmy from his Woodner Hotel suite to the Marble Palace early the next morning. Bobby drove himself in from Hickory Hill in his convertible, top up, his huge black dog, Brumus, in the back. Their respective buildings, Teamster International headquarters and the old Senate Office Building, were no more than two hundred yards apart; neither man could easily avoid laying eyes on the other's place of work.

Both had come awake that day with the exact same intention. Bob's first order issued was to Walt Sheridan: "Get me everything personal you can on Hoffa, from before he was born." He and his staff had already begun to accumulate data on the Teamster leader's professional past; now Kennedy needed better insight to the man himself. How much of Jimmy was bluster, braggadocio, rationalization . . . truth?

Hoffa demanded the same kind of information on Bob, from Sandy Farrell: ". . . And I mean everything! There I am, holdin' all the cards in the deck, and *he* thinks *he* can lean on *me!* Where's the snot get that?"

Knowledge isn't always power. Each man was *left* rather strangely affected by the other's story. An odd recognition happened for each, blurry as it was. Bob told Walt, "There's one ironic thing, he's from German-Dutch settlers, with some Irish thrown in—and they got here before my people did! So for all his poor-boy song, what the hell, it's not my fault my family hit it and his didn't."

Walt laughed. "Not his fault, either, Bob."

"I guess not. My God, you do have to give it to him —eighteen times in one day! He was telling the truth. He has been one fantastic fighter for the workingman, ever since he was a kid. What a leader he could make! What the hell does he have to mess with all that other crap for? Even so, by comparison Beck looks like a real nickel-and-dimer."

"Yeah, but that's why I think Hoffa's the real dangerous one. He doesn't care about the money. With him it's the power."

Jimmy told Sandy: "Ya know, in a way it must be a pain in the ass to come from so many bucks. Nobody notices nothin' ya do! Christ, this kid's been a hell of a little scrapper all the way, guess I never really gave him that. Jesus, what a partner he'd make!"

"You're looking for areas of negotiation," Farrell said, "and I'm telling you to forget it. He's the other side of the tracks, Jim. You say blue, he'll hear brown."

Sheridan advised Bob: "Hoffa's his own worst enemy. He talks progress and modernity, but he still thinks he has to go to bed with the underworld, and that's twenty years behind the times. Maybe it used to be true, but . . ."

"Isn't it more true, Walt, to say that if there's an upperworld and an underworld, you can't win at dealing with both? You've got to go one way or the other eventually?"

"Well . . ."

"Let's give him the benefit of the doubt," Bob decided. "Pull out all the stops and let's see exactly how deep he's in. Maybe it isn't too late to slow him down at least."

And Jimmy told Sandy: "Put the burner under Cy Cheasty's ass. I'm not buyin' the soft goods from him any more. Tell him I want the real hot stuff on the little bastard. Startin' yesterday!"

BOOK THREE

Battles

At ten o'clock on the morning of February 26, 1957, Senator John McClellan pounded his gavel in the Senate Caucus Room and announced to the members of his Committee and its staff, the press, and the public, "The Committee will come to order.

"The Chair wishes to make a brief opening statement. Senate Resolution Seventy-four, of the Eighty-fifth Congress, agreed to on January thirtieth, nineteen fifty-seven, established this Select Committee, which has been officially named the Senate Select Committee on Improper Activities in the Labor or Management Field.

"This Select Committee is authorized to conduct an investigation, and to study the extent to which criminal or other improper activities are or have been engaged in, in the field of Labor-Management relations, or in groups or organizations of employees or employers, to the detriment of the interest of the public, employers, or employees, and to determine whether any changes are required in the laws in order to protect such interests against the continued occurrence of such practices or activities.

"The urgency of this problem was recently demonstrated by organized Labor itself, when the AFL-CIO felt impelled to adopt strict codes of ethical practices covering the establishment of paper Locals, the administration of welfare funds, the infiltration of racketeers into the unions, and the threat of Fascist and Communist involvement in the American Labor Movement.

"Therefore, with respect to these frightening new

forces that are imposing themselves on organized labor, this Committee was formed. It shall be the purpose of this Committee to inquire into and to expose . . ."

And so the Hearings began. Movie cameras whirred. Photographers popped their flashbulbs on behalf of *Life, Look, Time, Newsweek,* and the other national newsmagazines and all the major newspapers. In the Caucus Room galleries and at home the public watched and listened. The testimony began to flow. Some was almost as formal as the Chairman's opening statement. Much wasn't.

Early occupants of the small witness table opposite the array of Senators, Chief Counsel Robert Kennedy, and various court recorders and staff assistants were reporters Wallace Turner and William Lambert:

MR. TURNER: As newspapermen, we have been visited in secret places at night by honorable workingmen who complained of their inability to stop the improper activities of their union leaders.

Without exception, they were in terrible fear that their visits to us might become known to their union bosses.

SEN. MCCLELLAN: I would like to remind this Committee that you make this statement as two reporters who were recently honored with an award for your work. That is the Heywood Broun Award, I believe.

MR. TURNER: Yes, sir.

SEN. MCCLELLAN: We congratulate you, and we are glad to have you here. Continue, please.

MR. TURNER: Thank you, Senator. As I was saying, the fear of retaliation is one of the most potent weapons to silence criticism from within the Teamsters Union in the Pa-

	cific Northwest. That fear pervades this organization.
SEN. MCCLELLAN:	Their fear is what?
MR. TURNER:	That their union cards at least will be taken up and that they will be out of employment.
SEN. MUNDT:	They fear they would lose their means of livelihood?
MR. TURNER:	That is one of the things they fear; yes.
SEN. MUNDT:	There are other types of retaliation which they fear?
MR. TURNER:	Yes, sir; that union has a history in our state of physical violence to people who disagreed with them.

When Portland racketeer Jim Elkins fulfilled his promise to testify, he told his story in much the same style as he had to Bob Kennedy in his screening sessions.

MR. ELKINS:	They called and told me and my wife, *We are just a minute away and we are coming over to break both your arms and legs.* So I just took a shotgun and sat by the door, but they didn't come.
SEN. MCCLELLAN:	Did they ever come?
MR. ELKINS:	Two fellows came when I wasn't home on two occasions, and my wife called me, and they left before I could get there.
MR. KENNEDY:	How did you finally catch them there?
MR. ELKINS:	Well, I left like I was going to leave and I doubled back in another car.
MR. KENNEDY:	Then what happened?
MR. ELKINS:	Well, I pulled up to the curb and I talked to them and they

	left and they didn't come back no more.
SEN. MCCLELLAN:	You did what?
MR. ELKINS:	I talked to them. Well, I pointed the shotgun at them and I talked to them, and they didn't come back anymore.

He said this in such a monotone and with such a straight face that the crowd, including some Senators, broke out laughing. Bob waited for it to quiet down.

MR. KENNEDY:	Did you do anything else to them?
MR. ELKINS:	Yes, I did. One of them, I treated a little bit rough.
MR. KENNEDY:	What did you do to him?
MR. ELKINS:	Well, I hit him on the head and knocked him around a little bit and put him back in the car and told his buddy that I was going to shoot the . . . butt off the next person that came in my yard.
MR. KENNEDY:	And they never came back?
MR. ELKINS:	They never came back.

The audience's murmurings of approval so closely approached outright applause that Bob Kennedy made a mental note: as courageous and forthright as Jim Elkins was to come forward like this, such accounts tended to paint the terrorists as somewhat less menacing than they were in actuality, especially to workingmen less ready with guns and fists than was Mr. Elkins. He would have to shuffle his witnesses and their stories more carefully in future.

That was a major problem in trying to expose to the public the more violent aspects of the abuses being suffered; the very words "gangster," "mob," "racketeer," "strong-arm," "muscle," and the rest had so thoroughly become the stuff of fiction to the pulpreaders and moviegoers of America that to let them

125

be used too often or too cavalierly ran the risk of having them backfire. In other testimony, Robert Kennedy took pains to more clearly identify the relationship between Organized Crime and Organized Labor, and the stranglehold he felt that was putting around the country's throat.

The truck advertising Aunt Dulcie's Cakes and Pies seemed to be making deliveries, but it wasn't. It was making movies, part two of a two-part series featuring John Cye Cheasty and James Riddle Hoffa. Cy wore a hat and topcoat against the chill winds and carried a brown envelope. Jimmy, who wore only a suit and was bareheaded, took the envelope, and the FBI agent operating the whirring camera inside the truck exulted, "I got it, I got it, the best yet!"

Jimmy got back into his Caddie and drove off. This time his trail was followed by two agents, one tailing in an unmarked car, the other in a room in a building opposite the Dupont Plaza Hotel. They communicated by walkie-talkie. Through his binoculars, the indoors agent watched Jimmy get out and head for the lobby. He said, "He's got the package in his hand. This is where it's got to be. We'd better take him."

The car agent responded, "Talk to the boss first."

J. Edgar Hoover was waiting calmly. "Is it on film?" he asked. "And is the package in his possession?"

"Yes, sir."

The indoors agent went to the window and signaled. Below, two waiting agents briskly followed Jimmy Hoffa into the lobby. Eddie Cheyfitz, waiting near the elevators with three union cohorts, said, "There he is now, I want to get a paper. Tell him I'll be up in a minute," and walked over to the newsstand.

Jimmy came through the crowded lobby all smiles. "Hi, guys, let's get upstairs, this is supposed to be the special one.

The two agents were joined by three others, and they closed on Jimmy Hoffa at the elevator, the lead man showing his credentials. "FBI, Mr. Hoffa."

126

"Big deal! What's—"

"You're under arrest, sir."

"What for?"

"You'll have to come with us, sir."

"I don't hafta nothin'! Johnny, get these geeks off me! Listen, you want this whole joint down on your heads?"

"We don't want trouble, Mr. Hoffa."

"I got some calls to make! You can goddamn wait!"

"Sorry, sir, let's go."

"For Christ's— All right, Johnny, get upstairs and call you-know. You! Where'll I be?"

"Federal District Courthouse, sir."

"Let's go, then, and make it snappy, I don't wanna miss my dinner!"

Eddie Cheyfitz had paused to check the headlines. He looked up, saw Jimmy being maneuvered across the lobby by five men, and gasped, "Oh my God!" He ran to a lobby phone, knocking a young woman roughly out of his way. To calm her, he thrust a twenty-dollar bill into her hand. "Emergency!" He dialed the operator and got the FBI. "Listen! This is Eddie Cheyfitz. I'm Mr. Jimmy Hoffa's attorney and I want to report he's right this minute being kidnapped! The Dupont Plaza Hotel! Five hoods! Hurry! They'll kill him! He . . . What? *What? For what?*"

Wearing just loafers, slacks, and a pullover sweater, Bob Kennedy took the courthouse steps two at a time, then ran down the echoing nighttime corridors, looking into the empty courtrooms. A side door opened and he saw Hoffa, handcuffed between two agents. He walked down the aisle. Seeing him, Jimmy snarled, "What took ya so long? We get ya outta bed?"

"Hello, Jimmy."

"Listen, you boys go get yourselves a cuppa coffee. Mr. Kennedy here'll keep me company."

Bob nodded, and the agents retired to the back of the small, empty courtroom.

Jimmy said, "You think you swallowed a canary, kid, but it's gonna stick in your throat!"

"What's the charge, Jim?"

"It's bullshit is what it is! Me bribe one of your investigators! I don't even know any of your little snoopers, how the hell could I bribe 'em? You smell tired, Bobby, you been runnin'? Ha! Just couldn't wait, could ya. Well, you're wasting your time and mine!"

Clark Mollenhoff appeared at the door, saw them, and came in. Jimmy laughed. "Jeez, even Mollenhoff! What is this, old home week?"

"I wouldn't have missed this for anything, Jimmy."

To Bob, Jimmy said, "Read all about it! Hoffa in handcuffs, huh? What'd you do, call every news rat in town?"

Bob grinned. "No, I asked my wife to."

"Finally slipped, huh, Jim?" Mollenhoff said.

Jimmy kept his gaze on Bob. "If I were you, and I'm glad as hell I ain't, I wouldn't go breakin' out the champagne yet. The fight's still young—and this is for the heavyweight title, right, Bobby?"

Mollenhoff whispered, "Speaking of heavyweights . . ."

Bob and Jimmy turned to see whom he was looking at. Jimmy beamed. "Ah, here's my boy now."

Bob Kennedy knew and admired this man too. He was Edward Bennett Williams, law-firm partner of Eddie Cheyfitz, and one of the nation's top criminal lawyers. Kennedy had met him when Williams defended Senator Joseph McCarthy in the Watkins Committee hearings. In fact, Williams had invited Bob to leave Government service and join his law firm. Now he asked, "Bob, what is this all about?"

"That's not for me to say, Ed."

Ethel Kennedy arrived. Jimmy was friendly, and they talked about horses. The small talk turned to banter about pushups between Jimmy and Bobby, each claiming to be able to do more than the other. Jimmy suggested that Bobby not wait any longer, "Run along, kid. I can take care of things here. You run your business and I'll run mine. There's nothing to it, nothing at all."

Outside, Mollenhoff congratulated him. "You've got him, Bob."

"Maybe. But you heard him—let's not break out any champagne yet."

At the end of the second day's testimony, Chairman John McClellan announced, ". . . Mr. Beck has shown flagrant disregard and disrespect for honest and reputable unionism and for the best interests and welfare of the laboring people of his country.

"Above all, he has shown arrogant contempt for the million and a half members, the honest laboring people in the Teamsters Union."

The day after the Dupont Plaza Hotel's excitement, he told the Caucus Room and cameras, "The arrest of Mr. Hoffa last night by Federal agents represents a disturbing new chapter for this Committee.

"The action taken by Mr. Hoffa is clearly indicative of the steps the gangster elements are taking, and will continue to undertake, to hinder, hamper, obstruct, and destroy the work of this Committee.

". . . We will try to meet them, and accept their challenge, and deal with them all accordingly."

The audience applauded, but he gaveled them to silence.

Burt Score was a reporter for the Detroit *Herald,* and he was late. Angie Novello thumbed him into Bob's inner office. Reporters occupied every available surface and space. They were all laughing when Burt entered, Bobby loudest of all. Burt said, "Damn—did I miss a good line?"

Bob threw the Baltimore game ball at him and cracked, "That's okay, Burt, you'll copy it from their early editions anyhow!" and everyone laughed again. By now, Bob had reconsidered and decided it was indeed time to celebrate.

Score asked him, "Will the bribery charge stick, Mr. Kennedy?"

"We've got it on film. Cheasty gives him documents, Hoffa accepts and gives Cheasty money. Would you say we needed anything else?"

"Well, I'm from Jimmy's home town, and, knowing him, you'd better have all you can get."

Somebody else asked, "Would you say Jimmy Hoffa's finished?"

Bob answered, "Yes, I would."

Burt Score said, "What would you do if he's acquitted?"

Bob thought. "Off the record?"

"Sure."

"If Jimmy Hoffa's acquitted, I'll . . . jump off the Capitol!"

Score wrote his story under the headline, BOBBY: 'IF JIMMY ACQUITTED, I'LL JUMP OFF THE CAPITOL!', and Edward Bennet Williams flourished it at the reporters who rushed around him and Jimmy Hoffa as they came out of the Federal Courthouse.

It was one of his first breaks. "There you have it, gentlemen," he announced, "a typical example of trial by media! Perhaps Mr. Kennedy is afraid to see this case go to a court of law. Perhaps he'd prefer to have his verdict now, in your newspapers. And perhaps I don't blame him a bit!"

The press laughed, writing it down. One yelled, "How are you, Jimmy?"

"Couldn't be better! And somebody tell Bobby, when he jumps, I'll be there—but I won't catch him!"

Bob regretted making the presumptuous remark, and the regret put him back on alert. He called for a brainstorming session with all available staff. While Angie was setting it up, he visited one of the Assistant U.S. Attorneys assigned to prosecute the Hoffa case and told him, "I just want you to know, if there's anything we can do to help you prepare the Government case, you've got it."

He was a thin young man who wore thick-lensed glasses. He said, "Thanks, but don't worry. It's open-and-shut."

"Never say that. Hoffa knows every trick in the book. He's been there before. And he's got the best possible attorney defending him."

"I know that, sir. But the case is made. We have the evidence, and we have the witness—John Cye Cheasty himself. Believe me—"

"Did you know Cheasty's heart is weak?"

"Well, no, but—"

"But witnesses with weak hearts can die on you! Now listen. I want this airtight and foolproof. With Hoffa, appearances are usually not the reality. We're learning more and more about him every day, and our

130

files are open to you. No reversible errors, all right? If there's anything we can do for you, at any time . . ."

"I won't hesitate to call on you, Mr. Kennedy. Trust me, I—"

"How many cases have you prosecuted?"

"Well, I—"

"Never mind, I don't want to know."

Back at his office, he and a ring of his men lounged about, eating sandwiches, drinking coffee, smoking, and second-guessing Edward Bennett Williams. Pierre Salinger said, "Never trust a man who uses his middle name."

"You can trust Williams," Bob warned, "to do everything right."

Sheridan said, "He's already requested change of venue, twice."

Duffy sighed. "Yeah, digging in on every technicality."

"Including six-month postponement!"

"Well, be glad he only got three weeks. Can he develop a case in that?"

"I think there's more going on than that," Bob said. "I think it's called 'get Hoffa elected.'"

Sheridan agreed. "If he can avoid a conviction before the September convention, Jimmy's got a better-than-good chance of becoming the new President of the International. Then, hell, he can go to jail for all he'll care!"

Salinger relit his cigar.

Joe Maher coughed. "Phew. What died inside that thing?"

Al Calabrese said, "Walt's right. Hoffa could win, then run the whole thing from behind bars."

"One thing's clear," Bob told them, "it's speedup time for us. We gotta get the works on Jimmy before Ed Williams . . ."

Jerry Adlerman, eating cottage cheese, asked Bob, "Justice going to stay open to new material, are they?"

"They'd better."

Sheridan nodded. "Yeah, they're going to have to be ready for any contingency. This baby's beaten trials and outrun Senate Committees before. Ask Wint Smith."

131

"Who's that?"

Adlerman said, "Another Committee taking a look at Jimmy Hoffa. Fifty-three. Smith was from Kansas, so Hoffa hired ex-Kansas Governor Payne Ratner as one of his attorneys."

"Jeez!"

Sheridan brightened. "Yeah, I got stuff on *that* magic act. Smith and Ratner were also bosom buddies, so two months after Ratner goes on payroll the investigation mysteriously starts to change direction— a hundred and eighty degrees away from Hoffa. In fact, just a couple days ago I came by a letter Ratner sent to Gibbons in 'fifty-four. In my book, it's collusion, writ large."

Kennedy sprang forward. "How?"

Sheridan shrugged. "I think they bribed Smith."

"Where's the letter?"

"You want it?"

"Jesus, yes, this sounds terrific, Walt!"

"I'll get it."

Sheridan passed Jack Kennedy coming in.

"Hey, Jack!" the men greeted him.

"Senator!"

"Don't stand, I'll only be in the area a moment. As you wuz. Bob, if you can break away from your card party soon, I'd like to—"

Sheridan was back. Bob said, "Just a second, Jack," and read the letter. "You got 'em, Walt! Jesus Christ, there it is! Listen, set it up—you and I and Carmine. Let's go see good Governor Ratner."

"Uh, he's not exactly co-operative so far, Bob. In fact, he's downright irritable."

Bob grinned. "I'll be charming. I'll be soothing."

The room laughed, then emptied.

When he and his brother were alone, he said, "How's your back?"

"Don't ask. Did I hear right? Who'd want to go to Wichita if he didn't have to?"

"Nobody. I have to."

"Oh really? Thought you were off the Hoffa Express for a while. He's Justice Department meat now."

"Frankly, I'm worried about the job they'll do, Jack. Ed Williams is a great trial lawyer."

132

"That he is."

"Dammit, why does a man with that kind of class take a case like this anyhow? Hoffa paid a goddamn bribe. We've got hard evidence. It ought to be open-and-shut, as I told somebody never to say today."

Jack laughed. "That's exactly why. Williams can't lose it. If Hoffa's convinced, well, hell, nobody could've gotten him off. But if it somehow goes the other way, and miracles do happen, then Ed's in the hall of fame. Clarence Darrow, Jerry Geisler, Edward Bennett . . ."

"Then that's exactly why I've got to keep the heat on Hoffa. If Justice doesn't . . ."

"That's Justice's problem, not yours. That's what I'm trying to tell you, Bob. Now, unless I'm mistaken and I'm not, we on *your* Committee have hearings coming up on the Bakery Workers. For which *you're* supposed to be preparing files, instead of flying off to grill Payne Ratner!"

"Ah, Jack, I—"

"Bobby, I'm worried about you. Going at it twenty-five hours a day is . . . well, it's hard to keep your overview, to put it mildly. I don't want you to let Hoffa get under your—"

Bob had opened his door. "Angie? Would you please bring us the Senator's copy of the Bakery Workers file?"

Half concealing his laugh, Jack muttered, "This better not be a fake hand-off."

"It isn't."

"Where'd you find the time?"

"I made the time."

"I was wrong. It isn't just Hoffa getting under your skin. It's *all* getting under your skin!"

Once inside Mr. Ratner's law offices in Wichita, Robert Kennedy found it difficult to be either charming or soothing, so he chose to let Sheridan and Bellino do most of the questioning. They sat in an arc around the front of his large desk. The ex-Governor didn't sit much: he was outraged, irascible, and paced impatiently. Once, when Carmine used the word "influence," Ratner jumped down his throat: "What 'influence'! I resent that! The implication is one of—I wielded absolutely no control over Congressman Smith. Wint Smith is a decent and honest man, with integrity. As am I!"

Sheridan inquired, "Sir, in nineteen fifty-three, did you ever discuss Mr. Hoffa with Congressman Smith?"

"That is an idiotic and irresponsible question! I was an *attorney* of Mr. Hoffa's in nineteen fifty-three. Wint Smith was a personal friend. It's perfectly natural that I may have discussed a client with a friend. 'Discuss' in no way translates to 'influence'! Wint Smith then and now is a decent and honest man, and I am proud to call him my friend."

Bob asked, "And Jimmy Hoffa?"

Ratner whirled. "No one has ever proven anything illegal or improper about this man, and until that's done I shall continue to regard Mr. Hoffa as a decent and honest man, and be proud to call *him* my friend as well!"

Sheridan presented Payne Ratner with the letter. "Governor? We have this letter from your files. It's addressed to Mr. Hoffa and signed—"

"What gave you the right to read my private correspondence!"

"A Federal subpoena, sir. It's signed by you and states, and I quote, 'I am pleased with the results we are getting, and I'm anxiously awaiting delivery of the package we discussed over the telephone.' "

"And?"

"And we're wondering what you meant by package," Bob said.

"I'll tell you gladly! It referred to a check for one thousand dollars, from the Teamsters, for tickets to a Republican Party dinner. Surely you, Mr. Kennedy, can't consider anything illegal about that!"

"No, sir. But why would you call a thousand-dollar check a 'package'?"

Fuming, Ratner said, "You're not in *Bahston,* New York, or Washington now, gentlemen—haven't you heard? Corny as Kansas in August? We're corny out here. We often do things in a jocular vein. Perhaps you find it difficult to understand—"

"Excuse me, sir?" Walt Sheridan interrupted. "But

I just noticed—the button on your interoffice phone is down. Are we being monitored?"

"Absolutely not. But if it'll make you feel any better . . ." He flicked it up.

Bellino said, "You declined our offer to have this interview recorded, sir."

Ratner's secretary appeared at the door, pad and pencil in hand. Ratner blushed and said, "Oh, all right, then—if you don't mind, my secretary will take notes. Now can we get on with this and get it over with? I have more important things to do with my time."

Sheridan returned to Washington. Kennedy and Bellino boarded a small commercial airliner to fly to Detroit. They strapped themselves into their seats and awaited takeoff. Bob was feeling tired, beat, derailed.

Carmine asked him, "Do you think Mr. Bluster was really able to maneuver Smith's investigation away from Hoffa?"

Bob turned his depressed stare away from the scratched window and sighed. "Nah. I don't think he could've had either the muscle or the nerve to do anything. I don't doubt that he talked a great storm to Jimmy, though. He might've promised he'd deliver . . . then was more surprised than anybody when he did!"

They laughed weakly.

"A grand," Carmine said.

"Ha, yeah, for tickets. In Wichita I bet that's a lot of chicken."

"And corn."

"Well, Jimmy's true to form in it. He had all his bets covered. Ratner couldn't have done him any harm, certainly."

"Well, listen, Bob, cheer up. I got a flash from Pierre. There may be more than we expect waiting for us in Detroit. He's very excited, he—"

"He's going to put Hoffa in my pocket."

Carmine chuckled. "His words exactly. Don't let it get to you, Bobby. Who knows, he might really be on to something. Gold's where you find it."

"God, just get me out of Wichita!" He slumped and shut his eyes.

The plane at last started to move. Carmine said,

"Here we go. Grab some sack time, Bob, I'll wake you when we get there."

The plane taxied to the end of the Wichita runway, turned, revved its engines until it vibrated enough to loosen teeth, then roared forward. At just the point when the passengers expected the sudden lift of take-off, they felt instead the abrupt slamming-on of brakes and a sickening lurch sideways: they were swerving madly to the left. A terrified voice screamed, *"It's going to hit us!"*

Some could see it: a small private Piper Cub was coming in at one o'clock. Bobby was full awake. The commercial pilot continued his severe turn, wheels screeching and skidding off tarmac onto grassy, rutty field. The stop felt as if they'd hit a wall. The engines cut off.

First: weird silence. Then: cries and gasps and shouts. The stewardess hurried along the aisle. "Please! We're all right! Stay in your seats! Sir! Please sit down! Everything is all right! Stay in your seats!"

"Oh my God!"

"Let us off!"

"Mama!"

Then the pilot's voice crackled through the loudspeaker: "Ladies and gentlemen, this is Captain Fitchen. We're fine. We, uh, had a young man flying his first solo. He made a very bad mistake. He's all right. There'll be a slight delay . . . I'm sorry, but we'll have to check out the aircraft for damage. If you have any problem, please report it to the cabin attendant. I'll be out to see you in just a few . . ."

Bellino was alarmed. "Bob! Bob?" He thought his chief was sobbing.

But Kennedy was laughing.

"That was funny?"

"No, no. Oh, Carmine! It's just . . . just six more inches and Hoffa would've been rid of Kennedy."

His near-silly giggling broke Bellino's tension, and he also began to laugh. "You . . . you want me to see who chartered that kid and his plane?"

Bob roared. Best joke he'd ever heard. Bellino joined him. They couldn't stop.

Somebody said, "Those two guys are crazy."

136

They related the incident to Pierre, driving them in from the Detroit airport. Through the cigar in his teeth he said, "Wow, one more Congressional investigation up in smoke, huh?"

Becalmed now, Bob said, "Well, at least delayed. Chief Counsels take, oh, three days to replace."

Carmine said, "It's accountants that take the time."

Salinger burst out, "Well, it was all worth it! Bob, I've really got it for you! Jimbo H. on a silver platter! I've been picking around Two Ninety-nine, right? Figure, try to see what's close to the bone, you know? Well, one tip led to another and . . . I felt it, I really did, I was getting warmer and warmer and I knew it! So, okay. It falls right into my lap. I locate this woman —a brave woman, gentlemen, a Teamster wife willing to break the conspiracy of silence we've—"

"Pierre . . ."

"Listen, will you? She's got the guts to tell me how her husband all of a sudden starts coming home with a smaller paycheck. Ten bucks light, every week. And for them that's a lot, right? Ten bucks, week in, week out. Like clockwork. Now, what's that sound like to you?"

"Kickback," Bellino said.

"You're damn right, kickback! And I know, because—get this—the trucker told her so! I mean, she finally confronts him with it, and he dodges, naturally, but then he breaks down. He says, 'Yeah, I gotta give the union back ten bucks every week.' Those bastards, huh?"

"Will *he* talk to us?" Bob asked.

"How's three o'clock tomorrow afternoon grab you? I've got it all set up. Perfect place. Secluded, quiet . . ."

It was on a highway out in the suburbs. STARLANE BOWLING. COCKTAILS. SNACK BAR. TV. BILLIARDS. GAMES. Inside, several women's-league teams were using the lanes at the far end of the eighty-lane hangar. Pierre said, "What'd I tell you? Few guys playing hooky from the office—who'd notice?"

"Perfect, Pierre. Very quiet."

They rented shoes and took a score sheet, requesting alleys next to the burly, solitary bowler in cover-

137

alls. In shirt-sleeves, they each bowled a set before acknowledging the trucker's presence. When they were sure it was safe, Pierre brought him over. "Robert, this is the gentleman I told you about."

Bob shook his hand. "Let's keep bowling while we talk. We have really only one question to ask you."

"Yes, sir."

Bellino asked it: "Who gets it?"

"What do you mean, who?"

"Can you give us the name of the person to whom you pay it?"

"No, I can't do that."

"Can you tell us how it gets to Hoffa?"

"Oh, my God."

Pierre said softly, "It's okay, Mike. I told you."

The man reddened deeply. "I'm sorry. I can't go through with this."

"You have to, Mike. You don't want your wife to . . . ?"

"Oh, Jesus, look, you guys, I'll tell you something. But you've gotta promise me—I want your word, this never gets to my wife."

"You've got it," Pierre assured him.

Going through the motions of drying his hands, the trucker told it to the ratty towel: "I'm lying to her. I'm not payin' no kickback to nobody."

Bob said, "Then where's the ten dollars going?"

"I got a girl on the side. I pay her rent for her. Forty a month. Ten a—"

"They got to you!" Pierre gritted.

"No, sir. Nobody got to me, except this girl. It don't hurt our house money none, and I hadda tell her something, so I made up the—"

Bob said, "Thanks, Mike. That's all. See you around."

Bellino was already getting back into his street shoes.

Crestfallen, Pierre said, "Well, I guess we'd better get out of here."

On the line, Bob said, "Not yet. I'm working on a spare."

Robert Kennedy pulled his car to the side of the

road and got out to look at the city. He was in a hurry to get where he was going, and at the same time wanted to never get there. He thought Washington a beautiful city, even in the rain. It was Jack who said it had all the charm of the North and all the efficiency of the South, but they agreed that physically it could stun. On the clearest of days, a mist clung to it: the mist of history. Its graceful buildings, set compatibly amid waters, hills, and woods, sang of human ability and aspirations. The architecture of its streets, the Wheel, looked glorious and ingenious from the sky; on the ground it practically guaranteed your getting lost in wrong turns.

The soft drizzle colored the air of the whole Basin lilac. It felt gentling to the taut skin of his sharp face, and kept his hair from blowing for once. He had been to Mass this day, and had received the Eucharist, for grace. He had his set of prayers and said them to himself now, viewing the city: for guidance, for strength, for release from anxiety and doubt; and for the happy recovery or speedy death of a friend lying sick at Bethesda Naval Hospital.

He couldn't help thinking of Jimmy Hoffa. He tried to hold focus: *the sin, not the sinner*. It was hard for him. He knew what Jimmy believed about law and religion: one was a swindle to protect those in power; the other was a drug to dope everybody. And he knew that Jimmy truly believed that there wasn't a person alive, male or female, who couldn't be bought. The man's cynicism and his behavior were repugnant and abhorrent to Robert Kennedy. Yet there was something else there in Hoffa, he sensed, that he somehow almost had to like and respect. He felt physical dread at the very thought of Hoffa's ever winning out over him. Yet he also felt almost an affectionate bond there between them. To the extent that Jimmy was still that man-boy in the crowd of poor, the one with the face with the sharp eyes, he felt compelled to wish him well.

This paradox didn't help lessen his anxieties. But it had no bearing on his doubts. About Jimmy Hoffa, Robert Kennedy suffered no doubts whatsoever.

He slipped into the hospital without ambush, but

139

when he came out they spotted him and once again pummeled him with their questions.

"How often do you visit him, anyhow?"

"Often as I can."

"How's McCarthy doing?"

"Senator McCarthy is seriously ill."

"How come you're about the only one from Capitol Hill to . . . ?"

"You'll have to ask them that."

"He is a personal friend, then?"

"He's one of my kids' godfather, what do you think?"

Just as he got his car door open, one last question stopped him. A reporter he didn't recognize yelled, "What are you getting out of this, Kennedy—tips on how to run your Teamster witch hunt?"

He stepped toward the man, pointed his index finger into the grinning face, remembered his "jump off the Capitol" mistake, and stopped. He came about, got in, and gunned the car away.

The John F. Kennedys lived in the Georgetown area of the city. Elegant, quaint, it was reminiscent of Boston's old Louisburg Square section of Beacon Hill with its townhouses, brownstones, cobblestone streets, polished brass doorknobs. Bob and Jack rarely got together after hours during the week, mainly because Jack regarded evenings as the time for rest, relaxation, socializing, and other diversionary pursuits, not as extension of the work day. Bobby, on the other hand, saw no distinctions between times of day or between work and play. He would often have Ethel bring some or all of the kids in to his office so they could eat supper together. Working with aides at Hickory Hill, he'd let any kid come to him with a question or cut knee to be inspected, without halting the proceedings. To him it was all one and the same, all equal parts of his life and world. So it wasn't a usual thing for him to be ringing Jack's doorbell this evening, in response to his brother's call. Something was up, he knew, and something was: Jack's temper.

"Dammit, look at me when I talk to you, Bobby.

140

We're trying to neutralize a problem here. Every time you see McCarthy, they ask *me* the questions!"

"What do they want from me? I quit his goddamn Committee, I wrote the goddamn minority report against him—what am I supposed to do now, go on TV and say I . . . ?"

Jack sighed. "Just underplay it, at least. That's all I'm asking—and strongly recommending. Jesus, kid, we got Labor pissed off on one side, what we really don't need is the liberals getting on their high horses!"

"I'll see what I can do."

"I love your loyalty, Bob. Nobody's saying give that up. But for God's sake, start avoiding publicity. There are political realities that—"

"I said okay!"

"I don't mean just me, either. You can jeopardize your whole investigation. Think about that! I know you'd rather get Hoffa on the real goods than on the bribery rap anyway. And how'll you do that if—"

"You didn't hear anything on the *Jencks* case yet, did you?"

"Not officially, but the scuttlebutt says the Supreme Court's going to go for it. That'll be any day now."

"That's what's worrying me."

"Well, it wouldn't exactly be a bad law, Bob, would it? Hell, why shouldn't prosecution's books be open to defense? That's only fair, isn't it?"

"It isn't the law, it's the goddamn *timing*. Ed Williams is already using every delaying action in the books as it is. If he gets *this* now . . ."

Jack had to laugh. "Yeah. Things have a way of working out in Mr Hoffa's favor, don't they."

When the Supreme Court's decision was handed down, Bob immediately visited U.S. Attorney Ed Troxell, to be told that Edward Bennett Williams had already filed a petition demanding access to all information used in developing the Government's bribery-conspiracy charge. Troxell sighed. "So now Jimmy Hoffa gets to look at our poker hand."

"Yes, a good *long* look. You can bet on that."

"Still, Mr. Kennedy, whether they get to see it or not, we do *have* the information, and that's—"

"They're also going to learn what you *don't* have,

141

Ed. Are you up on all the Hoffa material we've been feeding you?"

"Not . . . up, exactly. I've been trying to get at it, but . . ."

"Well, try harder. Has it crossed your mind—what if Williams should put Hoffa on the stand?"

"It'll never happen."

"But if it did, you'd be caught with your pants down!"

"It won't happen. They'd be crazy."

"I know. You're probably right. Actually, Clark Mollenhoff, the Cowles writer, told me he asked Williams point-blank if he'd ever consider it."

"And?"

"And Williams said that, contrary to common opinion, defendants who fail to testify in their own defense in Federal court usually get convicted."

"That's a bluff."

"Most likely," Bob said. "Clark thinks Williams was just teasing him. But I'm trying to get your guards up, Ed!"

"They're up! I know what I'm doing. And I don't know what he means by 'usually,' but for Hoffa to take the stand would be suicide!"   ..

"Really? For whom?"

The rains didn't end with April.

In May the rains fell heavily on the graveyard in Appleton, Wisconsin, and on the small bunch of people gathered around the priest reading the burial rite over the body of Senator Joseph McCarthy. The funeral services held in Washington previously had been only slightly better attended.

The thin, sad figure holding the umbrella over the weeping Jean McCarthy was that of Robert Kennedy. Outside the gates, and outnumbering the mourners, members of the press were waiting to ask him why he was there, when so many others weren't.

Judge Burnita S. Matthews was presiding.

The jury finally found acceptable to both Edward Bennett Williams and U.S. Attorney Troxell consisted of eight blacks and four whites.

Clark Mollenhoff rushed from the Federal Court-house to the Senate in search of Robert Kennedy. When he found him, Bob was loaded down with papers and half running down a hallway to a conference with Senator McClellan. He said, "See me later, Clark."

But I think Prosecution's already made a major mistake! And I've heard something else."

Bob slowed. "What's wrong?"

"First, they let Williams load the jury with blacks. Second, they say he's going to make race an issue."

"Race? What the hell's race got to do with it?"

"You're asking me?"

Bob stopped. "Damn. I figured he only had two real options—try to break Cy Cheasty and hope for reversible error."

"God, Bob, how can you not be there?"

"We're overloaded. I'm represented there, though, I've got somebody very reliable, honest, interested, and dedicated to give me nightly reports."

"Who?"

"Ethel."

Ethel attended, all day, every day. It was not pleasant duty.

John Cye Cheasty did indeed come under very heavy artillery fire. In the beginning, defense attorney Williams asked him, ". . . And you say you are an attorney?"

Cheasty said, "Yes. I am an attorney."

"From New York."

"Yes, from New York."

"Don't you do a little investigating on the side?"

"I have done some. Yes," Cheasty replied.

"And some spying."

"I have done some *investigatory* work."

Williams then asked, "Isn't it true that you once *investigated* the NAACP? The National Association for the Advancement of Colored People?"

"Objection!" Troxell shouted.

"Sustained," said Judge Matthews.

Cheasty pleaded, "There is no truth to that statement! No truth whatsoever!", but no statements heard can be unheard, and Williams's question had been heard by all, including the eight black jurors.

Jimmy Hoffa wasn't the only one who sat staring into Cheasty's face while he was on the stand. Mack Stenn sat staring at him too, from right behind Hoffa. Mack Stenn was primarily a sex man; sex and drugs. He was not a Teamster, but he worked on special projects for Jimmy Hoffa, when required. Stenn was also an enforcer, but not the usual kind. Short, suave, thin, and sharp as a stiletto, Mack Stenn did his for-hire enforcing not with his muscle, but with his eyes. His eyes seemed to be neither human nor recognizably animal, but rather something else, something out of another kind of place than Earth, murky and evil. They were so yellow they were almost white, and when he wanted them to, they seemed to shine forth, sending menace into a target's soul. Stenn was often paid to attend, say, a union meeting to do nothing more than be there, staring at the party requiring the intimidation. Mack Stenn was also a man of many hats literally changing them daily and wearing them all the time, indoors and out; this was because, to enhance the power and effect of his wizard's eyes, he kept his well-shaped head shaved bald to the olive skin. Staring now at the weak-hearted witness, Mack Stenn held his hat, a derby, on the lap of his razor-creased trousers.

John Cye Cheasty later told Ethel Kennedy, "My God, you have no idea how much it helped me just to be able to look out and find one friendly face watching me."

Cheasty was a Caspar Milquetoast only on the outside. He withstood Williams's grilling well, avoiding traps and dark alleys, by calmly and insistently sticking to the basic facts: Hoffa hired him; he went to Kennedy and worked against Hoffa under FBI supervision. At one point Williams remarked, "You're very long on detail, Mr. Cheasty."

Cheasty replied, "I believe in being accurate."

"And you don't feel *anything* could have *interfered* with your *comprehension* of those details?"

"Nothing. Not at all."

144

"Mr. Cheasty, do you take any *drugs?* On a regular basis?"

"Now just a minute!"

"Objection, Your Honor!" Troxell tried.

"Overruled."

Williams bore in: "Once again, Mr. Cheasty! *Have* you taken any form of narcotics? On a *regular* basis?"

Cheasty produced a small brown bottle from his jacket pocket and explained, "I . . . I do take nitroglycerin every day. It's for my heart condition, though, and in no way—"

"Nitro . . . glycerin!? Every day? Thank you, Mr. Cheasty, that's all I wanted to know. Your witness."

His part done, Cheasty was leaving the courtroom when Clark Mollenhoff intercepted him. "Cy? No interview, I know you're beat—just something personal?"

"Sure."

"Cy, this has intrigued me all alone—why? You've got all those kids in Brooklyn, a bum heart, you needed the money—why would you cross somebody as dangerous as Hoffa? And you must've expected the kind of abuse they threw at you in the cross-examination."

"I'm glad that part's over, I'll tell you that."

"That's not telling me why."

"Why?" He smiled. "Hell, you had stink on the one hand, and a kid eating a cheese sandwich in the Senate building! Who would you work for?"

His FBI escort surrounded him.

Clark said, "No regrets then, huh?"

"Just one," John Cye Cheasty said. "I can't do any more to help now."

In contrast, Robert Kennedy proved to be an awful witness under Edward Bennett Williams's hammering. His answers were correct, but his delivery was hesitant and nervous. It was his first experience of being a witness, of being on the receiving end of direct, shrewd, architected questioning. And though he hardly needed it, Williams got unsolicited help from his client. Jimmy knew the crowd was packed in his favor. He'd been kibitzing all along, but when Kennedy got

145

up there for the slugging and revealed he'd lost his cool en route, Jimmy had a field day.

After preliminary exposition of data, Williams suddenly hit him with: ". . . You have to admit, Mr. Kennedy, that there was no real danger to McClellan Committee operations, just because a few so-called confidential files were examined by persons not on *your* staff!"

Bob's anger blew: "I admit no such thing. Hoffa tried to destroy the Committee with spies, subterfuge, and every tool at his disposal!"

Williams smiled coolly. "Thank you for the speech, Mr. Kennedy . . . but a simple yes or no will suffice in the future."

Jimmy guffawed. "There ya go, Bobby! It's my pleasure, buyin' you this education!"

Judge Matthews gave him a dirty look and a pound of her gavel.

Williams went on. "Now, please tell the court, Mr. Kennedy, weren't you a millionaire at the age of four years?"

Bob almost stuttered, "I don't see what that has to do with it."

"Of course you don't," Williams commented with oil, "but I'm certain the *lawyers* in this room *will*."

"Gotcha again, Bob!"

The room roared. The judge gaveled them quiet and said, "Mr. Hoffa! Please restrain yourself. This is a court of law, after all."

"Sorry, Judge, couldn't help myself."

Pedantically, Williams explained, "I am just trying to establish, Mr. Kennedy, whether you have any compassion for the working man or the underprivileged in this country . . . or *is* your investigation simply a way to hunt phantoms of your own making . . . ?"

"Objection!" Justice Department Prosecutor Troxell shouted, only adding to the pandemonium this attack had caused in the courtroom. Jimmy was cackling, the Judge was gaveling, a clerk was trying to be heard announcing, "Recess! Recess!"

This was just what Mack Stenn had been instructed to wait for. He was posted outside the door, with his

146

mystery guest. Bob was leaving the stand, the jury was starting to file out, spectators were getting up and stretching and finding their belongings, Hoffa was standing at the defense table talking with Williams and his other lawyer, Martha Jefferson, a black from California. Stenn made his move, urging his companion ahead of him down the aisle. Jimmy looked up and hollered joyfully, "Hey, *Joe!* How the hell are ya? Hey, look folks, it's *Joe Louis! The greatest fighter of all time!*"

And all the folks stopped and turned to watch the lovable Brown Bomber go and put his famous right arm around Jimmy Hoffa's shoulder, and to hear him say, "What they tryin' to hang on you now, Jimmy?"

"Nothin' to worry about Joe—just Bobby Kennedy tryin' to tuck it to Organized Labor again!"

Louis comforted him: "You the best friend workin' people ever had in this country, Jimmy!"

The great fighter already knew Martha Jefferson; now Edward Bennet Williams introduced him to the other Negro lawyer helping him man the defense table. This reputable attorney was from Arkansas and a law-firm partner of Judge Matthews's brother. During the trial, Williams also posed for a picture with Martha Jefferson that appeared as an ad in the *Afro-American* applauding Jimmy Hoffa as a friend of the Negro race. When Judge Matthews learned that this ad had been delivered to every juror's doorstep, she ordered the jury locked up.

Disbelief, fury, and dread possessed Bob Kennedy now, and he got no relief from any of them at the swank cocktail party he was obliged to attend one evening at a Washington home. His new administrative assistant, Kenny O'Donnell, went with him. It was dressy. A large buffet was set out, and waiters served champagne from silver trays. There was an open bar, and many reporters were in attendance, so it was difficult to go unaccosted for long. Bob was learning to use his smile in the defense, and quipped his way through the inevitable series of "off-the-record" probings. When he spotted Eddie Cheyfitz's red hair weaving toward him through the crowd, he felt his

147

nerves relax: this was one glad-hander he wouldn't mind talking to at all.

"Cheers, Bob!" Eddie was into the champagne with zest.

"Hiya, Eddie. Eddie, meet Kenny O'Donnell."

"Sure, Kenny, very pleased to meet you. O'Donnell . . . oh, right, you're the one with the photographic memory, aren't you?"

O'Donnell fake-earnestly said, "I can't remember— isn't that Bellino?"

The three laughed. Eddie squinted puckishly and said, "So, Bob, what do you think so far? How we doing?"

"It isn't how, it's what you're doing that I don't like."

"For instance?"

"For instance, we have documentation that Jimmy's own Local Two Ninety-nine discriminates against Negro truckers left and right, and you've got him up there playing Abe Lincoln."

"All's fair in love and war, Bob. We're playing to win."

"You're playing dirty."

"Oh, I wouldn't go that far. We're simply—"

"Using a lot of showmanship because you don't have a case. I'll give you the psychological victories so far, Eddie—but don't think you've done enough to erase films and photographs and an honest man's story from the jury's mind. We're dealing in hard evidence. You're dealing in gamesmanship."

"And who knows which'll win, right, Bob?" Eddie swapped his empty glass for a full one from a passing tray.

Bob was intrigued. "You sound confident."

"I feel confident."

"Know something we don't?"

"Gentlemen, I'm the man's attorney!"

"He's sure got enough of those!"

Eddie laughed. "Hey, let me tell you a humorous sideline to all this serious stuff." His glass was empty. "You want to know whose ass Jimmy's kicking right now? His own! Oh, he's boiling. Seems he got word

148

from some, uh, contacts of his that they're laughing at him for being his own bag man with Cheasty!"

Kennedy and O'Donnell were too astonished to interrupt.

"Now he can't even believe it himself. Boy, he doesn't like coming off an amateur in *their* eyes, their respect is very important to him. I think it's hilarious. He's pounding the walls." When he noticed that they weren't joining him in the laugh, Eddie shrugged. "Ah well, you had to be there, I guess."

Bob's voice was dry as bones. "Do you realize what a confession you just made, Eddie?"

Eddie shook his head, looking for a waiter. "Naw, naw, I'm drunk, Bob, that's all. We're all drunk. We didn't even meet tonight."

"You drunk enough to let Hoffa testify?" O'Donnell asked.

Eddie wagged a finger at him. "Now you're trying to take advantage of a drunk! That's a no-no. But wait a second. Just for the sake of argument, why you so sure we won't? What'd be so wrong, puttin' him up there?"

"We're *not* sure you won't," Bob snapped. "But I'll tell you what's wrong with it: you *know* that man is guilty, and to knowingly put a guilty man on the stand in his own defense—"

Eddie Cheyfitz stopped him with a gentle hand on the shoulder and moved away. "Okay, Bobby, 's all right, I gotta shuffle off now, nice talkin' . . ."

Watching him leave, Kenny spoke without moving his lips. "Smile, Bob, keep smiling."

Bob clenched his teeth. "I am, I am. But I want to go kick in those windows. Christ, Kenny, they're gonna do it!"

"Let's get to Troxell."

"It's too late. He'd need a week to get *half* prepared to face Jimmy. And I don't think we've got twenty-four hours."

They had less.

The very next morning, Edward Bennett Williams stood up in court. "Your honor, I call Mr. James Riddle Hoffa to the witness stand."

A shock rippled through the courtroom. The impossible was happening. The spotlight was on Jimmy, and he quickly stole the show. By telling the truth, with a little English on it.

The key question was finally asked: Had Mr. Hoffa indeed met and exchanged envelopes with Mr. Cheasty?

"Sure I took the documents. What—did you miss that part of the movies? See, Mr. John Cye Cheasty was my lawyer. I paid him good money to serve as my attorney. Hell, you *saw* me pay him! He says, 'Meet me at such-and-such a place, I got something you should have.' What am I gonna do, not show up? Sure I show up. Now, what I didn't know was something else. How was I to know they were Committee documents?

"My *lawyer* never told me they were no Committee documents! What—can't a man take documents from his own lawyer any more? There a law against *that* now? There a law against trusting your lawyer? I'm supposed to hire him and then not trust him?

"How was I to know that Cheasty was violating the sacred lawyer-client relationship? I was always taught it's supposed to be like a priest in the confessional, or somethin' like that! Sacred! Like a marriage!

"How was I supposed to know that he was being bribed by Bobby Kennedy to violate our lawyer-client relationship?"

"Objection!" Troxell demanded.

Jimmy jumped. "Yes, I said bribery, and I'll say it again! Bobby Kennedy oughta be up here on trial for bribery! *Not me!*"

The two-word message reached Bob Kennedy on a piece of folded note paper handed to him while he was conducting hearings on the Textile Workers in the Senate Caucus room.

It read: "Hoffa acquitted."

It stunned him silent. Senator McClellan took up the questioning where he had left off.

On their jubilant way to the black Cadillacs waiting outside the Federal Courthouse, the Hoffa entourage gladly let themselves be swamped by the eager newspeople. Surrounded by Joe Louis, Martha Jefferson, and Edward Bennett Williams, Jimmy brandished the

150

Detroit paper with the Bobby-will-jump headline and laughed. "Hey, you all remember this?"

"What are you going to do now, Mr. Williams?"

"Why, I'm going to send Mr. Kennedy a parachute."

The remark was one of the first thrown at Bobby when the same reporters crowded around him in his outer office later. "A parachute, huh?" He blushed and laughed. "Well, I asked for that one, didn't I."

"You feel beaten, Mr. Kennedy?"

"I feel that Mr. Hoffa has won a battle. Speciously, but . . ."

"Are you saying the trial was rotten?"

"No, I'm not. The defendant was acquitted by a jury of twelve. That's our system of justice, and I wouldn't want to live under any other."

"Oh, come on."

"All right, I'll say this: what decided this case was a combination of effectiveness and ineffectiveness. Unfortunately, Mr. Williams was the one with the effectiveness."

"Jimmy was pretty good too, Bob"

Bob smiled. "He was." Jimmy outsmarted them all and Bob knew it. Nobody expected him to take the stand but he had, and he caught the Government attorneys unprepared. Bob had a better measure of his adversary now. Distracted, he said, "I might point out that the grueling cross-examination of Cy Cheasty lasted three days. Jimmy Hoffa's was thirty-two minutes." He vowed he'd never let anything like this happen to him again.

"How about Joe Louis?"

"He was a great fighter in his time. That's all for today. Thanks for coming by." He went back inside his office, where Walt Sheridan was waiting. "Walt, there's been an allegation that Louis was paid big to show. Move on it."

Hickory Hill was far enough out to escape the worst of the humidity that plagues Washington in the summertime. This day the July sun shone bright and warm through clear air. The limbs and leaves of the high old trees danced lazily in the light breezes. It was afternoon, and the place was noisy with life. Dogs

151

and children ran; music blared; teenagers and wives played tennis on the courts, or sat on the shaded terrace chatting and laughing. It was always dangerous to go near the Kennedy pool wearing clothes, especially at more formal evening affairs, but today a couple of Bob's staff men stayed dressed; though it was conducted poolside, the meeting was strictly business. Bob wore only khakis, some of the others just bathing trunks. They had gone for a swim, played some ball, lunched, talked about the tans they hoped to get.

In the teeth of Hoffa's acquittal, Bob wanted to rally their spirits, pull them back in close so they'd again feel their camaraderie and sense of mission. The work went round-robin, each investigator summarizing the current status of his area of responsibility in Operation Hoffa, then fielding questions from Bob and others. All were especially intrigued by Kenny O'Donnell's report that "Jimmy bugged the members of his own Detroit Local . . . and I know you don't want to hear this again, Bob, but Justice is confident of both indictment and conviction, on the basis of the documentation we've provided them."

"How fast can they get a trial?"

"Oh Christ—late November, early December?"

"Shit."

"Here we go again. That's *after* the convention!"

Bob punched his palm. "How many times can I say it? We've got to get the Hoffa story out to the public before the Teamsters meet in September, or else we're gonna be dealing with the President of the most powerful union in the world! Pierre, go back to Detroit. Start from scratch. Subpoena *all* financial records, *all* Locals."

"Good God, not again."

"Watch it, Pierre—God is a Teamster."

"LaVerne?"

"Yes, Bob. I'm onto some of Jimmy's dealings in the pension funds, and . . ."

"Again, I want no loopholes this time. No shortcuts. No mistakes. Nothing but perfection."

"Let me read you what I have so far." Before LaVerne Duffy could move his hand the six inches to the sheaf of onionskin papers on the light, tin tray-table beside him, a softball flew in out of nowhere, bounced, and came up under it, sending it and all the papers over into the green water of the swimming pool. Everyone yelled, "Oh no!"

The table came apart, the legs sinking, the top floating like a raft, not like the thin, square pieces of evidence against Jimmy Hoffa—they floated like dead leaves, absorbing water fast. Dismayed faces looked from the floating, sinking sheets of paper to LaVerne Duffy. He said nothing, simply walked to the shallow end of the pool, stepped down into it, and began wading, picking papers out of the water as he went.

Duffy was one of the investigators who had stayed fully dressed.

The heel of Walt Sheridan's right shoe caught on the step of the South Chicago bus. Walking in the heat up the street, he tried to pound it against the pavement, but the nails had bent. He limped along until he came to a shoe-repair shop that still called itself Cobbler. The cobbler fixed it while he waited. That's the kind of neighborhood it was. It reminded Walt of lower-middle-class neighborhoods in Utica, New York, Dorchester, Massachusetts, the District of Columbia: Irish, Italian, Jewish, or Slav, gone black. He found Joe Louis's address, entered, and climbed the stairs through the smells of cooking and cats, the sounds of families enduring summer in the city.

On the third floor, he came to Louis's door and knocked. Louis opened it, said, "I'm on the phone," and walked back inside. Sheridan stepped in, closed the door, and waited. A game show played silently on the TV; top-forty music blared from the radio. Newspapers and sports magazines lay scattered about the sparsely furnished room. "It's that Sheridan what called from Kennedy," Joe Louis said into the phone. And then, to Sheridan, he said, "What you gonna want now?"

Walt said, "I have an affi—a statement we want you to sign."

"Says I gotta sign sumpin', what you think?" Listening, he smiled. "Yeah, okay, that's right, that's good . . . Oh, you know, I missed a coupla gimmes, but I was aroun' the greens all day, not too bad, drives was good. Okay then. Later." Off the phone, he turned back to Sheridan. "Lemme see it."

Sheridan produced the affidavit. "It's only what you told us before, Mr. Louis. I just had it typed up, and we'd like you to sign it."

Louis moved his eyes over it. "Like what?"

"Just that you're an old friend of Mr. Hoffa's, and that . . ."

"Got a pen?"

Sheridan handed him a pen and watched while Louis, instead of signing, drew the pen through line after line of the statement.

"Is there something inaccurate, Mr. Louis?"

Louis didn't answer, just kept deleting. Walt noticed a framed photograph on the otherwise bare walls: Joe Louis in his prime, gloves up. The champion had obviously aged and thickened, but he was still a formidable, handsome athlete. He handed the papers and pen back to Sheridan. Walt saw that he had affixed his signature below only the final paragraph, which read, "I did not receive any money for the trip I took to Washington to visit Mr. Hoffa and Miss Jefferson."

Sheridan accepted it, then, a bit sheepishly, handed Joe Louis the pen again and a blank sheet of paper. "Uh, Bob Kennedy asked if you wouldn't mind signing your autograph. It's for his son."

Louis growled, "I'll do it for his son," and wrote, "To Joe Kennedy—best wishes—Joe Louis." He gave it to Walt, saying, "Kennedy can go jump off the Capitol."

Detroit was also sweltering. The shirt under Pierre Salinger's suit jacket was dark with sweat. His spirit was dark with frustration. I was late afternoon; he had started early in the morning, was close to the bottom of his list, and still had not collected his first subpoenaed document, record, or file. He had located and confronted officials in their Local offices, lawyers in their homes, and union goons in their cars and hangouts, all with the same result: none. He received curt dismissals and slammed doors, and when any words were offered at all, they were the same three: "Talk to Hoffa."

His burning feet reached the steps of Local 183, a shoebox establishment in a Detroit outskirt. He rebuttoned his collar, tightened his tie, dried his face, mustered his hopes and charm, and smiled at the receptionist. "Hello. Would you tell Mr. Kierdorf that Mr. Salinger is here from the Senate Committee? To collect the subpoenaed documents? Thanks."

She was wearing pink-rimmed starlet eyeglasses fastened behind her neck with a sequined cord and she looked like she might be somebody's sister-in-law. She smiled, pushed the lever on her intercom, and said, "Mr. Kierdorf, there's a Mr. Salinger here to—"

The disembodied voice boomed, "Tell that son of a bitch to drop fucking dead!" *Click!*

She looked apologetic.

Pierre leaned over, clicked her lever, and said, "Mr. Kierdorf! This is called defying a goddamn Federal subpoena, and you can—"

"You can get your ass outta here while you still got it!" *Click!*

Salinger straightened, waited until his boiling had cooled to a simmer, then as levelly as he could spoke into the machine again. "Mr. Kierdorf, the documents I—"

"Talk to Hoffa! *Click!*

He finally gave up and went back to the phone in his hotel room. "Bobby, somebody got to everybody. Yeah, they know it's defiance, they don't care. It's talk to Hoffa, talk to Hoffa. Know what I think we oughta do?"

"Let's talk to Hoffa."

Through his intercom, Jimmy Hoffa told his secretary, "Make 'em wait. I got a vital meeting goin' on in here." Then he grinned at the group of men sitting around his Local 299 office: Farrell, Kierdorf, and nine others. All except Sandy had received a Federal subpoena. Jimmy said, "You all got it with you right?"

"Right."

"Now you know what to do when I make the play? You know where to go?"

They knew.

Jimmy had prepared for this. Throughout his bribery trial he had kept thinking of Kennedy, kept seeing him out there on the edges, waiting. One thing about the acquittal that was even better than an appeal was that he was getting back to the Bobby problem without too much delay. The streets had made him all too well aware of the dangers in letting an enemy hold back too long: they came back at you too strong. After one mix, you had to hit them again, first and fast. It was true in anything, really. Think, move, and *blam,* that's it. Like when Jimmy Jr. Went to college—proud as he was that the kid turned out to be such a terrific athlete, the minute he heard it was going to run over into college he got on the phone to the school and put the kibosh on it just like that. Football was bullshit.

He leaned back in his chair now. "Whaddaya think, Sandy, let 'em stew a half hour or so?"

"At least."

The office door burst open and slammed back against the paneled wall. Bob Kennedy walked in, followed by Carmine Bellino and Pierre Salinger.

Jimmy flared. "What the hell you think *you're* doin' I told ya to wait!"

"I waited," Bob cracked back.

"Not long enough!"

"All I'm going to!"

Jimmy was out from behind his desk and up to Bobby's face. They stared. Neither spoke.

Farrell said, "Mr. Kennedy, you can't—"

Locked with Bob, Jimmy yelled, "I'm throwin' this brat outta here, Sandy!"

"I don't see it," Bobby hissed. "You touch me, and—"

Farrell and Bellino closed and separated them gingerly. Salinger scanned the lineup of ten glowering Hoffa men, all now on their feet. His mouth begged for a cigar.

Hoffa broke the silence. "So you want my financial records, do ya? You want my books?"

At this, the ten men backed into a straight line along the opposite wall.

156

"Well, I'm gonna show ya what I think of your goddamn committees and your goddamn subpoenas and your goddamn bunch of pryin' Pauls!" The ten had brought out their subpoenas. Ranting, Jimmy passed down the line, collecting one from each. Papers in hand, he stormed back to within an inch of Kennedy's chest. "And this is what I think of *you!*" he yelled, tearing the subpoenas to shreds and throwing them into Bobby's face.

Bob stared through the confetti.

Jimmy stayed eyeball-to-eyeball and raised his right fist, clenched. "Now you get the fuck outta my office and outta Detroit! And if you know anything, Kennedy, you'll get the fuck outta my life, and *stay* out!"

Bob's right fist was up now. "You've got exactly three minutes to figure out how you're going to turn over those documents to us, Hoffa! If you can't, I'm going to be back here with the goddamn Army! And I'll shut you down so goddamn fast it'll feel like a wildcat strike! And if you don't think I can do it, you can ask one of your four thousand goddamn lawyers! You meathead, you're fucking with the Government of the United States this time!"

"*I* know what you're tryin' to do! You're tryin' to stop me from becoming President of this great union! It must really eat your guts out that you can't *ever* get the workin'man in this country to turn against me!"

"We'll see about that!"

"You'll see shit! No matter what you say or do, it'll never happen! I'll see you dead first!"

Kennedy smiled. "No, you'll see me in court first." Then he turned and walked out, between Bellino and Salinger. Pierre followed.

Bellino said quietly, "Uh, Mr. Hoffa, we can discuss the terms for getting the documents we—"

Jimmy swung his guns away from the empty doorway onto Carmine. "I know you too, Bellino! You know, with seven kids to feed, you're gonna need work for a long, long time, and don't you forget that!"

"I won't. Thank you. Now, in lieu of the subpoenas, I think there's a formula we—"

Jimmy laughed. The coiled spring of his stance had finally relaxed. "You're all right, Bellino." Then he said to his men, "All of ya, outta here now. Me and the *paisan* here got some negotiatin' to do!" He returned to his chair behind his huge, mahogany desk. Carmine took a chair opposite. When they were alone, Jimmy said, "Ya know, I was readin' somewhere . . . ya know how some of your newspaper pals describe your boy? 'Elegant young roughneck.'"

Bellino smiled. "Yes, we've seen that. It's quoted, actually. It's how F. Scott Fitzgerald described the Great Gatsby."

"Well, I don't know about that, or about great, but it's the roughneck part. He better watch out for that. I got him fightin' my style there, didja see? That's risky business, that's pretty—"

"Maybe it's the best style, I wouldn't know. Now, in cases where subpoenaed material—"

"Aah, Bellino." Hoffa grinned. "You always mean trouble for me. Okay, lay it out, let's see how good you are."

At first all was more elegant than roughneck when the McClellan Committee opened its summer, 1957, hearings. The Caucus Room was filled to overflowing, which Senator McClellan noted in his opening remarks. ". . . We have quite an audience this morning. You are all welcome, but we must maintain order. Please be as comfortable as you can, but please also be quiet . . ."

James Riddle Hoffa was sworn in and identified himself as "business representative and Vice-President of the International Brotherhood of Teamsters." He spoke clearly and confidently and correctly. He was dressed in his usual businesslike attire: white shirt, dark tie and suit, black shoes. Sandy had suggested dark socks as well, instead of the white, but Jimmy prevailed.

Chief Counsel Robert Kennedy was calm and friendly as he asked, "Do you hold any other positions with the Teamsters Union at the present time?"

Mr. Hoffa replied politely. "I will give you the main

158

ones, and if you want more I will give them to you gladly," then did so.

"I believe you said you have been with the Teamsters since approximately nineteen thirty-two."

"Yes. Approximately."

"During that period you have been arrested a number of times, I believe."

"That is correct."

"How many times, approximately, do you think?" Kennedy asked, stiffly.

Hoffa, leaning back, crossing his legs, glancing up into his memory: "Well, I don't know, Bob, long time since I counted them up. I think maybe eighteen or nineteen times I have been picked up and taken into the custody of the police. And out of the nineteen, three of those times . . . in many instances these were dismissed, you see . . . but in three of those times"—spoiling Kennedy's punchline—"I received convictions."

Kennedy proceeded. "Now, I'd like to talk about a charge of conspiracy between you, and the union, and certain wastepaper companies."

"Talk," Jimmy said.

"Was there a conspiracy?"

"It was so charged."

"And it was *nolo contendere?*"

"Yes, sir, it was."

"And you paid a thousand-dollar fine?"

"Yes."

"And then you were indicted in nineteen forty-six on an extortion charge, I believe."

"That is correct." His eyes had already hardened; now his voice began too. "The extortion charge was a question of refusing to load—"

"Mr. Hoffa, I am not saying whether you are guilty or not, I'm just trying to get—"

"You are implying that I am guilty of extortion, and that isn't true."

Kennedy had facts. "You had to return the money that you collected from these various grocers. The court ordered you to do that. Some seven thousand five hundred dollars. Is that right?"

This hit an exposed flank. Hoffa hedged, mumbling

159

his words. "Approximately? Yes, that is . . . right, I . . ."

"Shall we go on?"

"Uh, if you . . . don't mind, I . . . need a few moments to check some facts with my . . ."

Kennedy smiled warmly. "Certainly, Mr. Hoffa. We don't want you to have any confusion."

A brief recess was called. Only a few stayed, including Senators; most preferred to seek a breath of air outside the muggy, sticky Caucus Room. Hoffa stayed bent to one side, conferring with an attorney. Kennedy pulled a briefcase up from the floor, dug out what he wanted, then leaned back perusing, putting his feet up on the edge of the committee table. Hoffa's voice made him look up. Smiling, Jimmy said, "Meant to tell you, kid, nice going on the timing of this. Right before our convention, huh?" He had come up to the table.

Bob shrugged.

Jimmy leaned down. "Finally got what you wanted, don'tcha. Last round for the heavyweight champeenship."

"That's your idea, Jimmy. That's not what I want."

"Oh yeah? What do you want?"

"The truth."

Hoffa cocked an eyebrow and his upper lip, trying to get Bob's deadpan to crack, but it didn't. "The truth, huh? All right, I'll give you this much truth, pally. Your good-lookin' brother there—I know what he wants in 'Sixty as well as you do." He spoke low, soft and friendly. "So listen. You do for me, I'll do for you."

Bob was surprised that he'd said it outright, but the second he heard it coming he dropped his eyes down to his papers: *I didn't hear what you just said.* Hoffa hung. When he realized no reply was coming, he returned casually to his witness chair and resumed huddling with his counselors. After the room had begun to refill, he suddenly turned back toward Kennedy and gibed loudly, "Hey, Bobby! You really shouldn't put your feet up on Government property, ya know! It's not nice to deface something that belongs to the people!" Under the scattered laughter this brought

160

from the audience, he slipped in, harder and lower: "Careful, kid—this ain't the last round by a long shot!"

Bob swung his feet down, smiling and blushing at the ribbing, then glowering at the threat. Jimmy Hoffa continued to baffle him: these swift, sudden changes—did he have some true madness, out of his control, or some super-shrewdness, totally in control? Or both? He had watched this man go up against solid evidence before, make a monkey of it, and walk away clean. Again he started to feel that dread of the unforeseeable rise in his heart. He willed it away. The conflict resumed:

". . . All right, Mr. Hoffa, let's see if I have this correct." Kennedy was saying later in the day. "Commercial Carriers, Incorporated, had a problem—their expensive rolling equipment was tied up in a strike. It was not rolling. So you settled the strike. Later, a friendly lawyer set up a company called Test Fleet. Which bought the heavy equipment from Commercial Carriers. Then leased it back to them. And this lawyer became the first president of Test Fleet?"

Mr. Hoffa answered sleepily, "That's your version of it. I don't expect you to get it entirely right."

"Who paid this attorney?"

"I don't know."

"You never paid him yourself?"

The rattler wasn't sleeping—it struck: "I didn't pay anybody in Test Fleet! Let's get this correct! I did not set up, nor did I run, nor did I have the stock of Test Fleet! Nor at any time did Test Fleet employ any drivers that came under the supervision of our organization!"

The other struck back: "But the Teamsters in your union *do* drive the trucks that you, Jimmy Hoffa, the boss of Test Fleet, lease to Commercial Carriers! Isn't that true?"

"Now, just a moment, just—a—moment! *Not* that I lease. Let's correct the record!"

"All right—Test Fleet leases."

"But not that *I* lease."

"Test Fleet leases."

"But *not* that I lease."

161

"That's fine. *Test Fleet* leases."

"Yes."

Kennedy didn't pause. "And the company was set up in the name of the friendly attorney and then the stock was transferred down to Tennessee, correct?"

"I think you are right."

"Who was the stock transferred to?"

"Josephine Poszywak and Alice Johnson."

Here Senator John Kennedy put in: "Who is Poszywak?"

Hoffa: "My wife is Josephine Poszywak, and Alice Johnson is Bert Brennan's wife."

Robert Kennedy, eyeglasses up in his hair, waited for the loud hum of spectators' voices to die down. Then he asked, "Has Test Fleet been a profitable operation, Mr. Hoffa?"

Hoffa: "*You* have the record. I think you could say that it was."

"Well, I am asking *you* the question."

"Since it was not my company, I can only say that I think it was."

Kennedy raised his eyebrows. "You do not know —your wife has not let you know how much money she made?"

Hoffa's eyes went nearly purple; his voice stayed dry and icy. "I think I know how much she made, I'm not sure."

"*Approximately* how much do you think she made?"

Jimmy glared. This was making him hot and hateful. The one thing that had made him even consider coming before the Committee to begin with was learning that they could subpoena his wife. "I can't tell you offhand, but I can guess."

"We have some figures here." Kennedy lifted a sheet of paper.

Hoffa waved his hand magnanimously. "Then read them off, brother, read them off!"

Kennedy began reading them off: "November fifteen, nineteen forty-nine, four thousand dollars each, to Mrs. Hoffa and Mrs. Brennan in their maiden names. In December of nineteen fifty, fifteen thousand dollars each. In October of nineteen fifty-one, thirty-

five hundred dollars. In July of nineteen fifty-two . . ."
The court recorder's fingers moved nimbly on his machine. Jimmy Hoffa was again bent to his attorney's ear; he might not have been even listening.

"Mr. Chairman?"

"Senator Kennedy?"

"Mr. Hoffa," JFK queried, "what I'm wondering is, when the Test Fleet Company was formed, how much money did your wife and Mr. Brennan's wife actually invest? What was their personal equity?"

The TV cameras panned to Jimmy Hoffa for his answer. "I think the financial report will show two checks, of fifteen hundred dollars each. And then there was an additional check of a thousand dollars that was put up for the capital—actual capital outlay for this operation."

"Yet it seems the total payment from Test Fleet to your wife and to Mrs. Brennan in the maiden names as of nineteen fifty-six amounted to over a hundred and twenty-five thousand dollars." John Kennedy smiled largely. "I admit, that's a decent return on a seven-thousand-dollar investment."

Hoffa squinted. "Are you against the free-enterprise system, Senator?"

"No, just its abuses, Mr. Hoffa," the Senator returned swiftly. "Now, I believe you stated—and I don't know if I am quoting you correctly—that *you* did *not* get any of this money. That this money was earned by your wife and Mrs. Brennan. *Did* you receive some of it? Or none of it?"

Hoffa grinned. "Well, we file a joint return, if that's what you mean." He listened for audience response, but heard silence. It also chafed him to hear Bobby's voice seem to come out of this senior man's lips.

"I do mean that," Senator Kennedy pressed. "So actually you *have* benefited from this too, haven't you, Mr. Hoffa."

"If you want to call it that, yes."

"Thank you. I do indeed want to call it that. Yes."

Hoffa's eyes slid away from John Kennedy's face only to land on Robert's; he was smiling. Jimmy felt had and didn't like it.

"The Committee will stand in recess until two o'clock."

Again the Senate Caucus room all but emptied; again Hoffa stayed in his chair, this time conferring with attorney George Fitzgerald, staunch, involved loyalist to both Hoffa and the Teamsters. Jimmy kept his ear bent to white-haired Fitzgerald, but his piercing eyes on Bobby Kennedy, still at the big table, packing papers into a briefcase.

Leaving, Kennedy passed Hoffa's table, and Jimmy suddenly lunged. It so looked and sounded like a physical attack that people stopped at the doors and turned back.

"Listen, you son of a bitch! I wanna tell you something—*leave my wife out of this!*"

Kennedy, coldly: "Are you speaking to me?"

"You're the only son of a bitch I see around here!"

"Jimmy, please!" Fitzgerald whispered.

Hoffa flung his arm away. "You shut the fuck up!" Then, to Bobby: "I don't want you dragging my wife through the mud, you understand?"

Kennedy was hot too. "*I* didn't bring your wife into this, *you* did! When you got her involved in Test Fleet!"

"My wife is as fine a woman as ever drew breath, and don't you dirty her name!"

"We're not out to dirty *anybody's* name!"

It was the Detroit showdown again. More and more people started flooding back into the room.

"The hell you're not!" Hoffa was crimson, leaning, pointing.

Kennedy was pointing back. "We're trying to get the truth. And if you'd start remembering better, we'd get at it faster!"

Hoffa exploded. "All you're trying to get is publicity for the beautiful Kennedys! Your brother's gonna run for President pretty soon, and you want Hoffa's scalp to show around! You're *not* lookin' for truth! You're lookin' for trial by newspaper! Conviction by innuendo! You're just a spoiled creep! You couldn't hold a job as a law clerk if you didn't have a rich daddy!"

"You *talk* tough!" Kennedy shouted back. "Well,

why aren't you tough enough to start answering questions for a change?"

"I never took the Fifth, and I never will!"

"But you hide behind your stooges who do!"

From the balcony it looked like a cockfight. Kennedy had flung his briefcase down. The small table between them was invisible. Nobody stopped it. It degenerated into venomous blather and came perilously close to fists. After this, Kennedy had a much harder time denying Hoffa's charges that it was personal, a blood feud between them.

"You can't take it, can you, Bobby! You couldn't take it when they acquitted me on that trumped-up bribery charge, either! You—"

"It wasn't trumped-up!"

"You had to go around tellin' everybody I was acquitted because the jury was mostly blacks! Because Joe Louis came in and let people know he was my friend!"

"Bull—"

"Well, he *is* my friend, and I'm proud of it! And you had to send that stooge of yours, Sheridan, out to harass him! Well, lemme remind you of something— that verdict was *unanimous!* Those four whites on that jury—"

"*I'll* tell *you* something about that jury, Hoffa. One juror had a police record of fourteen convictions! Another one had nine! Another one—"

Jimmy played to the gallery now. "Oh! Ain't that *terrible,* now!"

"Another one had a son in jail on a narcotics charge while the trial was goin on!"

"Had—a—son—in—jail. Had a son in jail! Mercy me!"

"I don't mean—"

"You're convicting him by association! Maybe he didn't have enough money to keep his kid outta jail! Ever think about that? Nah, how could you? What are you sayin'—these people got no right to pull jury duty? Huh? Speak up!"

"No, but they aren't people who want to side with the law!"

"Listen to that! He wants lily-white juries! Our

great jury system isn't good enough for Kennedy! Boy, I'd like to get *that* on record! I'd like to see your brother get elected with *that* hangin' around his neck!"

Bobby had come to his senses. He picked up his briefcase and began moving away. "See you at two o'clock."

Jimmy followed and caught up with him. "You wanna know what I'd like to do when this is over?"

"It's not going to be over for a long time!"

"I'd like to take you off by ourselves and give you the whippin' you need and never got!"

"You and who else—your three hundred lawyers or your Cadillacs full of animals? That's how *you* fight!"

That stuck in Jimmy's throat. When Bobby reached the door he yelled, "You never jumped!"

Bobby turned back, laughing. "And you would have!"

"You welshed!"

Bobby laughed again, but stopped; Jimmy was going further: "When I beat that chickenshit wiretap trial in New York! Will you jump then?" George Fitzgerald looked near a stroke, but Hoffa went on, addressing God knew whom. "This is a charade! You're just tryin' to make me look bad in front of my union! You're tryin' to keep me from bein' President! Well, it ain't gonna work, Bobby! You can't tell no Teamsters what to think! It ain't gonna work, Bobby!"

The Kennedy brothers ate sandwiches together that noon. Jack tried to calm him down. "It's psy-war, Bobby. He's just trying to get you to make it more personal. Don't let it. Don't lower yourself. Stick to the . . . this Test Fleet thing, now. Certainly sounds like a violation of Taft-Hartley to me."

"Sounds like! Taft-Hartley specifically forbids a Labor officer to accept money from an employer with whom he bargains. And that's exactly what Hoffa did. He's a union negotiator and an employer at the same time, no matter how well he hides behind wives and maiden names. And that's against the law."

"And that's where we should deal with him. You're the best organizer I've ever seen, Bob. It's that that

166

has produced so much solid evidence, and it's the solid evidence that the Committee can—"

Bob's intercom had buzzed. Angie's voice announced Walt Sheridan. Brightening, Bob told her, "Yes, send him in." To Jack he said, "I'll show you organization—if this is what I'm praying it is . . ."

It was. Sheridan came in holding a sheaf of stapled papers between a thumb and forefinger.

Bob grinned. "That hot?"

Walt gloated, "Hotter than that. Hi, Senator. Gentlemen, one for you and one for you. It's even better to hear it than to read it, but I sent the tapes straight to you at the Committee, Bob."

They were transcripts of conversations between Jimmy Hoffa and New York racketeer Johnny Dio. As the Senator and the Chief Counsel read them, the investigator said, "Read 'em and weep. Now I know why Hoffa believes every man's got his price—he's paid them! Look at them—bankers, corporate executives, cops, judges, Congressmen . . . Jesus, it gave me the chills. If we don't get that bastard, he's not going to run just his union, he's going to run this whole goddamn country!"

Jack Kennedy finished reading first and whistled. "Good God! No wonder he can sit up there like a rooster and look me straight in the eye and— Wait a minute, Walt, how did we get those tapes?"

Sheridan said, "Don't worry. New York D.A. Frank Hogan had Dio tapped, not Hoffa. Completely legit. Jimmy just happened to be one of the parties that turned up."

Robert Kennedy finished reading, threw the papers on his desk, and sat bent over, his head nearly between his knees.

Jack said, "Gonna throw up?"

"I'm so happy I can't believe it. And Jesus, you're right. I'm trading lipshit with him like two jerks in the schoolyard, while . . . Let's get back."

Bob had been right about Jimmy and the Fifth Amendment. During the proceedings Jack had even accused him outright: "Mr. Hoffa, I think you're pleading the Fifth by proxy!"

It was purely Hoffaesque. On the stand, Jimmy

would claim to not remember something, then refer the Committee to Bert Brennan or somebody who, he was sure, would remember. The Committee would call that party to testify, only to hear over and over: "I refuse to answer on the grounds that it may tend to incriminate me," or some allowable variation of syntax. Jimmy's vow never to plead the Fifth thus remained intact. As did the failure to disclose much information.

This day the Committee took no referrals and used the tapes to aid the witness's recall.

Robert Kennedy to Hoffa: "Did you discuss with Mr. Lacey the question of Mr. Dio getting a charter with the Teamsters?"

"I cannot recall that, whether or not it was discussed or not."

"Perhaps this recording will help. Mr. Chairman?"

Senator McClellan: "We will play another recording. This is Mr. Hoffa to Mr. Dio, May fourteen, nineteen fifty-three." Their voices filled the hushed room.

HOFFA: Hello, Johnny?
DIO: Yeah.
HOFFA: How ya doin'?
DIO: Oh, I'm tired.
HOFFA: Listen. I just came from that fella's office. And he, ah, positively definitely went on record as opposing you, in, ah, getting a charter.
DIO: Who was that? Marty?
HOFFA: Yeah. Marty.

Kennedy shut off the recorder. "Does that help, Mr. Hoffa?"

Against the tapes and the Committee's disallowing his referrals, Jimmy reverted to two of his other weapons, near-amnesia and a language best described as an ingenious combination of Danny Kaye and Professor Irwin Corey at their tongue-twisting heights. Right now he replied, "Well, I think it certainly concludes a considerable misunderstanding as to what really happened."

"Then will you tell this Committee what *really* happened?"

"I'm not sure I remember."

"Can you remember *where* it happened?"

"I think it was a hotel."

"What hotel?"

"I can't remember."

"Did Dio go into the hotel with you?"

"I don't remember."

"Did he go into the elevator with you?"

"I don't know."

"Do you know if he went to your room with you?"

"I can't answer that. I don't remember."

"You don't remember back—now this is three months ago—and you can't remember *three months ago* whether Johnny Dio was in your room? A man under indictment for throwing *acid* in Victor Riesel's eyes?"

Sleepy-eyed again and postured almost like a boy pouting, Hoffa said, "I cannot remember whether he was or not, as I said. It was that period of time and I just don't recall. I'm sorry."

Kennedy: "So am I, Mr. Hoffa. So am I."

The brothers had evolved into a battery, Jack often relieving Bob's dry, straightforward interrogations with his own more eloquent demands: ". . . And then I'd like to understand your union's violent and expensive opposition to the new Labor Reform Bill. A bill whose primary intent is to clear mobsters and organized crime out of union politics . . ."

"That bill is nothing but a strikebreaking, union-busting bill in my opinion!" Against Jack, Jimmy rarely played sleepy-eyed. It sometimes seemed, despite Jimmy's private claims of admiration for the Senator, that Jack inspired deeper and more hair-triggered anger in Hoffa than even Bob did.

Nor was Jack always able to practice the unemotionalism he preached to his younger brother. Anger begat anger: "Mr. Hoffa, this is *not* a strikebreaking, union-busting bill! *You're* the best argument I know for it! Your testimony here this afternoon, your complete indifference to the fact that numerous people who hold responsible positions in your union come

169

before this Committee and take the Fifth Amendment because an honest answer might tend to incriminate them—that attitude alone is enough to make this bill mandatory for the future of a decent and honest Labor Movement that will benefit the millions of honest and hardworking Americans that *you know nothing about!*"

Both barrels: "Are *you* telling *me* that I don't know the American workingman? Are *you* saying *I* don't know anything about the American workingman? A man who's never done a decent day's work in his life is telling *me?!*"

Rap! Rap! Rap! Rap! Rap! It took the Chairman many severe hammers of his gavel to finally restore some modicum of order.

Dave Thatcher was tired. But his adrenalin was flowing so strong that he felt suspended over the abyss of collapse, held upright by only his ever-thinning nerves. He had sought relief by a window in the quiet and space of the corridor outside the perfervid chaos of the Caucus Room. He was standing there, arms slumped upon the sill, forehead pressed against the glass, when the hearings broke for the day. That was why he wasn't noticed when Jimmy Hoffa came charging out between George Fitzgerald and Sandy Farrell.

Jimmy Hoffa said, "That son of a bitch, I'll break his back! Him and his brother too! *I'm gonna break his back!*" he swore, and Dave heard him. He swung about to see who else was in the crowd in Hoffa's wake.

Robert Kennedy used it next day as a change of pace and as a surprise in their assault upon Jimmy Hoffa's emplacement. Beginning casually, he asked, "When leaving the hearing room yesterday, and several people have testified to this matter, did you say, 'That son of a bitch, I'll break his back'?"

Jimmy had already been fixing "the Look" upon him, the seemingly unblinking, burning stare. Nor did he break it to answer, "Who?"

"You."

"Say to who?"

"To *anyone*. After several people testified before the Committee, *did* you make that statement?"

170

"I never talked to anyone after they talked to the Committee."

"I'm not asking if you said it *to* them. I'm asking *if* you said it."

"Not concerning them, far as I know of."

"Then who did you make it about?"

"I don't know. I might have been discussing somebody, I don't know . . . a figure of speech?"

"Well, whom did you make the statement about? Whose back were you going to break?"

The Look now projected impatience and contempt. They were trying to bait him into admitting he was still a man of violence, and he wasn't about to fall for that. "I don't remember it."

"Well? Whose back were you going to break, Mr. Hoffa? *Whose back?*"

As Kennedy had raised his voice, Hoffa lowered his, and spat, "Figure of speech. I don't even know who I was talking about, and I don't even know what *you're* talking about!"

Final clash: stalemate.

A week later, Senator McClellan closed that session of the Committee's hearings with a forty-eight-point summary that included: ". . . And in conclusion, we find Mr. Hoffa culpable in thirty-three criminal acts. We will present all our findings to the proper authorities, in the sincere hope that justice will be done."

Outside, Jimmy Hoffa regaled his chorus of reporters as usual by flinging a cross-arm of defiance to the whole affair.

"Jimmy! Think this'll hurt your chances in Miami?"

"Well, that's what it was all about, wasn't it? But I'll tell you the truth. It won't have *any* effect! My people know what this is, it's a personal vendetta on the part of one man named Bobby Kennedy. He's embarrassed that I beat him up, fair and square, in court, and he's trying to make up for it with phony, trumped-up charges!"

"What about the thirty-three criminal acts?"

"Listen, if McClellan's got somethin' on me, let him get the authorities and throw me in jail. I'm waiting, brother! And he knows where he can find me. I'll be in Miami in September. And after that I'll be right there

171

across the street in Teamster Headquarters. As President!"

He posed for big-smile pictures at the open door of his waiting black Cadillac. Then a reporter asked, "What about George Meany's threat that if you're elected he'll throw the Teamsters out of the AFL-CIO?"

He snapped, "No comment!" and vanished.

John English was like his name: distinguished, lean, gracious. Now in his late sixties, English had been a Teamster for most of his life, more than fifty years, and the Secretary-Treasurer of the International since the forties. He had provided key, inside co-operation to the McClellan Committee in bringing about the downfall of Frank Brewster and the rest of the Dave Beck oligarchy. Now Robert Kennedy was calling upon him again.

They met at a bench in a small, lovely vest-pocket park in Washington. Bobby supplied the lunch: sandwiches wrapped in wax paper, apples, cartons of milk. John English said, "This was a most pleasant idea, Bob. I get so tired of all those stuffy restaurants."

"Strictly my pleasure, sir. When do you leave for the convention?"

"Oh, early. I'll be flying down this Thursday."

"I see. Do you like Florida?"

The stately, senior man's pale eyes crinkled with humor. "The place or the event? I like the place for brief visits, the sun's good for these stiff old bones. And I . . . Oh, yes, indeed I do like a convention! Not the razzle-dazzle and the excesses so much as seeing the whole great union out in force, in person. It can be a moving experience, like a parade. But that's not what you want to hear, is it, son."

"I'm afraid this year's carries very ominous overtones to it, John."

"Ominous? Hmm. I know all too well the misgivings you have about Jimmy Hoffa, Robert. But any troubles he might have had, well, chalk them up to the mistakes of youth. Wouldn't you appreciate such allowances to be made on your own behalf by your elders?"

172

Bob smiled, eating. "I appreciate the sentiment and the wisdom, certainly. But this particular situation is much too serious to—"

"Robert, please try to expand your vision somewhat. You hail from a long line of politicos—tell me, do you know what a 'bucket of coal' means?"

"I ought to. A bucket of coal and a Christmas turkey. When my grandfather was still a saloon-keeper, that was how you bought, well, that was how you established loyalties in the wards that—"

"Exactly. That would later be returned in the form of votes. Not such a bad system altogether, either. Even now, it's the wise Senator or Congressman who leaves his ivory tower on a regular basis and goes home to his constituency. Sees who needs a bucket of coal or a turkey. A nephew in the fire department. What do people want or need, after all? Not so very much. But pity you if they don't get it . . . or if you let somebody else arrange it for them."

"I understand that, John, but—"

"For instance, if I asked you to name the most lurid thing you can remember about Boston's own James Michael Curley, what would it be?"

Bob thought, then grinned. "I guess that he once got re-elected Mayor from behind prison bars!"

English chuckled. *"Bah!* I must say I find your accent refreshing, So that's the most lurid, hey? My, my. But think—what does that incident tell you?"

"Well, that . . . that the people mustn't have known or cared, I suppose."

"Hmm. Interesting. If you aren't going to eat that other half, could I have it? Thank you. Excellent ham and cheese, nice and fresh. *Or,* Robert, that the people loved the man more than they disapproved of his deeds. That's something you ought to give more consideration to. The human realities. They don't always align with the laws and principles in the libraries, but they are nonetheless *there,* Robert. And room must be made for them."

"That can lead to some pretty flexible morality, John."

"Let me try to put it another way, then. I've often said this before, of Beck, and soon I suppose I'll be

173

able to say it of Mr. Hoffa—and it's this: Hoffa and I could split Teamster headquarters in two, and each take a half, and the members wouldn't give a damn as long as we took care of them."

"That's cynical."

"I don't know if it's cynical, but it's true. Reflect a bit on all this, would you, Robert? Consider Jimmy Hoffa's good side, his better qualities . . . then consider the alternatives. Who else might we have?"

"Well, your own union is putting up Haggerty."

"He could win it, but he could never run it."

Exasperated, Bob got up and walked a small circle on the stone path. "Dammit, John, I appreciate your philosophies, I really do. But I have a hard time dealing with them. I have to deal with the nuts and bolts, and here they are—we're gathering evidence that the convention is rigged. More than half the delegates may have been selected illegally. Hoffa's got the Credentials Committee in his back pocket. There won't even be serious challenges to questionable delegates. Your wonderful Mr. Hoffa must not be so sure that his people love him so much! He's *fixing* it, John!"

"What . . . what proof do you . . . ?"

"We have some, we're getting more as fast as we can. So far it's all from your own people, John."

Blood reddened the gaunt face of John English. "Jimmy Hoffa is a great organizer. He's a great negotiator. The union contract is his Bible! Beck did nothing for this union. Jimmy will do everything!"

"He'll fill it with syndicate criminals!"

"No! He'll hold them off! He's the only one who knows how to deal with . . ."

"You're kidding yourself. You believe that because you want to. You want it to be true. Well, it isn't. don't think even he knows how deep he's in."

"He resents people like you trying to tell him what to do. That's all, Bob. *That's* why he fights you!"

"No, that's only part of it. And that's something *you* should consider." He sat down beside the wavering, befuddled man. "John, it has to be you. You have the name, the reputation, the esteem. You have the integrity to stop him. I only hope you have the courage."

174

The pale eyes watered. More to the trees than to Kennedy, he said, "I don't know. I don't know. I don't have much longer. My pension . . . I . . . fifty years I've given to . . . if I tried to go against it now, I . . . From our own people, you say?"

"Yes, sir." He bled for John English at the same time he was trying to pray, to will the decision and courage into the man's aging heart. Eddie Cheyfitz had called Dave Beck "the grand old man," but here now on the park bench, near to tears, sat the real grand old man of the Teamsters, sad and confused.

John English stood. He had folded his square of wax paper into a small, neat wad. He dropped it into a litter basket, turned, and extended his hand. Robert Kennedy shook it. John English said, "Thank you, Mr. Kennedy. For the lunch and for the advice. I . . . I will look into these matters. I'll try . . . I . . . Good-bye."

A thousand balloons dropped.

Tens of thousands of voices roared in the smokey air of the great Convention Hall in Miami.

Banners and signs and streamers moved wildly above the faces and shoulders of the solid, raucous crowd of delegates, alternates, families, friends, cronies, cheerleading girls in straw boaters.

Bugles and drums played against other drums and bugles.

Joe Curran of the National Maritime Union made a speech.

Harry Bridges of the International Longshoreman Workers Union gave a speech.

Then the International Secretary-Treasurer, John English, the grand old man of the Teamsters, made his way across the speakers' platform to the podium and waited for the din to die down. He waited a long time. HOFFA! HOFFA! HOFFA! HOFFA! came the chant. "H-A-double-G-E, R-T-Y spells Haggerty!" came the rival song. Whistles shrieked. Hands wouldn't stop clapping. Male and female voices shouted. Finally the raging ocean settled enough for his straining voice to be heard, and John English shouted, ". . . As Secretary-Treasurer of this great

175

union! But more importantly, as a dues-paying member for over fifty years! . . . I am pleased and proud to place in nomination the name of the next General President of the International Brotherhood of Teamsters! . . ."

But that was only inside.

One cabbie told the story: "So I get him to the hotel, and he gets right out, right? Now, I know it's him all the way from the airport. I say, 'Hiya, Jimmy,' and he says, 'How ya doin', brother!' And he's with all these guys—five-hundred-dollar suits! Jimmy pays it himself. I look, and it's a fin. Now the fare's four eighty, right? So I says, 'Hey, Jimmy, what's this? You're my goddamn boss and you give me twenty measly cents?' He laughs. 'Jeez, I thought it was a ten!' And then he slips me another ten on top of the five!"

Jimmy, of course, had come in from the airport in a black Cadillac limousine.

Just as many of the Teamsters had never seen the likes of Miami, so Miami had never seen quite the likes of the Teamsters. Some came like huge, lumberjack-shirted Paul Bunyans from the northern wilds; some slinked in lean and drawling from the West, looking like carnival workers: intricate belt buckles and bad teeth. Sunday suits couldn't hide the cap-and-denim-shirt look of city truckers, or the fatigue-jacket-and-wool-sweater bulk of the over-the-roaders.

"That whole fuckin' swan is made outa liver?"

"Champagne! Right out of the fountain!"

Doormen often "owned" the doors they opened at the high, modern, garish Beach hotels in this sort-of tropical kingdom of beachboys, gigolos, B-girls and C-girls and semi-pros. Many services were offered. One doorman related: "This was one of the zoot-suiters, not the trucker type at all. White-on-white shirt and packing, I'm sure of it, you could practically see the holster. Anyway, he crosses my palm and he wants 'Duh, a broad.' He'll go fifty bucks. So I take his room number and I call Evelyn. Do you know Evelyn? Well, she's absolutely marvelous, and her specialty is her chest. I mean, this girl has made

176

movies! And tonight she's wearing this *fabulous* halter affair! God knows where she ever found it, Frederick's of Hollywood or something! These enormous young jugs, and just one little hook in the front, well I mean! Such a hussy. To make a short story even shorter, though, she's back down in less than five minutes! And she's laughing her head off. I ask her what happened, and she said, 'Oh, this will kill you! I sashay into the room. He's already down to just his underwear. White boxer shorts, natch. And he's sitting waiting on the edge of the bed. I unfasten the little hook, out they shoot, and off he pops! He pays me the fifty, I rehook, and that's it.' 'Evelyn,' I told her, 'this has to make you the fastest *hooker* in town!' My God, where do they find these cretins?"

In his suite at the Eden Roc Hotel, Jimmy Hoffa was giving one of his many press conferences.

". . . And what's the main question to be resolved down here, Jimmy?"

Hoffa was glowing. "Whether it'll be a landslide or just a huge victory!"

All the reporters laughed with him. Farrell tried to interject, "There are committees meeting all over town. We have many involved, complicated platforms to construct that are—"

But they wanted to hear Hoffa.

"Who do you consider your real competition, Jimmy?"

"Well, they're saying this Haggerty, but I don't buy it."

"Why not?"

"Because I don't believe I have *any* competition!"

Big Clark Mollenhoff was there and asked, "Are you saying the election *is* fixed, Jimmy?"

Jimmy grinned. "Aw, look at that—I give the jimoke a straight line and he falls for it!" He hastened to smooth it over: "All right, let me put it to you this way. I feel I don't have any real heavy competition because my people know who and what they're voting for. They know I'm not one of these pot-bellied, cigar-smoking clowns who really want to represent the employers and the management in this country!

I'm one of them, one of the little guys behind the wheel, and they know I am! And they know that *I'm* the one that's willing and ready, anytime, to stand up to the bosses! To stand up to the corrupt politicians and what-have-you that try to use the Teamsters for a stepping-stone!"

"Is that a reference to the Kennedys, Jimmy?"

"Hey, listen, if the shoe fits . . . jump off a building in it!"

"Jimmy, one of your men told us it's all over but the looting. Do you—"

"That's a bum joke."

"Well, do you give Haggerty any chance, or are you going to steamroller?"

"What's Haggerty think?"

"The Haggerty people claim tremendous delegate strength in the East, and that forty percent of the South is already committed to them."

Jimmy shot a look to Sandy, who smugly shook his head no. Then Jimmy scoffed, "South what? South Salt Lake? They're suckin' wind!"

Mollenhoff pressed: "What about the suit filed by the New York delegates?"

"Wimps! You always get a buncha winners. They're just crybabies who didn't get picked to come to the convention, so they went weeping to Bobby Kennedy instead."

"But the judge who heard their case voted to have this convention stopped, Jim."

"Dammit, Clark, play straight with me! The *Appeal* judge, overruled that decision! You forgot to mention that, huh? That whole thing was nonsense! Tears from sore losers, and sour grapes! Look, all of ya. I'll win this convention. Not because it's fixed, because it isn't. I'll win because the competition is lousy. Simple as that. It's lousy now, and it'll always be lousy when it runs against Hoffa—because *Hoffa works!* And I don't mean like Ex-Lax."

He pointed to the wide picture windows of his suite. "See that town out there? All them lights and honkytonks and hotel rooms and all? Well, I'll tell ya somethin'—while all the other guys are out there pattin' backs and shakin' hands and slingin' the bull-

178

shit around, and gettin' snockered and stayin' out all night and makin' each other promises they can't keep —know where I am? I ain't out there! I'm up here, and I'm thinkin' of new ways to win! And I'm on them phones! Convention or no convention, I'm talkin' contracts, and I'm talkin' to truckers who need me all over this country! And by the time all them blowhards and backslappers and drunks away from home for the first time go crawlin' back into bed at three, four in the mornin', they lost and they don't know it! I got 'em licked! It's *all over!* No contest! Because I work at it, and they don't know how ta even start!"

Only Mollenhoff wasn't too impressed to ask, "Then you're not worried about Kennedy any more, either?"

"Never was! He did his best, and Hoffa's still walkin'!" Then he turned almost ecclesiastical and solemnly pronounced, "It's all in the hands of the rank and file now. I'll leave my future to them."

Downstairs, one of those rank-and-file delegates, from Tamworth, New Hampshire, was telling his counterpart from Sweetwater, Texas: "And when this here dancah got down to her brasiair, damned if she didn't strip the thing off and was a goddamn *boy!*"

Kennedy was home in Hickory Hill, Virginia, telling one of his children, "All right, but hating a teacher's guts isn't reason enough to quit school, especially in the middle of a class. Now, I know how you feel, and it'll be rough, but tomorrow you'll have to just go to her and—"

"Phone, Bob—LaVerne!"

"LaVerne, hi, wait—Either shut up in there or I'll turn that thing off! If you're not going to watch it, leave the room! For God's sake, Ethel! Sorry, LaVerne, what have you got?"

"An informant, Bob!"

"Fantastic. Reliable?"

"Total. We're right—the Credentials Committee's a hoax. Total setup. Turning out Hoffa delegates like cookies."

"Can we prove it?"

"You tell me. We need the Committee's minutes."

"Hoover can do that. I'll get him."

"Tell him it's got to happen very fast, Bob. Hoffa's practically— Who's English going to nominate?"

"I don't know, LaVerne. I just don't know. Goodbye."

Ron Ahrens, a Midwest business representative and alternate delegate, sat at the bar of the Silver Seahorse drinking rye-and-gingers with water backups and imagining what he would do, if he got the chance, to the pink-haired girl above him on the stage, sweating and fingering her naked nipples to the thrums of *Bolero*. Of course, probably nothing would happen to him again tonight. You couldn't just go up to girls like her. And he hated the idea of offering money, but goddamn, he was getting randy! Maybe he should've brought Ginny along after all. Damn sunburn he got on the back of his legs wasn't doing him much good either. Maybe there was some signal you were supposed to give. Maybe the bartender. They were supposed to go all the way down to the bare hair and then some in this place. God, if that girl ever did that, he'd just . . . And damn, when would he ever get to a town like this again?

"Seven and a half minutes," the girl five stools away was telling the man pretending to be a magazine writer. That was her average time in a john's room when she worked the hotels. She'd give a guy the eye. If he responded, she'd go over and say, "Want a date?" If he did she'd tell him twenty dollars and ask for his room number. He'd go up, then she'd follow. "Blow jobs. That's all they all want. Haven't had my pants off in two years on the job. Just the suck. What they can't get at home, I guess. I don't care, makes it easy. Listerine's cheap. It's the ones who want to kiss and ask questions that slow you down and cut your income. I love the truckers. Big, dumb, and drunk. God, I could spend my life at Teamster conventions!"

In the Eden Roc, Jimmy Hoffa was just snapping out of a long stare at nothing. Mack Stenn was sitting silently on a sofa. Sandy Farrell was having a Scotch. Jimmy had been mulling two things: the

Presidency and Bobby Kennedy. It was so close he could taste it now. Yes, he wanted it and bad. But what guys like Kennedy could never get through their skulls was that he didn't want it for what Beck had, or even Tobin. That making believe you were some kind of Governor or Chairman of the Board or whatever was bullshit. And it wasn't even the bucks, either. Hell, there were a thousand ways to turn a dollar— every American citizen, union leader or not, had the Constitutional right to invest or otherwise make a profit in business, and nobody in the world had the right to dictate to you that you couldn't. No, no, what none of them could see was that the Teamsters was the greatest union in the world, with the greatest guys in the world in it! But it was like some big baby. Like some innocent girl. It was always in danger. The gold-smellers came at it from all directions. It could be raped, picked clean and thrown away, stripped, used and left lying in a million pieces. It needed somebody who knew how to keep it building, keep getting the more and the better for every member, while at the same time handling the wolves and vultures. You couldn't pretend they weren't there. You couldn't throw stones and expect them to go away. You had to know how, and he *did,* goddammit! How many times did he have to prove it? Why couldn't they understand that he was the only one who could pull it all off?

He tried to figure what he'd do if he were Kennedy. He'd flood the place with FBI investigators, just like he was doing. What else? He picked up the phone and didn't dial, just listened. Then he hung it up and yelled, "Mack, go over this joint with a fine-tooth comb!"

Stenn obeyed.

Sandy Farrell sighed. "It's already been done twice, Jim."

"Do it twice more! It's fuckin' bugged and I know it!"

"All right, Jimmy, all right."

"You don't believe me? You think I'm goin' ants? Pick up that phone and tell me you don't hear a click!"

The three of them went through the suite again,

181

fingering lampshades, drapes, the undersides of tables; they looked under rugs and beds and into air vents and the air-conditioning units. In the bedroom, Jimmy snapped his fingers and threw open his closet. "I'm crazy, huh? Well, come here and check this suit!"

Sandy did.

"Smell it!"

Sandy smelled it.

"Waddaya call that?"

"Dry-cleaning fluid? I don't know, it—"

"Bullshit, drycleaning fluid! It's a special powder. I read about it. FBI's got this special electronic device. I wear this suit, they know where I go from a mile away! Maybe they can even hear what I say off it, I don't know. Well, okay! They wanna play that game? Mack!"

"Yeah, chief."

"Get a driver, and put this fuckin' suit in a car to Chicago! . . . Yeah—nonstop ta Chicago, tonight! Let the fuckin' FBI sneaks tell Hoover and Kennedy they're hot on my trail ta Chicago! Ha! That'll fix the bastards!" Now, he thought—what else? "Keep searchin', Sandy. And you get right back up here, Mack. I gotta think. I gotta think!" Mack made a call and left with the suit.

An unusual number of young Registered Nurses always found their way to Miami Beach. With so many retired people there, hospital and private-duty work was plentiful, but it was more than that: for young, fresh females who were not show-business types or worse, life could be enjoyed at a very attractive level. There were very many wealthy men in the market for pretty, "nice" dinner and gambling and sailing and dancing and nightclubbing and swimming and tennis and drinking and golf and flying partners. These lonely men tended to act fatherly, and only rarely made much in the way of physical demands. Nursing never paid better than minimum sustenance; what was wrong with providing some poor old geezer an evening's or a day's companionship in return for dining well and having some expensive fun?

And besides, the "real" Miami crowd was such a

ball. The doormen and beachboys, strippers, waiters, cocktail waitresses and all were such a gas to hang around with. They worked nights mostly, as did most nurses, and what made it easy for the nurses to enter this lively society was, of course, their access to the more interesting drugs. Amphetamines, for instance, weren't even called "speed" yet; and amyl nitrate was almost as available as adhesive tape. The Beach was an advanced bunch, and kicky.

As I rule, nurses stayed home when any real, big-noise conventions hit town; they weren't among the girls one saw at bars and around pools. Lucy Smithers, from Sioux Falls and Geriatrics, was an exception. Her beachboy had become an addict. To make ends meet, Lucy had had to stretch a few customs here and there. She began accepting tips from grateful families and patients at the hospital, and gifts of clothes and jewelry from generous dining partners. One desperate weekend, guided by an experienced chum from the Beach, she turned a trick at the Fountainbleau. She hated the pawing, but he came in two seconds and it was the easiest fifty dollars she'd ever made. She never let herself fall into the habit, but from time to time . . . and this was one of those times. She spotted Ron Ahrens in the Silver Seahorse and took the stool next to his.

Slugger, Phil, Andy, and Zeke had one suite; Everett, Pete, Tom, and Bill had the adjoining one. They had opened the connecting door, so they had practically a basketball court to run around in, with beds, couches, chairs, music, bathtubs full of beer and ice, desktops loaded with liquor and setups. Jo, Helen, Wendy, Phyllis, the one with the garters, Georgette, Candida, and the other one seemed born to party. They were dancing around and sitting on laps, singing, pushing boobs into mouths, drinking, laughing, grabbing meat. Georgette was wearing Ev's cowboy hat. Candida had been busy with Zeke before and now was in a corner with Slugger, giving him her full attention. Tom was singing dirty to Jo in a corner. Phil had passed out sitting on the hopper.

183

Ron Ahrens's heart was drumming; his knees felt as if he were going into a fight. He unlocked his hotel-room door and let Lucy go in first. She smelled like flowers. He'd make believe she had pink hair. She was quick, but that was okay. And God, she didn't wear a panty girdle! He hated panty girdles, though he'd never tell Ginny, it would hurt her feelings. He hated trying to peel it off, hated even watching her squeeze out of it. But this red-hot little baby wore just white little things with lace—and she was tanned almost black, but not there or there!

"Broads!" Jimmy Hoffa announced. Mack Stenn looked up in disbelief. Sandy Farrell just stared. "I bet they're usin' all them women out there as spies!" Hoffa divined. "Get on them phones! I want the word out right now! No messin' with any bimbos! Them whores are paid off! I want every swingin' dick at this convention to get the word—Hoffa says anyone, and I mean *anyone,* gets caught foolin' with a dame is outta work *permanent!*"

Mack started calling.

Sandy pleaded gingerly. "Jimmy, that's crazy. We can't—"

"Do what I told you, or you're out too!"

Sandy started calling. He used their network: from the top down, key men had lists of numbers, then each of those numbers had a list.

Ron Ahrens's phone rang within ten minutes; he was still only at third base. It sounded to him like an act of God, like a call from home. He whimpered, "Oh no, no."

Candida passed Slugger the phone. "Are you shittin' me?" His face fell. "Jesus Christ . . . Yeah, yeah, all right, all *right!*" He hung up. "Party's over, you Kennedy whores! Out."

Like General Patton in Italy, Jimmy Hoffa moved through the Eden Roc lobby on his way to the convention floor. He was mobbed by adoring well-wishers. Laughing, he called many by name. Clark Mollenhoff stepped out of the crowd. Jimmy said, "Hey, poison-pen! Happy day for you, huh?"

"What do you think of the coalition, Jim?"

"What coalition?"

"Haggerty, Lee, and Hickey. They're talking about pooling their delegates against—"

"That desperate, huh?"

John English at the podium was building to his pay-off: ". . . The name of the next General President of the International Brotherhood of Teamsters! The man with the most guts in America, *Mr. James R. Hoffa!*"

As Jimmy walked to him across the stage, white socks flashing, the sea of people erupted with hurricane force: HOFFA! HOFFA! HOFFA! HOFFA! HOFFA! John English took Jimmy's hand, held it aloft as a referee holds a winner's, and yelled into the mike: "I love this little fella—I love him!"

HOFFA! HOFFA! HOFFA! . . . Jimmy saw no reason to end it too quickly. He waited, smiling, pointing down to faces he recognized in the closest rows. "Good to see ya, Lonny! . . . Hey, Crackers, what you doin' here? . . . Dolobowski, they takin' care of ya? . . ."

Finally he tapped the mike and raised his arms for quiet. "All right, thank you. . . . All right now— you're all big boys with big voices, now calm down and let a little guy talk!"

A voice broke clear: "C'mon, Jimmy, let's get this election over with!"

Jimmy laughed. "Oh no, no way—we do this thing accordin' to Hoyle! No one's gonna accuse *this* convention of not bein' democratic!"

At Hickory Hill, the news was coming on. Bob was reading Dr. Seuss with only one eye on the page: "'. . . Then over the housetops and trees of Katroo, You see that bird coming! To you. *Just to you!* That Bird pops—' Oh, hold it, guys, I wanna hear this." He jounced the little girl from his lap and rolled forward onto his knees, his face up close to the screen. Another kid mounted him like a horse.

The announcer was reading: ". . . And in Miami today, Jimmy Hoffa, Labor's controversial firebrand, was elected President of the International . . ."

"Goddammit!"

"Mama! Daddy said goddamn!"

"I did not. Ssh!"

". . . Brotherhood of Teamsters. In his address to the Convention, Hoffa said . . ."

Suddenly Jimmy's face filled the tube, not three inches away from Bobby's.

"I have no fight with the McClellan Committee! But! When a Congressional committee concentrates on a personal attack or misuses its power, it can be *dangerous!* For *all* of us!"

Ethel watched from the doorway.

Jimmy went on, "Something is wrong when a man may be judged guilty in a court of public opinion because some enemy or some ambitious person . . ."

"That's your father he's talking about, children."

". . . Accuses him of wrongdoing by *hearsay* or *inference!* . . ."

Bob gladly ran to answer the phone. It was reporter Fletcher Knebel, asking, "Any comment on Hoffa's address, Bob?"

"I was just watching it, I only caught part of—"

"Well, he's claiming that Senator McClellan sent telegrams to Teamsters officials in Miami saying that most of the delegates might not have been legally chosen. Is that true?"

"Is which true?" He had to dodge and hedge. This wasn't the call he'd been praying for. The other hadn't come yet. He said, "Uh, Fletch, lemme just say that situation will be clarified in a short period of time."

"You saying I should hang in down here?"

"Ah, that might be a good idea, yes, Fletch. 'Bye."

"Every party has a pooper, that's why we invited you, party pooper, party pooper," some drunks in Jimmy Hoffa's packed suite started singing at the somber-looking intruder at the door. Jimmy wasn't taking it so lightly. The man was an FBI agent, interrupting the victory celebration to say, "It's my duty to inform you, Mr. Hoffa, that the minutes of the Credentials Committee have been subpoenaed. Agents from our Miami office are now trying to—"

Jimmy barked, "Let's go!" to Sandy and Mack, and

186

they pushed past the agent, heading for another floor at the Eden Roc. The agent followed.

The Teamster official in charge of the suite housing the Credentials Committee was trying to hide the smile on his face as he told a second FBI man, "I'm sorry, but a terrible accident has happened. A tragedy. I'm afraid I couldn't give you the Committee's minutes even if I wanted to."

"Why not?"

"One of the hotel's maids was cleaning up in here, and by mistake she took them along with a bunch of other stuff. We ran after her as soon as we discovered it, of course, but we were too late."

Jimmy and company arrived. His man threw him a wink, and he relaxed.

The agent said, "What do you mean, too late?"

The Teamster shrugged sadly. "She had already thrown all her refuse down the incinerator chute. There was nothing we could do."

LaVerne Duffy came running up the hall in time to hear this last and said, "Which chute did she use?"

The Teamster came out into the hall and led the way to a wall chute. "This one."

Hoffa said, "What a shame. Burned to a crisp."

The first FBI agent grinned. "Are you sure it was this chute, sir?"

"Positive."

"This is a laundry chute, sir."

Duffy yelped a war cry and ran to the elevators, followed by the two agents, then by Jimmy Hoffa and his people.

In the Eden Roc's basement, the agents scavenged through the laundry bin, gathering the papers together. Duffy examined them and smiled into Jimmy Hoffa's stone face. "They're all here." He passed them to the FBI. "Good night, Mr. Hoffa."

When they were gone, the Teamster official stuttered, "I, I'm sorry, Mr. Hoffa, I thought . . ."

Without looking up from the cement floor, Hoffa said, "You're through, fired. Get out of my sight."

"But I tried, Jimmy, I—"

"*Now! Out!*"

Sandy walked the broken man to the elevator, arm around his shoulder, whispering something to him.

When he was back, Hoffa said thinly, "How do you like that. My first act as President is to fire some poor little jerk!"

Their voices echoed harshly off the concrete walls of the dark empty corridors.

"Sandy? The minutes. How bad can that be?"

"Bad, Jimmy. It can constitute hard evidence that—"

"Spell it out."

"We can fight it in the courts, but they might be able to bar you from taking office."

In the lobby, LaVerne Duffy dropped a dime in a pay phone and asked for the Hickory Hill number. "Yes, operator. Collect."

Jimmy was punching the heap of dirty laundry. "That bastard! That son of a bitch! He's taking it away from me! He's trying to take my union. Well, I ain't gonna let him! I'll see that little fucker *dead* before I—"

"Easy, Jimmy," Sandy warned.

Mack Stenn stayed apart, staring into the gloom.

Jimmy quit yelling. He straightened away from the bin and said to the empty, damp corridor, "I'll see him in a coffin first." He started walking. "Him and his brother both!"

BOOK FOUR

The War

Luckily, Judge F. Dixon Letts had already left his Washington courtroom and closed the door to his chambers before Jimmy Hoffa snapped out of his shock and screamed, "You're bought! They paid you off! The Kennedys got to you!"

Eddie Cheyfitz and Sandy Farrell urged him to regain control of himself, but it was difficult. His rage was understandable: Judge Letts had just announced, "Due to the evidence placed before me, I have but one recourse. The question of tampering with a free election, and violating the Teamsters' constitution, is a matter that will have to be decided in a court of law. In the interim. I am barring Mr. Hoffa from taking office as President of the International Brotherhood of Teamsters."

It was all he wanted in his life. He had won it, and now they were taking it away from him. His bride was being carried off the altar and locked away in a tower.

He was being attacked from all sides. On October 24, 1957, twenty-nine labor leaders, including Walter Reuther, gathered around the great table in the AFL-CIO Executive Council Hearing Room.

George Meany presided. "The final vote is twenty-five to four," he declared. "The measure is passed." Looking past Hoffa, he said, "Take this message back to your union, Mr. English—if Jimmy Hoffa continues as an officer on any level in your union, the Teamsters will be expelled from the AFL-CIO. We will then—"

"Button that lip, Meany!" Jimmy exploded. They had tried to ignore him at their peril. "You're just afraid Kennedy'll start investigatin' *you!* And I'll tell you somethin' else—we have more dues-paying members in the Teamsters than you have in all your two-bit unions put together! We don't need you, you need us! You don't have the guts to expel the Teamsters—your rank and file will never permit it, and you know it!"

He left the table. English, Farrell, and the other Teamster vice-presidents moved away with him. From the door he added, "You unload us? Hell, the Teamsters'll unload *you . . . all* of you! Then where'll you be?"

But the pressure was getting to him. Outside, a flock of waiting reporters were amazed when he so uncharacteristically turned his venom on them: "No comment, I said! Don't you understand? Then I'll arrange your education—there'll be no statement! That's it, brother, *no statement!* Period!" He slammed the black Cadillac's door behind him.

His closest associates rallied. The instinctive, deep-seated loyalty he had shown them over the long, tough years was returned to him in this time of crisis. Jimmy had a favorite restaurant in Washington, a small steak place near the Woodner Hotel. Eddie Cheyfitz and Sandy Farrell thought it would be a cheerful setting. They had some news to spring on their boss, and a proposition that required as much delicacy as they could arrange. The tension entered the restaurant with them. The place had been renovated since any of them had dined there last. Jimmy Hoffa was a man who had once walked himself, his wife, and his two children out of the Copacabana in New York because he found the floor show offensive. Eddie and Sandy were dismayed to discover that the simple eatery had overnight been transformed into a mock Merry Olde England Taverne, complete with waitresses costumed as wenches—if wenches' dresses ever ended at their crotches, with bosoms displayed like bread on platters. Hoffa seemed not to notice, and ordered his usual evening steak as habitually as he ordered his cold crab or lobster for lunch.

Sandy said, "You tell him, Eddie."

Eddie told him. "Jimmy, we've worked a deal with Letts."

"A good deal or what?"

"Mostly good. He'll accept a three-man Board of Monitors to oversee your operations as President!"

He kept scowling, but they could see some brightness return at last to his eyes. "Be thankful for small favors, huh?"

"It's better than staying barred, Jimmy."

"Mostly good. What's the hook?"

"Well, none, really—except you're not exactly used to working with three overseers sitting on your shoulder."

"I'll survive. Can we get control?"

"Well, we can certainly try to neutralize. Get at least one good member on the board. But I wouldn't bet the ranch."

"Monitors, huh? How'll they get paid, who'll pay 'em?"

"Well . . . that's funny, we never thought . . . I guess the union will."

"Of which I'm the President, right? There's your neutralization, gents, get to work on that. Yeah, I guess I can live with that all right."

The three shared their first good laugh in a long time.

"Jesus, Jimmy, you sure go straight to the bone."

"They call this bread? Look at that, like sponge for cryin' out loud!"

"Well, at least they heat it up."

"It'll sit like a ball in your stomach."

Cheyfitz and Farrell exchanged leery glances. It wasn't easy to soften up a guy who never drank and critiqued the bread. Again, Eddie took the task. "Jimmy, there's something else we want to talk to you about."

"Couple a busy little bees you two are turnin' into, huh? What's on your minds?"

"Well, Jimmy, you might call it your image."

"Don't start on the socks again."

"No, no, it's, uh, more important than anything like that. we think," Sandy said.

Eddie said, "Jimmy, we don't have to tell you how

everything's coming down on your head lately. You're under very serious fire from all points of the compass."

"So I noticed."

"Well, you're President now, monitors or no monitors, and whether Bobby Kennedy likes it or not. But with Meany and Reuther getting blowy, the whole world's going to be watching you . . . You with me, Jimmy?"

"I'm listenin'."

"How's your steak? It looks perfect. Mine's—"

"Will you can it! If you got somethin' to say, say it."

"Jimmy, you have to start coming off classier. A pillar of propriety. A leader who's doing something about all the criticism."

"You've got to start getting the powers off your back."

"Doing what somethin'?"

"You've got to clean some house."

"I don't *got* to anything. Tell me without the *gots* in it."

"Jimmy," Eddie said, "please, get rid of some of the hard cases. Just one ex-con in a few big cities, nobody you'll miss. It'll do wonders for your name, and for the face of the Teamsters. All the big lights are on us, and you—"

He pointed his fork at Cheyfitz's nose. "Who do you think you are, firing people out of the Teamsters! I don't do that for nobody! I don't forget my friends, I don't care who they are or what they done!"

"That was all right before, Jimmy. Not now."

"Eddie's right, Jim."

"My ass he's right."

"Think about it for a minute, Jimmy," Eddie reasoned. "Look, a Federal Court is ordering you to clean up your union. You've got a Board of Monitors sampling your breakfast every morning, watching you shave."

"It's the perfect cover, Jim."

"Exactly! It's an umbrella. Who's going to blame you for unloading under that kind of heat? They'll know you had no choice! And as I said, just a token shakedown will do the trick. Ten, maybe a dozen heavy-hitters, that's all."

"But I do have a choice, and my choice is no! You guys don't know what the fuck you're talkin' about!"

"Jimmy, you're making a tragic mistake."

"I don't desert people I . . . I don't desert my friends!"

Eddie added, "Jimmy, this could be the biggest mistake you ever made."

It seemed to be the last straw. Hoffa was red. He threw his fork down. He signaled for the waitress to bring the bill. He wiped his mouth, then pitched the napkin onto his half-eaten food on the plate. When the girl came over he turned on her. "Why don't you go put some clothes on! Cover yourself up! Shame on you!" Other patrons were staring and listening now, but he didn't care. "If you belonged to my union, you wouldn't have to wear slutty costumes like that! If you were a Teamster, you wouldn't have to shame yourself like some two-dollar whore!"

Sandy Farrell tipped her extravagantly, then hurried outside to try to catch up with Eddie and their enraged leader.

It was Robert Barney Baker's turn to face chief counsel Robert Kennedy at the McClellan Committee. The 325-pound Baker was an ex-convict, Mob confidant, and roving, strong-arm Teamster "organizer" for Jimmy Hoffa. Mr. Baker's demeanor on the witness stand was in ironic contrast to his reputation and awesome enormity. He was polite, respectful, good-humored anything but violent.

"And Connie Noonan?" RFK asked. "Do you know Connie Noonan?"

"I know him, yes, sir, I do."

"He's a friend of yours?"

"Yes, sir."

"And Eddie McGrath?"

"Well, I didn't know Eddie too well."

"Did you also know Cockeyed Dunn?"

"I didn't know him as Cockeyed Dunn. I knew him as John Dunn."

"Where is he now?"

"He has met his Maker."

"How did he do that?"

"I believe through electrocution," Barney Baker said gently, "in the City of New York, or the State of New York."

Kennedy waited for the light laughter to end. "And what about Squint Sheridan? Did you know him?"

"Are you talking of Andrew Sheridan, sir?"

"Yes."

"He has also met his Maker."

"How did he die?"

"With Mr. John Dunn," Barney Baker explained solemnly. "In New York. As a guest of the State."

The Caucus Room found this hilarious. Senator McClellan had to employ his gavel once again.

There was football again that Saturday at Hickory Hill, live on the lawn in the morning, then on TV in the afternoon. Jack gave Bob the high sign. They left Dave Thatcher, Kenny O'Donnell, Salinger, and the others to the game, got beers out of the kitchen, then went walking out around Bob's yard. Jack kidded him. "Ever think of raking this place?"

"Ah, it'd just encourage the rest to fall, then we'd have winter."

"Good point. Saw Eddie Cheyfitz."

"And?"

"Oh, you know Eddie. His line this season is that Hoffa's been wanting to get rid of the hoods all along —not that there are *that* many! And now that he's got the Presidency we'll start seeing it happen. Of course, unfairly strapped, we must understand . . ."

"By the Board of Monitors. Ha! Would that it were true. Jimmy's got too many IOU's being waved in his face. He couldn't clean house now if he wanted to, which he doesn't. What's the word among your fellow nobles?"

"That's getting a bit shaky, I'm afraid. You have to admit, our Republican friends have been patient and co-operative up to—"

"Now what's the bitch?"

"Oh, that maybe it's time to leave Hoffa for a while and start casting our nets in other waters. You know what that means."

"Meany and Reuther."

195

"Yup. And there are rumblings too that maybe you're getting too far afield."

"Bullshit!"

"It is starting to look like a police lineup."

"But it's connected! I'm not hauling people up there for the hell of it. It's all Teamster business. You tell them that, don't you?"

Jack laughed. "I tell them what I've been telling them so long, I can't stand to hear it any more."

"You're not your brother's keeper."

"It was a pretty neat line for a while. Too bad."

"You'll think of another. Have Ted write you one."

"*Do* you see a pattern in all of it, Bob?"

"Yes, and I'm glad we're alone. Anytime I mention it to somebody else they start mumbling about overwork and go for the straitjackets. I'm convinced, Jack. Call it syndicate, call it the Mob, or whatever, there is such a thing as organized crime in this country, and it's taking a big bite out of every dollar every guy brings home Friday night."

"Can you prove it?"

"Not yet."

"Your friend J. Edgar Hoopla denies it outright, did you know that?"

"That should be proof enough right there!"

"Now, now."

"Dammit, Jack, that's half the problem. The Justice Department is a joke. Last year they completed only twenty-five prosecutions against organized crime. Twenty goddamn five, when there should have been hundreds, thousands! And of the twenty-five, know how many they won?"

"Half?"

"Two."

"Christ."

"Yeah. Fucking Eisenhower's off playing golf, and Hoover's chasing bank robbers like it was nineteen twenty-seven or something!"

"All right, but you and I are operating inside nothing more than a Senate Select Committee on Labor. If there is such a thing as organized—"

"There is."

"If you say so, I'll believe it, and I'll argue your

case before the Committee. But it's only a Committee, and we don't even have a decent budget yet. But you have to admit one thing."

"What?"

"It's a hell of a lot of fun."

"Fun. Like hell it's fun. Now I know Hoffa's only the tip of the iceberg. There's just so much more to do!"

"Don't worry, Bob—legislation will come out of this."

"That the damned Justice Department will sit on!"

"It's like Satan, isn't it. Like Lucifer."

"What is?"

"The underworld, or whatever you want to call it. Its greatest strength is our denial of its existence."

"My God, you're right—even to the making it funny. How could there be this jerk in red underwear, horns and a tail and a pitchfork? And what is it that makes us kind of laugh when you mention gangsters and mobsters and all that?"

"Perfect cover."

"Yeah, except they *are* real, and anything but funny."

Through the Committee, they both knew now some of the stark realities behind the masks: that over ten million dollars of union funds had been stolen, embezzled, or misused by union officials in a fifteen-year period, involving gangster infiltration of seven unions and domination of some fifty jukebox, vending-machine, and garbage-collection companies.

"It's evil," Bob said.

Jack grinned. "Indeed it is . . . Ahab."

"Oh God, did you read that too?"

"I wonder if Hoffa knows what Moby Dick is. It didn't really bother you, did it?"

Bob shrugged. "No. It was always clear to me that *somebody* had to get that damned whale."

November, 1957.

Sergeant Edgar Crosswell of the New York State Police walked sleepily from his patrol car to the office of the Mountainside Motel. "Morning, Nancy."

"Morning, Ed."

197

He didn't notice the unusual flush in her cheeks. He said, "Nice nip in the air."

"Yup. Foliage is staying real late this year. Lovely."

"Well, I got some fella going around writing checks on money he don't have—can I have a look at your registry?"

"You surely can!" She turned the ledger book around on the desk for him. "I been dying to show somebody!"

Crosswell looked, and his eyes popped.

She pointed to the window behind her. "Look at that parking lot!"

Filling the rear parking lot were more shiny new black Cadillacs and Lincoln Continentals than Ed Crosswell had ever seen before in his life.

Nancy gushed, "You'd think we were opening a car dealer's, wouldn't you?"

"They sure as hell ain't hunters! What in the hell, Nancy?"

She told him all she knew, and to Sergeant Crosswell it was the sweetest, most exciting music his ears had ever received. He gasped, "Barbara!" and ran for his car.

They had begun arriving the evening before, Nancy said. Some had already driven up to Joseph Barbara's house. She had overheard—that was where they were all going.

Year in, year out, Appalachin, New York, a little north of the Pennsylvania line in the center of the state, was a pretty quiet beat for an officer of the law. For twenty-odd years, Edgar Crosswell had fought boredom by keeping alive a single hunch he had: that Mr. Joseph Barbara, wealthy owner of a local soft-drink bottling plant, was more than he appeared to be. Crosswell knew Barbara carried a gun, knew that he was involved in at least two murder cases, and was pretty sure he'd gotten his start as a bootlegger during Prohibition. Crosswell had never stopped watching him, sure in his heart that he'd live to see the day Barbara would make a false move. He'd see it, and he'd be there. Radioing for assistance, he could barely control his voice. This, whatever in God's creation it was, *was it!*

Meanwhile, Barbara's guests were arriving at his home. Aside from the fact that a hundred limousine-riding men could hardly expect to come together unnoticed in such a tiny town, it was an idyllic setting for this congress. Barbara's estate was large, roomy, elegantly appointed and lushly landscaped, complete with a long, wide circular driveway that climbed from a heavy, ornate gate and opened at the front of the house into a parking area ample enough even for such a huge fleet of luxurious motorcars. The two guards at the entrance knew Mack Stenn and passed him inside with only friendly touches of welcome. He wore a pearl-gray fedora. Mr. Barbara greeted him as he did all the attending notables: "My home is your home." There was food and drink fit for emperors. Mack circulated through the spacious rooms busy with men, extending his greetings, paying his respects and being introduced to his fellow guests.

Carlo Gambino, the "Boss of Bosses," was there, as were the Falcone brothers from New York, Vito Genovese from New Jersey, James Colletti from Colorado, Russell Bufalino of Pennsylvania. To Frank Tanella of Florida, Mack said, "Hey, look at the tan, we should all live in Key West, eh?"

Tanella laughed. "A suit like that I could never find in Key West!"

"Ho, so you get it in Havana, come on!"

"No, Mack, not even in Havana—what is this, silk, but not silk either! Beautiful."

This was Mafia. This was Cosa Nostra. This was a special meeting of the "National Commission." There would be very serious business discussed, but not until the personal and social amenities of brotherhood had been properly enjoyed.

One indirect beneficiary of Joseph Barbara's largesse was Lou Felippa, proprietor of Appalachin's Main Street Fish Store. He left the Barbara kitchen's rear door and danced up into the cab of his delivery truck, whistling. He had catered some affairs in his time, a few in fact for Barbara, but this? Nobody'd believe it. He jump-started his truck in second, rolling down the incline of the service entrance, then swung up and around to intersect with the main driveway.

He had just begun to brake for the gateway when the space suddenly filled with two State Police cars screaming in from the public road. Lou thought they were only the first two of what must be a convoy. He sent his brake pedal to the floorboard, whipped his truck into a tight U-turn on the pebbled drive, and roared speeding back up to the main house.

He started yelling out his window before skidding to a stop at the front door: "Police! Cops!" The guards disappeared inside. Felippa made bold enough to follow them in, still sounding his frantic cries of "Police! There's cops all over the place! They're comin' in from everywhere!"

For most of the guests, instincts reacted faster than brains. Some sixty-three princely-dressed Mafiosi dropped their drinks and plates and evacuated the premises at once. They ran through doors, they jumped out of windows. Outside, they scattered, running stiff-shoed across lawns, making for the apparent safety of the woods surrounding Barbara's grounds. Silk suits plunged into briar patches.

Sergeant Crosswell stood gape-jawed in the open door of his patrol car. Was there a fire in the house? His men also watched the stampede: they were one patrolman and two agents of the Treasury Department's Alcohol and Tobacco Tax Unit. Edgar had called them in, figuring this mysteriously huge conclave might have some connection to Barbara's wartime conviction for illegal sugar.

Inside, forty cooler and wiser heads had prevailed, including those of Vito Genovese, Carlo Gambino, Mack Stenn, Vincent Cisco, and assorted other powers and their lieutenants. They simply stayed put, knowing they were invited guests having a meeting on private property; they could have been Elks or Lions or a Holy Name Society.

"Christ A'mighty, I can't believe my eyes!"

"I said it before. Big meetings a mistake."

"Friggin' assholes!"

"Joseph, ask the policemen to come in for a drink or else go away."

"Yes, Godfather."

"One thing. We have lost our quorum."

200

"Jesus, Mary, and Joseph!"

"Shitheads!"

"Well, we can discuss at least."

Informally, then, they exchanged their views on at least three pressing issues: the meeting to their future operations of the Narcotics Control Act of 1956 ("A judge gotta hand down the minimum. Profit's not worth the gamble."); the recent shooting of Frank Costello and assassination of Albert Anastasia and Frank Scalise ("Mean big changes."); and various increased pressures being felt as the result of the aggressiveness of the McClellan Committee's investigations and hearings.

Vincent Cisco said, "Mack, here, now—Mack, we should tell you, we are sorry about the troubles you are having. You are a good man. But soon, well, I am afraid your trouble is becoming our trouble. They are starting the investigating of the vending and the construction on the East coast, the olive oil and the cheese down South, the laundry and the bakery in the West. In Pennsylvania and New York, of course, it's the garments, this Anthracite Workers scam is coming apart . . ."

"This Kennedy," another senior voice put in, "is coming to be a pebble in the shoe! When you start to walk, it hurts."

"I think he must be stupid, is all. This singling out of Hoffa. This kind of encounter. This can be very delicate. He must know this."

"But he's young yet, and too ambitious, that's all. He wants to make good deeds that make good headlines."

"Yes, he'll grow up soon."

"He better."

"But what if he doesn't?"

"So?" Vincent Cisco said. "What do you do to the pebble in your shoe?"

God knows what Sergeant Crosswell would have done about the situation if the Scattering of the Sixty hadn't happened. As it was, he simply withdrew from Joseph Barbara's property, marshaled sufficient help, and staked out the surrounding highways and byways. Eventually, out they all came. From the fields and meadows, forests, swamps, and glens, the men in the suits came staggering, soiled, wet, lost. Once on the roads, of course, they were required by state motor vehicle laws to provide identification on official request, which Edgar Crosswell and his deputies duly and promptly made.

Sergeant Crosswell assembled all the names and submitted them in his report to his superiors.

But the lists of names and news of the incident fast reached the papers and magazines, matching photographs were supplied, and soon the story was front-page headlines all over the world.

Appalachin was called "A Convention of Crime."

Lucifer's existence could no longer be denied.

Senator John Kennedy couldn't keep his face straight for long. "I'm sorry, Bobby, but you have to admit, the sight of all those sharpies running through the woods must've been funny as hell! What did they think was happening?"

Robert Kennedy was all smiles too, but from gratification. He had Jack's desk covered with newspaper pages and glossies. "My boy Mack Stenn, Civillo, Colletti, Genovese, Gambino . . . It goes on and on. *Fifty* with arrest records, thirty-five with convictions! California, Texas, Colorado! Eighteen arrested in connection with murder, fifteen with narcotics, twenty-three for illegal use of firearms. It's like finding out about Dachau, Jack! And twenty-two *directly* involved in the unions, in Labor or in Labor-Management relations! That's a bingo, pal! That's a jackpot! God, this is terrific."

"And now?"

"Now you've got to back me, Jack, all the way. You've got to let us go on this."

"What's your next move?"

"New York. The Attorney General's started a Special Group on Organized Crime in the United States, but he's getting mostly the narcs to staff it. Hoover won't lend the Bureau. He says it's a fishing expedition and that he's got neither the time nor the manpower to waste on 'speculative ventures.' I don't know what he needs more than Appalachin to convince him."

"Oh, I think he's convinced, but won't go in against bad odds."

"Well, the hell with him. I've been talking with Frank Hogan in New York. He's got a Crime Intelligence Unit loaded with information we need if we want to broaden our investigation."

"And we do want to broaden—hell, we have to, it's staring us in the face. All right, go to New York. I'll go to the Committee."

New York District Attorney Frank Hogan didn't try to bargain, but he did ask Robert Kennedy if there was anything that could be done for him in Washington. "We really could use more Federal funds in this." Bob said he would try to get the Senator to intercede in his behalf. Then he left Hogan's office in the Foley Square Federal Courthouse building, his briefcases loaded with copies of information gathered by Hogan's Crime Intelligence Unit. At the elevator, he put one heavy case down to push the button. The doors finally opened. There was one passenger in the elevator, and he held the doors back while Kennedy retrieved his case. Bob heard "Pretty heavy load for a skinny little fella," and looked up. His helper was Jimmy Hoffa.

They rode down together. They exchanged pleasantries awkwardly, then resumed their more customary sparring.

"Like your new job, Jimmy?"

"That's okay, Bobby, you can just call me Mr. President."

"Shouldn't I ask one of the Monitors first?"

"Nah, I can speak for them."

It was an agonizingly slow elevator.

"How's your wiretap trial going, Jimmy?"

"Well, you know. You can never tell with juries. Like shooting fish in a barrel. But I'm not worried. Who the hell'd believe I'd buy my own people?"

"I believe it.

"Lucky you ain't on the jury."

The elevator stopped at a floor. The man waiting

looked inside and recognized them and froze for a moment. Jimmy pushed the close button, laughing. "Get the next one, it'll be safer!" Alone again, he asked Bob, "You didn't come all the way to the Apple to see me, did ya? Whose keyholes you got your ear in now?"

"Appalachin's."

"Them the mountains, right?"

"You know what I mean—the little party a bunch of your friends had?"

"My friends? Beats me, I didn't hear nothin' about it."

"Maybe your invitation got lost in the mails."

"That's big talk, Bob. You wouldn't want to get hit with a slander suit, would ya?"

"You're starting to sound like one of your lawyers."

Hoffa laughed. "Christ, I've been spending so much time in court, I oughta!"

"You'd make a good lawyer, Jim."

"Better than you, kid, better than you."

Halfway through the lobby, Jimmy stopped, and with something approaching genuine concern he said to Bobby, "Kid, lemme try to tell you something. You can take this any way you want to. I been around a lot longer and a lot more than you. You're young and you're bright, but you don't always act it, huh? I know you think you're playing a smart game, but I also know you're not, you're . . . you're in where the trees grow thick and mixin' with things you don't understand. Go easy, Bobby."

"Is that a warning?"

"Call it advice from a guy who knows."

They walked on through the lobby, out the doors, and down the great steps. This time it was Bob who stopped; it was vague, but he had been touched and felt the need to return the contact. He said, "Jimmy, okay, maybe there is a lot I don't or can't understand. But are you still so sure you do? Your whole battle cry has always been the little guy—how much good you do for him, how much he loves you for it. But the AFL-CIO *did* kick you out. Now, hasn't it occurred to you that for Meany to pull that off he had to get ten million rank-and-file little guys to vote against you? And they did? Jimmy, please—clean it up before you lose it. Dump the trash."

Jimmy Hoffa's face was clenched as tight as a fist, but no bombast came. He said, "You tryin' to make a deal?"

Bob said, "Same as you—advice from a guy who knows."

"But you don't!" His voice was wrenched with conflict. "Look at you, Bob . . . when they was all pissin' on you for stayin' tight with Joe McCarthy, you said somethin' like if he was good enough to be your friend when you needed him, then you were gonna be his friend when he needed you. Now, I liked that. That much I understood about you. Why can't you understand that about me, goddammit? I'm talkin' *loyalty,* and what the hell else is there?"

Bob had no answer to that.

It was over.

Each withdrew to his battle station.

Hoffa said, "I'm goin' uptown, can I give you a lift?"

Kennedy looked across the street and saw Mack Stenn waiting at the black Cadillac. "No, thanks, I'll grab a cab to La Guardia."

"Yeah, that's way outta my way anyhow."

"See you, Jimmy."

"See you, Bobby."

Hoffa telephoned his family from his uptown hotel. He tried to calm their fears about the outcome of his wiretap trial, and promised to be home as soon as he could. Then he summoned Mack Stenn to bring the car around. Jimmy claimed he had never written more than one check in his life. He went to his store of cash, grabbed two handfuls of big bills, threw on his overcoat, and went downstairs. "Macy's!" he told Stenn. On the way he stopped at Saks and at Lord and Taylor. A light snow was falling over the city, just starting to stick to taxi roofs, awnings, streets crowded with last-minute shoppers. Bare legs and skate blades flashed beneath the giant tree at Rockefeller Plaza, ablaze with a million bulbs. Santas clanked their bells at every corner. Christmas music filled the air in front of every store. Salvation Army members rattled their tambourines, tooted their trumpets, and sang into microphones. A seeing-eye dog slept at the feet of his begging master, a wreath of holly fixed to its reins. Jimmy felt homesick and vulnerable. He bought practically everything that caught his eye that he knew would please his wife, his children, his friends. The jury was still out. He couldn't move fast enough, couldn't buy enough things to let him keep it off his mind for a minute.

Sandy Farrell had no trouble spotting them. He'd found their Caddie parked in a Kinney lot, and waited. Jimmy had Mack Stenn overwhelmed with packages and shopping bags, and was himself barely visible under his load of gifts. Sandy roared at the spectacle weaving toward him through the snow, but he'd already been brimming with happiness anyhow, and soon the gifts were flying through the air. The three men whooped and jumped up and down and whacked each other on the backs and arms. A hung jury. He had won again.

From a distance it looked like a winter scene from a Vermont calendar. It was early evening, blue changing swiftly to black. The roof of the house was white with snow. Icicles hung from the gutters and eaves. The snow on the ground had that thin crust on it where no boot had trampled, no arms and legs had spread and flapped to make angels, no path had been cleared by snowballs rolled into snowmen. The house's outside lights were on as well as the inside ones, and Christmas trees glittered both inside and out, and all the lights seemed to find tiny diamonds shining where they hit the thin top crust of unbroken snow. It was an outside party. They were ready to move it inside, but it was still too beautiful out there, and the temperature was still strangely warm, perhaps for the lack of any wind, and it was such a gas to be standing around with drinks and stuff all bundled up like Eskimos or skiers.

There was little unbroken snow on the terrace or in the yard close by the house where the outside tree winked all colors: Bob and Ethel had asked not only every investigator on the staff, with their spouses and dates, but every secretary, clerk, messenger, and assistant who had ever lifted a pencil or phone on behalf of the McClellan Committee's tasks. Almost all had showed up, including several reporters based in the area or staying there through the holidays. All had come eagerly, not because they had to but because they needed to, which was why it was being given in the first place. "Holidays are so depressing!" was already a cliché there and then, but rarely ever true when the Kennedys were involved. This was turning out to be an exception. The punch, grog and nog were "super," the food "terrific," but it wasn't working. Somebody mumbled to somebody else, "Now I know what Valley Forge felt like."

"Yeah, but they survived."

That was it. They were an army, albeit small, and they had tasted defeat too many times. The side of right was supposed to overcome; so maybe they were not the side of right after all. The hung jury in New York had landed like the one mortar round the place wasn't built to take. The stereo played songs and carols through speakers. "Jingle Bells" sounded stupid. "White Christmas" and "Silent Night" drew the wrong kinds of tears. Bob had tried. He had stood atop the terrace wall and said, "This may be the appropriate moment to tell you something that, well, maybe I should have been saying more often to you all over the year. And that is how fantastic you all are. And how much I have to thank you all for. I am more proud of each and every one of you than I can ever express . . . and I want you to be just as proud of yourselves. Now, this is Christmas. And Christmas is something to celebrate, even if . . . Look, I know what you're feeling, but please, don't allow yourselves to be disappointed. This war of ours is an enormous undertaking. You are the first brave few to undertake it. You are serving a cause of the highest order, you couldn't give your lives to anything more important. We must expect setbacks. We cannot let setbacks be defeats. We must learn to take setback after setback without weakening, without despair. If there weren't setbacks, if disappointment didn't meet us at every turn, we would have to question the true magnificence

207

of our undertaking. We are being tried, and tried sorely. Know this. There is something out there that is against our winning. That something is evil, and that something is resisting us with such an ever-increasing intensity that that resistance itself should be a sign of hope for us! We *are* winning!" Then he looked down, smiled, and added, "It just doesn't feel like it!"

They laughed; then the laugh spread and rose into cheer. They applauded and sent him back shouts of approval, vows of allegiance. "Okay!" "We'll get 'em, Bob!" But the spirit rising just as abruptly quit and fell back. It was into this strange, dark, lingering gloom-amid-false-cheer that, later, a surprising act was made by an unexpected person. Clark Mollenhoff had been standing toward the back edge of the gathering, talking and drinking with friends, when he suddenly turned and left them, made his lumbering way to the terrace, and stood on the top step. His head reached almost as high as Bobby's had from atop the wall. His voice was soft but deep, and they listened:

"Uh . . . excuse me? People? Thank you. For those who don't know me, I'm Clark Mollenhoff, but most of you do, and you know how really out of my line this is. But something's got to be said here tonight. Now, I'm an outsider in this, but I sure don't feel like one, and this moping is teeing me off. Look. Two years ago I wouldn't have bet a plugged nickel on anybody ever getting Dave Beck. Well, you got him. When this started, I was one of the ones feeding you the information. I'm proud of that, and I'm not too humble to say so. But it's been working the other way around for a long time now. And I'm even prouder of that. That's the way it's supposed to work. And it's finally working that way because *you're* doing it!"

"So he beat a bribery trial last year and a wiretap trial last week. Big deal. He *was tried*. And he's going to be re-tried on the wiretap charge! Before you people, there wouldn't have been any of those trials. You think that's nothing? He's under a Board of Monitors and Meany booted him out of the AFL-CIO. You think that's nothing?"

Bob Kennedy had gone into the house to stop a scrap in one of the kids' upstairs bedrooms. Ethel found him and said, "You'd better get back outside. Something great is happening."

Mollenhoff went on: "Now I'll tell you two other things, and then I'll shut up. One you don't have to hear but I'll tell you anyhow. Because it's Christmas or something. Watching you people work has changed me. I've been a reporter a long time. It makes you a cynic, a total skeptic. Well, I'm feeling something inside that I thought died someplace back in high school. I don't even know what to call it. But it's whatever the opposite of cynicism is called. It's . . . I'm beginning to think, to actually believe that great good, right things are possible to accomplish again. You did that, and how dare you feel discouraged. All right. Bob tried to tell you something earlier, and he was right—you're getting close. You're getting too close, I think. It's going to get very hot for you. Nobody has ever come as close as you people have to Jimmy Hoffa and the men behind Jimmy Hoffa. They don't like it, and they are going, I'm afraid, to let you know how much they don't like it.

"I was wrong. I do have something else to say— Merry Christmas and Happy New Year to the smartest, toughest and most dedicated group of public servants it has ever been my privilege to know!"

They had stayed spellbound up to his "Merry Christmas," and then they broke, and this time their spirits flew and didn't quit. Robert Kennedy had tears in his eyes when he embraced Clark Mollenhoff and thanked him.

The man waiting in the parked car had to keep flicking on his windshield wipers to see out. His was one of only a half dozen pleasure vehicles in the vast, muddy, deeply rutted lot; the rest were huge, diesel tractor-trailers. The big truckers' stop near the Tennessee-Virginia state line was typical: diner out front, bunks and billiards out back. The fierce March winds were blowing horizontal all along the highway, whipping dirt as well as rain against the traffic. All the over-the-road, long-distance rigs at TRUCK-EATS-RATES stood smeared with upflung mud, anonymous as houses. Now and again a trucker would rev, throw on his lights against the bleak day's grayness, and roar off, back on his way. Now and again, another trucker would come barreling in off the road, breaks farting, and park. Some drove partners, some drove solo. The man in the grit-and-rain-splattered new car would switch his wipers on, look, then shut them off again, to wait some more.

Tony Belson, heading north, had to pee so bad he slipped her in nose-first, swung down out of his cab, and ran through the mud for the diner. He yelled hello to Gus and Florence behind the counter, hit the latrine, and came back out, peeling off his soaked jacket. He'd dried his hair with paper towels. D.D. Tompkins was eating chili in a booth. "Hey, Tony!"

"D.! Hey, whaddaya say." He slid across the red leatherette seat opposite the other trucker. Florence sent Kitty over, and Tony ordered eggs, sausage, pan-fries, and coffee. Grits came. "Where you goin'?"

210

"Nashville," D.D. said. "Paper. You highballin' to D.C., right?"

"Um. Toilet bowls and bathroom fixtures. How'd you know that?"

"Didn't know the freight, knew D.C. Know somethin' else, too."

Belson stiffened, but D.D. was a friend. "What's that?"

D.D. kept looking at his chili and lowered his voice. "What you're gonna do after you git there."

"Yeah, I'm gonna unload and look for another load to bring back! Stick it, D.D.!" His food came, and he attacked it.

"That's all, huh, Tone?"

His mouth full, Belson said angrily, "You start shuttin' that mouth, Tompkins, hear?"

"No need to get henshit with me, Tone, you know that."

Tony calmed a bit. Also talking to his food, he whispered, "Where'd you hear?"

"I heard. Point is, shit, if *I* did anybody might've. I'm tryin' a save your life, Tone."

"Save your breath."

"Don't do it."

"Fuck you, don't do it. You hear so much, you didn't hear what they did to me? Well, nobody fucks me like that and gets away with it. All right, so I'm an independent, I've always been an independent, I *like* being an independent. That means they blow up your rig? Right outside your house? So it knocks your wife out of bed so hard she bleeds and we . . . we lost that kid, D.D. Seven *months,* man!" He was nearly crying.

"Hey, Tone, I . . ."

He'd kept whispering all along, and continued to whisper. He said, "Fuck me? Fuck Hoffa! I wanted that kid, D.D.! And for that kid, I got a U.S. Senator waitin' on me! I am gonna fuckin' testify my goddamn guts out! They think I—"

The man from the car entered the diner, hung his hat and raincoat on a hook, and sat up on a stool at the counter. He was exceptionally well dressed for the place, but nobody took any notice. He ordered a cup of coffee and a piece of pecan pie from Gus, and sat

211

looking straight ahead at the case of assorted pies and pastries. They were laid flat, but the case had mirrors so you could see how much of the pies and cakes had already sold.

D.D. was almost sorry now that he'd mentioned it to Tony Belson at all. It was certain he wasn't going to be able to talk or warn him out of doing it. It seemed all he'd accomplished was to get him so riled up that he wasn't even trying to eat his food any more, was just smoking his cigarette fast, practically biting the end off it. Abruptly, he had shoved it into his grits and was up, putting on his jacket. D.D. said, "You just got here, Tone."

"I gotta go," he said, throwing some bills on the table. "See you next time, D." And was out the door. The diner's windows were too steamed up to see through, but just before the ear-blasting, floor-shaking, glass-rattling explosion, a fierce red-and-yellow flash appeared through the gray. Almost everyone ran at once to the side windows. D.D. ran outside, crying, "Oh Christ, no! Tone! Tone!"

The man with the pecan pie didn't run at all, just kept eating and looking at the sweets in the mirrors. He was Frank Malcolm, enforcer and killer. He liked being back on the road; sticking around his Teamster local office had got on his nerves. When the truckers were sure all Belson's tanks had blown, they ran outside too. They had wiped the steam off the windows with their hands and, looking now, Frank Malcolm could see them silhouetted against the raging fire where Belson's cab had been. Sirens sounded in the distance. Through the smoke, the ribs of the trailer end were starting to reveal themselves. Malcolm had to be sure, but he didn't want to get soaking wet and filthy, either. So he waited. The shocked truckers began drifting back in, describing it. The blond one who had been eating with the fink finally said it: "Aw lord, they'll never dig 'em out . . . fuckin' steel melted like solder. Like a goddamn bug in a furnace."

Malcolm could leave now. Only the crust was left on the pie anyhow. The coffee was still too hot to drink fast, so he poured extra milk into it. The blond guy was still babbling on. When Malcolm heard him

curse—"them fuckers, them goddamn, dirty killers"—
he took a better look at him. That was reckless talk
after a terrible accident. It might come in handy to remember the face of somebody who had the thoughts
that led to talk like that.

Malcolm paid his chek, got five dollars in small silver from Florence, and headed through the wind and
rain for Clarksville.

In Chicago, Committee investigators Gerry Gotch
and Jim Kelly found the address Joey Aiuppa had
given them. It was a narrow-door, dilapidated old hotel, the Whitney House, in a block of taverns and
small factories and junkyards. The desk clerk sat on a
stool by his silent, tiny switchboard, reading a racing
form in near-darkness. His shirt was very dirty and
he had the shakes. He said, "Aiuppa? Uh, I'm supposed to see I.D.'s."

They showed him their credentials.

He said, "Okay. I got a message. He said, when
you come, he wants to meet you outside. Take a right
out front. Walk up this side till you come to Reznick's
That's old car parts. It'll be the long wire fence, only
one this side. Wait there."

They thanked him and followed the directions.
With no tall buildings near, the lake wind was using
the street as a tunnel, sucking paper and refuse against
poles and walls, whisking filth out of the gutters. The
car came from behind them, straddling the low curb,
going sixty. Kelly threw himself up the cyclone fence
and started climbing. The side of the car grazed the
back of his right leg. Gotch had been walking on the
outside. Turning at the noise, he threw himself straight
up onto the car's hood, bounced off the windshield,
then off the fence, landing on the sidewalk close
enough to the car's passing rear bumper to get exhaust
in his face.

Kelly dropped down and helped his partner to his
feet. Gotch said, "Get a number?"

"Are you kidding?"

"Jesus . . . Well, he met us all right."

Frank Malcolm started making his calls about an

hour outside Clarksville. From a gas station, he simply said, "Mrs. Molsen?"

"Yes?"

"Mrs. . . . *Gloria* Molsen?"

Gloria Molsen realized she said yes the second time into a dead line. Her customer at the counter of her dry-cleaning shop said, "My goodness, woman—you all right?"

Detroit Teamster Business Agent Roland McMasters was no Barney Baker, but at two hundred and forty-five pounds he didn't exactly melt into crowds. He was obscuring a radiator in the union hall, smoking a cigar and chewing the fat with four of his associates, loitering around on desktops and folding chairs. McMasters spotted thin, young Joe Maher come through the outer door and cross the vacant entry hall, but ignored him. A pint of Three Feathers was being passed around. When Joe Maher stopped in the doorway and said, "Mr. McMasters?" some of the others turned to look, but McMasters didn't. He was saying, ". . . So Jocko says, I don't give a rat's ass if they put three shortstops and two left-fielders out there, I'll still give yez even money on the Tigers!"

"Mr. Roland McMasters?" Joe Maher said. He had now taken the paper from his inside pocket and walked to the edge of the group.

McMasters still didn't look at him. "Who wants to know?"

Maher began, "I'm an investigator for the McClellan Committee, and I have a subpoena here for you to—"

"Well, bring it here and lemme see it!"

Maher walked forward. McMasters stayed on the radiator. He took the subpoena with one hand and with the other grabbed and held Joe Maher's lapel. His friends laughed. McMasters finally looked at Maher's face as he crumpled the subpoena into a ball with his free hand, telling him, "You tell Kennedy he can shove this up his ass."

Maher was too amazed by the fist that came flying into his face to even try to block it or move, not that he could have moved far with the huge man's other hand holding him tightly now by his coat. McMasters hit him in the face again, then, coming off his perch, drove it deep, twice, into Maher's stomach. Joe doubled over. McMasters straightened him up and began back-handing him across the face and head.

"Lay off, Mac! You'll—"

"They think we don't mean it!" McMasters raged, working his hammer into Maher's gut and kidneys again.

Vision blurred with blood, Maher felt the hands both close around his neck, thumbs trying to break into his throat. He heard yells and shoes scuffing, then felt his maddened attacker being pulled and pried off and away from him. Heaped small on the splintery old floor, Maher wiped his eyes clear and saw shoes, all wingtipped brogues, some new. He looked higher. McMasters was still being held but lightly, puffing and sweating, his immense belly moving in his shirt like a floating medicine ball. Nearly delirious with pain, fear, and fury, Maher lunged to his feet and swung the roundhouse at the same time. He seemed to feel the impact and the fire in his arm only after he was already running for the door and escape.

On his second call, from a roadside pay phone about twenty minutes outside Clarksville, Frank Malcolm said, "We told you not to go to Washington any more, Gloria Molsen. But you went again, didn't you, Gloria Molsen." He listened to her whimper for a while this time, then hung up.

In Washington, Eddie Cheyfitz was feeling upset. This new push wasn't his style; the pressures were throwing him off his pace. He had Jimmy egging him on with the lean-harder orders on one hand, and now he had an irate Bob Kennedy blasting at him on the phone. Eddie preferred making calls to getting them, and tirades like this . . . He finally bolstered his nerve and said, "Bob, this tough-guy routine doesn't wash with me, and you ought to know better! Hell, you used illegal wiretaps yourselves, so how can you—"

"Don't pull that on me, Eddie! That was before the Supreme Court's ruling and you goddamn well know

215

it! Isn't there anything you guys won't try? *Somebody* offered a hundred grand to the Chairman of the Board of Monitors, and it sure as Christ wasn't Walter Reuther!"

"Are you saying *I . . . ?*"

"I'm saying this, Cheyfitz, and get it straight. He'd better lay off my investigators, that's all. You're flirting with murder!"

"Now cool off, Bob, we—"

"You think terrorizing my people is the way to cool me off? Jesus . . . Eddie, I will *swear* to you here and now—your boy can beat the next three hundred raps for all I care, and he'll still have me breathing down his neck!"

A concerned Angie Novello finally peered into Robert Kennedy's office. He had hung up, but was still seething.

"You okay?"

"Get me some aspirins. About ninety!"

"That wasn't Eddie *Cheyfitz?*"

"Yes, that was Eddie Cheyfitz!"

"He offer to make Jack President again?"

"God, that's all I would've needed."

The triumphant Jimmy Hoffa emerged victorious from his second wiretap trial in New York and greeted his waiting gallery of reporters with open arms. Laughing he stilled their initial babble of questions with "Ladies and gentlemen, please, please! The verdict speaks for itself!"

"How'd you beat it, Jimmy?"

"A bum rap! It beat itself!" He clapped the shoulder of Edward Bennett Williams, beside him in his glory. "Take a bow, Ed! Ed here said it best—you can't tap wires with one hand and prosecute wiretappers with the other!"

"Jimmy! What was the—"

"Hey, fellas, come on—you want me to hang around this place and write your copy for ya? I'll tell ya this, though—if you all belonged to our Teamster Local here in New York, you'd be gettin' better pay for shorter hours!"

They laughed. Then one asked, "How do you think Bobby Kennedy's going to take this, Jimmy?"

"Lyin' down!"

"Is he still fighting your election to . . . ?"

"What's that one know about gettin' elected? He never gets elected to anything, he gets appointed! He's got a relative in the business!" They laughed again, but he went on, "And that's all that McClellan thing's about, you know! Just spendin' millions of your bucks and mine to keep Jack Kennedy and his little brother in the public eye! Jack's tryin' to ride in on my back!"

It was raining again when Frank Malcolm parked his car at the curb in front of Gloria Molsen's dry-cleaning shop. He could see her inside, pulling a paper wrapper down over a hanger holding pressed slacks for one of the people waiting at the counter. He left his engine running, but shut off the wipers. He didn't need to see any more, and didn't wish to be seen. He reached the quart Scotch bottle of gasoline out of the glove compartment, unscrewed its cap, inserted the gas-saturated rag for a wick, opened his door, stepped only his left leg out, flicked his Zippo, ignited the wick, threw the result hard with his right arm at the plate glass window, and gunned the car away down the street, switching the wipers back on. In his rear-view mirror he saw the store go flying out into the street through the air: glass, wood, clothing, maybe an arm. His window was cracked open a bit and he heard the explosion and the screams. He didn't need to wait around on this one: she had already talked, so death wasn't strictly required.

It was close to midnight by the time all the top investigators summoned had got the word and made it to Robert Kennedy's box of an office. They drank coffee, smoked, and felt like yawning, but the situation was too critical for any of them to permit their fatigue to show. There were no maps posted, but it still felt like the operations tent of a heavily besieged infantry battalion. Walt Sheridan was saying bitterly, "He's not only muscling us, now he's turning into the sweet-heart of the press!"

LaVerne Duffy: "The little bastard's good copy."

Pierre Salinger shrugged. "Let's face it, as news, corruption gets boring after a while. And they've had it for over a year and a half. A *ruthless Committee,* on the other hand, *marshaling forces* against one cocky little guy . . ."

"And losing," Sheridan added.

"Never mind," Kennedy snapped. "What do we do?"

Joe Maher sighed. "Have to get to be the good guys again."

Bob asked, "Their systematic, violent attack on both investigators and witnesses—why isn't that news?"

Sheridan said, *"We* know it's systematic, but . . ."

"Yeah," Maher said, "even Brophy in the *Post* sees it as isolated incidents, not premeditated or coordinated against us. Just panicky thugs lashing—"

"Well, *can* we show it's an organized effort?" Bob asked. "Dammit, they're waging an all-out war against this Committee!"

Kenny O'Donnell spoke up. "I think I might have something. There's a Frank Malcolm . . ."

"What about him, Kenny?"

"Go, memory, go!"

Kenny sat up out of his slouch. "Going through it all, I found a pattern . . . There were three incidents around Tennessee, and another five, at least five, around Flint, Michigan—all with only one thing in common besides the violence, and that's Malcolm's name. I *can* recite a brief bio. He was in the Illinois pen for armed robbery; when he got out, Hoffa gave him Teamster Local Three Eighteen in Flint; since then he's been booked seven or eight times, all for assault with intent to kill—and all charges dropped, of course. But he's a known enforcer, at work in at least two states. We might squeeze him with a Federal rap."

"That's enough," Bob said. "Who'll go talk to him?"

Joe Maher shuddered. "I'm up, Bob, but if it's all the same to you . . ."

"Thanks, Joe, I knew you'd do it."

Under cover of night, Frank Malcolm cut a hand-size square hole in a side window with a glass cutter, outside the putty line. He tapped it gently, pulling gingerly on the tape he had stuck to it, and it came out into his hands with a neat, quiet *clink*. This was a home-town job, so he was using two underlings, one as lookout, one as driver. He reached his gloved hand in through the hole, unlocked the window, and swung it open. He lowered the two five-gallon cans of gasoline onto the inside floor, then climbed in after them. His eyes had already acquired their visual purple, night vision, so he went to work at once.

It was a laundry. He carried one can into the small front office to his left. He checked the door for alarms; there were none, so he unlocked the front door from the inside. This would be his exit. Wooden shelves to the ceiling on three sides behind the counter held bundles of laundry wrapped in heavy brown paper, with names grease-penciled on. He saw no need to soak any of those higher than the second shelf, and emptied three quarters of the first can over them and over the rolls of wrapping paper stored beneath the counter.

The rear was a long, garagelike room with brick walls and cement floor holding four wide wooden benches piled high with linens and sheets. Huge canvas hampers on wheels stood about, overflowing with shirts and napkins and other cloth material ready to go into the six cylindrical washing bins. Frank Malcolm emptied the first can into two hampers, then started at the back on the benches with the other. This second can had a small leak in one bottom corner. As Malcolm went splashing and pouring the gas over the innards of the laundry, the leak splashed and poured gas over the front of his jacket and trousers. He didn't notice. At the doorway to the front, he flung the empty can back into the gas-drenched room, bent down, and set his lighter to the end of the thin stream he had poured along the floor from the first hamper. It took, and the little river of flame ran coursing away from him, spreading fast. It was when he bent to light the saturated paper rolls in the front that the flames backfired on him and went climbing up his pants leg.

He was instantly a human torch. and went screaming out the front door. His lookout and his driver came running. He was rolling himself around on the street, but was still flaming so high they couldn't get to him right away. By the time they did and had him rolled and slapped flameless, he lay crumpled, charred and smoldering, moaning. The lookout cried, "Should we ring the alarm?"

"Don't be a moron!"

"We gotta get 'im to a hospital!"

"How the fuck are *we* gonna go to a hospital?"

Frank Malcolm's car tore up to the emergency room of the Flint General Hospital and delivered its package. A rear door flew open, and something big and black and smoking was pushed out onto the driveway. The car disappeared into the city.

In the corridor outside Malcolm's room, the Flint District Attorney told Joe Maher the doctor's report: "He's got third-degree burns over ninety-five percent of his body. They don't give him the night."

"Can we see him? I want to try to get a statement."

"Yes, we can go in anytime. I want one myself. Let me do the talking."

Frank Malcolm was a mummy in the bed. Even his eyes were covered in bandage. Only his nostrils and his mouth showed through the white swaddling. The D.A. identified himself, speaking low and up close, and also identified Joe Maher. Then he said, "Frank, we have to know what happened. Who were you working for?"

A rattle from far away, through the mouth hole: *"No."*

The D.A. reasoned. "Frank. Mr. Malcolm. You're dying. Get it off your soul. Tell us the names. This is your last chance! For God's sake, for your own salvation, Frank, talk to me!"

Dying, Frank Malcolm made his statement. Putting their ears even closer to his mouth, they heard, very clearly, *"Go fuck yourself."*

Robert Kennedy in Washington was getting about the same amount of satisfaction from all quarters as

Joe Maher got from Frank Malcolm in Flint, and roughly the same message. The Republican Senators began to exert increasing pressure for the shifting of concentration away from Hoffa and onto Walter Reuther. Robert and John Kennedy and the other Democrats kept insisting that preliminary probings into the United Auto Workers had revealed certain discrepancies and procedural fuzziness in some areas, but certainly nothing to compare to the widespread rot evident in the Teamsters.

Robert Kennedy was convinced that the two best shots at revealing Hoffa's corruption were still the Test Fleet issue and the notorious Sun Valley scheme. Sun Valley was a parcel of virtually worthless land in Florida, undeveloped and largely under water. Teamsters were officially encouraged to buy shares in it for their retirement happiness. Through an operative, Hoffa swung the deal by depositing Teamster pension funds into Florida bank accounts—accounts that paid no interest. Kennedy badly wanted to use these two blatant examples of mismanagement as final proof of Hoffa & Company's outright and enormous screwing of the Teamster rank-and-file. He met resistance.

Hoffa's longtime sidekick, Owen Bert Brennan, took the witness chair before the Committee.

"Mr. Brennan . . . according to Mr. Hoffa, some of the initial capital used to build your Test Fleet trucking firm was raised by you. At the racetrack, I might add. Is that statement accurate?"

Brennan resembled actor William Holden playing a successful business executive. In conservative suit and dark-rimmed glasses, his appearance didn't belie his reputation for cool toughness. Neither did his behavior. "I respectfully refuse to answer, pursuant to my rights under the First, the Fifth, and the Fourteenth Amendments of the United States Constitution."

"It's a simple question, Mr. Brennan—did you raise money for Test Fleet at the races? Or was there another source of your income?"

"I respectfully refuse to answer, pursuant to my rights under the First, the Fifth, and the Fourteenth Amendments of the United States—"

"Mr. Hoffa couldn't remember where a large portion

of the money came from. He referred us to you. Is this how you answer his question?"

"I respectfully refuse to answer, pursuant to—"

"Or is this simply a way for Mr. Hoffa to avoid taking the Fifth Amendment?" Kennedy's finger jabbed the air between them like a hammer. "He refers us to you . . . and you take it for him! Mr. Brennan. We want here to—"

"Mr. Chairman!"

Republican Senator Karl Mundt stood up. "I resent this line of questioning from our illustrious chief counsel. The people of South Dakota, whom I have the honor to represent, respect and admire the Constitution of the United States, and permit anyone to take refuge in it. That is a basic of American law.

"We also, in South Dakota, respect the great Labor Movement in this country, and are tired of seeing only one corner of it constantly assaulted by our friend from Massachusetts. We have asked, time and again, for this investigation to move on.

"Or is Jimmy Hoffa the only labor leader of questionable morality in this nation?

"We feel an investigation into the great bastion of American decency known as the United Auto Workers is long overdue. Or is Walter Reuther going to escape the intense gaze of our investigative microscope?"

Senator McClellan looked weary. "Senator, this does not seem the proper time to raise a question of procedure."

"Mr. Brennan—" Kennedy resumed.

"When is the proper time, Mr. Chairman?" Mundt demanded. "When *is* the proper time?"

The chief counsel was summoned later to the Chairman's office. His Arkansas drawl sounded more tired than gentle. "Just where are we, Bob, with the UAW?"

"We've had two full teams of investigators on them, sir. Carmine Bellino has already spent several days auditing their books. I've initiated a special investigation into Walter Reuther himself, based on certain allegations, which so far continue to appear unsubstantiated. What can I say—we're doing all that can be done."

"There are no questionable areas at all?"

"Well, sure, we've picked up a few discrepancies

here and there. But not enough to justify a full Committee session. Not yet, anyhow. In my opinion."

"Mmm. Thing is, Bob, I don't know how long I can hold the Republicans off."

"I know, sir. But damnit, what we're looking at now is far more important. We've found nothing in the UAW or Reuther that even comes close to the scale of Hoffa's corruption."

"Thing is, if this starts degenerating into squabbles and speeches and partisan politics, the whole Committee goes down the drain."

"Well, it is an—"

"I know it's an election year, Bob. And I also know what pressure the Teamster lobby can bring to bear when it wants to."

"Which it does."

"Which it surely does. And I'm afraid it's going to get worse long before it gets better."

The Massachusetts Council of the Knights of Columbus held the swell affair at Blinstrub's, the favorite Boston nightclub of Archbishop Richard Cushing. Plumes, swords and sashes abounded, and the dress was formal. Robert and Ethel, Rose and other Kennedy family members sat at the head table.

Archbishop Cushing had developed his stentorian style of preaching and public speaking in the same place as, and often at the side of, his boyhood buddy, the fabled ex-mayor James Michael Curley: on the tailgates of electioneering trucks in South Boston. He was a big, shining-eyed man. The severe asthma he suffered seemed only to heighten the nasality and timbre of his glass-shattering voice. He could make a five-minute talk last an hour, but attention wouldn't drift; he was Moses. His was the keynote speech.

". . . And now, I am greatly pleased, to present, the Council's Annual Lantern Award, for outstanding patriotism, to Mr. Robert Francis Kennedy, who is, after all, a Massachusetts man and, therefore, a reminder that New England is still producing men of vision, integrity and leadership!"

Bob blushed at the applause and moved to the podium, accepted the plaque from the Archbishop, and waited for the prelate to be seated. "Thank you, your Excellency. It's a great privilege to receive this—I'm, uh, deeply honored. In many ways, this award seems even greater to me because it *is* given for patriotism. I have long felt that this nation faces disaster unless it begins to reinstill in all its citizens the toughness and the moral idealism which, a hundred and sixty years ago, guided George Washington in his . . ."

One of his sisters side-mouthed delicately to Ethel, "I think Bobby's been spending too much time around Barry Goldwater."

"Lord, whatever you do, don't mention Goldwater to him!"

Bob and the Archbishop sat beside each other for the dinner. "Well, young fella, we've been hearing a lot about you up here lately."

"Some of it good, I hope, Father."

"I think it would be good to have you as our Attorney General, any truth to that, Bob?"

"None. Sheer rumor, Father."

"Hm, never believe everything you read in the papers, huh? Still, as they say, it would be a steppingstone to the governorship."

"I have no time for that kind of thinking, Father."

"Yes, well, I guess you do have your hands full."

"I'll say."

"Just don't get disheartened, Bob. Tell Senator McClellan I said so. You people have been doing an outstanding job down there. Too important to let the GOP start throwing all those monkey wrenches into the works."

"I heard a good one tonight, your Excellency—they say we'll all know the day you make Cardinal . . ."

". . . by the white smoke rising from Blinstrub's! Ha, that's an old one. Smartalecks. But I learned many years ago, Bob, as long as they're still talking about you, good or bad, you're still alive and okay."

"I'll try to remember that, Father."

Driving south, home to the Cape, his mother knew enough not to mention Bob's speeding directly. She merely said, "Maybe we should have stayed over in town." He slowed down.

"So, Bob," his sister said, "how's Barry Goldwater these days?"

Ethel sighed.

"He's a rat is how he is!"

"I've always loved those silver-haired jet pilots. I thought you kind of liked him?"

"Aw, I do, I guess, but know what he pulled on me?"

"Tell us, tell us!"

"Well, you know how he and Mundt and the rest have been trying to sabotage us left and right with their damn filibusters . . . and they're constantly leaking crap to the press, me and Jack, mostly, how we're protecting Reuther and persecuting Hoffa. And then, of course, when you call them on it, they deny it outright, like a bunch of kids!"

"Tell them the latest denials," Ethel said.

"Oh, yeah, this is just terrific, as if they'd rehearsed it. Goldwater said, Oh, no, what, *me?* 'Why, I'm as happy as a squirrel in a little cage.' "

"Squirrel!"

"Then Mundt says he's *perfectly* happy, *he's* happy as—you ready for this?—he's as happy as a South Dakota pheasant in a South Dakota cornfield!"

"Bob knows one of the reporters who got the leak from Mundt," Ethel added, "and when he told him the guy said, 'When's the hunting season open on South Dakota pheasants?' "

After the laughter, Rose said, "Maybe we should've stayed the night in town." Bob slowed down again.

"Anyway, then I hear that Goldwater has said outright that the Democrats, guess who, were running out on the investigation of Reuther. Well, I blow. I corner him in the hall and ask him point blank: *does* he think any more should be done than we're doing? And he says, No, not at all! He just wants to get back to Arizona and admits he doesn't want any more hearings, that's all. So I say, then why the hell did you *say* something like that?"

"That's politics," said his sister.

"Exactly! Well, then I really blow, and say, God-damn it, it's been run as a bipartisan committee all along, we've done all our investigations on a strictly nonpolitical basis . . . Well then he just gives me the grin and says, 'Bob, you're in politics whether you like it or not,' and goes off to Arizona."

Rose leaned forward. "Your father's been telling you that for ages. Please slow down, Bob."

Jack was eating clam chowder in the kitchen of the main house. The father had already turned in. "Hey, you pick up another award for me? Thanks a lot."

"Any time."

"Here's one for you."

Bob looked at the cartoon in the folded newspaper. A cat, labeled *The McClellan Committee,* was chasing its own tail. "Those bastards!" He threw the paper down and snapped open a can of beer. The women had gone to the living room.

Jack got more chowder from the stove. "I don't see why they had to make it a shitty old alley cat. A Siamese, maybe, or even a Cheshire I would've—"

"They're trying to close us down, Jack!"

"Ah, relax. Think of what Harry Truman said."

"What?"

"Nobody spoils a good story like an eyewitness, or *If you can't stand the heat . . ."*

"We're *in* the goddamn kitchen!"

"Shall we join the ladies?"

"No."

"Then we'll stay, right? You really shouldn't drink beer in a tuxedo, you know."

"It's rented. Damn it, how long can it keep going Hoffa's way? That bastard declared war on us. He beat up our investigators, and terrified or killed our witnesses, and we kept right on going. It didn't work. Now he's waging war from the inside. He's got the Republicans and the fucking newspapers doing his dirty work for him."

"And he seems to be winning."

"Yeah. Even McClellan's finally rolling over."

"McClellan's right—we have to begin hearings on Reuther and the UAW. It's got to be done, Bob."

"What has to be done? Does pressure have to be taken off the Teamsters? Do you have to be embarrassed?"

"How will I be embarrassed?"

"Well, Christ, you know it's going to look like we're using peashooters up there. Those two fuck-up investigators the Republicans put on it. Hell, they don't have a goddamn thing to show for all the time and money they . . . Ah, it's just going to make all our work look as shabby as everyone's claiming. The Reuther-Kennedy alliance. Just as we suspected. Jack, they're going to take the UAW and hit you over the head with it."

"Well, they think we've been beating them over the head with the Teamsters."

"Just politics as usual, right?"

"Politics as usual. Loosen your tie, at least. You really shouldn't drink beer in a tuxedo."

Bob took his tie off, and his jacket.

"It still has to be done, Bob."

"I know." He opened the kitchen door and stepped outside onto the porch and looked up at the late-September, two-in-the-morning sky. "Good God, I've never seen it so dark."

Then light cracked. In Weehawken, New Jersey.

Walter Sheridan had been following a lead. He came to dead end after dead end. In the verge of writing the lead off as false, he pulled into a filling station, a small two-pumper on a quiet country road. Sheridan got out for air and to stretch his cramped legs. The attendant set the gas nozzle and raised the hood to check the oil.

"Know a guy named Harry Gross?" Walt asked him. "Used to live around here?" It was a shot in the dark.

"Might."

"Here's a picture of him."

"That might be him. Who're you?"

Sheridan identified himself. The man brightened. "Oh, the McClellan Committee! Sure! Say, I think I saw you on the TV, didn't I?"

Walt didn't say no.

"Sure, I know Harry Gross. Cash his paycheck for him, in fact, once a month, regular as anything—was in here just last night, matter of fact." Yes, he did happen to still have the check. Would he let Walt see it? "Hey, this make me part of this Senate investigation of yours, would it?" Yes, it would. He showed the check. "You won't want to keep it, I hope, I ain't been to the bank yet."

"No, here, you keep it. This Neo-Gravure Company —what do they do?"

"Printin', I suppose. Printin' and publishin', somethin' or other, ain't far from here."

"Are Mr. Gross's checks always from the same place?"

"Oh, sure. Must work for them."

"By the month, huh?"

"Yup. Once a month he comes and I cash it. This help you any?"

Sheridan almost hugged him. "You might say so. You might say you helped break a case wide open!"

The manager of the Neo-Gravure Company of Weehawken and his assistants weren't so direct.

". . . And Mr. Gross gets paid by the month?"

The manager did the talking. The three others sat and leaned around in his office looking sheepish and wary.

"Yes, sir. By the month."

"And he's not here right now?"

"No. Where'd Harry go off to this afternoon, you know? No, we're not sure where he—"

"Exactly what does he do for you?"

"He's, uh, platform foreman. Shipping department. Good man."

"Will he be back later?"

"No. Actually, I just remembered—he went on vacation today. Huntin' someplace. Anything else?"

"Yes, gentlemen, I think there is. Could you explain to me how a man with a criminal record like Mr. Gross's gets to be a foreman in your company? And could you tell me how he manages to run your shipping platform in New Jersey while he's running a Teamster Local in Miami, Florida? That's one hell of a commute, wouldn't you say? You don't have to answer now. You'll be hearing from us again very soon. Thanks."

The Neo-Gravure manager did hear very soon, and he told Robert Kennedy and Walter Sheridan such a remarkable story that Senator John Kennedy found himself being detained in his Senate office late into the night. He listened, then recapped, "All right, so he gets out of Sing Sing and starts getting a grand a month from Neo-Gravure to guarantee them 'labor peace'—

229

this is hardly the first Teamster payoff we've come across."

"There's more, Jack. Tell him, Walt."

"In nineteen forty-eight, a Teamster strike hit the entire city of New York. A total shutdown."

"I remember."

"But the shutdown wasn't as total as everybody thought. You ready for this? The venerable New York *Times* and also the New York *Mirror* were both somehow able to continue distribution."

"What?"

"Yeah. Neo-Gravure. The *Times Sunday Magazine* and the *Mirror's* Sunday supplement were both printed there."

Bob said, "Jack, they both made secret payoffs to Harry Gross—forty-five thousand dollars to keep their papers on the streets. Jack, that's the New York *Times* making a deal with Organized Crime!"

JFK whistled soundlessly and leaned way back in his chair, kneading his face with his two hands, then saying to the ceiling, *"Say it ain't so, Joe, say it ain't so!"* Then he came forward. "The evidence is there?"

"Yes, sir."

"Christ, Bob, this is big."

"That's why we had to bring it to you. The Committee's got to *see*—if they can make the *Times* stop or go for a few thousand bucks—"

Jack finished it: "Then it's possible next time they can tell them what to print. Good God, that's manipulating a free press! Hell, that makes the Mob, through the union, more powerful than the Federal Government itself!"

"Damnit, the Committee has to understand this, Jack!"

Jack sighed. "Unfortunately, their most urgent desire right now is to get the hell out of business."

Sheridan spoke up. "I want to tell both of you, I'm sorry it took so long to dig out the *Times* connection."

JFK said, "No, Walt. The very least this has done is remind all of us what none of us should ever have doubted—it's real, it's everywhere, and one way or another, it's got to be stopped."

Robert Kennedy sat with his forearms resting on his legs. He said, "*I* never doubted it."

Jack laughed. "I didn't say all of us doubted it, I said none of us should have."

"All right. That's better," Bob said.

Sandy Farrell got a little careless—he opened the door to Jimmy Hoffa's hotel bedroom without knocking first. A form sprang out of the bed, rolled once. and came up in a crouch, pistol in hand and pointed at Farrell's chest.

"Jimmy! It's me!"

Hoffa rose and put the revolver away. He didn't speak.

"I'm, uh, sorry, Jim, I thought you were sleeping. It's about time to get ready to go down to the meeting."

"I'm watchin' the time!"

The massive rallying meeting was to be at Jimmy's Local 299 in Detroit; every member and officer within reach was summoned to be there and hear for themselves, to allay their fears and understand how things really were, the truth of the matter between Jimmy and the Government. Between Hoffa and Kennedy. It was well attended and very well covered by the press, the photographers, the TV cameras, the tape recorders. Hoffa was measuring, refortifying, and dispalying his power base. His rank-and-file Teamsters.

It was a concert any symphony conductor could have envied.

They clapped at all the right places, they cheered, they yelled out, they obeyed every direction the baton of his voice gave them. He orated:

"Tomorrow, with my last appearance, it'll all be over. The McClellan Committee will be out of business, and Bobby Kennedy will be out of a job! And what has it all added up to? Absolutely nothing!

"A few accusations that weren't worth the paper they were printed on, and a few court cases that only wasted the taxpayers money. Hoffa is still here . . . and Hoffa will always be here . . . *if* that's the way *you* want it!

"Yes! There are still other questions that are being asked of me. Yes"—he looked at the press—"there are individuals in this audience who ask the questions about Hoffa—where did Hoffa get the right to run this Union?

"Where did he get the right to borrow in advance on his paycheck?

"Where did he get the right to be in business for himself?

"Well, I've answered that question *to you* hundreds of times! And each time, before it happened, I brought it up with you . . . and you gave me the authority to do it!

"And I say to you that no man in this room who attends meetings regular will ever say, under oath or not under oath, to reporters or to any individual, that there were secrets in Hoffa's life that *you* don't know about!

"Because *I* tell *you* what's happening! And you know I do!"

He let the rafters ring, signaled for quiet, then resumed: "Yes. As you all know, I've been called back to appear before the Committee again—"

A Teamster interrupted: "I think the day you go back, we should all give them the biggest damn strike they ever seen in this country!"

Jimmy looked genuinely outraged, went over to the podium, and rapped for order. "Out of order! Out—of —*order!*" They went silent. "This is a legal matter, not to be resolved in this room!"

A second Teamster rose and asked to be recognized, which he was. He said, "Well, maybe we can't go on strike. But the day you're on the stand, we can get awful sick, and brother, everyone knows when you're sick you just can't work!"

Jimmy again stopped their laughter and applause: "Now look—let's get serious now . . . and I know you are . . . and I know your heart's in the right place! But I want to tell you something again—this is a court matter, this is not a problem that we can resolve in this meeting hall!

"I say to you men tonight, be patient.

"Be patient . . . but be vigilant.

"Be on guard . . . that nobody destroys this Union!

"Be on guard, and remember the days of 'thirty-two, 'thirty-three, 'thirty-four, 'thirty-five, and 'thirty-seven. Remember!

"All the weary hours of the nights we spent on strike.

"Remember the strikebreakers.

"Remember the armed guards.

"Remember the injunctions.

"And remember—*not one single person came to your rescue!*

"Not one single newspaper, not one TV reporter, not one commentator on the air did anything except *blast* you because you were tying up the trucks!

"Yet today they say the *poor, poor drivers.* The poor *Teamster* members! Somebody is *mistreatin'* em!

"Well, I don't know of anybody in this room—and I know most all of ya—that has got to *back off* and *ask for help!*

"You're all pretty husky, healthful people!"

Again he let them roar, and when they were satisfied he ended: "Now I wanna . . . I say to you as your President . . . and I repeat my pledge—the only one I ever made to ya—and that is, I will work for you.

"I will do the best I can do, and whatever it may be necessary to do we will do, *to support the Teamster members of Local Two Ninety-nine!* Thank you."

He let them overflow the stage to touch him and say things to him, chanting as a group, as at the Convention: HOFFA! HOFFA! Reaching out for him, patting his back. Touching his clothes. Truckdrivers, touched by emotion, touching Hoffa. Touching their man.

The evidence was being made public and officially recorded. Legislation would come from this. But on the surface, his last tangle with the McClellan Committee went all Jimmy Hoffa's way. Remaining curt and almost disdainful throughout, he deflected every punch thrown at him. Robert Kennedy asked, "Mr Hoffa, do you have any evidence of the twenty-thousand dollars that you put into the Sun Valley Business?"

Hoffa squinted. "I don't need any evidence. You will take my word for it, as the Internal Revenue has."

Kennedy: "Was it in cash that you put it in?"

Hoffa: "Yes."

Senator John Kennedy asked, "Do you have any record of it?"

Hoffa: "No."

JFK: "Can you tell us where you got the cash?"

"I accumulated it."

"Did any of it come out of the 'winnings' that Mr. Brennan made for you at the racetrack?"

"Very easily it could have."

John Kennedy fixed his angry smile on Jimmy Hoffa. "I have never been completely convinced, Mr. Hoffa, to be frank with you, that Mr. Brennan did win this money at the racetrack."

Jimmy shrugged. "Why don't you ask him?"

"I did, and he took the Fifth Amendment!"

Hoffa smiled. "Maybe he had a reason."

Heating, Senator Kennedy said, "I think he does have a reason. I just can't accept the explanation that this was won in a casual way at the racetrack!"

"Then *you* disprove it," Hoffa advised.

"It is extremely difficult because you do deal in cash."

"And I am going to continue."

"To deal in cash?"

"I think it is the American way."

Robert Kennedy resumed the questioning. "How much cash do you have now, Mr. Hoffa?"

"I don't know."

"You haven't any idea how much cash you have?"

He lashed out: "This is not the Internal Revenue! I refused to give them a net-worth statement, and I do not believe I am required to give it here."

"Do you have ten thousand dollars in cash?"

"I don't know."

"A hundred thousand dollars?"

Senator McClellan reluctantly intervened. "The witness will not be required to answer how much cash he has at the moment. He states he handles everything in cash. That will have to be enough. Unless we can tie it in with some particular transaction, no other answer will be required of the witness."

In the corridor outside the Senate Caucus Room, Jimmy Hoffa was mobbed by reporters, TV cameras, and spectators, and once again made the most of the opportunity to fire at will at his enemy: ". . . Whaddaya mean, am I glad it's over? It's not over! Bobby ain't got Hoffa yet, and until he does, it ain't over. Which

234

means it'll never be over . . . because he ain't never gonna git me!

"But maybe I'm wrong. Maybe he's tired of losing—which he should be! Maybe he's tired of pickin' on the Teamsters—which he should be!"

"Why do you think he singled out the Teamsters?"

"Because he hates Hoffa!"

Walter Sheridan had been trying to make his way through, then lingered to listen. When Jimmy threw up one of his favorite challenges—"And who'd they go after besides us, not countin' a few feeble passes? Nobody, that's who"—Sheridan recited loudly: "The Bakery Workers, the Textile Workers, the Hotel and Restaurant Workers, the Sheetmetal Workers, the Hod Carriers Union, the Carpenters, Walter Reuther, the UAW . . ." But Jimmy ignored him completely and kept on: "Nobody, that's who, nobody! Lemme ask all you smart people somethin'! What's the *name* of these hearings, huh?"

"The McClellan Committee!" somebody offered.

Another shouted, "The Senate Rackets Committee!"

"Wrong!" Jimmy said, "All wrong! You there, young fella—do you know?"

A young spectator, flustered, tried, "The Senate Select Committee on Unfair Labor Practices?"

"Ha! You all hear that? 'Unfair Labor Practices!' No! Wrong again! Well, okay—now that it's all over till they find some other gimmick to waste my time and your money, lemme educate you ta something! Their real name was the Senate Select Committee on Improper Activities in the Labor or Management Field!

"Didja get that? *Or Management!* Or *Management!* Big surprise, huh? Who ever heard of that? What *Management* did they investigate?"

Sheridan started to speak out again, to be drowned out by: "Whitewash jobs! A few whitewash jobs, and that was it! You wanna know who they shoulda started with? Bobby Kennedy, that's who! And lemme tell ya this, too—when big brother Jack runs for President, the Teamsters are gonna be out there workin'—for the *other* guy! Who*ever* he is!"

235

J ohn Fitzgerald Kennedy did indeed run for the Presidency of the United States in 1960. His brother Robert resigned as chief counsel of the Senate Committee to be his Campaign Manager.

There was a Kennedy machine, backstage, and it was operated chiefly by Jack's father, Joseph Sr., and by Bob. Bob Kennedy plunged into this national campaign energized by a vast array of skills and motivations: he was always being told he was in politics whether he liked or admitted it or not, so he would now, by God, be in politics all the way; and he was coming out of his years with the McClellan Committee at full speed, armed with comprehensive experience in the organizing of men and material, and burning with pent-up frustration at only imperfectly pursuing Hoffa and Organized Crime. He went to work like a demon, or like Michael the Archangel, sword flashing.

By the time of the Democratic National Convention in July in Los Angeles, it was down to Jack Kennedy and Lyndon Johnson, the "other guy" behind whom Jimmy Hoffa had thrown his mighty Teamster support.

A Democratic Convention is traditionally much closer to a Teamster convention than to a Republican one. The Democrats love to enjoy a convention city to its fullest, they love to party, and they love to *politic,* as long and as loudly as lungs and arguments will last. By and large they're more at home in a union or political-club hall than in a Chamber of Commerce meeting. In convention, they relish the cheerleading teams of pretty girls, the balloons and crepe paper, the straw hats, the hoopla of hotel room and convention-floor crossfirings of give-and-take. Nineteen sixty was one of those, and then some. Before the voting, sides switched like goldfish in a tank; bitter rivals became bosom buddies in a nonce, and vice versa. Lyndon Baines Johnson, Texan-cowboy eyes crinkled and twinkling, saddle-sized jaw dominating the wry grin and lined cheeks, was a lifelong master at the free-for-alls. At one of his countless impromptu press conferences, this one in the poster-bedecked lobby of the Biltmore Hotel, a reporter confronted him with "Because the Teamsters are backing you, Bobby Kennedy claims there's an 'unholy alliance' between you and Jimmy Hoffa."

Johnson grinned. "Ah think it's time the Kennedy camp quit trying to smear candidates with guilt by association. Now, our man with the Madison Avenue Smile, his daddy, and his brother have been running against Mr. Hoffa for several years now . . . it's time they all realize there are other issues facing this country!" There was none, but one seemed to be able to see a wad of chewing tobacco slide from one cheek to the other as he added, "Of course, frankly, I think Senator Kennedy would make one fine running mate—the Vice-Presidency's a pretty good place for a young man in need of experience, and I'd be proud . . ."

Bob Kennedy was inside the Convention Hall, picking his way through the smoking, talking, loud, close-packed throng with murder in his eyes. At last he spotted the man he had been searching for, coming in a door from the lobby, and met him at the edge of the floor. "Bob! Hi! You know we—"

"Where were you?"

"When?"

"For the last goddamn fifteen minutes! I was supposed to get Dakota numbers from you fifteen minutes ago!"

"Oh! Yeah, well, my damn walkie-talkie—"

"Check out and go home. You're through." He spun and walked away without another word. It was time for the special meeting he had called up in the Kennedy suite, their headquarters for the Convention campaign. The rooms were so packed he vaulted to the top of a

237

desk and announced, "Keep answering those phones, but listen to me. I'll be quick about it. I know about all the bitching, and I'm sick of it. You're not here to go to Disneyland. I've been here before, four years ago, and I watched defeat. Defeat because of nothing but disorganization and sloppiness. Everybody had a marvelous time and made a lot of friends and went home losers! That's not going to happen this time. The only reason we've made it here tonight is because we've done it right.

"Get this clear. Jack's the nice guy. Not me. Every candidate needs a son of a bitch, and I'm Jack's. You can hate me. Feel free. Just obey me. If you don't like it, leave now. We're going to get him nominated! And if you think I've been rude or hard or whatever on you up to now . . . wait until we go for his election!"

They laughed; he smiled. "Okay. Enough. Now, I want every delegation double-checked, then triple-checked. I don't want hunches or guesses, and I don't want wishful thinking. I only want to know the votes we are *guaranteed* on the first ballot. Then we'll know where we—Jerome?"

"Bob, we're having a hard time getting any straight dope out of most of the Southern delegates. It's the civil rights platform, I think, and they're—"

"I know. All right, here's your procedure on that. They're probably all going to John Baines Wayne anyhow, but lay it out—we have the best civil rights plank any Party has had since Lincoln! We're totally behind it, and we want it passed at this Convention—make sure they understand that. It's not negotiable, and don't leave them thinking or hoping it might be. And don't go begging them for their support on it, either. The votes we might get now wouldn't be worth the bad feelings later. Anything else? Okay, get at it. You're all doing fine."

That night, John F. Kennedy won the nomination on the first ballot.

Water sprinkled softly from underground pipes on the shrubs and flowers and lawns of actress Marian Davies's splendid Beverly Hills manion. She had been a good family friend since Joe Kennedy's Hollywood days. He and two of his sons were lounging about her lovely swimming pool this clear, sunshiny California afternoon. Bob had just been told the first part of some very disturbing news, and he blew. "No! No! Jack, you can't *do* this!"

Their father said, "He can and he should, Bob."

"Bobby, the Vice-Presidency doesn't mean a thing anyway. We need a—"

"Johnson tried to rob you of the nomination! It's been very ugly and very personal between them and us the last couple of months. Damnit, he's a vindictive . . . And he's been to the well with Hoffa."

"We need him, Bobby. He owns the South. We'll never make it without Texas."

"But he's voted against everything you ever stood for! Consistently!"

"All right, then this way we'll be getting him out of the leadership of the Senate. Look at it that way."

It was hard and hurtful for Robert Kennedy to look at it in any way but: the dream was not going to be so clean after all. At that time, Lyndon Johnson, in Bob's estimation, personified the wheeling-dealing, back-room good-old-boy brand of politician he believed government should rid itself of. To finger him as Jack's running mate seemed to be a mockery of all they had said and stood for throughout the campaign. Crestfallen, he could only mumble, "Jesus, I even told Jackson already he . . . What makes you so sure he'll accept?"

The father said, "He'll accept."

"The Convention will fall apart!" Bob argued. "The liberals will bolt faster than—"

The old man said, "No, they'll be confused at first, but in two weeks they'll be saying it's the smartest move Jack ever made. Which it will be."

Jack said, "Don't you want to win, Bob?"

The second part of the news grieved him even more deeply. He received it with a wooden, expressionless face, stood, and left them. He'd do it, but at least he could make them wonder about him for a while.

"Well, well, this is a surprise, thought somebody

239

must've got the message wrong. Pull up a chair, get a load off your mind, young fella."

"Thank you, sir. Senator, my brother has asked me to be the one to personally offer you second place on the ticket."

One huge hand flew to Lyndon Johnson's chin. He leaned back and looked away. The two sat there together in silence, the air between them electric with the implications. Robert was Johnson's strongest opponent in the Kennedy camp; he was also the nominee's beloved brother and partner. The man must mean it. "Tell the next President of the United States the Senator from Texas is honored to accept."

Sandy Farrell found Jimmy Hoffa out in the woods at his lakeside home in Michigan, chopping wood, laying in logs for the winter, swinging the ax vigorously, running with sweat. *"Johnson!"* Jimmy screamed. *"Johnson!"* He drove the ax deep into the tree-stump chopping block, yanked it free, and flung it into the woods. "They fly all over the fuckin' country in their goddamn daddy-bought plane tellin' everybody Hoffa's for Johnson, so Johnson's a crook—then they *name* him?"

"And he accepted."

"I don't fuckin' *believe* those guys! They call *me* a crook! Goddamn hypocrites! God *damn* it, Sandy, I mean *God damn it!* All right! Get on it! We go for Nixon!"

"A Republican? You want the Teamsters to go against the Democrats?"

"You heard me!"

Robert Kennedy ran Jack's campaign for election with the same rigor as he had the race for the nomination. Now, more people than staff and volunteers got a taste of his impatience with laggards. When the powerful New York Democrats slowed and then jammed the spinning gears with their internal strife, Bob flew there himself. At the head of a conference table in a literally smoke-filled meeting room, he listened to the various old-pro contingents from the Boroughs and Albany air their grievances. His briefcase stayed on the table before him, unopened. At the end, he stood, picked it up, and told them: "It seems you have a serious split here. Eleanor Roosevelt and you so-called Reform Democrats over there, and Tammany Hall over there. That seems to leave a middle. Well, that's a middle that we are not going to fall into. I neither know nor care what all this means to you, but to me it comes out simply as the New York Democrats are fighting among themselves . . . at a time when any and all infighting is not going to be tolerated! If you continue, it becomes seriously questionable whether any of you will survive after November. So let me put it to you—that question will better be resolved if John F. Kennedy and the Democratic Party win! Frankly, I don't care if you survive or not, but I'm telling you—knock it off, put up a united front, get back to business and get Kennedy elected, or God help you!" Then he walked out.

One Brooklyn pol said, "He mentions God as if he just talked to Him!"

"I'm willing to bet he did!"

"The New Frontiersmen," they came to be called, the Kennedy men, their programs, their goals. Throughout the campaign, the young Senator's messages to the people were carefully constructed to project a balance of general, stirring imagery and ideas with a backbone of specific, hard issues and themes. One issue that was purposely and consistently repeated was that of "Jimmy Hoffa," by now a code name for corruption associated with Organized Crime. Its recurrence in speeches and debates and interviews was meant to act as a warning to the enemy and as a reminder to the public that as Hoffa himself had said, "it's not all over." One element that helped them keep this issue in high visibility was the man himself.

Stumping for Richard M. Nixon, pugnacious Jimmy Hoffa was popping up all over the Republican roast-beef-dinner circuit. He steered fairly clear of the Labor-Management relationship, in deference to the leanings of most of his audiences, and concentrated on hearty diatribes against the Kennedys, spicing his harangues with heavy reference to the family fortunes. ". . . Old Joe's really a cheapskate, though. Oh, yeah. There's a story goin' around now, in fact, that he's told his boys not to buy one more vote than is necessary. Seems he's willing to finance a victory, but he's damned if he'll pay for a landslide!"

Point for Hoffa.

Even in his famous television debate against Richard Nixon, Jack Kennedy managed, by deft if rather odd bridging, to include a reference to that issue: ". . . I think we should have an educational system second to none! I'm not satisfied when many of our teachers are inadequately paid, or when our children go to school in part-time shifts. I'm not satisfied when I see men like Jimmy Hoffa, in charge of the largest union in the United States, still free."

Point for Kennedy.

"Well, I've got news for little Bobby's big brother. Hoffa is free because he's never been convicted of anything. But that's a distinction the Kennedys don't make. If they think somebody ought to be in the pen, then to hell with due process. Is that kind of man going to be elected to the highest office in this land?"

Point for Hoffa.

Rising, the winter sun makes a pale yellow sky to the east of Cape Cod. The last waves of Canada geese go barking south overhead in arrows. The fierce, slate-gray sea cuts cliffs in the beaches. Sea glass, sanded smooth, abounds along the tidemark among the shells, kelp, and driftwood. Nearly rock-hard, the sand is easier to walk on than in the gentler seasons. The wind whips and whistles, salty and cold. At Hyannisport, the two Kennedy brothers walked, heavy coat collars up, bareheaded. Robert said, "You could never call it anything but nepotism."

"You're my brother, not my nepot."

"You're sure you know what you're doing?"

"Can you think of somebody better?"

"No."

"Neither can I. You're the best. And that's all I want."

"Well, then, thank you. I accept . . . Mr. President."

Jimmy Hoffa was on one of his phones in his Marble Palace office when he got the word. "Will you quit yapping about who's President and who isn't and tell me why you called? . . . No, no, I didn't hear . . . Jesus . . . Yeah, thanks." He hung up, swiveled around and stared out at the Capitol, gleaming white against the cold, clear blue sky. Then he hit a button on his intercom. "Yuki, get Sandy in here."

Farrell came.

"You hear?" Jimmy said. "He made Bobby Attorney General!"

"Jesus Christ."

"Yeah. Now it really gets rough."

Abashed, Sandy muttered, "They do have guts, don't they."

"More guts than brains. They're fuckin' crazy."

Bob Kennedy now had an office every bit as large and opulent as anything in the Marble Palace. Kenny O'Donnell, Dave Thatcher, Angie, and the rest all kidded him about it the first few days, but he laughed. "Well, it's good for two things anyhow—we can play some real ball without going outside, and I can fit every lawyer in the whole Department in here at one time!"

It was his. The whole Justice Department. It could now no longer be a thorn in his side. He was the Attorney General of the United States, and he had the complete support and encouragement of the President in all his acts and decisions. Such a combination of power might have existed before in the country's history, but if it had he had never read about it. He wasted no time taking over and putting his thumbprint on the plate. Just as Jimmy Hoffa had installed a gymnasium for all employees when he took charge in the Marble Palace, so Bobby Kennedy had one built in the Department of Justice. Hoffa had replaced Dave Beck's free movies with calisthenics classes; Kennedy only put out the word that it would behoove everyone to use the physical-fitness facilities.

Bob went strolling throughout the labyrinths of Justice, opening closets, introducing himself to copymachine operators. Down an aisle in the silent stacks

243

of a library, he came upon a young man reading a paperback beside an outside window. The kid was a clerk, he said. Bob smiled. "Well, I'm the Attorney General, and if you don't find something to do around here, you'll be an unemployed clerk. Read on your own time, like I do."

And he did fill his office one day with not only all the Department's lawyers, but some hundred others. He mounted his desk, laid down his guidelines of operating as he had to his staff at the McClellan Committee, then smiled. "Now, I know a lot of you must be wondering how a lawyer with absolutely no trial experience gets to be the Attorney General, so I'll tell you. I started in the Department as a young lawyer in nineteen fifty for four grand a year.

"But I worked hard.

"I was ambitious.

"I studied.

"I applied myself.

"Then my brother was elected President of the United States."

He identified their new primary missions to be civil rights and Organized Crime. "We're going to improve one and destroy the other. Last year, this Department had only seventy-four crime figures targeted for prosecution. Only thirty-five ever went to trial. Only eight of those were convicted. Eight, out of this entire nation. Well, that's the past. Welcome to the beginning of a new era for the Justice Department in this country.

"People, I want you to hear this and hear it well: I am here and now declaring war on crime in this country! They have an army out there, and never think they don't. You, all of you, are my army. Each of you is a soldier of an army in combat, at war against a most vicious and powerful enemy. Your performance will be judged accordingly.

"I will offer you now what I always do, and that's a chance to get out on your own. If you're going to do it, do it now. To stay is to commit yourself totally to the cause of justice in the United States. The choice is yours. That's all."

The office emptied slowly and noisily, until only one man was left, in the rear, leaning against a wall

244

and grinning. Bob laughed. "Well? You in or out?"

Ted Lerner lost his grin. "What? I thought I was only . . ."

"Visiting? I want to offer you a job, Ted."

"From Tacoma? No, I—"

"No, you'll have to move. Hey, I came to you once, now it's your turn."

"To do what, Bob?"

"Handle my press work, cover public information for the Department, I don't know, everything, anything you want to do."

"Wow. When do I start?"

"Thanks, Ted. Right now. Consider yourself on payroll. Now, there's a guy out in—"

"Hey, wait, listen, I'm grateful and excited, but I'll have to give the paper two weeks' notice at least, and move, and . . . I couldn't be here before the sixth or the tenth of the month."

"Great. I'll look for you on the sixth. This guy, though, he was one of the prosecutors on Beck, a black, very common name but I can't . . ."

"Charlie Smith?"

"You got it! What's he doing?"

"Charlie went into private practice in Portland."

"Terrific trial lawyer. Listen, Ted, I'm setting up a special, elite group to handle nothing but Hoffa cases. How about giving Smith a call and see if he'd be interested in coming to see me."

"Well, sure—but there's one thing about Charlie you ought to know: he was head of Lawyers for Nixon in King's County."

"I'm not interested in his politics, Ted. He's one of the best lawyers I've ever seen, and that's all I want. Call him."

Charlie Smith signed on. So did other new, hand-picked legal or investigatory experts, along with many of the veterans of the McClellan years. At their preliminary briefing session, Robert Kennedy told them: "This unit is to be considered top secret. Meaning only three people know about it: me, the President, and probably Jimmy Hoffa."

Walt Sheridan quipped, "The Get-Hoffa Squad!"

"Call it what you will, but get him and get him

solid. Legally solid. Clark Mollenhoff is here because he knows more about Hoffa than anybody, and is available to all of you at any time. Anytime you can't reach me, get Jack." This meant Herbert J. Miller, Kennedy's Assistant Attorney General. "This time, I want to get him all the way . . . or leave him alone. And I don't want to leave him alone."

Bob got out of his chair, walked to the wall and removed a framed quotation. "Uh, I've been gearing up the Department with a lot of military language, because I think it works and I know it's accurate. But, you guys—well, some of you are already familiar with this, but let me read it to the rest of you so you . . . see how I want us to be. It's Shakespeare. It's from King Henry the Fifth, and it goes:

We few, we happy few, we band of brothers
For he today that sheds his blood with me
Shall be my brother. . . .
And gentlemen . . . now a-bed,
Shall think themselves accursed
they were not here . . .

That'll be all for tonight, I guess. Good luck."

Attorney General Robert Kennedy's fresh, strong army went on the attack and never stopped. All over the United States the underworld was struck more heavily than had ever happened before. Jail cells started to fill.

Their appeals run out, Dave Beck and Barney Baker went to prison. Indictments and convictions multiplied rapidly in Miami, Cleveland, New York, Louisville, Kansas City, Chicago, Detroit. Racketeering Teamsters and Mafia figures even at the Appalachin level were being nailed left and right.

Sam (Moe) Giancanna was indicted.

Six of Jimmy Hoffa's closest pals in Detroit and Pontiac were indicted.

Inside informants talked more and more.

Vito Genovese was indicted.

Johnny Dio was indicted.

Cincinnati, Los Angeles, Philadelphia felt the heat. Carlo Gambino was indicted.

Chieftains, bosses, underbosses, captains, lieutenants of the Cosa Nostra, Mafia soldiers—none were invincible any longer.

Louisiana overlord Carlos Marcello, having lunched with Vincent Cisco, walked to the door of the small New Orleans restaurant and stopped. His bodyguard opened the door and stepped out into the warm sun on the sidewalk. He surveyed the street, then crossed to the waiting Cadillac. Marcello followed, Cisco close behind. He was halfway to the car when the FBI closed in, identifying themselves quickly and clearly to insure the guard's hands came back out of his pockets empty. "Mr. Carlos Marcello?"

"You know who I am."

"You'll have to come with us, sir."

"You can't arrest me."

"No, sir. Pursuant to an order issued by the Immigration Department and signed by the Attorney General of the United States, you are hereby being deported."

"I want my lawyer!"

"No time, sir. Your plane to Guatemala leaves in fifteen minutes."

His bodyguard could only watch as he was escorted into the waiting car. "Fucking Kennedy," Cisco said. "He'll pay for this."

One of Marcello's Florida counterparts, Frank Tanella, didn't have to be hit by the Justice Department forces. When Fidel Castro grasped power in Cuba, Tanella had been caught there, running his casino operations, and thrown into the Havana prison. But something was being done about that . . .

Wiry, leather-skinned Robert McKeon was in his Miami Beach bar early one morning, washing glassware and sweeping up in preparation for opening. The venetian blinds on his windows and his door were down and closed against the sun. A dark shadow appeared at the door and knocked.

McKeon called, "Not open yet! Come back in two hours!"

247

The form moved closer into the doorway and spoke through the crack in the doorjamb. "Mr. McKeon, I'm the man who talked to you last night."

"Fort Worth?"

"That's right."

McKeon unlocked the door. His visitor stepped in, smiling friendly, offering his hand. He was pleasant-looking, a bit pasty-skinned despite the beginnings of a tan, well dressed and tending to the slick side. McKeon said, "Sure didn't take you long to get here."

"I flew. This is very important to me."

McKeon poured two mugs of coffee at the bar. He said, "Well, like I said, I can maybe give you some advice is all."

"Mr. McKeon—the individual I'm talking about is Frank Tanella."

McKeon nodded. "I've heard of him, all right. But that only makes it harder, not easier."

The stranger's tone was ingratiating. "I understand you ran guns for Castro, and that you and him are pretty good friends. Now I want very badly to help my friend get out of jail down there, and all I'm asking from you is a simple letter of introduction to your friend."

"No, I wouldn't want to do that, I don't think."

"I'm prepared to make it real worth your while."

"What's 'real' worth?"

"Twenty-five thousand dollars. Cash money. Just for a letter." He looked around the modest tavern and smiled, "That doesn't happen to you every day, does it, Mr. McKeon?"

McKeon stirred his coffee with a spoon for a long while, thinking. Then he said, "Tanella. No, I'm sorry, but I'll have to pass."

The man from Texas looked genuinely disappointed, but didn't press it. "I'm sorry we can't do business this time. Anytime you find yourself in Fort Worth or Dallas, you know how to find me—the fun'll be on the house."

"Thank you kindly."

"This never happened, of course."

"Of course."

Outside, the man from Texas put his sunglasses

back on and headed for his car. Well, nothing ventured, nothing gained. He'd just have to go on to Havana without the letter, and take his chances there; he wasn't too worried.

In Washington, it was after midnight when Robert Kennedy and Walt Sheridan left the Justice Building and headed for their cars in the parking lot. Bob had been so engaged in other matters, Walt had had to wait until ten to brief him on the latest developments. Jimmy Hoffa had succeeded in forcing the surrender of the court-appointed monitorship, and was hurrying the staging of a new Teamsters convention; under attack, hurting, he wanted a mammoth demonstration to display his continuing popularity as President.

Sheridan had also informed Kennedy: ". . . The Federal Judge in Tampa dismissed the Sun Valley case on a technicality in selection of a grand jury."

"We'll resubmit?"

"Right. By then we'll be able to broaden the charge. Dismissal might work for us, actually. Going after low-level Teamster officials turns out to be a good idea. We're hitting everyone who destroys evidence or gives false testimony. All of a sudden more and more of them are finding it easier to talk to us than to face perjury raps."

"Terrific."

"Yeah—they're starting to be more afraid of you than they are of Hoffa. We're coming across two basic kinds of guys, the ones who've been getting screwed and want it cleaned up and the ones who see themselves getting ahead faster if Hoffa's out of the way."

"And how close is he to that?"

"Well, there is one more thing I wanted to talk to you about—we've got enough evidence in the Test Fleet deal to nail Jimmy on a conflict of interest."

"Shit, that's nothing but violation of Taft-Hartley, Walt. Thirty days and a fine, with a suspended sentence, if I know him!"

"I know, but it's solid, Bob. A guaranteed conviction. I think we should go for it. It'll be his first, and the timing's—"

"Okay, go."

"Good. Also, what do you think about seeking the indictment in Nashville instead of Detroit?"

"Can we get it there?"

"I think so. It's where the outfit operated."

"Absolutely. I'd hate to go after Jimmy in Detroit!"

In the lot, Bob had his car keys out where he stopped and looked up. "That bastard." The Marble Palace was all in darkness, except for one office: Hoffa's.

Walt said, "Jimmy's burning the midnight oil."

Kennedy put his keys away and turned to head back to the door of the Justice Building. "See you tomorrow, Walt."

"Where the hell are you going?"

"If that son of a bitch can find something to do at twelve-twenty in the morning, so can I!"

Jimmy Hoffa wasn't exactly working; he was talking to Edward Grady Partin, Teamster Boss of Local 5, Baton Rouge, Louisiana. Partin was in trouble, and, a loyal Hoffa man for all of his twelve years in the union, had come to Jimmy for help.

"How many charges they got on you, Ed?"

"Twenty-six! I don't—"

"Yeah, I know, join the crowd. Bastards, they're beltin' all my good guys." Jimmy liked Ed. He ran his Local well, and wasn't afraid to use his fists when he had to. Partin had also done some special jobs for him over the years. He was the kind of guy you could call on Christmas Eve and he'd be right there, ready to do whatever you needed done. Big, tough, loyal guy—you could put him on the cover of the Teamsters' magazine.

Hoffa didn't know that his friend Ed Partin harbored a grudge against him for some of those Christmas Eves. Partin loved kids, had five of his own, and was in the process of losing them; his wife was finally leaving him, and he knew his years of zealous service to Jimmy and the union had had a lot to do with it. It was only a grudge, though, and Partin kept it buried pretty deep inside himself. He was from the back-country South, around Woodville, Mississippi, where nobody sane ever told you life was supposed to be soft. He trusted Hoffa, and was willing to be patient. But he did wish the little guy would settle down and give his problems some attention.

Jimmy couldn't sit still. He'd drop for some push-ups every ten minutes or so, but it didn't seem to be helping him calm down. He was pacing about his great office, stopping to stare out at that goddamn Kennedy asylum, then turning to pace and prowl around some more. He had had a messy scene earlier. He'd called in one of his headquarters officers, to talk to him about his drinking problems. The man had given him some guff, and before he even realized what he was doing, 190-pound Jimmy was lacing into the skinny old geezer with everything he had. Took Sandy and three others to pull him off the guy. Probably didn't do the dope any harm, but he hated going out of control like that over nothing, and was hating even more the ones he knew were responsible for getting him into such a sorry state, them spoiled little rich kids over there playing with the power! Partin, Partin. Good man, good muscle. Lots of trouble right now. "Hey, Ed. I came by a .270 rifle. High-powered scope. Shoots a long way without droppin' any. Know where I could get a silencer for it?"

"What make is it, Jim?"

"Damned if I know. Ah, I'm just thinkin' out loud, but somebody's got to get that little son of a bitch one of these days!"

"What son of a—"

"Bobby Kennedy, who else! He's nuts, him and his brother, they're goddamn maniacs. How much, Ed?"

Jimmy was hard to follow tonight. "How much what?"

"Your bond!"

"Oh! Uh, fifty grand, Jim."

"Wow, them's big bucks, huh, kid? Fifty! Jesus."

He was at the window again, his back to Partin's chair. "You know, the little shit runs around in a

251

convertible, all the time? With the top down, and the dumb-ass dog hangin' out back!"

Partin tried to joke. "And I can't go to the funds, you know, that bein' what they're indictin' me on."

"And his goddamn house," Hoffa rambled, turning back to his desk and making diagrams with his hands for Ed, "sits right near the road, big as hell, and not even a fence, and no guards at all!"

"That right, Jim?"

Hoffa looked up; his eyes seemed to have changed back to normal again. "Hear this ain't your only problem, Ed—what the hell's this kidnapping rap about?"

"Aw, shoot, that's a whole other mess. One of the kids in the Local, nice boy, illiterate as all hell, but you know. I don't know how I got myself into the middle of it, but I did. He took his kids away from his wife, then went and holed up in a motel with his momma, his kids, and a shotgun. So I hear about it and go over—"

"Creeps got so many enemies now, they'd never know who done it! Someplace down South'd be the smart setup, let it look like some of the segregation people . . ."

Partin didn't like the feel of it; he pretended not to be hearing, and continued. "Well, don't his wife's kin pull up in a station wagon outside while I'm trying to talk some sense into him, and don't they have at it, a battle royal like you've never—"

"And they slam you with kidnapping?"

"Aggravated kidnapping! It'll never stick, I don't think, but—"

Jimmy Hoffa stood up. "Ed, you call Allen Dorfman in Chicago and ask him about the bond money." He walked to the door and opened it.

Ed Partin followed. "Thanks, Jim, I knew you'd—"

"One more thing, Ed—you know anything about these plastic bombs they got now?"

"Plastic?"

"Forget about it, we'll talk about it some other time. See you around, kid."

Ed Partin left in a daze. He decided Jimmy was cracking under the heat, and put it all down inside with the Christmas Eves.

Jimmy Hoffa had his convention.

The Kennedy Administration went brightly into its second year.

The Justice Department's assault on Organized Crime continued, indictments falling like shrapnel.

Early in September, 1962, a black Cadillac moved along a dirt road through a swamp outside New Orleans. Its headlights at last swept across the front of a seemingly deserted hunting lodge, and it stopped. The car doors opened and the door to the lodge opened, letting a narrow shaft of yellow light fall across the porch and onto the dirt yard. An elegantly dressed man appeared in the doorway and called his welcome in Italian. Coming up behind his bodyguards, Vincent Cisco returned the greeting in the same language.

Inside, a meal was set. Only Vincent Cisco and his host sat to partake and to talk. "It is time to remove the stone from my shoe," Cisco said bitterly.

The other man shook his head. "He is the Attorney General, and a brother. Nothing can be done. One cannot have a President angry for vengeance."

"Then . . .?"

"No!"

"Cut the head off the rooster, the rooster dies. Remove the President, and . . ."

"It is not possible. Only a crazy man would consider it."

"Crazy men can be found anywhere."

"Nothing can be done."

"Something *must* be done," Cisco said.

A few days later, two other men met and drank coffee together in the Carriage Hotel in Miami Beach. Pleasant sunshine washed the stucco outside walls and seeped inside through the graceful Spanish grating on the arched windows. One was a young man, a wealthy Cuban exile named Alberto Pérez, and he said to Frank Tanella, "The loan. It is secure?"

Tanella said, "A million two hundred fifty thousand dollars. Hoffa has personally approved it."

"Aah, Hoffa! I don't know. He is besieged with too many troubles of his own. I must be certain that the

253

loan is secure, Frank." Pérez in fact had to be certain and cautious about many things. He was a double agent, also employed by the Federal Bureau of Investigation.

Tanella sipped and reassured him. "Don't worry. Jimmy's problems will be corrected. This man Kennedy is in trouble."

"No, believe *me*, Frank. This President Kennedy is very popular and will most surely be re-elected."

Frank Tanella put his empty cup delicately into its saucer. He wiped his mouth with a napkin and said, "No, Alberto, he is going to be hit."

BOOK FIVE

Occupation Forces

Edward Grady Partin lay on his back on his cot in his East Baton Rouge Parish, Louisiana, jail cell, unable to sleep. The single, small window was too high in the wall for him to see out, but through it he could hear the nighttime sounds of wind in the trees, insects, highway traffic and railroad trains. Light from the prison yard below reached his ceiling in separated, jagged shapes. The light on the floor outside his cell was straighter, though also faint; it came from the guard's office at the end of the cell block. Other prisoners snored, moaned, turned in their blankets, uttered clipped pieces of words in their sleep.

This was not the first night Partin had spent in the eerie half-world of insomnia. He had met Allen Dorfman in Miami and had been told the Teamsters would come through with the fifty grand. They hadn't. He was in now on the kidnapping rap. He had friends on the outside trying to raise the bond money for the other charge. His wife had left; he had weekend visiting privileges with his kids, but little good that would do him if he was going to be locked away for God knew how long. He could see them in the dim fragments of light on his ceiling these fretful nights, laughing, playing, weeping, looking for him. His heart hurt. More and more, Jimmy Hoffa's years of Christmas Eves tore loose from the bottom and came floating to the top of Ed Partin's melancholy. And now he was being double-crossed on the fifty grand. He was sure of it, they were going to dump him, and the only reason

256

he could think of had to be that crazy night with Jimmy: he hadn't answered Hoffa's call, and was being punished for it.

He had visions of the man and the dog and the blue convertible going up. They didn't disturb him so much as the visions of the house going up. In that waking dream of explosions and flames there came sounds of children screaming in terror and pain. That terrible scene played over and over in Partin's desperate mind. For many nights it simply scraped against his one soft, sentimental spot: his deep, instinctive fondness for babies and little people. But lately, it had been sort of enlarging and distancing itself from his feelings. The reality of it . . . the possibility of it had begun to loom in his brain, and it scared him.

Tonight, he couldn't abide it any longer. He abruptly rose off the bunk and went to his cell door. Bars touching his cheeks, he spoke once, low, into he hallway: "Leroy!" He gave the clod another few seconds then said it again, louder: "Leroy!"

The guard came out through the light in the doorway and along came the block, making impatient sounds. He curled his Batman-and-Robin comic books into a roll and waved it at Partin. "What you want, Partin? You tryin' to wake the whole—"

"I want to see the warden."

"Sure. In the middle of the night! I'll just go right now and—"

"You want that funnybook down your throat, Leroy?"

"Haw. Take more'n some old baby-snatcher to—"

"Ain't going to be in here forever, Leroy."

"Hell, what you goin' on about this time of night anyhow, Partin?"

"You go call Edwards now. You tell him Ed Partin got to see him right away."

"You crazy? I can't—"

"Shut that fool mouth! You tell him I know something the Feds will want to know about. Matter of national security."

"National . . . ! Aw, Jesus, I . . ."

"Leroy—please. It's life-and-death, man."

257

The guard caught the big man's sincerity. "All right, Ed, but it'll be your ass if—"

"Shut up and go."

Warden Edwards made him wait until early the next morning, then saw him in his office. Partin spoke clearly and steadily, telling of his meeting with Teamsters President Jimmy Hoffa. Edwards knew who Partin was, and knew the kidnapping time was a fluke. When Partin said the words "plastic explosives," the warden threw up his hand.

"Hold it, Ed. I've heard enough. If any of this is true, it's too rich for my blood. It's got to go higher up. I'll make some calls for you."

Walt Sheridan was waiting in Robert Kennedy's parking slot when he arrived for work. "I wanted to catch you outside and alone."

"I thought you went to Nashville already."

Sheridan said. "I decided to wait until after a jury's been selected. My being in the same city might—"

"Right, they'll be looking for any out."

"Bob, we got a call from Baton Rouge last night. A man named Edward Grady Partin said Jimmy Hoffa asked to have you killed. Something about plastic explosives being thrown into your car or your house."

"Partin, yes. One of Jimmy's pale, right?"

"Frank Grimsley's on his way to talk to him now."

"Why FBI? Couldn't we—"

"This is assassination we're talking, Bob."

"Cut it out. That's the old agent in you coming out."

"Partin's no eight-ball. If he claims that Hoffa's talking about having you killed, we can't ignore it."

"Whatever you say, Walt. But hell, Jimmy's liable to *say* anything."

"Yeah, but do me a favor, will you? Start using one of the limo's for a while?"

Bob laughed. "Brumus couldn't stand being closed in like that."

A kid named Hoagie was on duty and came for Partin. Walking him out, he said, "Why's the D.A.

wantin' to see you at three in the mornin' anyhow?"

"Harassment, Hoagie," Partin said, "just more harassment."

In Warden Edwards's office, District Attorney Sargent Pitcher introduced Ed Partin to Frank Grimsley. Partin told his whole story again, into a tape recorder. When he finished, Grimsley asked, "Ed, are you sore at Hoffa for something?"

"Sore? No. I got a few bones to pick with him, but no, Jimmy's still my friend, and my boss. I can't live with it any more, that's all."

"Are you telling us the truth, Mr. Partin?"

"Yes. I have kids of my own."

"Was there anyone else with you and Hoffa in his office or nearby? Who could confirm your story?"

"No, nobody. Jimmy plays close to the vest."

"Then how do I know you're telling the truth?"

"I don't know."

"Are you willing to submit to a polygraph? A lie-detector test?"

"I am."

Sheridan reported to Kennedy: "Partin's telling the truth. The polygraph backs him up."

"Now what do we do?"

"First, we'll have to call the Secret Service."

"Oh, Lord, won't Hoffa love that, seeing me being escorted around by—"

"I know, but it's got to be done. Now comes the interesting part. Grimsley and the local DA got together down there, and Partin can get out on bail if . . . Partin's willing to work for us, Bob. We want to put a phone patch on him and let him see if he can get in close to Jimmy during the Nashville trial."

Bob Kennedy whistled. "Shades of John Cye Cheasty, huh?"

"Like you said, it's war, Bob."

"Can we trust him?"

"I think so. Even if he's only trying to save his ass, he's risking it, too. They'll snuff him in a second. Partin knows that better than we do. He calls it 'the old Swiss cheese disease.' I think he's legit, Bob."

Home alone, Ed Partin attached the patch to the reciver of the phone, activated the tape recorder, and dialed Jimmy Hoffa's number at the Marble Palace. "Jimmy? Ed Partin."

"Hiya, Ed, how's it going?"

"I'm back on the street, Jim."

"That's good."

"Yeah, they finally gave me bail on the stupid kidnap thing."

"God. What's on your mind, Ed?"

"I got some things I'd like to see you about, Jim. Some union business and you know."

"Sure. Listen, why don't you meet me down in Nashville?"

"Nashville?"

"Hell, yeah, I thought everybody knew—goddamn Kennedy's got another trial rigged up to waste my time on. I'll be in Nashville the weekend before the twenty-second. Meet me there, huh? We can talk, and there's maybe a couple things you could help me out on."

"My pleasure, Jim. I'll be there." Now Partin tried to elicit harder goods. "By the way—I did hear where we can get that plastic package." He was telling the truth. There had been a hijacking of a truck full of various explosives in Louisiana; Partin knew who and where.

Hoffa cut him off: "Talk to you in Nashville."

Hoffa's invitation led Sheridan and Grimsley to use Partin for more than the alleged assassination threat, so long as he was willing. The word was out that Hoffa was overreacting to his Test Fleet misdemeanor trial. He didn't want to be convicted of anything. He was probably going to try to put a fix in.

Partin was willing. He'd go to Nashville and keep his ears and eyes open for any indication of possible tampering with the jury. He'd report same to Walt Sheridan, via pay-phone calls to an unlisted number, using the pseudonym "Andy Anderson."

Jimmy Hoffa hit Nashville like thunder. He arrived on the Teamsters' twin-engine Lodestar, and was met by the press. He called Kennedy the "Boy Attorney General," compared him to Hitler, then proceeded to the Andrew Jackson Hotel. He occupied an entire floor there; where Hoffa was, Teamsters International Headquarters was.

Ed Partin made his contact with Hoffa, and was welcomed as a friend and trusted lieutenant. Inside information started coming to him fast. Down in the Andrew Jackson's coffee shop, he met Allen Dorfman and a swarthy man who introduced himself as Anthony Quinn, but then admitted he was Nick Tweel, in from West Virginia "to help Jimmy with the jury." Partin went to a pay phone and Andy Anderson called Walt Sheridan at the Noel Hotel. Sheridan dashed right over to the Teamsters' hotel, sauntered through the lobby and coffee shop, made the man sitting with Dorfman, then walked close to the big guy coming out of the phone booth, the one with the "P on the handkerchief in my pocket."

"The Noel. Room Five Four Two," Sheridan side-mouthed.

"Got you," Partin-Anderson said, then returned to his friends.

For every Teamster official and union-connected racketeer who descended upon Nashville that October, there seemed to be at least one FBI agent also arriving. The people of Nashville were only mildly interested in the Hoffa trial to begin with. Then they and the rest of the world were further distracted by the larger and more terrifying news announced on television by President John F. Kennedy: Soviet-made missiles had been positively discovered ninety miles offshore, in Cuba. He was blockading all Cuban ports against any further traffic by Soviet ships. This might be it.

Hiroshima. Nagasaki. World War III. The Nuclear Holocaust.

In addition to all the *this might be it!* horrors he shared with the rest of mankind, Walt Sheridan bore the immediate burden of knowing that the Hoffa showdown was all in his own hands now. The President's brother would be at his side in this monumental, cataclysmic crisis, from beginning to end. Sheridan was still in a state of shock and dread when the knock came on his door in the Noel Hotel. "Yeah!"

"Anderson."

He let Ed Pardin in. They shook hands. "Were you careful, Ed?"

"Are you kidding?"

"I meant this to be brief, we ought to have one face-to-face if we're going to be doing this together, but . . . Did you hear?"

"Sure did. You got a bottle around?"

They poured Scotch and sat. Ed Partin said, "Christ. Nuclear war. It's so weird—you, me, Hoffa, all of us. Boom."

"Well, we can't just sit around."

"Okay. Jimmy's already said to me he might have something to pass to somebody. He patted his wallet pocket, so I guess he means money. He said, too, they're going to try a few scattered jurors and take their chances."

"So it's real. We're not fooling with maybes anymore."

"Jimmy never fools around," Partin said. "Kennedy don't either, I guess."

"The President, you mean?"

"Yeah. Sometimes I like that about a guy, takes no crap from anybody. But sometimes it can scare the hell out of you, can't it."

"You scared, Ed?"

"Sure am."

"I might as well tell you now—they've dropped the kidnapping charges against you."

"Good. Thanks. Uh, the phone calls have started, too."

"What phone calls?"

"You know. Standard practice. Just reaching out to prospective jurors, all over the lot."

"Hoffa does that, does he?"

"Makes sense, Mr. Sheridan. Later, you can always say it could've been anybody. Newspaper reporters, cranks, do-gooders."

"And any contact with the defendant can disqualify a juror. Clever."

"Sure. Let me ask you, if the jury stays straight, can Jimmy be got on this thing?"

"He's wide open for it. A lot of his own people have

been telling him for years to let Test Fleet go, but he wouldn't. He let the payments flow in right through nineteen sixty. About a million eight to the firm, almost two hundred and fifty grand to his wife and Bert Brennan's. Add to that the— Is something amusing?"

Partin was grinning. "You straight-arrows really get all hot over that, don't you."

"You're a Teamster, Ed, that's *your* money going to—"

"Oh, hell, that don't bother anybody. We don't care too much about what they do at the top, probably do the same or worse if we had their jobs."

"Just as long as Jimmy delivers good contracts, right? I know. That's one of the things that make it so hard for us to get him."

Ed Partin got up and poured them both more whiskey. "It ain't that kind of money that got Jimmy into this dutch, Mr. Sheridan. He's gone over. He wants to kill people, and he don't care *who* any more." He downed his shot, waved a huge arm, and was at the open door. "Better get along now. See you on the phone."

Late that night Sheridan was brought from bomb-haunted sleep by the phone.

"Andy?"

"Walt?"

"Bob!"

"How's it going down there?"

"Never mind down here, how's it going there?"

"It's, uh, all very . . . stretched thin here."

"You sound like you're in a hole!"

"I'm okay. How're you and—"

"Bob? Listen. You worry about Cuba, let *me* worry about Hoffa! Go get some sleep. And don't worry— we'll nail his ass to the roof of the Grand Ol' Opry for you."

Their man in court against Hoffa was Tennesseean James Neal. Sheridan informed him of the "reaching-out" calls, and Neal informed Judge Willaim. E. Miller. In Miller's chambers, Jimmy did exactly what Ed Partin had predicted. Overstepping his own defense counsel, William Bufalino and Tommy Osborn, he ranted, "That's a lotta crap! You can't say them calls, *if* they were made at all, weren't some out-of-town reporter who you *don't* know about! You bimbos don't know everything, you know! This ain't a police state *yet!*" And the judge ruled in his favor. The Government prosecutors were overzealous, overconcerned. Miller saw no reason to sequester the prospective jury.

With Ed Partin now part of the close ring of men around him, Jimmy Hoffa continued to run the details of his enormous union, working his phones faster than any switchboard operator. Partin had never been exposed to the phenomenon for sustained periods of time before, and had to truly marvel at it. Hoffa seemed to be a whole different man from the one who spoke of high-powered rifles and plastic explosives and blatantly ordered the fixing of jurors. Jimmy was laughing: ". . . No, I wish I thought of it, but Cuba's no deal of mine, Ned—but listen, what's his bottom line? . . . Seven and a quarter? He there with you? Tell him it's a deal, yeah, we'll take it . . . What? He would've gone to a half? Tell him that's all right, I woulda gone to seven!"

Sandy Farrell was waiting for a lull. When it came, he presented the visitor, Ewing King, head of Teamster Local 327 in Nashville. Jimmy shook his hand. "Ewing, how are ya? How's Janet and the kids?"

"Jan—? Why, she's fine, thank you! I'm amazed you remember her name, Mr.—"

"Hey, what kinda President you think I am?"

"Well, sir, that's what I came up here to tell you—we all love you down here, Jimmy, we're behind you a hundred and ten percent!' And if there's *anything* you want from us, anything at all . . ."

"Sit down, Ewing, sit down."

When jury-selection proceedings ended that Tuesday afternoon, insurance man James Tippens found himself sitting in the #12 chair in the box. He left for home fairly certain he'd be chosen the next day to sit on the Hoffa trial. Heading for the bus stop, he was glad to see the Dodge sedan pull up. "Hey, Jim, need a lift?"

"Sure do!"

He got in, and the man drove him home. He was an old friend and lived in the same neighborhood. They laughed, talked about sports and the weather and the Cuban Missile Crisis. Then his friend said it. "Jim? How'd you be interested in making some easy money?"

"Never seen that kind yet, what you got cooking?"

"Ten thousand dollars."

Tippens had no reason to connect his friend to anything, but some bell went off in his head. He said, "Hold it right there. This have anything to do with my jury duty?"

"Well, yes."

"Then don't say one more word." He got out at his door, went in and ate his dinner, read his paper, watched his television, and went to bed. He worried about it all night. He didn't want to get his friend into any trouble.

Just before nine the next morning, Tippens was with Judge Miller in his quarters, telling him the whole story. Miller excused him from jury duty and cautioned him to mention the matter to no one until the FBI could question him.

Once again Judge Miller ordered prosecution, defense, and the defendant to meet in private. Once again Jimmy was fiesty. "We gonna spend this whole trial in your quarters or what?"

"I have never heard of such a bold attempt to subvert the jury system in all my twenty-seven years as lawyer and judge!" Miller solemnly declared.

Accusations, denials and counteraccusations flew back and forth.

Miller prevailed finally with some vehemence. "I am indignant that such a thing has occurred in my courtroom. I want it known that I will take the strongest possible steps to punish anyone who is apprehended and proven to be engaged in this kind of activity! I will take Mr. Osborn's opinion, and not sequester the jury. In the face of my warning, only a fool or a totally corrupt scoundrel would attempt any further tampering!"

Walking back into the courtroom, Jimmy grinned at Bufalino. "Cutie-pie when he's mad, ain't he?"

As Hoffa's behind-the-scenes onslaught on jurors continued, Tommy Osborn's interrogations of them in court got longer and slower and more detailed. Osborn was as Tennessean as Neal; he had taken Hoffa's offer because he believed the Justice Department was indeed persecuting the Teamster boss. His lines of questioning would even reach to the prospective jurors' viewing habits: did they ever watch *The Untouchables? The Huntley-Brinkley Report?* Had they ever read Robert Kennedy's book on Hoffa and the McClellan Committee. *The Enemy Within?* Finally Judge Miller got weary of it and warned he would soon put an end to the selection process.

At the end of eight days, the Cuban Missile Crisis was over. One of the most potentially expensive bluffs in history had been called, war narrowly averted. The world let out its breath, succumbed to the momentary shakes, then tried to pick up normal life where it had been frozen. Robert Kennedy could at last turn his attention back to Nashville. From his home, he dialed Walt Sheridan's secret number. It was busy.

"Yeah," Andy Anderson was telling Walt, from a drugstore, "Jimmy was real upset over the Tippens thing, whatever that was." Partin had been back in Baton Rouge when that had happened. "Says they're going to lay low for a while. But I picked up something from Ewing King—know him?"

"Yup," Sheridan said, "go on."

"There's a Mrs. Paschal on the jury. Her husband's a Tennessee highway patrolman, and—"

"And Hoffa's got Ewing King in charge of getting to Betty Paschal through her husband," Sheridan relayed to Kennedy.

"How?"

"King says he can offer Paschal a promotion—knows the Governor and the incoming Governor, all that jazz."

"You still believing Anderson, Walt?"

"Yes. Listen, the local Bureau down here's been triple-checking every word he passes. They'd love to

266

prove he's a double, but so far he's good as gold."

"Jimmy's got the locals cracking too, huh?"

"I'll say. Andy says he's coming down hard on King now, claiming he's been doing a lot of talking and no delivering. The patrolman is King's big chance to make good."

"How's the trial itself going?"

"I stay pretty well clear of it, but from what I hear we're fine. Of course, Jimmy's raising holy hell in there every day."

"He's good at that."

"Yeah, poor Neal and Charlie Shaffer, he's giving them the evil eye calling them names and jumping up and down every two seconds. Real circus."

"How are you, Walt?"

"Hey, having a hell of a time. I ate with Clark Mollenhoff the other night, says to say hello. He thinks our case is airtight this time, and he's in that courtroom every second."

"Great."

"I can see what makes him such a great reporter—he smells I've got a plant in, and you should've seen him trying to get me to tip my hand."

"Well, Clark's safe."

"Oh, I know, Bob, but . . . Jesus, I'm afraid for my guy's life in there!"

"Ewing King and the cop—can you—"

"Bob, I think we've said enough tonight."

"Okay. The walls have ears, right?"

"At least."

Ewing King was tall and thin and had practically no chin, so the FBI gave him the code name "Gump," after the chinless cartoon character Andy Gump.

On a Saturday night, Gump sped along a highway away from Nashville in his red Thunderbird. An FBI pursuit car followed. It was a white Plymouth. Agent One drove. Agent Two maintained radio contact with FBI headquarters back in the Nashville Federal Building at Eighth and Broadway. Walt Sheridan was there, listening and waiting. The white car's call name was "88." Agent Two broadcast, "Forty-four, Forty-four, come in Forty-four. This is Eighty-eight, over."

"This is Forty-four, over." Forty-four was a green Chevrolet.

"Forty-four, Gump is pulling into a roadhouse up ahead . . . the Countryside Inn . . . He's watching for the tail . . . we're passing him by . . . Please pick it up, over."

"Eighty-eight, this is Forty-four, we roger. We're in sight of the place and are— Oops, Gump is moving, Eighty-eight, Gump is on the road again, over!"

"This is Eighty-eight, roger, we've got him in the mirror, we'll let him pass—out."

Just as green forty-four was passing the Countryside Inn, a blue Pontiac exited onto the highway, heading in the opposite direction. The radio agent, Four, caught a fleeting glimpse of the driver and pushed his transmit button: "Eighty-eight! Pass your T-Bird and make the driver, over!"

"Roger, Forty-four . . . God-*damn!*"

Ewing King's red Thunderbird was now being driven by Teamster official Mutt Pitts.

Walt Sheridan listened to the frantic inter-car jabber cracking through the receivers.

"This is Forty-four. Gump now in blue Pontiac, heading west. We're making the big U, out!"

The radio operator said, "He made a switch."

Sheridan ordered, "Tell both cars to proceed directly to Paschal's address."

"Good idea," the FBI operator said, and did so.

Walt said, "Thanks," and thought, *Thank you, Ed* —Partin had warned him exactly what would happen. As a precaution, they had a third vehicle staked at Paschal's house, blocking his driveway, in fact, with a fake flat tire, rear bumper jacked up. When the Tennessee highway patrolman pulled up he asked if he could help. "No, sir," the agent said, "I'll be out of your way in no time at all." When the blue Pontiac arrived shortly after, the patrolman went over to talk to the driver. Just after the green Chevrolet cruised past and vanished around the corner, the stakeout agent went over to the Pontiac, identified the driver as Ewing King, and told Paschal, "I'm all set now, sorry if I inconvenienced you, sir."

Around the corner, Agent Four was radioing, "This

is Forty-four, we've made Gump and Paschal . . . they're talking together . . . blue Pontiac license plate number . . ."

By Sunday morning, even Robert Kennedy in Washington knew—they had it, verified contact between the Teamsters officer, King, and the juror's husband, Patrolman Paschal.

In secret, Edward Grady Partin signed the affidavit prepared by Walt Sheridan. It was presented in a sealed envelope to Judge Miller. He read it, resealed it, and, being apprised now of the Anderson-assassination aspect, he called only the defense lawyers to his chambers. Protecting Partin's identity, Miller declared the existence of proof that the jury was being influenced. Tommy Osborn resigned from the case, Judge Miller still refused to sequester the jury. It took something more bizarre to bring that about.

One day in court, Jimmy had just finished testifying and was talking to Bufalino at the defense table. The jury had left the room. Federal marshals, clerks, reporters, and a few students and curious spectators were milling about, talking and stretching and leaving for smoke breaks. A strange-looking young man suddenly walked down the center aisle. He wore a soiled raincoat and his hair looked as if he had cut it himself, with a razor. He stopped, pulled a pistol from his pocket, aimed it point-blank at Hoffa, and fired. It was a pellet target pistol, but nobody knew that then. Jimmy alone kept cool. He bolted straight through the panicky confusion and coldcocked the kid right on the chin. The burly marshals and others then proceeded to pounce on the gunman, a deranged patient on the loose somehow from a nearby mental hospital. If the jury had been present, it could have meant an immediate mistrial. Now Judge Miller ordered them locked up for the rest of the trial.

By now, though, Jimmy was feeling hounded, cornered, and betrayed. He hired six off-duty policemen as a special security force around his person, his office and his living quarters, under the charge of the one close associate he felt he could still trust. To him he said, "Ed? I got word there's a double working in here. Any idea who the hell's the sleazy rat?"

"Beats me, Jim," Partin said. "You know your other guys better than I do."

They discussed the abortive King-Paschal affair. Hoffa said, "Don't worry, I still got a lock on this thing."

"The Paschal woman's off, though, right?"

"Yeah, but I still got one juror in my hip pocket. He's kin to one of my business agents, who came from down here. He won't take any money, but he won't go against his own people."

"That's still just one guy, Jim."

"Ed, one man is a hung jury, and a hung jury's as good as an acquittal. They'd never try this thing again.

Andy Anderson reported this to Walt Sheridan.

The trial concluded. The jury went out. It stayed out a long time. A deadlock was reported after the seventh hour. Four hours after that the jury came back and announced it was hung.

Two special planes drew attention at the Nashville Airport. One was the Teamsters' Lodestar, the other the Air Force transport Robert Kennedy had dispatched to bring his men home. All the reporters clustered around the Lodestar to hear Jimmy, once again jubilant. "The jury was deadlocked because, in spite of Bobby-Boy's brainwash squad, several jurors refused to vote the way he said they should. If the trial hadn't been rigged by the so-called Justice Department, I would've been acquitted outright! Judge Miller was prejudiced! And Jim Neal was one of the most vicious prosecutors who ever handled a criminal case in this country! For anyone to make a statement that this jury had been tampered with was a disgrace! A disgrace and a lie!"

Clark Mollenhoff split from the rest of the reporters and made his way across the tarmac through the freezing winter wind to the Air Force plane, starting its engines. Inside, he found the long cabin crowded with gloomy staff people. The Attorney General's men were once more eating defeat. Robert Kennedy had had the plane hung inside with bright banners proclaiming

MERRY CHRISTMAS! and CONGRATULATIONS! A couple of the despondent investigator-prosecutors were moving along the aisle, tearing down the CONGRATULATIONS posters.

Dropping hellos and halfhearted words of commiseration, Mollenhoff wove through the busy aisles toward the curtain at the rear, behind which he'd been told he'd find Walt Sheridan, Jim Neal, Charlie Shaffer. He dreaded the morose scene he expected to find there. But the closer he got, the surer he was that it was laughter he was hearing.

There they were, making drinks and celebrating.

Clark said, "For guys who've just lost the Government's first major, airtight case against Hoffa, you seem pretty giddy! Finally go around the bend, Walt?'

"Aw, sit down and have a pop, Clark!"

"Merry Christmas, Clark."

"Thanks, but what's the gag?"

"No gag," Sheridan said. "Judge Miller's turning all the jury-tampering evidence over to a grand jury. This time, Jimmy 'improved' himself out of a misdemeanor and right into a felony!"

Jim Neal said, "Jury-tampering's a felony—no thirty days and a fine. He'll be looking at a year to five!"

Mollenhoff laughed. "Jimmy's improvers at work again! Shouldn't somebody tell the good news to the funeral up front?"

"No, Bob's waiting to do that when we land. He says it'll do them good to see how losing feels!"

The small, sleek Lodestar zipped down the runway and took off into the Nashville sky, heading for Detroit. The Air Force transport followed. It was bigger, heavier, and more clumsy, casting a great, dark shadow beneath it. But once it was airborne, its enormous power soon outdistanced the luxury craft carrying Jimmy Hoffa.

Robert Kennedy and Vice-President Lyndon B. Johnson still passed each other in the Oval Office like two strange, wary housecats.

"Morning, Mr. Johnson."

"*Good* mornin', Mr. Kennedy," Johnson answered, leaving.

Bob looked at his brother and saw the same wry smile that LBJ had worn. "Uh-oh, this smells a bit too cozy for my taste."

"Nah, it's right down your alley."

"What is?"

"This." The President held up a paper. "It's an old Executive Order I found. Teddy Roosevelt, nineteen oh eight. He decreed that every Marine Captain and Lieutenant should be able to hike fifty miles in twenty hours. So I sent a copy over to General Shoup and told him to shape up the Corps!"

"Bet he loved that."

"Yeah, he said he'd take care of the Marines if I'd take care of the White House. I asked Lyndon who the right man for the job would be."

"Oh no!"

Jack laughed. "What's the matter, Bob? He recommended Pierre, of course."

"You bastard."

"You will go out though, won't you?"

"Fifty miles? Ask the Senator from Massachusetts!"

"I did."

"What did he say?"

Jack grinned. "He smiled sardonically."

The two brothers laughed. Ted Kennedy had been elected the previous November, setting the historic precedent of having three members of the same family in Federal office at the same time. During his campaign, *Time* magazine had made the "smile" remark, to which Jack had objected: "Bobby and I smile sardonically. Teddy will learn how to smile sardonically in two or three years, but he doesn't know how yet."

The President turned serious. "Where's Nashville?"

The Attorney General said, "Walt says there'll be an indictment for jury tampering. With the help of our man on the inside, I think we'll go all the way this time."

"I hope so—read Dick Starnes this morning?"

"No."

"Allow me: 'For all I know, Jimmy Hoffa may be guilty of wholesale mopery. But is the Attorney General entitled to dedicate the immense power of the Federal Government to chucking him in jail? I've followed Hoffa's career with passing interest, and all I can swear to is that he makes lousy speeches. He may set fire to orphan asylums for kicks, but does that deprive him of the right to due process? During the nineteen-sixty campaign, Candidate Kennedy stated flatly that an effective Attorney General, with the present laws on the books, could remove Mr. Hoffa from office. It is now nineteen sixty-three, and Mr. Hoffa has still not been removed. What are we to conclude? Does our new Attorney General need dictatorial powers? Or do we need a new Attorney General?' "

Bob stood by the window, glowering. "He's never heard Jimmy make a speech."

Jack smiled and threw the paper into the waste-basket. "It's a good thing I'm too busy to have the time to read garbage like that."

In his Marble Palace office, Jimmy Hoffa was greeting his old friend, the venemous Mack Stenn. "Hey! You been out of the slammer over two months! How come I haven't seen ya?"

"Oh, been busy, Jimmy, you know. L.A., Detroit, Nashville."

"Nashville! Sure wish you were there when I was. Well, what can I do for ya, Mack?"

"Uh, I'm afraid I came up to do somethin' to you, Jimmy, and it's lousy. A friend of mine in Nashville tipped me: they're gonna indict you, Jim."

Hoffa slumped. "Son of a bitch! That fucking Bobby Kennedy! Damn, the biggest mistake I ever made in my life was crossin' that bastard's path!"

Mack shrugged. "Well, he's made a few mistakes of his own." He removed an envelope from his pocket and handed it to Hoffa. "Here, Jim. From our friend in Vegas."

"Good, thanks—I was expectin' this in the mail."

"Who trusts the mail any more?"

"Jesus, you got that right, Mack! We got an eight-hundred-thousand-dollar new Local goin' up in Detroit, you know? And the contractor just comes to me and says the whole joint's wired already! I go bananas. I hire my own private cop to check out my house, and he comes up with twenty-three bugs! In my own home!

273

I gotta watch what I say to my own wife and family in my own private home!"

"Yeah, it's a sin, Jim. Well, I'll be in touch, I've got to—"

"Hey, what's your hurry, Mack? You just got here. Stick around, I maybe got a couple things you can . . ."

"I'm due in New Orleans. Sorry I had to be the one to tell you about the Nashville rap."

"Aw, not your fault, Mack, thanks. New Orleans, huh? What, goin' down for the Mardi Gras?"

Mack Stenn winked and smiled. "Yeah, Jim. The Mardi Gras."

Robert Kennedy was feeling no less bedeviled than Jimmy Hoffa. In his office, Walt Sheridan had just informed him that the Nashville grand jury had subpoenaed Edward Grady Partin to testify about Jimmy's jury-tampering charge.

"God*damn,* won't this thing ever straighten up and fly right!"

"Hoffa's lawyers have instructed him to plead the Fifth."

"But if he does that, how the hell could we ever use him later, if it goes to trial?"

"If he doesn't, Bob . . ."

"Hoffa will know, and Partin will be dead."

"Of course, the grand jury *is* in secret session."

"Yeah. Tell me about juries keeping secrets from Jimmy Hoffa."

"Ed's got to plead the Fifth, Bob. It's the only way."

"I know. It's the only way to keep him alive. Okay."

"Are you all right? You look . . ."

"I'm . . . I don't know, Walt. Jesus, won't it ever end? Is it me and Jimmy for the rest of our lives?"

"We'll, worrying won't help, Bob."

"God, you sound like my mother and Ethel! I know worrying won't help! That's what I'm worried about!"

They laughed, but Sheridan could see Kennedy was still in knots. He was at last beginning to show his age. Some gray was coming into his hair, his cheeks were hollow, the skin bagged heavily beneath his eyes. Even sitting with his legs propped up on his desk, his body didn't appear relaxed, but rather like a wound spring.

A couple of nights later, Sheridan's bedside phone rang him out of a deep sleep at three in the morning. It was Bob. "Come on, let's hit it, today's the day!"

"What day?"

"The day to uphold our honor!"

"Oh, Jesus, not the hike."

"Yes, the hike. We're going to meet at—"

"Bob? The Nashville grand jury's supposed to come in today. Somebody *has* to stick around and wait for the word! I—"

Kennedy laughed. "Quick thinking, Sheridan. All right, go back to sleep. I'm just glad you're on my side, that's all—you weasel better than Hoffa!"

The stalwart band met at dawn where the Chesapeake & Ohio Canal runs under the Chain Bridge. Ted Lerner, Dave Thatcher, Kenny O'Donnell, Joe Maher, and the others looked like guerrillas in their odd pieces of military gear: combat boots, fatigue jackets, wool O.D. trousers mixed with L.L. Bean hiking boots, MacGregor hunting coats, Sears fishing pants. Thatcher sported a green beret. They called him "Special Forces Davy." Ted looked like a lumberjack. They all clapped their hands and stomped in place for warmth. Their breaths made clouds like the mist off the Canal. Then the blue convertible tore up with the horn blaring. Bob and Brumus got out. The others yelled, "Aw, he ain't gonna make it! Jack'll never let you live this down, Bob!"

Bareheaded, Bob asked innocently, "Who's not going to make it? Let's go." He wore dress oxfords, light slacks, and a plaid wool shirt over a sweater. Stuart Symington said, "We aren't going to class, Bob. This is a fifty-mile forced march!"

Teeth flashing white, Bob said, "Then let's go! The Tow Path all the way to Camp David, right? Ted, you look like Paul Bunyon."

They agreed to keep to the infantry pace, a hundred and six steps a minute for fifty minutes, then a ten-minute break. Brumus galloped off, taking the lead, barking merrily, rousing the birds in the bushes and trees. Moving, their bodies warmed rapidly. The sun rose, burning away the mist. It stayed bearably cold and dry all day. They naturally strung out into groups of twos and threes and talked. Bob stayed alone and silent. He walked and walked, forgetting for long stretches of time and ground the presence of the others behind him.

The farther they hiked, the less they talked. In two hours it was an almost totally silent march. By the end of three hours, the dropouts had begun, hard upon the arrival of open blisters and leg cramps. Bob was a considerable distance ahead now. He had forgotten to take the ten-minute breaks.

The rest of Washington rose and went to work, including Jimmy Hoffa. He hadn't slept well. He had come awake at three in the morning and hadn't been able to fall back to sleep. He'd lain there acutely aware of the presence of listening devices surrounding him. Once, he snapped on his light and leaped from the covers and crouched to feel the underside of his mattress and bedspring. He quickly realized the folly of it and quit. He went to his office even earlier than usual. Only in work had he found any relief lately—in the frenzy of the all-day phone dealings, in putting his brain exclusively into the intricacies of the various contracts being negotiated countrywide.

He busied himself with paperwork until the secretaries and staff began arriving. Then, blessedly, his phones began to ring—but this was the day that even they turned against him. It was on his third call. He had rung Sandy Farrell and barked, ". . . Yeah, and get me everything we've got on the three-million loan to Vegas. They're looking for another two-five now, and I don't wanna go ahead until you and me see all the details in black and white."

"I'll be over in twenty minutes, Jim," Sandy said and hung up.

Jimmy was about to set the receiver into its cradle when the second *click* reached his ears. "Who's that?" he yelled into the mouthpiece. "You still there, Sandy?" Silence. "Is that you, Kennedy? Are you listening to me, you jerk?" Silence. He slammed it down and ran to his door. "Yuki! Did you touch that phone just now?"

"No, Mr. Hoffa, I—"

He yelled at the row of lesser secretaries. "Did any of you fiddle with my phones just now?"

They sang their frightened no's.

Enraged, he slammed the door. Then he went and tore the three phones out of their wall outlets. His instincts signaled to drop for some pushups, but he couldn't. Ever since Nashville, even before, the awareness of being under constant surveillance had worked on him like some insidious torture. Now he sought escape in violence. He yanked all the drawers out of his great desk one by one, hurling them against the walls, their contents spilling everywhere. Then he squatted and heaved the whole desk over onto its back with a heavy crash. There were bugs hiding somewhere in this room, he was positive. And he was going to by God find and smash every single one of them. He ran to the edge of the enormous Persian carpet and began rolling it up, separately from its felt underliner. He'd roll that up next. Then he'd run a knife down every crack in the wooden floor.

By noon, the line of marchers had thinned down to a trickle, widely spaced along the Tow Path leading to Camp David. But Robert Kennedy was unaware of anything except the earth in front of his shoes, and the sound of the dog panting by his side. Ted Lerner and Dave Thatcher were the closest, about a quarter mile behind, and Thatcher was fading fast. He said, "It's like he's possessed! Maybe he's seeing Hoffa's face in the ground."

"I hope not. He'll walk to the Gulf of Mexico."

"Think he's all right? I keep expecting to find him out cold around every bend."

Lerner said, "I know. But he's such a Spartan. That isn't good, though, that solitary . . . we ought to start catching up."

"Not me, Ted. I'd do anything for that guy, but I'm biting the dust any minute now."

"Don't feel bad, you've already outlasted a lot of young Marines."

"You think that's his depression coming out, huh?"

"Yeah. It's probably good for him. But you know him. He can brood himself into a—"

"What's keeping you going, Ted, you that depressed too?"

"No, I just keep making believe it's Italy again. If I stop I'll get shot."

Thatcher stopped and dropped to lie out on the grassy embankment. "That is all she wrote!"

Lerner kept on, running double-time in spurts until he caught sight of Kennedy ahead on the trail, then called out. "Bob! Hey, wait up!"

Sandy Farrell opened the door to Jimmy Hoffa's office and couldn't believe what he saw. The place was a shambles. Legs had been ripped off chairs. Cushions on the sofas had been cut open. File cabinets stood open-holed, their drawers empty on the floor all around. Hoffa was at the far end of the wall of bookshelves, ravaging through all the books, one by one. "Jimmy! What's happening?"

"Get me Danny! Get Danny Doolan for me!" Doolan was a professional, an expert in installing and detecting electronic surveillance equipment.

"Jimmy, this is—" Farrell bit off the word crazy before it came out. He saw the dead phones and went back outside to make the call.

Ted Lerner and Robert Kennedy, side by side, kept putting one foot in front of the other. Lerner said, "My legs are solid lead!"

"Mine too."

"You . . . you're moving kind of erratically too, you know, Bob. We really ought to stop for a while."

"I can't."

"Why not?"

"I'll never start again."

"It . . . it must be thirty, thirty-five miles by now. That's pretty good, screw it."

"It's not fifty."

A jeep came up alongside them. "Afternoon. I'm Adams, Park Ranger. You gents okay?"

"How far to Camp David?"

278

"Oh, lemme see. Ten miles, I'd say, no more than that."

They thanked him, and he drove on out of sight. Brumus didn't chase him. Ted said, "Well, I guess we can make another ten, huh?"

Bob said, "Easy."

They went on for what seemed forever. Lerner finally got him to break for ten, but Kennedy didn't sit. He peed in the woods, then kept pacing around. "Let's go, Ted."

"It's only been three or four minutes. Believe me, even the infantry says . . ."

"It's getting cold and dark."

"Okay, okay. You're making me tired just watching you!"

They resumed their trek.

What seemed like years later they again met Ranger Adams, parked by the side of the trail. "How much farther now?"

"Oh, five, seven miles or so!"

"Come on! I know we've come more than ten!"

"Well, give or take."

Even Kennedy stopped now.

Learner said, "I'm done, Bob, my ankles are swollen and . . ."

"Yeah, me too. Let's hitch a ride in the jeep. What the hell, we beat everybody else."

The treetops suddenly bent in the wind. A helicopter came chop-chopping in above them. Adams said, "What in hell's that for?"

Ted said, "Maybe Jack's worried."

"Maybe it's a national emergency and I'll *have* to give up!"

A figure appeared in the open side door, waved down, then brandished a large sign, LIFE MAGAZINE!! The figure took it away waved again, then reappeared with a camera Bob said, "Oh shit. Now we've gotta make the distance!"

"Not me."

"Well, me, then. You're lucky, Ted."

"How?"

"Your brother's not the President."

Ted lifted his weary bones into the jeep. "That really it, Bob?"

"I don't know any more, Ted. Probably not," he said somberly, and started walking toward Camp David again. His dog was beside him, the jeep behind, and the *Life* chopper was overhead, circling and following, camera clicking away.

Danny Doolan arrived from New York at about seven-thirty that night. Jimmy Hoffa was waiting, alone in his office. Doolan took one look around and whistled. "Somebody started without me again!"

Hoffa didn't smile. "Do your stuff, Danny, *I gotta know!*" He didn't know which to hope for, something or nothing. Beat down and dead tired, he watched the man open his suitcases, assemble his apparatus, and set to work. He let Jimmy hold a small, heavy metal box with knobs and a gauge in it. "Watch the needle, Mr. Hoffa." Jimmy watched the needle as the man began moving about the room, slowly and methodically, wielding his scanner. The needle stayed dead. Jimmy said, "I'm gonna look awful paranoid, Danny."

"We'll see. I don't talk shop to anybody, Mr. Hoffa. Don't worry about that."

"Good."

"But you could've saved yourself a lot of time, anguish, and—"

"Just do it, will ya?" He began wondering if the needle was connected to the rest of the junk or not. Just how good was this guy anyhow?

The helicopter hovered low over the Camp David gates for a long while, then lifted and flew off. The Attorney General had made it the whole way, the only one. Walt Sheridan came out of the cheering crowd and up to the exhausted, laughing Bob Kennedy, "Congratulations, Bobby! Fifty miles, Jesus!"

"Thanks, Walt. Where's that damned Ranger? He kept—"

"Congratulations again, Bob. They indicted! *Five* counts of jury tampering! Hoffa's charged with 'aiding, commanding and inducing!' It's felony time, Bob— hard time! We got him!"

It took a minute to set in. Then Bob said quietly, "No, Jimmy got himself."

"She moved, Danny."
Doolan moved back slightly. "Now, Mr. Hoffa?"
"She's goin' off the other end!"
"That's it then. Right in there."
Jimmy dropped the gauge box and crossed to the walnut wall paneling Doolan was tapping with his scanner. He grabbed a heavy screwdriver from Doolan's case and stabbed the wood with it, finally prying a chunk of the paneling away from the wall. There it was. *"I knew it! I knew it!"*

"You were right, Mr. Hoffa. Here, I'll get that out of there for you." He examined the small device. "Ah, yes. That'll mean there's another one outside. Somewhere in the building across from your window, I'd say. Listening post. They can hear your paper clips fall."

"I knew it, I knew it!"

But Jimmy's moment of relief didn't last long. Sandy Farrell came rushing through the deserted outer office and stopped in the open doorway. His face was as long as a horse's, his voice heavy with sadness and fear. He delivered the news from Nashville.

Hoffa shuddered, as if he'd been hit with a mallet. He turned and ran to the high, wide windows. One end panel was hinged to open, and he opened it and yelled at the building across the street, "Hear *this*, Kennedy! You ain't gonna get me! You little prick! You're not gonna win! You're not gonna get Hoffa! Hoffa wins! Hoffa. . . !"

Danny Doolan was repacking his equipment. He figured it wouldn't help anybody to mention that he'd disconnected the setup, so nobody was hearing any of it, except maybe some passersby down below on the street. Leaving, he said to the forlorn Sandy Farrell, "Call me after you get this fixed up. I'll sweep it clean for you."

"Yes," Farell said, "Thanks. We will."

The notes came out of Kid Thomas Valentine's trumpet and floated over the heads of the jazz lovers sitting on the floor of Preservation Hall. In the lush air outside they met and mingled with the other sounds of the streets of New Orleans's French Quarter: blues, ragtime, Mississippi River boat whistles, trolley wheels ringing along the steel tracks on St. Charles Avenue, the human voices of tourists mixing with the members of the city's *gumbo-mêlé*, all out walking and being accosted by the hawkers manning the doors of all the cabarets, offering tantalizing glimpses of the pretty women dancing naked inside, to more music.

This was the night Mack Stenn had been preparing for. He was taking his guest to the meeting. He had shown him the town, and had enjoyed doing so. In the week, they had dined together at Antoine's, Manale's, Brennan's, the Commander's Palace, Arnaud's, Galatoire's, even had the red beans and Chaurice sausage at Buster's. The guy could have been a stiff and Mack would still have had a good time entertaining him, but the little man from Texas was a good sport. In fact, Mack had known him from Chicago years ago, where he'd been a Teamsters business agent and other things, before going to Texas, where he now owned the Vegas and Carousel strip clubs in Dallas, and other things.

Walking through the Bourbon Street carnival now, well fed and nicely oiled, Stenn felt magnanimous. "Anytime you think you might like to add one of these to your string of joints, just let me know, okay?"

The slick Texan laughed. "Well, thanks a lot—you sure seem to be the man to see in New Orleans, all right!"

"Aw, no, just close. The man we'll be seeing in a couple of minutes now—he's the one."

The car was waiting for them on a side street, in the dark of the overhead Spanish moss hanging thickly from old oak trees. Mack opened the rear door, the light went on, and a man leaned forward, smiling. "Ah, hello. The friend of Frank Tanella, eh? Good, good."

Stenn said, "Vincent Cisco, let me introduce my friend, Jack Ruby."

Ruby joined Cisco in the back. Mack Stenn closed the door, walked around to the right front, and got in. The long black Cadillac cruised off into the New Orleans night.

The rugged, bull-dog handsomeness of the Director had in his latter years aged and thickened into a Buddha-like solidity. He seemed never to smile, and even when he spoke his lips seemed only barely to move. His eyes held all the animation, but his mind worked quicker than they; they seldom betrayed his true thoughts or feelings. Robert Kennedy did not relish their personal meetings, but was most often the one to bring them about: to keep his distance from J. Edgar Hoover would have been to seriously jeopardize his own authority as the Bureau's top leader. For the Director's part, the eager young Kennedy was hardly his first Attorney General; nor, he suspected, would he be his last.

Today Hoover sat behind his desk in the FBI Building, phlegmatic and fully suited. Kennedy had removed his jacket and loosened his tie. He moved about as he spoke. "Edgar, we really need to get more, faster, on this interstate jukebox situation."

"I've told you, Bob. This is a difficult and time-consuming operation. We must proceed carefully." One specific incident he still held against Kennedy was the time he had dined with Mr. Hoffa at the home of Mr. Cheyfitz, now deceased. On the very evening that the Bureau had got the hard goods on Hoffa! To

Hoover, it had been worse than an indiscretion; it had allowed Edward Bennett Williams, later in court, to throw doubt on Hoffa's sources of information: he might have learned things from Kennedy himself, never mind John Cye Cheasty. In the Director's mind, Kennedy had contributed directly to the Government's loss of the case.

"Carefully doesn't have to mean slowly!" Bob complained. "Put more men in the field on it, or whatever—but I want to see some results!"

The eyelids lowered and raised patiently. "I have also told you, Bob—my organization is simply not prepared to implement this so-called war on Organized Crime of yours. We need more time, more personnel, more information, more financing, more—"

"Look. You're doing splendidly, Edgar. I don't mean to be critical. I agree and, more important, the President agrees that the Bureau indeed needs more and better support. And we fully expect that you'll be given it, as soon as possible after his re-election. It has his highest priority. All I'm saying is, in the meantime, with the resources we have now, we can do better. I've seen it for myself! We have excellent men out there, all more than willing to—."

"I thought— Excuse me, I thought I asked you to cease making direct contact with the field agents. I thought I explained that you can get all the briefings you need on the crime situation from myself, from Mr. Evans, or from Mr. DeLoach. To have an Attorney General developing personal relationships with field agents is not conducive to—"

"Aw, come off it—it's great for their morale, and you know it."

"I know nothing of the kind. They are responsible to one, single authority for their actions and performance. Me. The unity of command, Mr. Kennedy. You can only divide and confuse . . ."

"Okay, okay, you may be right," Bob relented. Then he tried to bargain: "I'll receive my briefings from you, then. Once a month, beginning—"

"My briefings are made quarterly." The eyelids closed and opened. "And they are made to the President. I'm sure you will be welcomed to attend, or to receive copies as they are—"

"Monthly," Bob said. He put on his jacket and tightened his tie to the collar. "Your briefings to *me* will be once a month, starting next month."

"I don't deal that way. I deal directly with—"

"Your immediate superior, the Attorney General. That's how it's going to be under this Administration, Edgar."

"No one has ever talked to me like that, Bob."

"I'm sorry, but you pushed me to it. Listen, there's a joke going around, have you heard it? It's about how the FBI had to be dragged, kicking and screaming, into the war on crime. Well, it isn't funny, and I don't like it, and I'm doing everything in my power to prove it false, and I should think you'd want to do the same!"

The Director was rubbing his thumbs together slowly, atop his folded hands. He blinked again and said again, "No one has ever talked to me like that."

"That's terrific, Edgar. Well, nobody talks to me the way you do, either. But talk's talk, and all I want is action, co-operatioon, and results. You can work with me or against me, but you'd better start working!" At the door, he turned. "I'll expect your briefing the first week of December."

The thumbs stopped rubbing. The hands came apart calmly. The Director reached for his phone.

In Hyannisport, Rose Kennedy issued the order: all radios and television sets in the house were to be unplugged. Joseph P. Kennedy, senior, had suffered a severe stroke, and was weak. But they had a rule in the family anyhow, which said that all bad news is best presented early in the morning. They would keep this from him for the rest of the afternoon and evening and night.

Her daughters would be flying in from everywhere. Their arrival, too, must be kept from him. Ted would be there in the morning. He would be the one to tell the father then. It was Robert's duty to be with Jacqueline. He would meet her at Andrews Air Force Base, when the plane landed from Dallas.

That Friday, the news bulletin interrupted all radio

and TV programs. Most felt shock and disbelief: either it couldn't have happened at all, or it could never have ended as tragically as it did.

Walt Sheridan was in his office in Nashville, dictating reports to his secretary, Marcie. ". . . Judge Miller concluded therefore that Hoffa's attorney, Tommy Osborn, had talked to Vick about influencing a prospective juror, then lied to the court about it. He has decided to turn State's evidence, in order to avoid—"

"Walt!"

"What?"

The ashen-faced young assistant cried, "On the news! President Kennedy's been shot!"

Marcie's open-mouthed face was about to come apart. Walt shouted, "No! Get me Bob on the phone! Move!"

She did, but the moment she said, "Angie?" she collapsed into tears.

Walt took the phone, only to hear it in Angie's voice, too. Something lodged in his windpipe, but he said, "All right, when you hear from him, or find out anything, call me immediately, will you?"

Marcie held both fists to her mouth and wailed, "He's dead! Oh, my God! He's dead, *he's dead,* they *killed him!"*

Jimmy Hoffa looked up from his phone to Sandy Farrell, said, "That so?" then looked down and went on with his negotiations.

Clark Mollenhoff came out of the Pentagon, hailed a cab, and got in. He started to say, "The Federal Courthouse, on—" when the cabbie, practically shaking, yelled at him, "Wait a minute! Listen!" The radio was saying, ". . . Was rushed to the Parkland Memorial Hospital in Dallas, where at one-fifteen P.M. last rites were administered by . . ."

"What's that?"

"JFK! Somebody blew his head open!"

"Oh no. Oh, Jesus, no. Get me to the Justice Department, fast!"

There, as almost everywhere else, work was stopped. He rushed to the Attorney General's office through halls and corridors filled with people moving in zombie-like slow motion. Many sat or stood, weeping openly. Faces gnarled with pain and fear looked to others faces for some relief, some denial, some explanation, only to find nothing but more anguish looking back at them. Why? Why him? Who? Why? No, it wasn't true, it just wasn't—was it? Could God let this happen?

Even the Hoffa Squad offices were eerily still and quiet. Ted Lerner, Jim Neal, Dave Thatcher, Jack Miller seemed drugged and propped like mannequins. Robert Kennedy wasn't there. He was gone, they weren't sure where. Somebody named Lee Harvey Oswald had been arrested.

"Who the hell is he?" Mollenhoff asked.

"Nobody knows."

Thatcher sighed. "We don't know any more than anybody else, Clark. The Soviet, the crazy fucking Cubans, a maniac? Who knows. The guy's saying he's innocent, but . . ."

Mollenhoff turned to Lerner. "I'm going to try the house, wanna come?"

"Yeah."

They found him sitting alone with Ethel in his dark study, staring out the window. He looked at their faces. It seemed to take him several moments to re-member who they were. Ethel left, shutting the heavy door silently behind her. Clark said, "We can leave. We were worried, so we—"

"No, stay. I'm glad to see you." His voice came as if he were speaking through some filter in his throat.

"Jesus, Bob."

"Yeah."

"Are you . . . ?"

"I'll go meet the plane. I'm waiting."

"He . . . it's so hard to know what to say."

"That's all right," Bob said. "It's even harder to know what to think. He's gone. How can I believe that? It's so . . . you know, there's been so much bitterness, so much hatred coming out that . . . well, I did, I had the thought that somebody or other might try to get one of us. But Jack. Not Jack. He'd laugh it off when I . . . He never worried about it."

He got up, put his hands in his back pockets and

walked to the window. He looked broken. He told them, "You know? I got a letter, just last week. Someone in Texas. Warning me. Said, don't let the President go to Dallas, he was going to be killed. But we're always getting . . . So I, you know, passed it to Kenny and he passed it to Secret Service, but . . . God, I never thought this would happen! I thought, if they're going to, it'll be me. Now I wish it was."

"Bob, don't . . ."

"Oh no!" he said. They looked to where he was looking. Squads of police cars were pulling up outside. Cops were pouring out, carrying rifles and shotguns, taking up positions around the house and grounds. Bob covered his eyes with a hand. "No. I don't want this."

"It's probably best, Bob. For a while, anyhow."

"No. I won't live like that. An armed camp?"

"You'll be off a lot now, Bob, for a while. It'll be better for Ethel and the kids not to be alone. They can still get around, get back and forth to school and everything with those guys . . ."

"I suppose." He covered his face again, dropping his head. "But I can't . . . I've got to be able to work, to keep it all going. If I can't, I . . ."

"You will, Bob."

Robert McNamara, Ted Lerner and Robert Kennedy drove at night to Andrews Air Force Base. Into the dark silence, trying to comfort, Lerner said, "Maybe . . . maybe some good will come out of this. The enormity of this—when it dawns on people what's happened, maybe there'll be less bitterness: maybe people will start coming together, and—"

"No," Bob said from his corner in the back. "This will make it worse." They parked and waited, saying little. In the cold, damp night he kept seeing Jack alive again, and thanked God he wouldn't have to see him dead; the coffin would be closed. The steel car about him felt protective and he dreaded getting out of it. But when the time came he got out swiftly, ran across to the plane and up inside it, and brushed past the new President in order to be with his brother's bereaved widow.

General de Gaulle said it, speaking of Jackie: "She

gave an example to the whole world of how to behave."

The drumbeat. The riderless horse, saddle empty. The caisson. She stood erect, in black but not concealing her beauty; she attended to her small, bewildered children. Just as Jack's next eldest brother, equally erect, attended to her, through it all. Courage, he would have wanted; courage and grace and the affirmation of ongoing life. They would try to do as he would have done.

Not all of mankind mourned that day.

Jimmy Hoffa entered Teamsters Headquarters in a rage, phoned the building's superintendent, and demanded that the flag outside be returned to full mast.

Television coverage of the funeral of John Fitzgerald Kennedy brought the awful event to the entire nation and to most of the world, first live, then in seemingly endless successions of replay. The news that night cut away to report the aftermath as it progressed, and showed the alleged assassin, Lee Harvey Oswald, manacled and surrounded by burly Dallas police officers. The announcer was saying, ". . . is being transferred to . . ." when he stopped abruptly, as stunned as anybody. A murky form had suddenly come up from the bottom of the screen and moved in close to the boyish-looking prisoner. Gunfire sounded. *"He's been shot!"* the announcer screamed. *"Lee Harvey Oswald has been shot!"*

Millions watched it happen, and saw the killer being overcome by the police. One viewer was Robert McKeon, tending bar in his crowded Miami Beach tavern. He said to himself, "That's Jack Ruby!" and put away for good the qualms he'd sometimes had about not taking the twenty-five grand that time.

Another viewer of the macabre second murder was Edward Grady Partin. In his Nashville motel room, he dropped his half-eaten take-out hamburger. "Jesus Christ!" He ran outside in his shirt sleeves to the pay phone by the candy machines and dialed the number. "This is Andy Anderson. All right, but did you see it? Yeah, well listen—you better bury me someplace, fast.

And I mean deep and safe. If you want me to testify ... I gotta be alive."

The terrifying reality of it all was felt more deeply, and better believed, when it started appearing in print. In the unmoving still photographs in the newspapers and magazines. In the re-readable words and sentences and paragraphs. In print, you could feel it in your hands. By the time Lyndon B. Johnson's image came on the television screens, the reality of his being President had been undeniably established in headlines and stories and unmoving pictures. Still, the image of his head and face above the Seal on the rostrum seemed to only trigger the image of the head and face no longer filling that space, and to bring back yet again the chill of what had happened. He said, "My fellow Americans" and asked for courage and support.

Watching from Michigan, Jimmy Hoffa cackled, "Well, Bobby Kennedy's just another lawyer now."

Robert Kennedy stood waiting alone in the Oval Office. It was the first time he'd been in there since Jack's murder. All traces of his brother's presence had been removed, but only physically; he could still see the photographs and hear the voices, still half expected to see John-John pop out of the kneehole in the desk, or Caroline come running in with drawings to show. Was the faint scent of cigar smoke still in the air, or only in his mind? He hoped this would be over with fast. He wanted to get out of there. He knew what was going to be said. Did the bastard still hate him so much that he had to do it in the flesh?

LBJ came in and went behind the desk. "Mornin', Bob."

"Good morning, Mr. President."

Clark Mollenhoff was so excited he dropped his change all over the phone booth. He finally got a dime in and dialing, prayed fervently that he was the first. "Mr. Hoffa, please. Clark Mollenhoff, of—"

"Hello, trouble, what blows you my way?"

It was how Hoffa always answered calls from Mollenhoff. Today it didn't grate. "I wanted to get your comments, Jimmy."

"On what?"

"On Johnson asking Kennedy to stay on as Attorney General!"

There was no pause. Hoffa yelled, *"Son of a bitch!"* and hung up.

Mollenhoff stayed in the booth for a moment, savoring the taste of it, thinking, *There—that's one twist nobody ever expected!*

Jimmy Hoffa had succeeded in having his jury tampering trial moved from Nashville to Chattanooga, Tennessee. Court convened in January, 1964.

In the courtroom, the situation seemed heavily lopsided. At the Government table sat Jim Neal, John Hooker, and Jack Reddy. The defense table had to accommodate Jimmy Hoffa, his co-defendants Tom Parks, Larry Campbell, Ewing King, Allen Dorfman, and Nicholas Tweel; and the attorneys: James Haggerty, Harry Berke, Jacques Schiffer, Cecil Brandstetter, Harold Brown, Harvey Silets, Dave Alexander, and Henry Brady.

Frank Grimsley had come up from Baton Rouge. He and Walt Sheridan sat together in the back row, near the door. Examinations, cross-examinations, outbursts, warnings, objections, rulings, conferences. Nick Tweel's secretary, Hazel Fulton from West Virginia, testified. So did highway patrolman James Paschal. Hoffa employed his evil eye on all hostile witnesses and prosecutors, and when necessary on Judge Frank W. Wilson, presiding. Day in, day out.

When the right time came, at a little before ten one morning, Sheridan tapped Grimsley and they slipped away, hopefully unnoticed. They left the Courthouse and walked to Sheridan's car. Grimsley grinned. "Think we're being careful enough, Walt?"

"Look, I know what I'm doing, Frank. We've come too goddamn far to lose another one. I take *no* chances any more. Even the look on Hoffa's face has me growing ulcers—he doesn't look worried enough."

"But he *couldn't* have been tipped."

"Every time we've ever said 'couldn't' with Hoffa, he *did!*"

Driving, Grimsley asked, "How's Bob holding up, anyhow?"

Sheridan said, "He's . . . very different. Ethel got him to go to Florida for a while. When they got back he looked more like he'd been in Siberia or . . . but he wants this bad. We've got to get it for him."

"Sure been a long haul, all right."

"Lifetime, it seems. He's . . . distracted a lot, lately. Find him staring out his window, hardly hears you come in. When it's me, though, when it's Hoffa, he snaps out of it."

It was an hour there and an hour back. They were relieved to have a difficult time getting in to the cabin up on Lookout Mountain: the deputy marshals were good. One of them rode with Sheridan and the witness on the way back, rifle on his lap. Grimsley followed in the other car, driving it so the armed officer would be free to maneuver if he had to.

They pulled up close to the rear door of the Chattanooga Federal Building, and got out. The Court had been adjourned for the noon recess. Justice Department aide Jack Thiede was waiting; he took the wheel of Sheridan's car and drove it down into the basement garage. His cohort Bill French stood ready inside with two more deputy marshals. French led the way to the small elevator. When the doors closed he said, "This is a one-way key. Nobody can stop us until we reach the fifth floor. Cassidy's covering the coast up there."

John Cassidy gave them the okay sign and pointed to the correct stairwell door, then led the way down the two flights to the third floor. There, he reconnoitered the corridor and signaled that it was all clear. He and Grimsley took up watch while Sheridan and the witness hurried along the corridor, then down the small passageway. Sheridan said, "Stay here. You're totally covered. When John Hooker makes his call, you'll get a tap from inside. Just open the door and go in."

"Can I smoke?"

"You can do anything you want, except leave."

"Don't worry."

"How do you feel?"

"Same as I've felt all year. Scared to death."

Joe Rudis was a staff photographer for the Nashville *Tennessean*. On the stand, he produced a photograph. John Hooker had it passed from juror to juror, explaining that it was simply a shot taken outside the Nashville Courthouse, showing James Hoffa closely surrounded by his entourage, whom he identified by name and location in the picture. He then excused Rudis and called his next witness, one of the faces in the picture, "Mr. *Edward Grady Partin!*"

The door opened, Andy Anderson stepped through. There was an audible gasp from the defense table. Then all hell broke loose. While Judge Wilson gaveled for silence and order, the clerk swore the witness in. Lawyers for his co-defendants were screaming for mistrial and severance of their clients. Jimmy was screaming, "You're the snitch! That bum was planted on me by the Government! Intrusion of rights! Plant! Snitch! Plant!"

Judge Wilson called prosecution and defense attorneys to his chambers, and insisted upon a sane discussion of grievances and motions. Harry Berke spoke for defense and challenged Partin's fitness as a witness: ". . . A convicted criminal, an accused kidnapper *mysteriously* released from prison! His testimony here is totally unacceptable!"

Jim Neal explained, "We have affidavits to prove that Mr. Partin is not and has never been in the employ of—"

"Bullshit," Berke said, "you planted him on Hoffa."

"Partin volunteered to go to Nashville of his own accord. We—"

"To save his own ass!"

"Gentlemen," the judge intervened, "it is not the business of this court to adjudicate the motives of Mr.—"

"Why not?" Berke demanded. "It's totally germane! *What* prompted him to go to the Justice Department, if in fact he did?"

"I have ruled that we shall not discuss that," Wilson said. "It's a matter of national security, and may prejudice your client."

This stopped them.

Berke said, "Excuse me, your honor? Just what is a matter of national security here?"

Jim Neal sighed. "Mr. Partin made contact with a law enforcement agency, in order to divulge what he termed an assassination plot."

"Whose?"

"Mr. Partin reported a threat, on the part of your client, James Hoffa, to have the Attorney General of the United States killed!"

Berke said, "Your honor, a moment to consult, please?"

"Of course."

Harry Berke and the other attorneys went into a brief and animated huddle in a corner. Berke came out. "Judge Wilson, my colleagues and I agree unanimously that we have no objection at all to allowing that testimony. Frankly, we find it utterly fantastic and unbelievable. We have no desire to suppress it. In fact, we'd love to hear it come out in court!"

"Well, I would not," Wilson replied. "Especially in light of the recent events in this country, such admission would be bound to turn this case into one involving questions of conspiracies, assassination plots, and so on. Which would totally confuse the issue for which we have convened, namely jury-tampering. Gentlemen, jury-tampering is the only question that will be resolved in my courtroom."

And so it was. Of the five counts, the jury found Jimmy Hoffa guilty on two. Judge Wilson sentenced him to serve eight years in a Federal pentitentiary. Of his co-defendants, only Tweel and Dorfman were found not guilty.

As his hung juries and acquittals had seemed to reproduce themselves, so now with his conviction.

In April of the same year Hoffa went on trial again, with seven others, in Chicago. He was charged with twenty-eight counts of fraud, stemming from his misuse of Teamster pension funds and alleged diversion of more than a million dollars of those funds for his own personal use.

In July, the jury found all eight defendants "Guilty as charged."

For once, Hoffa had the wind knocked out of him. No shouting, no screaming, no ranting or raving.

Awaiting his sentencing, about the only rancor and chagrin he displayed was toward Clark Mollenhoff, covering the trial. They met as they almost always had, in a courthouse corridor. Jimmy said, "You know, maybe it's you who shoulda hit a river with a rock around your neck, big man!"

"Why me?"

"Because it was you who put fuckin' Kennedy on my back in the first place! Way back when."

"I did. But come on, Jim, you had a little something to do with it yourself, don't forget."

"Baloney!"

"You're not even slightly at fault, I suppose?"

"Don't worry about me, pal. I ain't done yet."

"Sure looks it."

"You don't know what you're talkin' about. As usual!"

"Come off it, Jimmy—it's all falling apart for you, and you know it. Even your own union's starting to dump you."

"How you figure that?"

"They voted to stop paying your attorney fees with Teamster money."

"That's nothin'."

"Most of your real old buddies are already in jail, and there's more and more talk about a new President."

"That's really nothin'."

"You're going away, Mr. Hoffa."

"We'll see. I'll tell you somethin', Mollenhoff—you'll be six feet under before *I'm* stopped!"

When Robert Kennedy heard the long-awaited news of Hoffa's first conviction in Chattanooga, he instinctively reached for the other phone to report and share the victory. In his excitement, he had forgotten. He froze there, hand on the phone. Jack wasn't there to call any more. They had worked so hard and so long for this day, and now only he was here to know about it. He removed his hand from the receiver, got up, and put on his jacket. He'd go home. But then he stopped again. Outside his door, the staff would be whooping it up with joy, deservedly. He didn't want to throw a damper on it. Nor did he feel up to going out to them and faking it. He returned to his chair and turned it to face the window.

After Chicago, the news reached him at home. He wasn't alone, and he wasn't closed away somewhere inside. He was out with all his own kids, quarterbacking a game on the lawn for nearly a hundred other kids, and what kids—they were white and yellow, brown and black, big and little; some were disabled or disturbed, some were not; all were from a home for the underprivileged. Ethel had been getting him to traipse around visiting kids like these all over the place. He was aware that she meant it as therapy for himself, and he was aware too that it was working—at least for the time he was with them. Unlike Will Rogers's famous, fatuous claim that he'd never met a man he didn't like, Bob had met plenty whom he loathed easily. But he truly hadn't ever met a kid he didn't like. They were so little, for one thing. And so open, so full of wonder. Such reminders of the possibility of another kind of world and life.

He wasn't doing much passing, not only because with nearly fifty on a side it would have been throwing it away, but because when he ran with it, they all got so much glee out of piling on him, even those on his own side. "No tickling! . . . And no fair taking my shoes off!" There was at least one kid in every monkey pile who tried to wrench the ball away from him; maybe it was more than one kid, but whoever he, she, or they were, he wanted to catch them at it, and tell them that was right to do, that was how to play the game. But he never saw them; only felt the hands tugging.

A few reporters had heard about the Kids Day at Hickory Hill and were there, snapping shots and accepting hospitality. But they and the school personnel were the only outsiders. The place hadn't been an "armed camp" since he had ordered the guard lifted after a few weeks. He didn't know that he and his family were still being covered secretly, from careful distances.

Catholic, he didn't fear his own death. Nor did he hate death; it wasn't an end, only a passage to new and better life. Remembering this helped him deal with the loss of Jack, but it wasn't easy to remember most times. Death was not loss; loss was something the living suffered. It was loss that he hated.

When he came up out of the latest mammoth monkey-pile, Ethel was hitting a saucepan with a spoon on the terrace, yelling "Ice cream!" As the mob dispersed, he noticed a lone, small black boy, about seven, standing and staring at him with huge chestnut eyes. He was about to toss the ball to him when the kid mumbled something.

"What did you say? You want to what?" He went over to him.

"Your brotha's dead, ain't he?" was what the boy said, more as a question than a statement. Somebody had told.

Bob knelt on one knee beside him, put his free arm around his shoulders, and said, "That's all right. I have another one. Let's go get some ice cream, huh?"

At the house, the phone was for him—Mollenhoff from Chicago. Hoffa had just got another five years. He went and told Ethel. "Thirteen years. My God. Thirteen years in prison. After running the most powerful union in the country."

"At least it's all over. It's finished at last."

"I guess so."

They had dined together once before; neither wanted to do that again.

There was no public place in Washington where one or both wouldn't be recognized in daylight. Any nighttime rendezvous was dangerous, and neither could suggest a place acceptable to the other anyhow.

Then Hoffa mentioned that he was going to Boston to conduct some union business. Kennedy was planning to be in Hyannisport around the same time.

They met, early in the morning, in front of the Shell on the Esplanade on the bank of the Charles River. Only a few sailboats were out on the water yet. The August day's heat wouldn't descend until later. A lone park attendant drifted around, spiking litter into his burlap bag; no students had come yet to lay on blankets or play frisbee. Storrow Drive curved close there, heavy with fast-moving traffic, mostly in-town. Each had to find a parking space somewhere nearby and walk, crossing the Drive by the overhead footbridge. The State House's gold dome glistened above the rooftops of Beacon Hill. Subway trains whined in and out of the Charles Street Station high over the old Jailhouse, crossing the bridge to Cambridge or diving into the tunnel under Back Bay.

They didn't shake hands.

Jimmy Hoffa said, "Sure you're safe here?"

Robert Kennedy said, "Sure you are?"

Hoffa laughed. "No—pal of mine told me to watch you, says you Boston pols got a saying up here, 'Don't get mad, get even.' "

"It's a pretty strong Teamster town, too."

"You bet. So spill it, Bob, how you think you're gonna screw me now?"

"It's simple enough. It's occurred to me that you and I are finding ourselves at pretty much the same crossroads. I'm leaving the Justice Department . . ." In fact, he was now Attorney General in name only. They had had their ceremonies and celebrations. His "Band of Brothers," including the Get-Hoffa Squad and the rest of his staff of investigators, prosecutors, secretaries, and all, were disbanding and dispersing. Ted Lerner was returning to the newspaper game, probably in Tacoma. Pierre Salinger was going to run for the Senate in California. Carmine Bellino was eyeing a banking job in Florida. Walt Sheridan was talking to NBC about becoming a correspondent for them. Many of them and the others were "keeping a bag packed," waiting to hear more about Bob's thoughts of running for the Senate from New York.

". . . And you're leaving the Teamsters," he said.

"We'll see." Jimmy grinned. "But Johnson finally gave you the sack, huh?"

"No. But he'll have a better chance of defining his own Presidency without a Kennedy around. It's mutually agreeable."

"That's your story, stick to it."

"I'm still Attorney General, Jimmy."

"Meaning what—you wanna make a deal?"

298

"Yes."

Hoffa's smile left. He studied Kennedy's eyes. "Your move, Mr. Kennedy."

"All right. I'm offering you amnesty."

Hoffa looked away. He gazed across the river. Kennedy couldn't read his face. Jimmy said, "Amnesty. How would it work?"

"If you'll step down, on your own, from the Presidency of the Teamsters, and guarantee to remove yourself from all union politics in the future, I'll see to it that you'll have to serve virtually no real time in prison. I'll guarantee a pardon that will reduce your sentence to no more than a few months, at the most. Also, all future charges against you, based on any investigations still going on, will be dropped."

Hoffa stayed staring down the Charles. The sun was behind them, but he was squinting. "That's it? Hoffa gets out of the Teamsters, does a little time, and Kennedy's a happy man?"

"That's it."

And that was where the civility ended.

Hoffa's head whipped back around. "Shove it up your ass, Bobby! You still think . . . You dumb, rich little jerk, you still think all you gotta do is get rid of Hoffa and everything comes up roses? Whaddaya think's gonna come *after* me?"

"A cleanup!"

"Bullshit! How do you know there ain't somethin' out there *worse* than Hoffa?"

"That's hard to imagine!"

"You just wanna take my union away from me!"

"It's not your union!"

"Oh no? Then whose is it?"

"Your goddamn friends! The goddamn gangsters you sold out to! The ones you sold your rank and file to, that you're supposed to love so much!"

"I never sold them out!"

Their shouted words ricocheted off the walls of the big orchestra Shell behind them, coming out like staccato gunshots.

"Tell *them* that! When they come to collect their pension money! That isn't there! Because you spent it on companies that were going broke and on hotels that were never built and on—"

"That's it, brother! End of conversation!"

"You've taken the fall, Jimmy! They don't want to know you any more! You're a leper, even with—"

"Like you, you mean? With Johnson and Hoover? Don't give me that 'resigning' horseshit, kid—you're running, and you know it'"

"You're making another big mistake, Hoffa! I'm offering you—"

"Somethin' I don't need! I'm gonna have those pissant convictions of yours overturned! And if you don't think so, take a gander at this!" He yanked a sheaf of papers from his inside pocket and shook it at Kennedy's face. "You oughta know an affidavit when you see one, huh? Well, this one's by a guy named Ben Nichols, sayin' you paid him two hundred clams to bug my hotel room in Chattanooga! Read it and weep, brother!"

Kennedy snatched it and started reading.

Hoffa berated him, "Take a good look, 'cause you're gonna be seein' it again, plastered all over the front pages of every newspaper in the country!"

"This is a put-up job, Jimmy, it's—"

"My ass, put-up! Shit, even your big buddy Hoover's already accusin' you of authorizing a million illegal wiretaps!"

"That's a misunderstanding Hoover and I are going to clear up. *This* is a stunt! If you think you're going to win with this kind of a joke, you're—"

"Joke, huh?" He grabbed it back. "A stunt, is it? Jesus, some hot-shit investigator you are! Some Attorney General! Hey—maybe you *don't* know! Wouldn't that be a riot! You think your convictions are gonna stick? Christ, you don't even know what's goin' on in your own FBI!"

Now the Shell went silent. Only the traffic along the Esplanade could be heard, and the racket of the subway trains.

J. Edgar Hoover's secretary smiled nicely. "I'm sorry, Mr. Kennedy, but the Director can't be disturbed at the moment. He's in a meeting."

"Then buzz Mr. DeLoach for me, please."

"I'm sorry, Mr. DeLoach is also in the meeting."

"This is urgent!"

"So, I'm afraid, is the meeting. Mr. Hoover left explicit instructions that—"

"When will he be done?"

"That's difficult to—"

"Tell him to call me as soon as he's finished."

"I'll do my best, Mr.—"

"You do better than that! You tell the Director that the Attorney General of the United States orders that he make himself available to me at five o'clock this afternoon. Five o'clock *sharp!* Understand me?"

"Yes, sir."

"Thank you."

At five he was back, throwing a very thick file heavily onto Hoover's desk. It was marked, "FBI Surveillance." Robert Kennedy said to the Buddha, "Why the hell wasn't I informed?"

"You knew, Mr. Kennedy," the Director said flatly. "I have your authorization for—"

"For some of it, yes! But Jesus Christ, not for all *that!*"

The hooded eyes slid to the right. "I have here . . . memos, passed through Mr. DeLoach and Mr. Evans, to me."

"I know all about those memos, too! DeLoach and Evans—they'd attend the same meetings, then submit one version to me and an entirely different one to you! Look for yourself! I've got them all together there!"

The eyelids blinked slowly, the thumbs rubbed.

"Do you intimidate your people so much, Mr. Hoover, that they tell you only what you want to hear?"

The Director's heavy chest heaved slightly. "I believe these memoranda represent your attitude, Mr. Kennedy, if not precisely your intent. It was clear to me with the Martin Luther King incident, and it was equally clear to me with these other—"

"The King thing I told you, I was wrong, dammit. I authorized and I was wrong. But these I did *not* authorize! I did *not* know!"

"You . . . asked for information. You demanded.

301

You insisted. I informed you that such an intensive investigation into Organized Crime was premature and ill-advised. You ignored my estimations. As my *direct superior* in the Department of Justice, you ordered me to provide your office with the maximum amount of information at the maximum possible speed. I complied."

"You smug bastard, you—"

"You accepted the information. You read all the field reports without question, you read the transcripts of all the phone conversations, you—"

"Goddammit, Edgar, I was told distinctly that the Bureau was getting that information from local law enforcement agencies, working on local criminal cases And I believed what I was told!"

"Or, as you so rudely accuse me, you believed what was convenient for you to believe, what you wanted to believe. Oh, you *liked* the flow of information, didn't you, Mr. Kennedy. You wanted it to never end, you—"

"I . . . I may have been naive, all right, but . . ."

"You may give it any name you desire, but understand this—I will not see this Bureau tarnished by your actions!"

Robert Kennedy thought, *God help you if I'm ever back around here with any kind of clout!* but he was too astonished and abashed to speak.

The Director added, "By the way—Hoffa and his Mr. Nichols. There is no truth to it. Desperate ramblings by a desperate man. It will never stand up in court. Now, you will have to excuse me, I have an appointment with the President of the United States. Good-bye, Mr. Kennedy."

Bob left without answering. Alone, he made the long walk away from Hoover's office and out of the FBI Building, heel clicks echoing eerily in the empty, polished hallways and staircases. Seven years, he thought, seven years since it all began. Seven. The mystical number, always, in the Bible. Seven, nay, seventy times seven . . . so it certainly felt.

Beck, Seattle, the angry ones, the frightened ones, the flashy mobsters, McClellan . . . Hoffa. The Band of Brothers. Jack. Oh, Jack . . . Had it been Jack?

Or Walt? Somebody—Dave? Ted? Clark? Somebody quoting Hemingway, about the men daring life. They were the ones whom life broke. But then, sometimes they got stronger, in the broken places. Bob walked faster. That seemed too . . . fatalistic, somehow. But life did not turn out to be so simple, did it. No, God, anything but simple, seven opposites of simple at least. Outside, he broke into a run, heading for his car. He suddenly needed to get home, to be home, fast.

Even after the Supreme Court upheld his conviction, Jimmy Hoffa kept trying to negotiate a better contract for himself. Right down to the wire, he kept his batteries of lawyers working. One night in his office at the Marble Palace, surrounded by attorneys all wracking their brains for ploys, he snapped his fingers. "Sandy! How about tryin' for a stay of execution on the grounds that I'm in the middle of negotiatin' a six-hundred-million dollar contract—I'm the only one who can do it, and it'll be benefitin' workers nationwide. They gotta give me the time!"

Everyone looked doubtful and made appropriate sounds. He shot, "Well, give it a try, dammit! Hit up a motion for a new trial based on my value to the American Labor community. Go ahead, work it up, and I'll look it over. Where *you* goin'?"

"To my office, to—"

"Do it right here! I got enough law books here to start a school! Come on, you guys, think! Get those asses in gear!"

The venerable John English was there, but could only sit and hold his head in his hands, distraught with sorrow and shame.

Farrell answered the phone. "Jimmy? Another one."

Jimmy said, "Hi! Where are ya? Pittsboro, North Carolina!"

The trucker said, "Jimmy, I got my rig right here at the side of the road! Just say the word and she's across the highway without a key! They're railroading you, Jimmy! Gimme the say-so and I won't move outta here till they give ya a decent break for once!"

Jimmy told him what he had been telling the scores of others who had been calling him from all over the country: "Thanks, brother! Your heart's in the right place, but that ain't the way to handle this. I appreciate it, but you get back on the job, now, and don't let nothin' interfere with the work of this great union, hear me? Thatta boy, thanks again."

Sandy said, "Dammit, Jimmy, *that's* your last best hope and you keep telling them no! Christ, let them do it! You could paralyze the whole country in ten minutes! Then they'd *have* to come to terms with us!"

"That's stupid and you know it. I refuse to discuss it."

"Every highway, every bridge . . . Think of it, Jim, you—"

"No strike! No strike! They boys keep movin', and the trucks keep movin', and that's it!" Then he surprised them. He sat down, let out his breath, and said quietly, "Hey, guys, gimme an idea—how much time can I do? Real time?"

One guessed, "I figure twenty-two months with good behavior."

"How about you?"

"I calculate twenty-four, outside."

"Sandy?"

"I pass, Jim."

"Bill?"

Bufalino said, "I've checked the Federal statutes, Jimmy. It's thirty-four, at least."

"Son of a bitch, you just gave me another ten months in the clinker! . . . But you ain't one to bullshit me, are ya, Buf. My God, three years." He looked broken.

"Freeze it, Jimmy!" Sandy had never seen Hoffa like this before. "Call a national, Jim! Bury the bastards!"

Hoffa sighed and smiled. "Go crank up that tape recorder for me, Sandy. I wanna make a statement for you and the rank and file. Somethin' to be played when I go in."

"If you go in, Jimmy."

305

"Just do what I tell ya."
John English was near tears.

Teamster President James R. Hoffa himself drove the car that took him to the Federal penitentiary in Lewisburg, Pennsylvania. It was March, 1967. The seventh.

There, Marshals put him into handcuffs and ankle chains. He said, "Assholes, if I was gonna run, I coulda just kept on drivin'!" as Sandy Farrell had only half kiddingly suggested. Before entering, he performed two of his most characteristic acts. First, he organized the large party of newspeople there to record this fateful event: "I want you TV guys with the cameras over there . . . and you radio guys with the mikes over here. Okay. Now, the rest of ya—don't shoot no questions at me. I'll say what I wanna say. No more, no less."

Then he delivered his last press conference for a long time to come, and he did it with flair and bombast. He attacked Bobby Kennedy, Judge Wilson, his whole Chattanooga trial in general and Edward Grady Partin in particular: ". . . Ready for Partin's list of qualifications as a Government witness? Bad Conduct Discharge from the Marine Corps! Three years in Washington State Penitentiary for burglary! Ninety days in Mississippi for petty larceny! Accused by his own union for embezzlement! Indicted in Alabama on manslaughter in the first degree! In jail, behind bars, in Baton Rouge, Louisiana, for *kidnapping* when he . . ."

For his finale, he took a sheet of paper out and read aloud the dissenting opinion of a Supreme Court Judge. "Now, this isn't any old Justice, this is the *Chief* Justice of the Surreme Court, Earl Warren! It's a lot longer than this, but I'm in a hurry, so just listen to this: '. . . And we have before us a case, where the *Government* went into the *jailhouse* to employ a man who was himself facing indictments *far more serious* than the one confronting the man against whom he offered to inform. The Government then employed the man, not for the purpose of testifying to something that had already happened, but rather for the purpose

306

of infiltration, to see if crimes would in the future be committed. I cannot agree that what happened in this case was in keeping with the standards of justice in our Federal system, and I must, therefore, dissent.' See you later, boys." He waved, and was gone.

Inside, he grimly and silently submitted to the internment procedure, being fingerprinted, photographed front and profile over the number 33-298 NE, stripped, sprayed, deloused, dressed in prison uniform, and placed in a detention cell.

Here sat the dynamic President of the International Brotherhood of Teamsters, staring at his shoes, thinking about the outside, trying not to think about the inside. Quite apart from the personal humiliation and defeat, the outrage of being physically taken away from work, wife, children, home, friends, the public streets, restaurants, to be caged like an ape in cramped, cruel spaces, Jimmy Hoffa had reason to feel real fears. Not just the normal terror of possible male rape. But there were men inside here who knew him. Some had cause to hate him. He was afraid someone was going to try to kill him. He'd never see the outside world again.

In 1961, a New Jersey hood had decided that his boss was getting too large a cut of the proceeds, and decided out loud. His name was Anthony Castellito, and he became dead. Many years later, his boss, Teamster chief Anthony (Tony Pro) Provenzano, would be convicted of Castellito's murder. But right now, in 1967, he was doing time in Lewisburg only for extortion. When Jimmy Hoffa entered the prison dining hall for his first meal, an ominous sound rumbled over the tables of convicts, like falling rocks. Hoffa straightened into his cockiest stance. Then he felt a hand touch his shoulder. "Good to see you again, Jimmy, you'll be eatin' with me at my table," his old Teamster comrade Tony Pro said, and the rumbling stopped. Hoffa was safe from bodily harm. In here, Tony Pro was boss.

That same week Teamster locals all across America filled their halls for special Jimmy Hoffa Meetings. Most men showed up expecting to hear the go-ahead for a national strike. They were more than ready to do it for the little guy, after all he'd done for them. But that wasn't what they heard. Every local president or business agent had been delivered a copy of the tape recording Hoffa had dictated before turning himself in. As if played, Jimmy's voice and words quieted them down as no presiding union officers had been able to do. From his prison cell, in effect, their leaders Jimmy Hoffa told them, ". . . These are tough, dark days. And I know there's talk going around about a National Strike. And it makes my heart feel good that you would do this for me.

"But you can't do it."

At many gatherings, the leaders had to shut the tape off here and wait until the booing ended. Then they resumed playing his message:

"You cannot let one man hurt this great union! A strike would be crippling."

They listened in Charlottesville.

"Not only to this country."

They listened in Waco.

"But to this union."

They listened in Des Moines.

"And I won't permit it!"

They listened in Indianapolis.

"If you care about my future, you must return to work."

They listened in Phoenix.

"And remember this—Jimmy will be back!"

They listened everywhere.

"This is my promise to you. Only the second that I ever made to you! . . . I'LL BE BACK!"

If all the cheering in all the locals could have been put together and heard at once, it would have sounded like a hurricane and been softer only than the roar that all the trucks in America made when their drivers returned to them, started them up, and thundered back to work.

LET'S PUT ROBERT KENNEDY TO WORK FOR NEW YORK, said the campaign ads and posters, cannily showing Bob in his shirt sleeves: sharp-featured, youthful, experienced, tough. And New York did put him to work, as their Democratic Senator. He surprised his enemies and fulfilled the highest hopes of his allies.

He didn't mellow; he matured. A subtle sign of the way he engaged and was engaged by the unprecedented tumult of the Sixties was his hair. He let it grow. Nowhere near the Jesus length he permitted on his sons, but nowhere near, either, the high-edged clip his mother would have preferred. The real and significant shiftings happened inside him. For these he had his years in the civil rights movement to thank, as well as, ironically enough, his years of combat with Jimmy Hoffa: from long, close-in exposure, he knew that those needing the most attention and help were the poor, and the workingman. The black unemployed, and the blue-collar laborer. As he had mixed in the streets of East Cambridge in his youth, now he went out into the streets of Bedford-Stuyvesant, Queens, and upstate hamlets. And from Washington, he finally looked at Vietnam and said Johnson won't bring peace there by burning it to the ground.

Finally, he was in politics, and he liked it. He brought his passion to it, has energy and zeal for efficiency. By himself now, he came to flex a certain new freedom of thought and action. Other men reaching their forties clung to their philosophies; Bob questioned his and resolved them in light of the new realities he saw.

But freedom is a spinning mirror. Bob's new solitude had been imposed. As often as it gave him the excitement of re-evaluation and renewal it afflicted him with its dark sides: doubt and fear. His recurring moods of blackness were still haunted by the same question: Jack. In their pursuit of Jimmy Hoffa, in their crackdown on Organized Crime, had there been something he should have—or shoud not have—done that might have prevented his brother's death? That question never stopped plaguing him. His only hope of deliverance seemed to lie in moving forward, in listening to the directions of his own soul and acting upon them.

When the Senator-poet Eugene McCarthy began marshaling the "flower power" and leading the "children's crusade" into an anti-war candidacy for the Presidency, Robert Kennedy looked and saw that it was right. He also saw that the man had no realistic, political chance of ever beating out Hubert Humphrey for their party's nomination. In the teeth of criticism from all sides, then, he entered the primaries himself.

This time, there was no notorious Kennedy Machine to set in motion. In a world turned upside down, in a time ripped by serious, bitter divisions, and crazy-quilted by Woodstocks, acid, pot, rock concerts, sit-ins, riots, raids, marches, Haight-Ashbury, Tim Leary, draft-card burnings, a "Silent Majority," carousing football heroes, the arrests of priests and nuns and scholars, of dropping-out, turning-on and turning-off and bombings; against these, chart-making, phone-calling, doorbell-pushing, chit-returning, and the other time-honored methods of organizational compaigning were useless, even if they had been available to him.

Kennedy hit the streets. He went out into the people. He said, "I've got every establishment in America against me. I want to work for all who are not represented. I want to be their President." He was sure that if he could reconcile blue-collar whites and Negroes, and add the kids, he could turn the country around.

He went out and touched the people, and the people touched him back. He won his first two primaries, then went for the big one. California.

On June 5, 1968, he was waiting in his room in the Ambassador Hotel in Los Angeles when Dave Thatcher ran in with the news. "You did it, Bob! It's fifty-five to forty-two over McCarthy!"

"Terrific!"

"Three in a row! It's like 'sixty again! Next step, the convention and Humphrey's ass!"

"No, next step is Chicago. Chicago'll be—"

"Aw, the hell with that, the real next step is downstairs, and right now! They're screaming for you—got the speech ready?"

He did, and went down to the mobbed Embassy Room, delirious with victory and hope, and, with Ethel behind him at the podium, delivered his victory speech. The crowd kept chanting, "Sock it to 'em, Bobby!" but he didn't. He simply thanked those deserving it and, once more, described his hopes and goals.

People, touched by emotion, touched him. Their man.

Done, he stepped down off the stage. Accompanied by about a hundred people—friends, aides, well-wishers, and others—he walked through a door in the rear wall. It led to another door, the one that opened to the pantry of the kitchen of the Ambassador Hotel.

Both doors closed behind him.

Jimmy Hoffa was in his cell at Lewisburg when a prison guard told him of Robert Kennedy's assassination. All he said was "What do you expect me to do, feel sorry about it?"

He surely already had enough to be sorry about. His friendly liaison with Tony Pro had been short-lived. When Provenzano started detailing the amount of Teamster turf he expected to be dealt when they got out, Hoffa said, "Bullshit! Look—you guys are gonna hafta be on your own from here on out!" It swiftly erupted into flying fists.

Not all the FREE HOFFA! bumper stickers in the world helped. Although deprived, cold-turkey, of telephones, Hoffa managed to keep in constant contact with the outside. He waged a relentless campaign to obtain a release from imprisonment. Year after year passed. Kennedy had been right: nobody wanted to know him any more. At least not enough of the ones with any power to help him. The "puppet" regime he had left in charge of his union cut the strings: life was most rewarding at the top of the mountain. Hoffa's "friends" also liked things better without him.

Even the pardon when it came had a hook in it. In December, 1971, James Hoffa's thirteen-year sentence was finally commuted, by President Richard Nixon. Hoffa signed it and flew home to Detroit. He thought the reporters were excited by his being free. When they asked him what he thought about the rider he said, "What rider?" Told, he claimed that the paper he had signed had not included the rider that made it illegal for him to be involved in union politics, directly or indirectly, for nine years—longer than if he had stayed inside and waited for parole. "That's that fucking Colson!" he charged, referring to White House aide Charles Colson, later General Counsel for the Teamsters International.

In 1974, Jimmy Hoffa filed suit in the U.S. District Court in Washington against President Nixon, charging that the conditions imposed had been done for "impermissible and illegal purposes." All along, he continued to fight for readmission to the union. Complying with the law, he traveled the length and breadth of the country speaking publicly on behalf of the National Association of Justice, an organization for the reform of prisons in which he became actively involved while at Lewisburg.

These lecture tours kept him in the public eye and the eyes of his Teamsters, but as time wore on he found himself spending more and more hours of his days tending his lawn and at his basement workbench in Michigan, repairing toys for his grandchildren.

That was where he was the day Tony Luizo showed up at his doorstep in person, all the way from his home, an industrial city on the East Coast. Jimmy left his workbench, went up and outside. "Like I told you a hundred times," he barked at the old Teamster, "I can't talk to you at all. But I can't even look at you anywheres inside the house. Fine thing, huh? Come on, let's walk. Maybe they haven't bugged the trees on me yet."

He already knew Luizo's story better than he wanted to. After thirty-odd years in the Teamsters, the man wanted to retire. He'd gone to his Local to apply for his pension, only to be told that because of some thirty-day lapse several years back, he was ineligible for even a nickel. His business representative had passed him up to his Joint Council; they told him he'd have to take it to the Marble Palace itself. He'd called Washington time and again but was never able to get through to anyone able or willing to help. Then he'd started phoning Jimmy direct, in Michigan. Hoffa took his calls every time but always had to tell him the same thing: "I'm out. I can't even chew the fat with you, unless it's about baseball or something. I'm sorry.

But listen—next time you call the International, tell 'em *I* said for you to talk to . . ."

"I still got no place, Mr. Hoffa," Luizo repeated now in Jimmy's yard, and began again to sing his tale of sorrow. Jimmy felt so bad for the guy he wanted to belt him. His voice on the phone had been frustrating enough; in person now it was unbearable.

"How'd you get here anyhow, Tony?" he asked, trying to change the subject.

"An old buddy let me ride shotgun far as Detroit. From there I caught a bus. I hate to barge into your home like this, but I . . ."

Yeah, yeah, Jimmy thought, but you're desperate. Not one other son-of-a-bitch in the world to turn to. And the thirty-day rap was bullshit. He himself could've fixed it in two seconds if he were still . . . Ah, but he wasn't . . . how many times did he have to learn it? Just seeing this poor bastard was not only agonizing, it was stupid. He had to get rid of him, for both their sakes.

He hated to, but he turned tough on him: "Get this through your skull once and for all, will ya? You're pissin' into the wind talking to me! I can't do a goddamn thing for ya, so hit the road!"

"But, Jimmy, I—"

"End of conversation!"

"But I always stuck up for ya, Jimmy! One bad word about you out of anyone and I'd be swingin' away!" Into his sixties, Luiso still stood big and burly. The tears in his eyes now welled so pathetically, Jimmy couldn't look at the man's face. Cut it out, he thought. Go away! . . . "Jimmy, I gotta know just one thing—all that talk about you fiddling with the pension funds all these years—*this* ain't what they meant, is it? I'll get out and leave you alone, but tell me that much, at least. Say that didn't have anything to do with this, Mr. Hoffa! It didn't, did it, Jimmy. It was somethin' else, somethin' big time, wasn't it, Jim. It wasn't you!"

Long after Luiso left, Jimmy stayed silent, staring at the ground. Then he snapped out of it and went back into his house, back down to the broken toys on his basement workbench.

He didn't like it, but finally had to accept the fact that Tony Pro had become the man to see.

On July 30, 1975, Jimmy drove from his home to Bloomfield Township, where he met Sandy Farrell waiting outside the Machus Red Fox restaurant. He hugged his old companion and laughed. "Hey, whaddaya look so nervous about, kid? It's all gonna work! I'm comin' back! The pardon's on Ford's desk right now!"

"That's great, Jim, but—"

"And I'll tell ya something, just between you and me, Sandy, when Hoffa's back, you're gonna see a lotta fuckin' heads roll. There's a lot of dues to be paid."

"Jimmy, listen . . ."

"You all right? You sick or somethin'?"

"No, but listen to me, Jimmy. Things are pretty . . . Just watch what you say, will you? I mean it. They're in a panic, Jim. Across the whole country. The only other time I've seen them like this was when Kennedy was hitting them so hard, and—"

"Now it's Hoffa's Comeback? Well, tough shit. I'm—"

"Jimmy, please, the lip. Just don't—"

"End of conversation! Nobody tells Hoffa what to say."

"All right, Jim, all right. I'm sorry." They stood in the cold silence for a minute. "Uh, Jim? Why don't you go inside and wait, huh? I'll do lookout and come and get you when they show."

"Good idea," he said. "Just me and Kennedy, huh? Only ones to put a scare in them. That's a hot one." Then he went into the roadhouse.

The door closed behind him.

Jack Ruby was sentenced to die on March 14, 1964. He won a retrial, scheduled for February, 1967. In November, 1966, he granted an interview and in it he said, ". . . Everything pertaining to what's happening has never come to the surface. The world will never know the true facts of what occurred: my motive. Uh, in other words, I'm the only person in the back ground who knows the truth pertaining to everything relating to my circumstances."

The interviewer, Harry Kendall, asked, "Do you think it'll ever come out?"

Jack Ruby, looking gaunt, sitting in a pewlike bench, answered, "No, because, unfortunately, the people who have so much to gain . . . and have such a material motive to put me in the position I'm in . . . will never let the true facts come aboveboard to the world."

"Are these people in very high positions, Jack?"

"Yes," Jack Ruby said, in conclusion.

A month before his new trial, on January 3, 1967, Jack Ruby died. Of cancer, it was reported.

This is 1979.

Jimmy Hoffa has never been seen again.

Doors close.

Trucks roll.

And sailboats sail. They leave harbors under power, then, on the open sea, they unfurl their sails. Motors are cut. When the wind is right and the sails catch it right, the speed can be great and exhilarating, and seldom does such power come accompanied by such stillness, such quiet, such grace. And you often can see men together sailing such boats, at the tiller, at the lines, talking to each other all the while, and laughing. But when you get up close you always see that whoever they are they are not John and Robert Kennedy.

The
Best Modern Fiction
from
BALLANTINE